Rain Cloud

John Summerlin

PublishAmerica
Baltimore

ISBN: 1-4241-6180-0
PUBLISHED BY PUBLISHAMERICA, LLLP
www.publishamerica.com
Baltimore

Printed in the United States of America

Chapter 1

Chief Charlie Rain Cloud, sat in the place of honor, located in the center of the council circle. His name was not really Charlie, this was a name he had been given by the white government, while conducting official business between the government and the Native American tribes. Nor was he a chief in the traditional way. He had been given the honorary title because of his age, and the vast knowledge he had of the history of all Native American people.

Nobody knew where Charlie came from, or when he arrived. However, he was always present on the first morning of this important council.

No one really knew how old Charlie was, not even Charlie himself. It was suspected that he had seen the coming and going of over eighty summers. He was the oldest living Native American that was alive in the entire nation. He had outlived the normal life span of his people by well over thirty summers. He could recall actual events that had transpired over seventy years before. These recollections came not from stories handed down to him. Rather they came from the memory of actually being alive during the time that they had transpired.

His physical appearance gave evidence to his age. His face bore sign of the many days he had spent in the harsh environment of the great southwest. There were many scars scattered among the deep wrinkles that surrounded his eyes and mouth. His skin lay loose over his entire body, and his hair had long since lost the glossy black sheen that once covered his scalp lock. His eyes were deep set, but they still retained the quality of alertness and wisdom, that was now lost in the eyes of many of the people sitting before him. It was quite clear to all at the council that his mind was just as alert as were his eyes. His mental actions could respond to any situation, even though his physical actions could not.

Beyond the council circle, there were the many dwellings of the people of the village. Most were thatched mud and brush huts. A few were worn ragged tepees that had been retained by some of the tribes. The tepee was a constant reminder to them of their previous life.

These tepees were only a shell of the original ones that had been brought to the area. The original buffalo hides, had deteriorated to the point that some had to be replaced with the hides of the cattle that the government had provided in limited numbers. When proper leather was not available, pieces of the white man's canvas had been used to shore up the walls. There were only a few of the picture stories remaining on the tepees. Most of these were not complete.

Some of the dwellings bore signs of the white man. They were shabby make shift huts, partially constructed with tarpaper. The entire village was in disarray, and unlike the villages of their former life. The ponies, once the prize processions, and were few in number, they were very lank from the improper care. The dogs also showed the signs of extended hunger. These things were not by the choice of the people. They were simply not supplied enough food and material by the Federal Government, so that they could maintain life as it should be maintained. The tribes assembled here felt they had been betrayed by the promises of the White Generals of the Federal Government.

Nevertheless, Charlie sat there in his finest dress. He wore an original war bonnet that had been reworked thru the years. Where this brightly colored feathered bonnet had once extended to the waist, it now flowed within inches of the ground. His breeches and vest were decorated with the cheap beads that had been obtained from the white trader many years prior to the people being relocated to this reservation. The weapons and tools for hunting had been replaced with the tools for cultivating the very poor soil that surrounded the village.

This village was located on the land between the Red and Canadian Rivers. The Quachita Mountains were to the east. This village was the scene of an annual celebration attended by the Creek, Cherokee, Chickasaw, and Seminole tribes. It was now the main village of the Choctaw people.

Charlie said he was a Choctaw by birth, and was the product of much moving from the lands along the Mississippi. He was finally settled on a reservation in southeastern section of the Indian Territory. He was revered by all of the Native American Tribes, and many tribes were in attendance at this annual meeting.

Finally, the singing and dancing was over and the drums were silent. There was great excitement among those gathered there; they were almost breathless as they waited for Charlie to start telling the stories. Stories, that told the history of the Red Man. Many of them had heard some of the stories before; but each time Charlie made them seem new and refreshing to their otherwise dull lives.

The silence seemed endless; finally Charlie raised his hand to signify that he was ready to pass on some of his wisdom, memories, and hope to the huge gathering.

"I have witnessed the first coming of the White Man to the land of the great river. The spreading of the white invader, into our land, was as a prairie fire that devours everything in its path. While the invasion of the white man was happening from the east, the same was happening from the south by a brown skinned people known as Spaniards. The movement of these two bands of strangers caused many of our brother tribes to move. When moving was no longer acceptable to these invaders, great wars were fought. After many battles, both won and lost, our numbers were reduced to the point that we were forced to sign a peace treaty with the invaders. The White Man, not known to keep his word, made many promises. Most of these promises have been broken between then and now. Therefore, we now find ourselves on this thing they call a reservation, and under the control of the White Government. It seems that it is the desire of this government to make us totally dependent on it for our survival."

Charlie paused and reflected for a few minutes while he refreshed his memory and caught his breath.

"These things I have just told you is common knowledge to most of you. That being the case I will tell you of three lifetimes long ago that had a great effect on all our lives. It will include the story of the first marriage between a white trader and one of the women of my tribe. This was the beginning of our ability to speak their language, and them ours.

To tell you of these three lifetimes it will take three days. These lifetimes were lived by at least three very unordinary warriors from three different tribes of the Midwest. These three stories will cover more than the domestic life and training of our people. They will also cover the great battles to survive and finally the building of a great nation.

So just as the case of all stories of historical value, I will start at the beginning in the land of our Zuni brothers, which was at that time several days ride to the northwest of where we are now gathered".

Charlie again paused and allowed his thoughts to gather the details of the story he was about to tell. The entire assembly was silent and hung on his every word.

"I will now tell of the life the Zuni, Red Feather. This story will also tell of the power of the spirit of the hawk. Red Feather's tribe lived in a pueblo built high in the side of a cliff in the central section of what is now known as the Territory of New Mexico. This story may not contain feats of great courage or many battles. It does contain much that must be learned by those that are to young to have experienced what this man was taught. These lessons must be handed down to the following generations; that they may retain all the beliefs and customs that are essential to extend the future of the Native Americans. This story contains the training of a young warrior's growth to manhood. The training may seem simple at times, however, it contains what he was taught early in life. This must be taught to all young people. These lessons can be applied to every situation that arises during a lifetime."

Having said this, Charlie began to relate the following story.

Part Two

Red Feather

Chapter 2

The first sign of the fresh morning light was bathing the upper ledge, that was the main entrance to the pueblo, found a young Zuni boy lying flat on his belly and peering down into the darkness of the canyon far below. This was the daily ritual that he had preformed ever day since he was old enough to walk. Today however it was quite different, he was expecting his world to change forever today. He was alone in front of the stone and mud pueblo that was his home.

This pueblo was recessed in a large opening under the overhanging bluff high on the north side of a cliff above the deep canyon. This particular pueblo had been there for many lifetimes. It had been constructed at this place with great care to ward off the enemies that were both man and nature. Great care had been taken in the construction and location many centuries ago.

No other person from the pueblo was up at this early hour. While he lay on the hard wind swept rock surface, and anxiously waited for the arrival of the lighted day, his ever-present companion joined him. Even though this was not the normal time for the boy to be up and about, he was never alone.

This constant companion, a grown red tail hawk had been with him constantly ever since he was a boy of only six summers. At that time, four summers ago, the boy had been walking on the level just below the pueblo when he discovered a fully feathered baby hawk. The hawk had apparently fallen from the nest. He spent a long time pondering what to do about this helpless bird that was not yet ready for flight, and it could not feed itself. The hawk offered no resistance as the boy picked it from the ground and carefully wrapped it in a soft deerskin pouch. It was as if the bird had been handled by human hands all its life. With the tiny bird safely in the pouch, the youngster climbed high into the tree where he had discovered the nest. Upon reaching the nest, he found it occupied by a second young bird. He removed the first bird from the pouch, and placed the small creature into the nest alongside its sibling. Then he climbed back to the ground below.

Just as his feet touched the earth again, the little hawk came fluttering down and landed at his feet. Shortly after the tiny bird came to rest at his feet, a lone loose feather floated to the ground.

The small boy determined that the return of the hawk to him was a sign, from the spirits, that he was not to return the bird again to the nest. He decided that the spirits must have intended for him to care for the bird until it was old enough to fly and hunt. At that time it would be free to do as it wished. He picked up the loose feather and carefully placed it in his headband. He then took the young hawk to his sleeping quarters. His father had given the boy permission to keep the bird with the understanding that the bird would not be restricted from the freedom that any bird enjoyed. For weeks he fed it small bits of fresh meat and insects, until the bird was no longer dependent on him for survival. By the time that this had come to past the boy, and the bird had formed a lasting relationship.

From the very first flight the bird was never out of sight of the youngster, for any length of time. It would only leave for short periods to hunt for something to eat and to get its daily exercise.

The boy had turned ten summers of age, the sun before, and he was looking forward to the return of his father this morning. His father, Walks Long, had been away hunting for two suns. He had promised the young boy that upon his return; he would begin the training that would transform him; from the small boy he was now, into the Zuni Brave he was to become.

With the sun not yet to the top of the mountains to the east, there was really nothing that the boy could see. The canyon below was covered with a dense growth of trees and brush, and therefore in total darkness, there was no movement visible at this time of the morning. Never the less, the boy lay there very still and searched the darkness for some sign of movement on the trail along the stream that ran through the canyon from west to east. This was the trail that would bring his father from the valley to the east. Below the pueblo, this trail would join the narrow winding trail that rose from the floor of the canyon below to the ledge where his home was located.

He knew that even if the sun was shining he could not see far below because of the thick stand of trees between the ledge and the stream below. Still he waited as the excitement grew.

While waiting he was eating a piece of wheat cake, which his mother had made from wild wheat, he could hardly contain because of the excitement. Wild wheat grew all over the mesa to the south.

As he waited, a small ground squirrel scampered across the protective rock wall that had been constructed to protect the people of the dwelling from the drop into the canyon below.

Neither the squirrel, nor the hawk, paid any attention to the other for they had seen each other on many occasions. "Little squirrel, I will soon have the same freedom to roam from this place, just as you and the other creatures of the world." The boy thought to himself as he fed the squirrel small bits of the wheat cake he was eating.

The crisp mourning air chilled him somewhat. He was clad only in a loincloth made of soft deerskin, and a pair of moccasins of the thicker leather from the back of an elk. He had covered his body with a fresh layer of buffalo grease, a daily ritual, to ward of the insects and had carefully placed his woven headband around his long straight black hair. He was very proud of this headband. His mother had stripped the fibers from the reeds that grew along the stream below. With the various dyes that she made from the many plants, she had colored and woven the fibers into this one of a kind headband for him on the completion of his ninth summer. Into this headband his mother had placed pictures of all the things that a young Zuni boy was interested in. The boy always wore the red tail feather, which had apparently belonged to the mother Hawk, in his headband. He had been told that this would help the bond between himself and his hawk companion.

He really never noticed that the air was cold. It was the excitement of the day that kept his body warm from the inside out.

With the cake eaten, and the sun still hidden, he lay there searching the darkness. In his heart, he knew that his father would not return until the sun was well above the top of the trees, still he waited.

The hawk sat motionless on the upper most rock that was a part of the retaining barrier. The sky above him began to gain a little of the brightness of the day, and he could hear the birds of the forest began to talk. Off in the distance he could hear the wolves making their last run of the night. "It will be soon," he told himself.

Looking to the east he could see the first orange rim of the morning sun. His heart leaped as he heard something among the stones far below him. Searching the spot where the sound came from, he was finally able to locate a doe and her fawn slipping along an unseen trail. "Soon I too will be able to walk that very trail as free as you do now."

In spite of the tension and the excitement, he was finally overtaken by the dream world of a small boy. He dozed and wandered in a world of make believe. Even the cry of the circling eagle, hunting high above, did not arouse him from this magnificent dream world of the young.

While he lay there on the ledge in peaceful sleep, the dream carried him into the world where he was a grown and strong brave stalking a mighty bull elk. He was carrying the finest long bow, and wore a necklace of many bear claws.

This elk he had stalked, for hours, up the side of a mighty mountain that could be climbed by only the strongest of men. Finally he had mastered the trick of slipping close enough for a shot with his bow. He carefully drew the arrow the full length of its shaft and let it fly.

He would never know the outcome of the flight of the arrow. Far below and to the south of where the boy was waiting, a weary hunter was making his way home from a successful hunt.

The hunter, Walks Long, had left the pueblo long before dawn two mornings before. To leave at this time of the day was necessary because of the distance between his home, and the place where the hunt was to take place. The valley to the east, of the pueblo, was over hunted. It was reserved for the older men that could not with stand the longer journey into the forest beyond. These older men still needed to feel useful. They also need the experience offering them the needed exercise to maintain their health.

By daybreak he was securely hidden on a ledge that overlooked a frequently used game trail. The first sighting was that of a doe and a fawn. Throughout the day, this would be repeated several times. Some of the fawns that had been born late in the season still retained their white spots. He remained motionless for the entire day and then relaxed for a nights rest. It was not yet time for the mating season; therefore, the movement of the bucks was limited to the hours of darkness.

When daylight again returned, Walks Long was again at the same place as he had been the day before. For the first half of the day, the results of the day before were the same. Finally, in the middle of the day the wind began to blow very hard. The noises created by the wind made the creatures of the forest restless. With the blowing wind, they could nether hear or smell danger. As was their nature, the bucks began to move to a position where they could face the wind. This would give them advanced warning of any danger. This was the case with the buck that happened to pass below the patiently waiting hunter. Under normal circumstances, this would not be the buck of choice. However, the hunter decided that this might be the only chance that he would have this day. As the buck worked his way cautiously along the trail, Walks Long readied his bow, for the shot. The buck finally worked his way to a point below and a few paces beyond the poised hunter.

The sharp twang of the bowstring sent the arrow through the short distance. The arrow severed the backbone just forward of the shoulders. With the shot so precisely placed, the buck dropped where he stood. Walks Long, waited for a short time to make sure that the deer was indeed dead. Then climbed down from the ledge to prepare his kill for the journey back to the pueblo. At this time of the year the buck was just beginning to grow the new antlers; therefore, they were covered with the thin skin like covering. This meant that the bone underneath would not be hardened enough to be of any use. Therefore, he would not take them back to the pueblo. This was the reason he had intended to take a smaller young buck but his luck being what it was, he had changed his choice. The deer weighed as much as a large Zuni Brave. He removed the useable portions of the deer, and he carefully packed them into a pouch that he made from the hide. He had laced it together with strips of cured rawhide.

Shouldering his burden of fresh meat, Walks Long started the long trek back to his home. This was certain to take him the entire night.

After reaching the base of the cliff, the hunter laid aside his bounty. He sat for a while resting and allowing the blood to return to his arms and shoulders. He sat there in the dimness of the valley, and peered up the side of the cliff. The Sun God was just beginning to show the face of the dwelling, high in the recesses of the mountain above.

After a short rest the hunter rose, gathered his burden of meat. He started up the narrow trail. This trail would take him from where he now sat, to the point where the series of wooden ladders would finally take him up to the pueblo. He knew his son was waiting, even at this early hour.

Arriving on the ledge, Walks Long saw the youngster sleeping with a broad smile on his lips. The hawk merely turned its head to acknowledge his arrival.

"Wake up my son; it is time that you rise from the world of a boy, and enter the world of a man."

The boy jumped to his feet. He seemed embarrassed that his father had found him asleep at this time of the day. Before him, stood his father with his long bow across his shoulder, and a deer skin pouch at his feet.

His father was a man of average height, for a Zuni Warrior. He was however, very powerful and carried himself with the pride and dignity of a man capable of controlling his own destiny.

Walks Long stood there looking proudly down at his son. Although the hunt of the last few days had made him weary, he would not let this be shown to his son.

"Come my son sit with me, we have much to do in the coming summers. We have to crowd the lifetime of knowledge, which has been handed down to me, into the several moons ahead. Today you start the journey that will lead you through a life, as you have never suspected. You are no longer to be called Little One, You must be known through the land as Red Feather. It is that name that the Spirits sent to you when the small bird was placed in your hands. This is one of the first things that you must learn; always look for a vision, or sign and obey the will and call of The Great Spirits."

Walks Long took his son under the protection of the overhanging shelter of the cliff above. He laid aside his bow and quiver of arrows, and there they sat with their backs supported by the face of the mountain. It was then that Walks Long explained that the spirit of the hawk was very powerful, and often carried messages from the other spirits. To many of their people, the hawk was a more powerful spirit than even that of the eagle.

They sat there in silence for a period of time, with the excitement building inside the young boy. The father was quite aware of this excitement. He also knew that it would sharpen the boy's quest for knowledge.

Just as the boy thought he could wait no longer, his father began to speak. A young Zuni boy would have never been forward enough to ask a question of any older person, or to interrupt even their silence.

"First my son you must learn of your people and your home. Next you must go out into the land. There you learn the ways of other people and their customs. This will not be accomplished over a short period. It will, in fact, cover your entire lifetime. What we do, in the coming moons, will only serve to give you a start into the world of manhood. The trail you are to follow will bring you sorrow and pain, as well as joy and happiness.

However, the sorrow and pain you will endure, because your life will be rewarded with the happiness and joy. You will learn the things that man must know and do. You must also, know the ways and duties of the women of our land. All of this knowledge is necessary for a Zuni to live, and enjoy the abundant life that has been placed on this land."

Chapter 3

After the short rest, the boy and his father picked up the pouch of meat. They carried it into the pueblo, and turned it over to the boy's mother, Misty Night.

Returning to the exterior of the home, they again sat with crossed legs, and their backs against the wall of the building. They looked out across the canyon, which had now become very active with the sounds of the creatures of the land.

"One of the first things you must know is how, and why our people are here at this particular place. Many lifetimes ago, The Anasazi began the search for a better life, and a better place to live. These ancient ones were at that time one tribe. The numbers were too great to be supported by the land where they lived. They began to search the unknown lands, towards the rising sun. These people, at that time, lived in a land that was far to the Northwest. The food supply was growing very limited. There was simply not enough room for the expanding tribe. Through the generations, there came many Great Chiefs. These Chiefs in turn selected members of their family along with their wives. They formed other smaller tribes. It is the custom of the Zuni to take wives from other tribes; therefore, they can obtain other ideas and customs. These ideas can be changed, or adapted to our way of life.

These other tribes of this world you will learn of at a future time. For the time, we will only discuss the Zuni people, and how we came to live here in this canyon.

Over the lifetimes, there was the development of many tribes, during which there arose a tribe of our brothers that developed a warlike style of life. These brothers were called Apache. They chose to occupy the lands, to the south and west. There they lived, on the open land, among the rocks and cactus, of the lower mountains and desert. These people became great hunters, and adapted themselves to living off what the Spirits had placed in this seemingly barren land. As a result of this development, it was then that they became the enemy of many of our other red brothers.

There is, farther to the south and east, another tribe of people, who also live in the same manner as the Apache. These people are called Comanche, and are also enemies to others of the world. By their nature, they live in isolation. They are not social to any other tribes. It is said, that they will even raid and steal from their own people. However, most of their efforts are spent raiding the brown men, called Spaniards. These brown skinned people live south of the Apache land. The only contact that our people have with these Apache and Comanche, are at Pow Wows that are arranged under the sign of peace. There, other tribes meet with them to trade for horses that they have taken from the south. These trades can be accomplished because it is the custom of all people to honor the sign of peace. Regardless of their nature or desires, all Red Brothers will never break some of the rules of society. One of these is the honoring of the peace sign and a man's word. These two things are held sacred to all mankind.

The Chief of the Zuni tribe, Heavy Cloud, was determined to find a place that his people could live safely. This must be a place where access was limited. It must be a place that could be defended with a minimum of fighting. He desired that his people live in peace if at all possible. He led his people down from the north through a deep valley to the point where this canyon entered the valley. When they reached the entrance of this canyon, they turned to the west began to explore what they had discovered. When they came to the large rock on the edge of the stream below, they paused. Heavy Cloud climbed to this very spot where we sit. He looked out across the land. Below him he saw a heavy forest and a good water supply. Beyond, to the south, he could see high mountains.

Between this place and the mountains he could see open lands. To the west he could see that the canyon stopped at a wall that could not be climbed. Behind and above him, was this cliff that provided the protection of an overhanging shelter. He was in the mouth of a cave that had been carved into the mountain by the spirits of wind, water, and time.

He then returned to the floor of the canyon. There he told his people that this is the place where they would remain for all time.

While the Zuni were in the process of doing this, Heavy Cloud's brother, Three Beavers, took a second group and started out in the same manner. This group would be called Hopi. They would eventually build their pueblo on the rim of a great canyon to the west. Of these people you will learn more during the coming summer."

Walks Long then sat back and became silent. The boy knew that his father was at that very moment living in the dream world of the past. Red Feather could hardly contain his emotions; however, he knew that he must not mutter a sound and break up what must be a beautiful dream.

Walks Long continued to speak. "Heavy Cloud and his followers remained at the base of the cliff. They made their camp near the foot of a narrow game trail.

Day by day, they began to clear the rocks and fallen trees from this trail. When they finally reached the base of the ledge that is just below the large cave, they constructed pole ladders to reach from that ledge to the level where we now live. These ladders were constructed so that they could be pulled upon the final ledge; thereby, keeping out any unwanted visitors.

The women of the tribe then began the long task of building this Pueblo, where we now live. The building of this pueblo took many summers. The rocks had to be carried from the valley below. Also, there was water and clay needed to hold the rocks. It was also needed to keep the cold winter wind out. This too, had to be carried up the trail and the ladders to the building site.

Summers turned into lifetimes, finally, our home was completed. As each young Brave went out into the world and took a wife, a room was added. We, now have many rooms, and a Kiva for all people.

When the Pueblo was finally completed, the tribe abandoned the camp in the canyon. Then they moved to their new home.

The women of the tribe had constructed a place that would withstand the many summers between that time long ago and this day.

With their safety now assured, the tribe set about the making of a normal life. Small clearings were established along the stream. The soil there was very rich and easy to work. Ditches were dug to carry water from the stream to the clearings. Pumpkins, squash, beans, and corn were planted.

The men went into the field, while the construction was in progress, and took deer and elk for meat and the leather to make our clothing.

By the time all this had been done; Heavy Cloud had gone to live with The Great Spirits, and there had been at least two other Chiefs.

With new Chiefs and the addition of others, the Zuni way of life never changed. We live today in the same manner that our people have always lived.

For the most part we are not a war like people. We only fight to protect our home and what is ours.

You will be taught to live in peace; however, it is also necessary that you learn the art of war. I, Walks Long, was born in this place and have lived here all my days. This was not the case with your mother, Misty Night. She belonged to the Sioux tribe of the northwest. There was a time when a large celebration was held in the land of the Two Knives, the mighty chief of the Shoshone people. All tribes that wanted to attend were invited. My father, Many Arrows, was the chief of the tribe here at the pueblo. I had just been promoted to the level of senior warrior. My older brother, Little Knife, was also a senior warrior. My father determined, that we should go to this meeting to learn of the ways of the other tribes. It was well known that Little Knife would someday become the chief, and I would be a sub chief. As you know this has come to past; now that our father has gone on to the land of The Great Spirits. My only intentions when we went to that meeting were to observe, and learn all that I could while at the celebration. However, it did not turn out to be that way.

When it came time for the dance of the maidens, Misty Night entered the circle of dancers. On her third time around the circle, she chose me to be her husband. Although this was a total surprise to me, I was very happy to be chosen. After the celebration I returned here to our pueblo, and gathered six of my finest horses. I took them to the land of the Sioux, and presented them to Misty Night's father as a gift. You see my son it is the custom of all Red Men to give a gift to one who has presented them with a gift. From that day forward we lived here alone until the spirit of life presented you to us."

Walks Long, then took the boy by the hand and they placed the ladder down to the next ledge, and began to descend to the trail below.

There were many questions in the mind of Red Feather. He knew not to question his father. He was quite sure that in time all questions would be answered. He wondered what they were going to do next, but he remained silent.

When they reached the floor of the canyon, Walks Long turned away from the entrance. He started to the west where the canyon stopped, and the small stream began.

Arriving at the beginning of the stream the boy saw a large pool of clear cool water.

Unnoticed by anyone, the red tailed hawk had been circling above. He was just in front of the two as they made their way along the trail. It was as if the hawk had been dispatched to guide them along.

As the boy gazed at the pool with water splashing into it from above, his eyes wandered up along the path of the cascading water. When his eyes reached the summit, he could see his hawk perched on the out stretched limb of a dead pine tree. How he wished that he could be at the top, and looking at all the sights that the hawk must be seeing.

"Every thing in this land has a beginning, my son. This is the beginning of a small stream that will go on its way until it joins with other streams. Finally it will become a part of a large river. Once that the streams have formed a river, they will flow on forever. The waters from the rivers and stream gradually return to the sky forming clouds. After this is done, they will return to earth in the form of rain, or snow. It is then that the entire process is repeated.

It is the same with you. You started out very small when sent to us by the Great Spirit of Life. You will continue to grow in body and knowledge, and your spirit will go on forever. You will join with others of your kind. Together you will become a mighty tribe of people. It is here that your knowledge is to have it's beginning."

Walks Long then went to a stand of small slender trees that stood on either side of the water. Here he began to select some of the younger ones that were about the size of a small finger. He would carefully examine each to assure himself that they were straight and true.

"Watch carefully my son, this is the material that we will use to make shafts for our arrows. They must be very straight, and long enough to accommodate a man of any size. Once we have selected all that we need, we will return to the Pueblo and prepare them for the next step."

The boy stood to the side, and watched his father carefully. Finally after a while, his father handed him the flint axe. He told Red Feather to select some of the shafts for himself. Red Feather was very reluctant at first because this was the first time he had ever attempted anything under the watchful eye of his father. He was amazed that the stone axe could cut so deeply into the wood of a growing tree.

After selecting a handful of these smaller trees he gathered them, and turned to see his father nodding in approval. This made his heart jump. He so much wanted to please his father, and learn all this wise man could teach.

Returning to the base of the trail, they began the climb to the ledge. There one of the older braves lowered the ladder for them.

Once they were back at the Pueblo, they sat in their regular spot. They begin to strip the bark from the young saplings. Each was again carefully examined for defects, and then laid aside to dry in the sun. The drying process would take several days; they were secured together with strips of deer hide to prevent them from warping, during the drying process. Red Feather was so engrossed in what they were doing that he hardly noticed the others that were working around them. Nor did he notice that the hawk was sitting silently on the retaining wall, and observing everything that they did.

Now it was time to prepare the arrowheads from the stock of raw flint that had been gathered on a previous occasion, from a field of rocks far to the southwest.

Walks Long selected several pieces of flint of different sizes, then returned to sit beside the boy.

"There are many uses for the arrow, for each use there must be a special type and size. For birds there will be a very small arrow made. To use on all small animals, such as the rabbit or fox, we will make one a little larger. The deer and elk require a much larger arrow. There will be a very large one for the spear. Also there will be a larger pieces made for the tomahawk.

To make these arrowheads, there are two methods that we use. One method is by chipping small flakes from the flint with the tip of a deer antler. The second method requires the use of fire and water. Today we will use the deer antler. Each piece of flint must be selected carefully as to size. It is very important that we waste none. It takes many lifetimes for a stone to grow and work itself from the earth."

Walks Long then selected a small flat piece, and told the boy that they would first make an arrow for the deer. This he explained would be the easier to make because it would be larger.

He laid the flint on the flat stone before him. This stone had been worn flat and smooth from the many years of use. After carefully examining the flint before him, he began the slow and careful process of chipping away tiny bits from all sides.

"The deer antler is the hardest bone that there is, and the deer gives us new ones each year."

By the time the first arrowhead was completed the sun was lowering itself to the rim of the western mountains. The once pure white clouds were now turning a soft orange that seemed to say that it is time for rest.

With the craftsmanship of many years of practice, the arrowhead was one of perfection.

"Tomorrow my son you will make your first, of many arrows."

Chapter 4

Red Feather woke with a start; he threw back the elk skin blanket, and bound down from the stone platform that was his sleeping place. The sleeping place was covered with many deerskins that were placed over layers of straw. The top most layers, of straw, were covered with the soft fur of the beaver and the fox. As his feet hit the floor, the hawk flew down from the peg high in the wall. It came to rest on the boy's shoulder. Quickly Red Feather pulled on his moccasins, and rushed out into the big room. To his dismay, his father was not there. He knew that it was very early; still he knew that he had never gotten up before his father before. He turned, and went to look into the place where his father and mother slept. There was no one there either.

He peered into the darkened Kiva. There he could see his father sitting cross-legged before the ritual fire. Never had he been allowed in the Kiva. It was said that he was still too young to talk to The Spirits, or join in the affairs of the men. He knew that his father was asking guidance for the coming day. He also knew that this could take a long time, depending on what The Spirits had planned.

He and his companion went to the outer ledge and waited impatiently for the time when his father would join them.

His Mother, Misty Night, called Red Feathered into the Pueblo, to eat his morning meal. He had completely forgotten to eat, in his excitement about the prospects of this day.

After a meal of mush made from crushed corn and wild wheat topped with honey, he was again faced with the task of waiting.

Finally the wait was over. His father returned to the big room, and joined him. He began to eat his morning meal also. The hawk had gone out into the forest, and captured its morning meal. It was perched nearby eating also.

"Today you will make your first arrowhead. After you have finished; we will go the floor of the canyon, and search for a proper tree, or tree limb to make you a long bow."

It was with nervous hands, that the small boy began to chip away small pieces of flint from the piece selected, and given him by his father. The sun had just reached the center of the sky when he completed the work.

After the completion of his project, he turned and handed it to his father.

Walks Long said nothing, but the boy thought that he saw a pleased look on his fathers face.

They then lowered the ladder, and started their descent to the floor below.

"The long bow is the most important tool that you will have. It must be made from wood that is carefully selected. It must have the ability to spring back to its normal curve when the arrow is released. In time this natural ability will leave any piece of wood that we may select. Therefore, it will be replaced often over a period of time. The wood for this we will find in the valley to the east. Once I have selected the proper piece, it will be you that will construct your first, of many bows.

As they made their way along the trail, they startled a mother bear and her two young. However, after a momentary start, the bears just moved away. There they observed, from a distance, the passing of those that had disturbed them.

When the man and boy reached the point where the canyon stream joined the river of the valley, they entered a thick stand of tall cane. Beyond the cane there was a large grove of small trees. These trees were all about the same size, and about as tall as two men would be. The hawk circled for a while, and then settled onto a limb to watch the proceedings. Walks Long carefully examined each tree, until he apparently found what he was looking for. He carefully chopped the tree with his flint axe. Using short precise blows, he was able to bring down the tree, without allowing it to split or tear away at the bottom. He carefully removed each limb, and twig from the entire length of the trunk. He announced that this was the one that they would use for the new bow.

With the small tree in hand, and the boy and his hawk closely behind, Walks Long started the journey back to the canyon. On the way back up the trail, they observed the mother bear gathering honey from a bee tree. The young cubs were playing at the base of the tree. They paid no attention to the passing pair. The bees were swarming around the bears, but they seemed not to notice. Walks Long told the boy that in the future he would show him the Zuni way to gather the honey without the interference of the bees. He said that the honey, from the bee, was a healthy source of energy as well as being very good to eat.

Back at the Pueblo the boy was handed a small flint knife. He was instructed as to how to remove the bark from the pole that they had selected. Once the bark was removed, there was a necessary scrapping process to make the entire piece as smooth as still water.

From the wider center, the ends were tapered to a smaller size. Walks Long had Red Feather stand. He held the finished piece with the center at the point of the boys nose. The lower end was cut at the level just above the boy's knees. The upper end was cut at the same distance from the center. Placing one end on the ground, Walks Long began to bend the stick. The stick bowed the same on either side of the center, and when released it returned to the original shape.

When this test was completed he handed the finished product back to Red Feather. He instructed the boy how he must cut the proper notch on each end.

Walks Long then produced a long thin string of platted hair that had been rubbed with the wax of the bee. One end of the string was secured to one end of the bow by using an over and under knot. This was the knot, always used when tying anything. This type of knot would not slip. After carefully measuring the string of hair, a loop was placed on the loose end. Once the string was prepared, Walks Long placed the end of the bow that had the string tied to it on the ground. He carefully bent the bow, and slipped the looped end up and over the notch on the opposite end. He carefully tested the bow several times. Being satisfied, he removed the string from one end and placed the bow aside.

"Never lay the bow aside with the string stretched. If you do it will shorten the life of the wood. Now, my son, it is time to make the arrow. Go and select the straightest of the shafts from those we have prepared."

The boy did as he was told. When he returned, Walks Long showed him how to notch one end with a small groove entirely around one end. He was told that this was where the arrowhead would be secured.

Walks Long had the boy stand, and hold his fist straight out in front of his shoulder. He placed the notch on the end just forward of the boy's fist. He held the shaft level to the ground marking, a spot on it even with the eye. He cut off the end of the shaft at that point.

"This is the proper length for a boy of your size. As you grow this length will change. It must always be measured in this manner. When you pull the arrow in the bow, the arrowhead will be just beyond your hand, and the center of the bow. The string and the other end will be level with your eye. This will give the proper power to throw the arrow about twenty-five paces. That is the distance at which the arrow has the most killing power."

After the arrowhead was secured to the shaft, Red Feather went inside. There he got two turkey feathers from those that were kept in a deerskin pouch in the big room. The feathers were carefully trimmed to the proper size and shape. They were placed on the opposite end, of the shaft. These feathers will assist the arrow to fly true." Walks Long told the boy.

"Now that we have completed the arrow, it must be marked. Every tribe has a special mark. It will also accompanied by the mark of the brave that made the arrow. We will now have to determine what mark you will use on your arrows."

After the arrow was properly marked, Red Feather watched carefully as his father instructed him how to hold the bow, and pull the arrow to a shooting position.

"Tomorrow we will hang an elk skin, by two ends, on a tree. It must be hung so that the bottom end will swing free. Each day you will practice shooting at this skin. When the arrow hits the loose skin it will fall to the ground to be used again. This you will continue, until you have reached the point where the arrow has enough force to stick into the skin. At that point you will advance to the next phase of the shooting process. Now lay the bow and arrow aside, and come sit with me."

They sat once again with their legs crossed, and their backs against the wall of the cliff. Walks Long took a strip of soft deerskin from his loincloth. Then removed a bear claw from the necklace around his neck. He placed the bear claw on the new strip, and gently tied it in a loop. He placed the loop around the boy's neck.

The hawk flew from his perch on the retaining wall and landed on the shoulder of the young boy. After the hawk had carefully examined the new necklace the boy wore, he returned to his perch.

"This string, with the bear claw, is a symbol that you have achieved one of the lessons that you must learn. Each time you have accomplished another goal, I will give you another claw for your necklace. In time you will obtain other bear claws for accomplishing great deeds."

Red Feather was very pleased with the new necklace, and his accomplishments of the day. The sun was beginning to close its eyes beyond the mountains. It was preparing for the sleep of the night. The two went into the big room, and sat to eat the prepared meal that had been place there by Misty Night. Tonight Red Feather, and his feathered companion would sleep in a dream world. When his night world was filled with good dreams, they never seemed long. Tonight he would dream of the flight of his arrow. In this dream the arrow would fly as far as the hawk could fly. The hawk would then return the arrow, and he would shoot it again into the sky.

The sleep was good, and the dream seemed to be a reality. In this dream Red Feather had grown from childhood to become a man among his people. In the dream he wore a necklace of many bear claws. Sometimes in his dreams the hawk would speak to him with words of wisdom or caution. After the dream disappeared the boy awoke, and he and the hawk went out into the big room to join his father and mother.

"Today we will study the tracks. It is necessary that each brave learn to read the tracks, and follow the trail they make. This will be the lesson you will learn today."

As they started down the ladder to the ledge below, Red Feather noticed that the Pueblo was almost deserted. Apparently all the people had left for the canyon long before he had waked up. They did this quite often when the weather permitted.

Walking along the floor of the canyon in silence, Red Feather observed the women and older girls gathering beans and squash. These grew in the small patches of earth near the stream. He had been told that these plants had to be placed where the sun could reach them during the time when the sun was overhead. The sun was the giver of life to all plants, when accompanied by the water diverted from the stream.

They reached the floor of the canyon, and started down the trail towards the valley to the east. They continued across the river and out into the forest beyond. The sands of the riverbank carried much knowledge. There were the many tracks of all animals that had come to drink.

"See these little tracks that resemble the shape of a hand, these are the signs left by the raccoon. Of these there are many because the raccoon lives near the river. It is here that they drink and eat. The raccoon, whenever possible, will wash his food before he eats. The water is also a safety feature for the raccoon. When attacked, the raccoon will attempt to get its foe into the water. It is in the water that the raccoon does its best fighting.

Here, side by side and on the same trail is the track of the wolf and the mountain lion. These are very similar, with a large depression at the rear and little depressions across the front. The smaller dots of the track give the direction of travel.

The tracks of the wolf show small scratches in front part of the track. The wolf has claws that make these scratches. The track of the lion cat does not have these marks. This is true of any cat. A cat has the ability to hold its claws in close to its paws. These claws are only extended when necessary for climbing or fighting."

They spent much time along the river, with Walks Long explaining each track. He told Red Feather what animal had made the track, and what the tracks told an experienced tracker. He said that the same would be true of any trail, even that of a man.

Each time they moved to another spot, the hawk would perch nearby and observe what the boy was doing. It was as if the hawk was learning also.

On occasions, the hawk would hear something in the forest that man could not hear. When this happened it would turn its head listening carefully until the sound was identified, or it had gone away.

Finally they moved away from the river, and along a smaller trail.

"This my son is the sign of the deer; the larger is that of the mother, and the smaller one is of her fawn. There will be a similar trail off to the side that will have the sign of the buck."

They moved away from the trail and soon found the second trail that had the same kind of track. At least, it appeared so to the boy.

"You see that these seem the same as those before, however there is a great difference. Just behind the main part of the track there are two smaller impressions, these are made by the back part of the bucks foot. These are added to the track of the buck because he is heavier. His weight forces the foot to go deeper into the earth. It is important to know the difference. Whenever possible, we take only the buck for food. We do not take the doe, because she is the giver of new life. Only in case of extreme hunger will we take the life of a doe or a fawn.

Each time that the sun is shining, and you are not studying with me, you will come to the river. You will practice reading the signs. If you find something that you do recognize, it will be proper for you to ask me about it, when you return."

Walks Long and Red Feather, sat on a fallen tree trunk. Walks Long took, from the pouch at his waist, some corn cakes and strips of dried deer meat. While they were eating, the hawk flew into the forest. It soon returned with a small field mouse. As the three of them were eating, Walks Long said. "The hawk is a great hunter. You can learn much from him, and the spirit that guides him."

When the light of day came again, Red Feather and the bird went into the big room to find that there was no one there. They went out to the ledge, and peered down. The ladder had been lowered, but that was all that they could see. Below were only the trees, and the sounds of the canyon. The boy returned to the big room, and began to eat bits of meat and a corn cake. These he shared with his feathered companion.

Red Feather gathered up his new bow, along with the lone arrow. He descended to the floor of the canyon. Just to the west of the trail, he found that his father had already hung the elk hide. There he spent a long time shooting his one arrow at the elk hide.

His first attempt had been a complete failure. The arrow fell short, and so did the next few attempts. He wanted to place the blame on the bow, but he knew in his heart that this was not the case. He had carefully stepped off the required number of paces, yet his pull of the bowstring was not sufficient to propel the arrow to the target.

Finally, after many tries and much walking to retrieve the arrow, he managed to hit the elk hide. The arrow struck very low. It had been nowhere near the spot where he held his eye.

Finally, he grew tired. He laid the bow aside, and headed to the river to study the tracks. He was so engrossed in his studies that he never noticed the women of the tribe gathering the food from the growing area next to the stream.

This was a routine that he would follow every time the sun was awake. He knew not where his father had gone, and would have never been forward enough to ask the question of his mother.

During these practice sessions, the hawk would sit nearby and quietly observe everything the boy did.

It seemed to the boy that the hawk knew what he was going to do, even before he did it. When he started down a trail the hawk would fly away. When he arrived at his destination, the hawk would be perched nearby waiting for him. "If only I had the wisdom of the spirit of the hawk?" He thought.

Chapter 5

"Today, we will go to the mesa above the canyon. We will travel to the south. There is a place that you must learn about. You must carry with you a sleeping blanket. We will be gone while the sun sleeps three times. When the darkness arrives, it will be cold. We will be sleeping out in the open."

Red Feather was very excited at the prospect of being on the trail with his father. This was to be the first time that he had ever slept outside the pueblo. Again he wondered what the adventure would be today, and the days that they would be away. However, he would wait. He knew he would receive the information when his father thought it time.

When they reached the floor of the canyon, they walked slowly. They discussed all the signs that they encountered.

When they reached the big valley they turned to the south.

After quite a walk, they left the valley, and began the long climb up the mountain. After a very difficult climb, they were finally at the summit. When they reached the top, the hawk was perched atop a pine tree, waiting for them.

"How did the hawk know the exact point where they would enter the mesa?" Red Feather wondered to himself.

After reaching the top, they selected a spot under a huge pine tree and sat. While they were resting, they ate a meal of dried meat and parched corn. They had not brought a water pouch, because his father had said that there would be fresh water along the way.

While they were resting, Red Feather had to work at staying awake. He was continually nodding and blinking his eyes.

Finally after the rest, the hawk rose from his perch, and circled over them.

Walks Long said, "the spirit of the hawk is telling us it is time to continue our journey."

As they started across the mesa, the land became more open. Red Feather could see far ahead of them.

As they eased along a much-traveled game trail, there were new tracks to be seen. Having been told that it was now proper to ask questions, Red Feather ask about each new track that he observed. His father would stop, and explain each as they were discovered.

First, Red Feather asked about the track that was somewhat like that of the deer or elk. He was told that this was the track of the antelope. "The antelope is similar, but somewhat different from that of the deer. They live out in the open country. They rely on their keen eyesight, and speed to keep them safe."

Next he asked about the track of the coyote that was the same as the wolf, except that the track was smaller. Then they found the track of the badger and the crooked line made by the rattlesnake.

Walks Long explained that the different parts of the country had different inhabitants. These tracks were those of the animals that lived on the prairie.

They had traveled far, and the sun was very low on the horizon. They found a secure place to place their sleeping blankets. They prepared for a restful night under the clear moon lit night sky. Theirs was a peaceful and rewarding night. The sounds that drifted across the mesa were altogether different from those that could be heard when sleeping in their pueblo.

At first light they were up; and eating a morning meal of dried meat, parched corn, and a dried wheat cake.

"We have only a short distance to travel today. At the end of this travel, we will be in the land that produces the soft rock. It will be there that I will show you how to gather rocks that contain a material that can be hammered into tools and decorations. Among these soft rocks there are three different kinds of soft material. One is a dirty rusty color, one is a yellow color, and the third is a shiny kind of a white color. All of these rocks can be hammered into the tools and decorations that we use back at our pueblo."

Arriving at the spot described by his father, Red Feather was amazed at all the different rocks that were in this large outcropping. Walks Long gathered some of the different rocks. They retired to the shade of one of the few trees that were in the area. He had gathered a few of each kind of the different rocks.

"These are the soft rocks, I have told you about. The yellow one is very soft and must be worked carefully. All of them can be polished to make them very shiny and beautiful. We will gather some of each and carry them back to the canyon. There you will learn how to form them into the things that you will want or need."

These rocks, which were referred to by color, by Walks Long, were abundant in the giant copper field that covered a large section of the mesa. Walks long went on to explain the copper, silver, and gold that was inside the various rocks could be used for many things. Their value was only in the many items that could be hammered from them.

"The spirits have placed many rocks in our land. Some will have no use at all to us. Others we will use in our every day lives. There is to the southwest of here, a great field of rock that have many tiny holes in it, this is one of the rocks that have no use that we know. They were placed there by a fire mountain, back in the days of the ancient ones."

After Walks Long had explained the use of each of the rocks that they had collected, they returned to the rock fields. They gathered as many of the different kinds that they could carry.

When they had completed the gathering of the rocks, they started their journey back to their canyon. Leaving the copper fields behind, they carried their burden of rocks, and discussed the various things that could be hammered from them. The hawk showed no interest in the gathering of the ore.

When they arrived back at their home, they placed the collection of rocks in a storage place, along side the collection of flint and turkey feathers.

"Soon the snows will come and the bear will sleep. During the time that the snow covers the land, we will sit with the others of the tribe, and make arrows and tools from the things that we have collected, and stored here. When the bear wakes from his long sleep, it will be time for our people to make the trip to the land of the Hopi."

Red Feather knew that every two summers most of the tribe went west to the great canyon. It was there that the Hopi people lived. Only the very old and very sick, along with the very young remained at the pueblo.

Tribes from great distances would travel to this place to observe, and take part in the Great Snake Dance.

Although Red Feather knew not what this dance was, he was looking forward to the return of the spring flowers, and the journey to the great canyon.

The days were getting shorter, and the sun was moving to the south. Much of Red Feather's time was spent in the forest practicing what he had learned. One morning he went out on the outer ledge, and saw that small snowflakes were beginning to fall. Red Feather knew that it was now time to secure everything from the long snow period ahead.

While the snow covered the ground, and the cold north wind blew over the canyon, the entire tribe remained in the pueblo. The women were all busy making blankets, baskets, and clay pots. The men spent much time in the Kiva telling stories, or talking to the spirits. However, much more time was spent making tools and arrows.

The winter was long, and Red Feather grew more restless with each passing day. The Red Tail Hawk spent most of its time perched near Red Feather. At least once a day, the hawk would leave the pueblo. It would go out in search of food. It required a certain amount of fresh meat. Although it ate the meat that Red Hawk had softened by soaking dried strips in water, it preferred the meat of small animals that it caught in the forest.

Finally the sun returned to the land. The snow was turning to water. The streams began to run once more. It was time to make the necessary preparations for the journey to the land of the Hopi.

With the entire tribe busy with these preparations there was little time for Red Feather, and his feathered companion to explore what the winter had brought to the canyon. The hawk was getting restless It would go on long hunting flights after first determining that Red Feather was not going into the canyon. After a successful hunt, it would bring its kill back to the pueblo. There it would have its meal while perched on the retaining wall of the outer ledge.

The tactics employed by the hawk amazed Red Feather it would circle high in the sky until it sighted its prey. Then it would cry out, this would momentarily freeze the intended victim. The hawk would then dive down to sweep the victim up in its sharp claws. After a period of time, the hawk had been taught to hunt and bring the catch back to Red Feather.

The ceremonial clothing and mask were carefully packed. These articles were the most important things that would be carried on the journey, aside from food.

The horses were retrieved from the mesa where they were normally kept. They were placed in an enclosed area in the valley near the entrance to the canyon. It took many days to carry every thing from the village down to the valley. Poles were cut and a travois was placed behind many of the ponies. After everything was loaded on these, it was announced that with the next rising of the sun the journey would began.

The entire tribe assembled, and each family was assigned a certain position in the travel unit. When the preparations had been completed, the long climb from the valley to the mesa above began. This would be the hardest portion of the trip. Finally the tribe had organized itself, and settled into the routine of travel.

They first went to the south. When they reached the copper fields they turned to the west.

When they came to the lava fields, days later, the travel became more difficult. Their progress was much slower.

From the place that was chosen for the crossing the rough red stones that had been produced by a fire mountain in ancient times, the field stretched as far as the eye could see in all directions. They had to pick a trail in and around huge hills and mounds of lava. The course texture of the lava cut into the soft leather of their moccasins. It was also very difficult for the horses.

There was no stopping as they passed through the valley of fire rocks. There was simply was no place large enough for a camp.

After crossing the valley of lava rock, the travel became easier. They continued to the west and made camp on the banks of the Rio Bravo.

They spent several days at this camp. While camped there, they replenished their food and water supply. The women gathered the fruit and melons, which were abundant this time of the year. They also filled the water pouches. The men spent the days hunting and fishing along the river.

After the supplies were gathered, and the repair of their footwear was made, it was time to once more pack and continue to the west.

Each day the hawk could be seen circling out in front of the travelers. Red Feather believed that his friend was scouting the trail, and would warn them if danger should it arise. At night the bird would sleep on a perch where he could watch over Red Feather, while the boy slept.

Although the desert was covered with the many different types of cactus and the ever-present clumps of white brush, the traveling was now much easier.

It was now midway through the summer. The sun and sand was very hot. The only relief the tribe had was in the knowledge that they were nearing the south rim of the great canyon. Within a short time they would be at the main village of the Hopi.

Chapter 6

Soft Rain, a young Hopi girl, was born and lived in a pueblo along the southern rim of the Great Canyon. Many times she had stood on the rim and wondered what was on the other side of this great canyon. When she stood on the rim, she looked to the north. It was impossible for her to see much that she could recognize. The distance was so great, that only a few of her people ever visited the north rim. She had been told that this was the greatest canyon in the land. It was as far to the bottom of the canyon as it was to the top of most mountains.

As she grew older, she began to go to the bottom to learn the art of raising crops. This she learned from the squaws of the village. The climb in and out of the canyon was a very difficult and demanding journey. Often the work parties would set up temporary camps at the bottom, and remain there for several days. The most demanding part, of the process of raising and harvesting the crops, was the transporting of the harvest to the village above.

The Hopi had farmed the rich land along the great river at the bottom, of the canyon, for many life times. On the south side of the river, and away from the roaring water there had been established many different fields. These fields were joined with a system of ditches, through which the water from the river could be directed to the plants.

Unlike the men of most tribes, the Hopi men were also engaged in the work of raising food crops. This caused a pleasant social climate that did not exist among others, of many villages.

Soft Rain had learned much while working at the bottom of the canyon. Her mother had taken great care to explain every thing that took place.

During the growing season, most of their time was spent with the growing of their food. The strongest members of the tribe would carry the harvest up the long climb to the pueblo on top. This climb would often take an entire day.

During the long winter days, Soft Rain kept busy learning how to weave baskets, and mold clay pottery. She also was taught how to make the paint used to decorate the baskets and pots.

In their society it was the duty of the women to record the many activities of the village. This they did by painting picture stories on the wall, or on stretched deer hides. These were special stories painted about ceremonies, and great successes of the tribe. As the braves sang of their experiences, the women would pay close attention to them. They would later record the event in a picture story.

Soft Rain spent many hours reading these stories, especially those, that told of events that had happened prior to her birth. She was very interested in the history of her people. Also this helped pass away the long dreary days when the weather would not permit her to go to the rim, and dream of the other side.

As she grew older she was allowed to join in the painting of these picture stories. After much practice she became one of the better painters in the village.

The only outside activity of the tribe, during the winter days, was the occasional hunts made by the men. This was only when the weather would permit. After a hunt was completed it became necessary, for all, to prepare the meat for eating and storage. Also the hides of the kill had to be prepared for use.

Soft Rain's mother had taken much time in the teaching of her daughter. She had told her of the ancient ones, and how their people had arrived at the place where the village was now located. She told of the various Spirits, and what was their purpose in the daily lives of the Hopi. She had taught, that all red people were the same in the eyes of the Spirits, even though some had adopted hostile war like ways.

Having learned of the ways of the Spirits and other tribes, she always looked forward to the time when other tribes came to their village for the celebration of the Snake Dance.

While standing on the rim looking across the vastness of space below her, she was very excited. This was the summer of the Snake Dance.

Every two summers there came to her village many tribes to observe, or take part in the ceremony. This ceremony was really to honor the Spirits, but to this young Hopi girl it represented a great social event.

She looked to the horizon in every direction to detect some sign that some of the tribes were arriving. Seeing no sign, she sat on a large rock and drifted into her own private dream world.

Chapter 7

As they approached the village, Red Feather could see that there were many temporary villages set all around the main pueblo. He had been told that many tribes would travel to this place. They gathered for the long period of dancing and celebrating.

During the celebration there would be many stories told in song. All those present would wear their best ceremonial clothing; and the traditional mask, and headdress of their respective tribes.

Red Feather has never seen such a variety of colorfully dressed people. He quickly made friends with those of his age. Of these he ask many questions. He knew that he could ask those of his age these questions, which he did, not dare, ask older people.

At the celebration, Red Feather met a young Hopi girl named Soft Rain. She was a little younger than Red Feather, but had learned more of her duties as a Hopi woman than he had as a Zuni man. The reason for this was the fact that she was in constant contact with all the people of the village. Thus she learned from both the men and women.

Red feather had not started his training until much later, and then most of this had come from his father.

Soft Rain was the daughter of a Hopi sub chief. As a daughter and only child of a chief she was privileged to things that other younger people were not. Since she was near the same age as Red Feather, it was from her that he learned many of the customs of Hopi people.

The celebration would last for a period of two weeks. Although the dance was called The Snake Dance, it was in reality a rain dance. The people were asking the Spirit of Rain to send the needed water to support the life of their land.

Prior to the arrival of the other tribes, the Hopi braves had collected several dozen snakes. They brought them to the village. These were kept in a special pit until it was time for the ceremony.

It was the belief of the people that the snake was the Spirit of some of their departed brothers, sent back to them, making the snake a brother to all.

Finally after eight days of secret meetings, the dancers were ready for the dance. This was a dance especially performed every two years in late summer, to ask the Spirit Of Rain to send rain. The entire event had many other reasons. The snake dance would only use half of the time set aside for the council.

Red Feather was very impressed by the dancers, and their handling of the snakes. He did not understand much about it, but was eager to learn.

He did know that the snakes would be returned to the wild after the ceremony. The snakes were expected to go out and spread the word that their human brothers were respectful of the Spirits that they represented. What amazed Red Feather the most was the many colorful costumes worn by the dancers. Many wore the headdress made from the skull of the buffalo. Others used the skull of the wolf or coyote for their ceremonial wear. Still others wore the traditional feathered war bonnets. Some of these bonnets reached almost to the ground. They were called war bonnets, but in reality they were worn only at ceremonies such as this. When engaged in battle these were worn only by the war chief, and he usually remained outside the actual battle. It was necessary for a War Chief to remain away from the battle. The wearer of the War Bonnet would be the main target of the enemy. In battle it was the desire, or intent to kill the leader of the opposing side.

After the ceremony, there was time for exploring the home of the Hopi people. Red Feather took full advantage of this time. He and several other boys were allowed to descend to the bottom of the great canyon. This was a journey that took an entire day.

At the bottom they found a great river, along which were many fields of pumpkin, squash, corn, and beans. There the men and women worked side by side to raise their crops. They produced much of their food at the bottom of the great canyon because of the available water. Also the soil was much better there. Along with the native fruits, nuts, and the meat provided by the hunters, they had a larger variety of food than those of other tribes.

The winters were very severe in this part of the land. This made the storage of food very important. The extra food was stored either in man-made caves or adobe buildings with very thick walls, and no windows.

This was the first time that Red Feather had ever come to the ceremony. He took full advantage of this opportunity to learn. He knew that this was a regular journey made by many tribes, and that he would be returning every two summers in the future.

After the main ceremony had been completed, there was a second ceremony that was to take place.

After two days at the bottom of the canyon, Red Feather returned to the village to find that the new ceremony was about to start.

The young girls, of all tribes, that were of age and wished to take a husband were gathered in a group. This also included squaws that had lost their husbands. These had served the necessary time in mourning.

All the braves that wished to take a bride were also gathered and dressed for the dance.

The requirements for taking a wife were very simple. A brave was to take a wife from a different tribe. The wife then would become a member of his tribe. She would return, with him, to his village to live.

There was much singing and dancing during this ceremony as all the girls danced before the entire assembly. It was then time for all the young bucks to take their turn dancing. After the brides were selected, the marriages were conducted in the customs of both tribes represented by the couple. This was a slow but happy ceremony, with the end results being that all that wished to marry did so.

Finally after the weeks of celebrating, it was time for the various tribes to return to their homes.

It was with a sad heart that Red Feather said goodbye to his new friends and prepared to leave the land of the great canyon.

Before coming to the big canyon, he had thought that his home was in a big canyon. He now realized that the world outside his canyon was very big and that he had much to learn.

As the various tribes departed, Soft Rain stood on the rim and looked to the north across the vastness of her homeland. Her long black hair blowing in the gentle winds that often swirled over the vastness of the great canyon. She did not want to watch as her new friends departed. She was sad to see all the people leave. She knew that once they were all gone, her life would return to the dull routine of daily life. It would be two full summers before these people would return.

Red Feather was traveling in the center of the group that headed to the east. He would look at the hawk circling in front of them, then back at the village of the Hopi. Finally they were so far from the village that he could no longer make out any of the details of the village. He would spend the long hours dreaming and remembering his experiences there.

Although they had been there only a short time, he had learned much. The return trip had none of the excitement that had been experienced on the way to the big canyon. The days seemed longer. The trail seemed rougher. The rocks in the lava fields seemed to be sharper and cover much more area than they had before.

After many days of uneventful travel they were at last on the mesa above their canyon. How small this canyon now seemed to Red Feather.

The hawk was circling high above the pueblo, and it would dip down very low to indicate the location of their home. It was as if he was telling Red Feather that he was happy to be back to his native home.

The return trip was now over, and the memories were put aside for the time being. Walks Long was preparing to continue the training of his son.

"When the sun again rises, we will go into the mountains and hunt the elk. The snow will soon be here and we must store meat for the coming winter."

With the excitement of the hunt now occupying his mind, the memory of Soft Rain and her people left Red Feather's thoughts for the time being.

The following sunrise found him and Walks Long on the trail leading to the north. His father had told him that this was the season when the elk were preparing to raise their young. The bulls would be calling and fighting for the cows. He told Red Feather that the spirits of all animals knew more about what the different seasons would bring than did man. The bear would be fat now, and prepared for its long sleep. The snow was already covering the highest tops of the mountains and would move lower day by day until it covered their valley and canyon.

At first, the excitement of the day caused Red Feather to forget some of his training. When they first started down the trail he was kicking small rocks and stepping on small twigs that would break. Walks Long had to remind him that he must walk quietly at all times. "A man must never allow himself to be heard when on a trail," he said. Finally Red Feather subdued the excitement. He began to pay attention to what his father was doing. Often he must learn by watching, because his father would not break the silence to tell him what he must do.

Higher into the mountains they climbed until it was time for the sun to sleep. There they unrolled the sleeping blankets, and prepared to spend the long darkness.

Long before the light of the day arrived, Red Feather and his father were awake and eating dried meat and wheat cakes that his mother had prepared for them. In the distance they could hear a long strange sound.

"That is the call of the bull elk. He is calling to his cows, and warning the other bulls that this was his territory. This is the call that will direct us to the location where we will make our kill. Once we have spotted the bull, we will move only when he had his head turned, or he has lowered it to eat. When a bull has his head lowered, he cannot see to the side. It will be then that we will take a few steps closer and stand still until the process is repeated. If we do this successfully we will soon be within the range of the arrow."

Red Feather heard something in the wind above his head. As he looked he saw hawk circling slowly above them. As he watched the hawk turned and flew in the direction of the sound of the bull elk.

The dry leaves on the ground made it very difficult to walk quietly. As they eased along the game trail that cut through the forest, they again heard the call of the bull elk. This time it was closer, and sounded more urgent. While pausing a while to listen to the sounds around him, Red Feather saw that the hawk was circling in a tight circle just ahead of them.

"We must always listen to the Spirit of the Hawk. Even now he is telling us where the elk is located."

Just as his father said, when they gained sight of the elk, the hawk was perched on a limb above the bull.

"It will be your arrow that will bring down the bull my son. You will shoot the first arrow. I the second if it should become necessary."

The elk was standing on a small rise with his head looking into the north wind. They had approached from the east therefore the elk was in perfect position for the shot. As if guided by a strange spirit they both drew their bows to the full extent of the arrow. Red Feather released the arrow. It flew true to the spot he had chosen. The elk lunged forward, and started running as the arrow entered his body and pierced the heart. The second arrow from Walks Long was not necessary. The many hours of practice had rewarded Red Feather with his first kill.

"We will now wait for death to take the bull. When this has happened, we will follow the trail of the blood and prepare the bull for the trip back down to the pueblo."

They sat for what seemed a long time, and then went to the spot where the elk had been standing. When they found no trail from this spot, they began a series of half circles in the direction the bull had run. After several passes they picked up traces of blood on the ground. They would follow this blood trail until they came to the place where the bull had last stopped. Along the trail they found several places where the bull had laid for a while. Finally they came to the place where the elk could no longer gain its feet. The elk seemed to be much bigger now than it had when they had first spotted it. As the bull lay on the ground the antlers reached from the ground almost to the shoulders of Walks Long. The hawk flew in and had a closer look at the bull. After he had satisfied himself, he perched on a limb high above them to keep watch over the proceedings.

"You have now earned another bear claw." Red Feather was told.

The return trip to the pueblo was very tiring, in fact it took three trips to carry the animal from the mountain to the pueblo.

When all this was completed, Red Feather was invited into the Kiva. It was the first time he had been in the Kiva, and allowed the same privileges as the older braves.

Chapter 8

He stood there clad only in a loincloth and moccasins. His body, covered with grease, glistened in the hot mid day sun. Two Coyotes, a Chirichua Apache brave, was giving his paint pony a rest while he searched the horizon in every direction. The careful search was necessary because the Apache had many enemies.

Many lifetimes ago a group of people had left the tribe from which they had originated and formed a new tribe. The original members of this new tribe were wild and reckless. They soon became the enemies of most other Red Men. They were known as Apache, and were feared by all other tribes, except the Comanche, to the southeast. It was only the Comanche that could have, and did in fact force the Apache from their original homeland. The Apache considered the braves of other tribes to be likened to women. They believed that what others had that they wanted was fair game. They spent much of their time raiding the villages of others.

As he rested his pony, he kept searching for he knew not what. All he could see was the heat waves rising from the earth and the lazy circle of the vultures.

He had refreshed himself with the water that he had gathered by piercing one of the giant barrel cacti that covered the vast land of the southwest. The land in every direction was flat and covered with only the many different cactus and plants that could survive this harsh desert.

He began to lead his pony to the east, which was in the direction of his village. His lived in one of the many tepees that comprised his village. The tepees were all made of buffalo hides, and were moved often as the people followed the buffalo herds. As he walked, he observed that his shadow was directly beneath his feet. By the time he reached the village, this shadow would be far out in front of him, if not gone entirely in the dusk of evening.

Having been assured that there was no danger in the area, his mind began to wander. His memory drifted back over the past ten summers to a point in time when he was a boy of only ten summers old. He was living in the portion of the village where all young Apache boys were to receive their training as warriors. The braves, in charge of the training, were giving instruction on the proper handling the bow and arrow. They taught that the arrow was drawn only for the purpose of killing. The bow and arrow were tools and never were they to be used for play, except in tribal competition. He wondered at the time how they were expected to develop the necessary skill if they were only to use it for these two purposes.

Later the instructors explained that these rules did not apply to a buck in training.

The training also taught them the proper way to use the spear, knife, and tomahawk. He would learn the secret of ambush, as well as the art of tracking.

Two Coyotes learned this all well. He soon mastered the skills of warfare. He had learned all this so well that he was made a junior warrior at the age of fourteen summers. He was promoted to the status of warrior two summers later.

The skills he had learned were often put to use. He would take part in many raids, with the purpose of taking anything useful from those of other tribes. Even if this act required the killing of the original owners. He did not consider this wrong, but rather a way of life. It was the way that his people had lived for many lifetimes. It was the only way he knew.

He had made many successful raids to the south, and taken many horses from the strange people that lived there. Most of the time these sneak raids were made at night, to avoid detection. However, his people were fierce warriors and enjoyed a good fight. These fights were preferably planed and often just for sport.

He had been away from the village for several suns, and was looking forward to a period of rest. It would not be long before the village would be moving. The people would be preparing for the great buffalo hunt. Everything in their life depended on the movement of the buffalo.

Two Coyotes enjoyed the buffalo hunt, but not nearly as much as raiding the villages of other tribes, and villages of the people of the south. He had gained much wealth from these raids. He had more horses than any warrior in the village. These horses presented a problem when the tribe moved the village. He had no wife and his mother had died several years earlier. Therefore, there was no squaw to cook and provide for him. His father was considered to be the greatest hunter in the tribe. From his father he had learned many lessons; one of which was riding his pony while leaning low over its side and shooting under the belly of his mount. This was also used to hide his body when stalking the buffalo.

Scouts had returned to the village and reported the location of the great buffalo herd. The entire village was preparing to move, when he awoke after his extended rest.

The village was moved shortly, and it was reestablished about a half days ride from the current grazing grounds of the great herd. While searching for the proper place to leave his ponies, Two Coyotes found an arrow that had markings he did not recognize. He took the arrow to the wise Medicine Man of the tribe.

"This is the arrow of a Hopi hunter. The Hopi is a tribe of corn raisers that live by the great canyon, to the north. They are a peaceful tribe of people and it is easy to raid their villages. They do not have many horses, but there one can acquire much corn and many squash. To raid their village one must do so during the day. It is at this time that most of the people are down at the bottom of the great canyon."

Two Coyotes told himself that after the hunt he must surely visit the land of the Hopi. He must see for himself these strange people. He had no desire to take their corn, but he must gain knowledge of these people. As was the custom of all Red Men, he must learn of anything new.

The hunters had much success because they had stampeded many animals across the prairie and over a bluff. This often left many wounded animals and required the use of the spear to complete the job of killing the buffalo. The women of the village had prepared the meat and hides. The travois were loaded and they carried every useable portion, of the kill, back to the village.

After the kill, the mans work was done, Two Coyotes thoughts turned to what the Medicine Man had said about the Hopi. He must surely travel to this place. He must see for himself these people that did not fight or raid.

It was not a common practice, for an Apache, to travel alone. They had many enemies. However, Two Coyotes was not one to conform to the ways of others.

When the sun began to show its orange rim above the land to the east, he was on his pony and headed to the north alone. He knew not where he was going, but it really made no difference. Any thing different was an adventure to Two Coyotes.

He traveled for many days in the general direction of the place where the Medicine Man had told him that the great canyon was located. He was traveling light. He ate the nuts and fruits of the different plants of the desert. He would kill small game such as rabbits and birds for his supply of meat. He knew from the words of the Medicine Man that he could not miss the canyon if he continued to follow the stars to the north. It was said that a great river traveled through the bottom of this canyon. This river entered the canyon from the northwest and traveled through out the canyon, and departed the canyon to the east.

He had hobbled his pony; and was preparing for the night, when a gentle breeze brought the odor of a cooking fire to him. He spent a long time gazing into the darkness, but had not detected the glow of the fire.

When the sun again returned to the land, he started north into the wind that had brought the smoke sign to him. After a short ride, he felt that he must be close to the canyon. The land had changed and he was no longer in the open prairie, but in a very rough and different territory. Now that he was sure that he must have arrived in the land of the Hopi; he hobbled his pony, and continued on foot.

About the middle of the day, he arrived at a place where the earth seemed to fall away into eternity. As he lay on the edge of this giant hole in the earth, he could see the river far below. He could also see a village along the side of the river. It was so far beneath him that he could not make out any details, but could detect movement in the village. He wondered to himself why any one would choose to live in this great hole in the earth. To him such a place was dangerous because it provided no easy escape route. The beauty of the canyon was completely lost to him because he was not sensitive to such things.

When darkness arrived he could hear the sounds of people to the west. He finally he detected the glow of fire coming from the direction of the sounds. When the sun returned, he would investigate along the rim of the canyon to the west.

Daybreak found him hidden on the rim overlooking the vast canyon. He could see thin trails of smoke rising from the small cooking fires below. At this distance there was no way that he could identify the people, or animals moving around inside the small encampment below.

He had also discovered a great pueblo to the west. He would be careful to avoid this village. He heard a scuffling sound coming down the trail that skirted the rim. Withdrawing deeper into the brush, he lay motionless barely even breathing. As the sounds came nearer he could tell that they were the sounds of a person walking. He moved only his eyes, because he feared detection.

Finally after a while, a young woman emerged from behind the rocks. She wore a soft doeskin dress and her moccasins were decorated with many different colored symbols. The decorations on these were strange to Two Coyotes. He was certain that he had never seen anyone from this tribe before. However, some of the markings were the same that he had seen on the arrow he had found earlier. He lay very still and watched as the woman sat on a large rock near the edge of the canyon. The woman was sitting no more than twenty paces from his hiding place. She was apparently taking in the beauty of the colorful vista below. Even Two Coyotes noticed that the colors changed with each passing moment. He dared not move for fear of being discovered.

The woman just sat there gazing out across the vast open space that occupied the area above the canyon. Two Coyotes could see that she was lost in a dream world. She probably would not have noticed if he did move.

Finally after an extended time, the woman stood up from the rock, and retreated back the way she had come. After allowing the woman time to get out of hearing distance, Two Coyotes rose and went to examine the place where she had been. He could tell that this place had been used often. He supposed that this was a regular habit or ritual. He told himself that for the next few days he would be at this place to see if she returned. He had determined that this was a young woman about his own age.

Each day the woman would return to the same rock. She just sat in silence, and look out across the canyon.

Two Coyotes knew by now that any day at this time, he could find her at this location. For now he would abandon this spot to explore the rest of the area. At night he would slip in very close to the village to observe the people there. Each day a group of new people would arrive from the village below. Finally the village at the bottom of the canyon was completely abandoned.

After determining that there was no longer anyone along the river, Two Coyotes descended the trail that led to the emptiness where the tepees had been. He could not understand what he saw there. He discovered tools that he did not recognize. There were also some mud and brush huts of a type he had never seen. There were empty cornstalks and beanstalks in the fields. He assumed that the corn and beans grown here had been harvested, and carried up the long trail to the village above for storage because there was none of it in the huts.

"These are strange people that do not hunt and raid as do the members of my village", he thought to himself. He vowed to himself that he would learn more of their ways before he left this place. He had long since returned to his pony and released it into the wild. It would not be fair to the pony to keep it hobbled for the many days that he would be in the land of the Hopi. He could always steal another pony, from some village, when it was time for him to leave. He also had the ability to walk, or run for great distances with out stopping to rest, therefore he really did not have to depend on the pony.

After the release of his pony, Two Coyotes returned to the rim of the canyon and began to explore the canyon, from the Hopi pueblo village, to the east. Later he would return and circle around the village to explore the west. There were many mountains and canyons around his homeland, but nothing like what he was now exploring.

The sun rose and set many times while he was in the process of scouting this country. So many in fact he had lost count of how long he had been away from his home.

Two Coyotes again returned to the place where he had first observed the young woman. The next morning she returned to her favorite spot, as usual. Two Coyotes decided that he would capture this woman and take her to his people. He would later make her his wife. He then set out to find and steal two ponies. He traveled to the southeast to a smaller village and waited until the time was right to steal the ponies that he would need for the journey home.

After he had slipped into the compound and selected two strong paint ponies he returned to the canyon and hobbled them nearby. Now he must wait until such time as he could capture the woman without the rest of the village being alarmed.

Chapter 9

Soft Rain sat on her favorite spot; looking out across the great canyon. She had often wondered what lay to the north of the opposite rim. She had been told that there was a giant valley to the north and east. It was said that in this valley there were giant rocks that rose from the floor like giant statues. She often dreamed of this place, and wanted to see something beyond her small world here around the giant canyon. She also dreamed that some day she would take a husband from a tribe that lived far from this place. She had a burning desire to see and learn much more about the land beyond.

Completely lost in her dream world, Soft Rain was unaware of the eyes that had watched her for so many days.

The days of the snow were approaching, and the men of the village were in the field hunting. The women were busy gathering wood for the winter fires. Also they had to prepare the food for storage. Therefore, the village had been almost deserted when she started for her morning walk.

Suddenly a hand covered her mouth; an arm encircled her waist. It happened so quickly that she had no time to struggle. A soft piece of deerskin was placed in her mouth, and another across her eyes. She did not even have the opportunity to see what her captor looked like.

She was led through the brush and rocks, and finally placed on the back of a pony. During all this she had not heard a sound from her capturer. She kept telling her self that this was a dream. That she would soon wake up, and she would find herself back in her village. All the while she was getting farther from her people. They would not miss her until darkness returned, and she could not be accounted for. She knew that by the time the village started searching for her, the next morning, she would be far away from the canyon.

Soft Rain could tell by the wind blowing at her back that she was traveling to the south. If this was true she was headed to the land of the Apache. The Hopi people would never enter this forbidden land of such a hostile tribe. She knew that if ever she entered the Apache Nation; it would be there that she would remain. She had known of several women that had vanished from the village never to return.

On the second night her bindings were removed as well as the deerskin from her mouth and eyes.

"I am Two Coyotes, an Apache Warrior, I mean you no harm. We are going to my village where you will remain until it is time for you to become my wife. I know that this is not the way of your people, but it is the Apache way. After you have learned our customs, and we are married you will become an Apache."

Soft Rain knew that she must never allow herself to be taken to the village of this man. She must search for a way to escape somewhere along the trail. Even though she knew not where she was, it made no difference to her. She would find a way back to the land of the big canyon. As she lay in total darkness, most of the night, she was trying to devise a plan.

Even though Two Coyotes seemed to be sleeping, ever time she moved he was awake. But there had to be a way for her to get away from the situation she was in. If only he would leave her side for a moment she would run and hide. She must wait and watch.

On the tenth day her chance came, the pony that Two Coyotes was riding stepped into a badger hole, and Two Coyotes tumbled to the ground. This spooked the pony, and it started running across the prairie. This was her chance; she turned her pony and raced back the way they had come. She was not trained in the art of tracking, but felt sure that she could find her way back to the place where he had removed the covering from her eyes. She hoped that by chance, she could trace their trail from there. If not, she would just wander along until she came across something that she recognized. She knew that the great canyon, or at least the river, went across the land to the north of where she was. If she could find the river, she knew that by watching the sun she could follow it to her village.

The days were overcast and the air was damp, the nights cold and long. She had nothing to eat, and she knew nothing about securing food. All she knew was the gathering of berries and nuts along the trail. This type of food was in short supply at this time of the year. She was free, that was all that mattered to her at this time.

Two Coyotes had injured his left hip in the fall, thus making it difficult for him to walk. He had also broken his bow that he had strung across his back. Now, he was faced with the task of recapturing his captive without a pony, or weapons, except his tomahawk and flint knife. This was a very unusual situation for an experienced Apache brave.

He could see his pony off in the distance but with his inability to walk normal; he could not catch up with the pony. Since he had stolen the pony, he was a stranger to it. Therefore, it would shy away when he got near.

By the time his leg healed so that he could walk, his captive had a six-day head start. Never the less he was determined to follow her and again capture her. No Apache could allow a captive to escape once they were captured. A captive must be retained or killed, but never allowed to escape. If he did not get her back, he would live in disgrace. With this though in mind he started to back track the way they had come. Since the girl was inexperienced, her trail was easy to follow.

Soft rain had slowed her rate of travel. She was constantly searching for something to eat. She knew that she must retain her strength. She was forever searching the horizon for something that she might recognize. The land in this area all looked the same to her. Her body was exhausted, but her heart was full of hope. Each day after she had rested during the night, she started out with renewed determination.

Searching the trail behind her she could see no sign that she was being followed. This was a good sign; maybe Two Coyotes had decided that she was not worth the chase. However, she could not be sure; therefore, she was ever watchful of the trail behind her.

Finally her luck began to change, at least for the time being. She came across a stream of fresh running water. Beside this stream she found several melons that were still growing, and the stream was full of water crest. She hobbled the pony near an outcropping of tall green grass. She then proceeded to refresh herself with food and water. She made a pouch from a portion of her skirt, and gathered some melons and seeds to carry with her when she left this place.

After she had eaten her fill and rested for a long while, her spirits were lifted and she was confident that she would find her way home.

She had traveled for days seeing no one, or any thing that even resembled her homeland. With the overcast sky there was no sun and she lost her bearings. Late one night the rain set in. It did not rain often in this part of the country.

When the rains did come the entire land seemed to flood. Every small depression in the earth became a torrent of running water. She took cover in an outcropping of huge rocks. There she remained for the entire next day.

The two preceding days had been a total loss, and she had lost her directions. Unknown to her she was now heading in the wrong direction. By the time the rain had stopped she was traveling east. This was the same direction as the flow of the river she was seeking. All trails and tracks had been washed out. When the sun returned she did not recognize anything around her. Her spirit also had been washed away. She was, for the first time, frightened. She believed that she was hopelessly lost with no chance of finding her way home. She spent much of her time searching the horizon hoping that she might find something or someone that might help her. Each day her hopes grew dimmer.

Soft Rain knew now that she was indeed hopelessly lost, and that she might perish in this barren wasteland. Her only option was to keep moving.

The stolen pony she had been riding had gotten free from the hobbles, and had run away during the storm. She was now not only alone but on foot. Her clothing, especially her moccasins were not fit for this type of travel. She was now wandering aimlessly around the prairie, first in one direction, then in another. Once she even came across her own trail. Of this she was sure because she spotted the place where she had spent a night. Loneliness, fatigue and fear over took her and she began to panic.

Late one afternoon she spotted riders off to the south. She sought a hiding place, and watched them approach. As they got closer, she determined that this was an Apache hunting party. To her dismay they chose to make camp just a short distance from her hiding place. She huddled in a small hole between two rocks where she was hidden from view by, a large growth of cactus.

After a long sleepless night, the sun finally returned, and she could see that the Apache hunting party was preparing to leave. After they had departed, she found a larger spot just outside of her hiding place. She laid down for the sleep that was much needed.

She was awakened by the sound of running horses. She peered out of her hiding place. She could see the hunting party of Apaches racing across the prairie back in the direction they had come. There was a large party of Kiowa Braves pursuing the Apaches. Soft Rain watched the departing warriors, from her hiding place, with great interest. She had no idea that she had wandered this close to the land of the Kiowa. This alarmed her greatly. She knew that if she had drifted into the land of the Kiowa, then she was far to the east of her home. She had heard that the Kiowa were equally as hostile as the Apache and Comanche. However she knew some of the Kiowa people, because even they attended the dance of the snake. This meant that she might receive assistance from the people of their villages. With this thought she gained some hope, if she had wandered that far to the east then it meant that she was to the southeast of the land of the Zuni. It was in the land of the Zuni that she also had friends. She knew that the Zuni people would help her, if she could only find their pueblo.

Apparently the Apaches that had camped close to her, had wandered into the Kiowa territory. The unwelcome hunters were being driven back to their own land. Under normal circumstances the Apaches would have stayed, and fought the pursuing Kiowa braves. In fact under other circumstances, they would have enjoyed the fight. This time was not the right time for a fight. They were painted and equipped for hunting and not war. Also they were outnumbered about three to one by this Kiowa war party. Any confrontation would only be attempted if the Kiowa pursuit carried them back into Apache land where they could gain reinforcements.

After the rain, Two Coyotes had lost the trail that he was following. Due to his injury, he was walking with the assistance of a stick. He began to cut back and forth across the prairie in the general direction that he had been traveling. Unknown to him, he was only a half days walk from the very spot where Soft Rain had been sleeping.

The following day he came across the camp that had been abandoned by Soft Rain. He could tell by the signs left that she was not too far away from this camp. It was here that he decided to camp for the night.

When dawn returned to the land, he was up and about removing any sign of the camp. About twenty paces to the north, he found a row of stones pointing in the direction that someone had traveled. He assumed that this was a trail sign left by Soft Rain. If he found no sign, or trail, he would circle around back to this spot and go in another direction. After all he thought that this might be a tactic to mislead any one following her. The circling process would be repeated until he had determined which direction Soft Rain had actually gone.

Chapter 10

Rain Cloud paused in the telling of the story. The moon was full and high in the sky. There were no clouds anywhere to be seen. He stood on shaking legs and peered in to the starlit sky. Once again he began to speak. "It is late and this has been a long day. I am very old, and I tire more now than as when I was a young buck. I will retire to my tepee for sleep. When the sun rises again, we will all gather here again. Then I will continue to tell you of this adventure."

Having said this he turned and walked the few paces to his tepee. All the people, around the council circle, wished that the sun were now once more shining, so that Charlie could continue. They all retired to their huts or tepees for the night.

The first light of day found the entire group again sitting at the council circle. Even if they did not wish to hear the words of Rain Cloud, they would never insult such a man by being absent.

Rain Cloud emerged from his tepee. He appeared as fresh as the morning air. He took up his position before the council to continue his story, where he had stopped the night before.

Red Feather and his hawk companion rose early in the predawn light. There was already much activity in the pueblo. The entire tribe was getting ready for their trip back to the land of the Hopi. This would be the fifth trip that Red Feather had made to the snake dance celebration.

He was looking forward to this trip more than usual. He had visions of joining in the ceremony, where the braves selected a wife. It was his intention to select his friend Soft Rain, should she enter the circle. Although he had only seen her for short periods every two summers, he was sure that he wanted her for his wife.

The hawk knew that something was going on. He fluttered about the pueblo much as a child would in anticipation, of an adventure.

Red Feather carefully packed the new shirt and moccasins that his mother had made for him.

"This will be a very pleasant journey for the two of us my friend. When we return to this place there will be three of us." He told the hawk.

After the tribe had carried their belongings to the valley, they loaded them on the travois. They were ready to depart on the long journey to the village, on the rim of the great canyon.

The climb out of the valley did not seem near as hard as it had in the past. Nor was the sun as hot out on the desert as before. In reality nothing was different, except the excitement felt by Red Feather. The hawk seemed to soar to a greater height than before. Red Feather noticed all this, even he though he was lost in his daydreams.

Finally the day he had anticipated arrived, they were in sight of the Hopi village. When they arrived in the village he carefully surveyed the people in search of Soft Rain. She was not to be found. This raised his hopes. Maybe, this meant she was in the pueblo for the women that were preparing for the wedding circle.

The many days of visiting and celebrating dragged by for Red Feather. For the most part he stayed to himself with his hawk companion.

The snakes had been captured and placed in their pit. The day of the dance finally arrived. All tribes gathered to observe the dance for rain. Time seemed to stand still while the dance was in progress. For several days Red Feather sat waiting anxiously for the next celebration to start. His heart fell when the women entered the circle, and there was no Soft Rain. Then he recalled something that Soft Rain had told him. She said that sometimes a girl would not join the dance until most of the brides had been selected. She said that by joining the circle later, the girl could then choose the brave of her choice by extending her hand to the chosen man. He could hardly contain himself through out the entire ceremony. As soon as the brides had been selected and the many wedding ceremonies were preformed, he searched out the Hopi Medicine Man.

"It is my desire to learn of the maiden Soft Rain."

The Medicine Man stood silent for a moment before he replied. "My son, Soft Rain is no longer in the village. Early last winter she disappeared from the village and has not been seen since. A search party found the tracks of two ponies going to the south. They went in the direction of the land of the Apache. They also found signs that it was indeed an Apache that had taken her. After many days searching a great rain came. This washed away all signs of the trail. No other sign, of your friend Soft Rain, has since been found."

It was with a heavy heart that Red Feather withdrew to himself to ponder this situation. The spirit of the hawk could offer no guidance in this matter.

After many hours of thought Red Feather decided that he would set out to find Soft Rain. This seemed to him the only way to save the woman that he desired to make his wife.

Early the next day he began to gather the necessary supplies that he would need for his journey, into the land of the Apache.

Red Feather sought out the braves that had first searched for Soft Rain. He wished to gain as much information from them as possible. From them he learned of the direction that they had searched. He also learned of the place where they had found the Apache sign.

Armed with little information and much hope, Red Feather set out to find Soft Rain. This seemed too many to be a hopeless journey. As he crossed the open lands to the south, of the great canyon, there was no reason to search for a trail. He had gotten information from the Hopi braves about this part of his journey. Alone on the prairie with nothing to do but ride, his mind began to wander. He recalled the first time he had encountered an Apache Tribe.

His people had been on a successful buffalo hunt to the southeast, of the pueblo. The meat and hides had been loaded and they were preparing to break camp to return to their home. Just as the sun was rising, there came a large band of Apache warriors. They were painted for war, and they outnumbered the hunting party about four to one. The Apache came in so swift that the hunters had no time to arm themselves and prepare for battle. Therefore there was very little fighting. While the hunters were seeking cover, the Apache warriors took the ponies with their loaded travois and rode off to the southwest. With their supply of arrows nearly depleted from the hunt, there was nothing that the hunters could do except return to their village to gather more arrows and braves. When they arrived back at the pueblo, they reported the attack, it was decided that they would paint for war, and go after their stolen ponies and bounty.

The attack had taken place far from the land of the Apache, and it was assumed that it would take more time for the raiders to return to their village than it would for the Zuni Warriors to overtake them. Within a very short time the men from the pueblo were on the trail back to the place where the raid had occurred.

Red Feather was chosen to be a part of the war party. He was only seventeen summers old at the time. The ride was a long, but very exciting for the young brave. This was to be his first time to actually be involved in battle. He knew that according to what the hunters had said, the odds had been reversed. The War Chief in charge felt sure that they would recover their ponies, however everyone was aware that the Apaches were fierce warriors. These were warriors, who would fight to retain the stolen bounty.

The Apache party was so sure that they had obtained such a complete victory, that they were traveling in a more relaxed mode. They were moving a lot slower than those that were following them. They would stop often to celebrate. They were so sure of themselves that they failed to keep lookout scouts behind. Therefore, they were not aware of the war party that was closing in on them.

Just before dusk on the third day, the Zuni scouts, returned to the war party with the news that the Apache raiders were preparing night camp.

The war party halted for a short period of time, to devise their plan of attack. They would enter the camp after most of the raiders were asleep. If they conducted this attack as they planned, the Apache would not know anything soon enough to prepare for battle.

It was not the custom of the Apache to attack or fight at night. Therefore, they never suspected that anyone would attack them in the dark.

Soon the Zuni warriors had surrounded the camp and subdued most of the lookouts. The only noise that could be heard was the milling of the ponies.

Red Feather heard a soft whistle and the attack was on. Unknown to them, there had been a lookout that they had not found. This lookout had slipped into the camp and alerted the other Apaches. When the Kiowa swarmed the campsite, the Apaches were preparing for battle. Many of the Apache were killed with out ever knowing what was happening. The rest put up the best fight they could under the circumstances. Then fled into the darkness with out their ponies. During the battle Red Feather had his first hand-to-hand encounter with an enemy. He was approaching a fallen brave, but as he drew near, the brave suddenly rose to his feet with drawn knife. The distance between them was so short that the arrow was useless. Red Feather drew his own knife and lunged forward striking the Apache in the face with his knife. The charge by Red Feather was so swift that it dislodged the knife from his enemy's hand. There was nothing the Apache could but flee into the night with blood streaming down his body from the huge cut across his face. At daylight there was no sign of the departed Apaches. Only the dead remained as evidence that there had ever been a battle.

The hawk circled the entire camp and carefully examined the remains of each fallen Apache. When he had completed this chore, he flew out onto the prairie to secure his breakfast.

Red Feather did not know if any of his arrows had succeeded in finding other targets. Never the less he would return to the pueblo a proud and victorious warrior. There would be much singing and dancing when they returned home. Each warrior would be required to tell, or sing of his part in the attack. The entire event would be recorded in pictures on the walls of the big room.

It was well into the third day; his memory had vanished from his mind, when Red Feather and the hawk reached the point described to him by the Hopi warriors. It was at this place that he set up camp, to search the area for signs. It had been too long and the winds and rain had long since destroyed any possible trail.

That night he went into council with the Great Spirits and asked for some sign or vision. He received no sign, and the spirit of the hawk had no solution.

After receiving no sign from the spirits, Red Feather stretched out on the sleeping blanket and prepared for a night's sleep.

Again the first encounter with the Apaches entered his thoughts. Could it be that the warrior, of whom he was searching, had been in that first raiding party long ago.

With that thought in mind he drifted off into the dream world of restful sleep.

When the dreams came they were not of raiding parties or battles. The dream that came to him this night was of his second trip to the land of the Hopi. In this dream, He was again in the great canyon. He and several other young braves were sitting along side the great river. They were receiving information, of the surrounding land, from one of the older Hopi braves. They were joined by a group of Hopi girls and their instructor. The girls were brought down into the canyon for instructions on the planting, caring, and harvest of the many crops that were raised there, and the selection of the many reeds used for weaving. One of these girls was the friend of Red Feathers. This friend was the girl called Soft Rain. They all sat and listened to the talk of the older brave, as though they had never heard the history of their land.

While Red Feather had not actually talked to Soft Rain on this occasion, it was still a pleasant day and made for a fond memory. Even in his sleep, it brought a smile to the lips of Red Feather.

The hawk seemed to know what they were doing out on the prairie alone. It would circle far ahead of Red Feather, when they started the wide circle of the area to the south.

Day after day Red Feather and the hawk moved further south. They were searching every inch of the ground along with every rock and bush. Each night was spent with a heavy heart. Red Feather was lost in despair. If only the Spirits would come to his aid, and show him some sign to renew his hopes.

Finally hope returned to him, when he rode upon, what had once been a small camp. Unknown to him at the time this was the very camp that Soft Rain had used twice when she had accidentally crossed her own path. Even though the camp had been covered over to make it appear that it did not exist, he could tell that this was a camp that had been used by two people on separate occasions.

What really raised his hopes was a group of small stones placed in a line pointing to the east. He found this sign several paces to the north of the original camp. Whoever had used this place for a camp was trying to tell someone, or anyone the direction they were traveling. It became apparent that there had been only one person there at any given time.

Could it be possible that Soft Rain had escaped her captor and was lost in this forbidden section of the land? Hope and anxiety told him that this was the case.

After refreshing himself with rest, food, and drink, Red Feather began to make his circle to the east, in the direction that the rocks had pointed. The direction he was traveling would carry him to the south of the copper fields and his homeland. If in fact it carried him near his pueblo he would visit his home to replenish his supplies. This would not be the case. The trail would continue to the east in the direction of the Kiowa Nation.

He knew that the Kiowa Apaches were a hostile tribe. He also knew that it was not their way to take captives. It might be that he could gain some information if he happened to meet some of the Kiowa people. However, most of the Kiowa people were probably still in the land of the Hopi for the dance of the snake, or at least on their way home.

Red Feather continued his search for a sign that might tell him that he was on the right trail. After the sun had risen and set several times he had found nothing to signify that he was indeed on the right trail, or any trail for that matter. The hawk had continually circled in front of him. Even this did not show any sign that was of promise to him.

It was with a heavy heart, he prepared his camp that night. He decided that if the next day did not show him a sign he would change his direction of search. As he lay down on his sleeping blanket he spoke to the Spirits. He asked for assistance with his search for Soft Rain. Receiving no sign from the Spirits he spent a long and restless night.

With the first sign of light, he arose and vowed that this would be the day that he would find some sign to guide him.

The earth had now become dry and was beginning to show recent signs. Finally on the outer reaches of his circle he discovered a footprint. He got off his pony and examined it more closely. He was certain it was the print of an Apache moccasin. The print was accompanied by a small impression in the ground. This was could have been made by the end of a spear, but more likely it was made by a stick. It showed that there had been much weight applied to it. A few feet away he discovered another print. The second print was that of a smaller person. He suddenly realized that he had found the trail of both Soft Rain and also her captor. The signs told him that they were not traveling together. It was apparent that Soft Rain had gotten free and was being pursued by this unknown Apache.

Panic seized him. He must overtake the Apache before Soft Rain was recaptured. He set the pony at a faster pace. All the while he was searching the ground so that he might not lose the trail.

Little did Red Feather know that at that moment he was less than a two days ride behind them. Since they were on foot it would only be a matter of time until he would overtake the pair.

Chapter 11

Soft Rain was making her way through a very rough and rocky section on the edge of a small river. She stepped on a loose stone. Her feet were very sore and her moccasins were worn ragged. The stone rolled and she fell. When she attempted to regain her footing, she was unable to stand. She had injured her ankle and had to drag herself to a safe hiding place. Now that she could not walk, fear overtook her. How was she to find her way home and what would she do if Two Coyotes found her?

Overcome with pain and fear she lay inside a small opening between two huge rocks. She had almost depleted her supply of food and she had no water. To her it seemed that the Spirits had forsaken her. Nevertheless she continued to seek some sign to tell her what she must do. For a day and a night she lay in her hiding place. The pain in her foot had subsided and at last she decided to try to stand. As soon as she placed her weight on the leg the pain returned and she tumbled back to the ground. The pain shot from her foot to every part of her body. This pain so great that it made her feel sick at her stomach and dizzy. She crawled deeper into her hiding place, and her heart cried out for help. She knew that help was not going to come. After all no one knew where she was, not even herself. Finally, total exhaustion overtook the pain, and she drifted off into a fitful sleep.

Two Coyotes was following what he believed to be the trail of his lost captive. His progress was slow because he was walking through very hard rocky terrain, and the signs were difficult to follow. Even though his lost captive was inexperienced, and had made no attempt to cover her trail, he sometimes lost the trail. He had to make wide circles to regain the trail, at times.

Finally, either by luck, or the will of the Spirits he came across a place where something, or some one had been dragged along the ground. He followed this trail into a cluster of rocks; there he found the sleeping maiden.

Since his approach had not aroused her, he decided that he would let her sleep while he himself would get some rest that he was in need of. This was being a mistake that he would soon regret.

Suddenly Two Coyotes awoke with a start. He was surrounded by a group of Kiowa braves. It well known the Chirichua Apache was enemies of the Kiowa Apache; and Two Coyotes was alone, and had no weapons except his tomahawk and knife. This being the case he decided that he would not offer any resistance to any thing that these men did. These Kiowa braves were fierce warriors, but they were not ruthless. They had been so preoccupied with the discovery of the Apache that they had not yet discovered the sleeping woman.

"What are you doing here alone in the land of the Kiowa?" He was asked. "You know it is against our law for you to be here without being told that you could enter."

Two Coyotes decided that it was in his best interest to tell them the truth. He started his story, at the point, where he had arrived at the great canyon. He told them of the capture of the Hopi woman. He told of her escape, and how he had followed her trail. He lied when he told them that he was unaware that he had crossed into their land. This last part they did not believe because all Apache people know the limits of their own land.

When asked where this woman was now, he directed them to the place where the ill woman was sleeping.

One of the younger braves called, Running Fox, recognized Soft Rain from a trip he had made to the dance of the snake.

The Kiowa braves held council among them selves; it was decided that they would remove the tomahawk and knife from Two Coyotes, and have him escorted from their land. Running Fox then dispatched two braves to escort the Apache away from their land.

Soft Rain was awakened by the noise outside her hiding place. In her feverish state, she could not understand what was going on. She only knew that she heard voices. At first she thought that she was still in the world of her dreams. She slowly dragged her self into position where she could see out of the opening. The harsh sunlight, from the outside, made it impossible for her to recognize the several men she could see blocking the entrance to her hiding place. Then she heard a voice that sounded like a young man.

"I am Running Fox of the Kiowa Nation. We mean you no harm. We have sent your Apache captor back to his land. We need to know the nature of your illness, or injury so that we may assist you getting back to your home. I know you are of the Hopi Pueblo from the rim of the great canyon. There I have seen you when attending the celebration and the dance of the snake. You will need much assistance because you are many days from your home. In fact you are on the border between the Zuni and the Kiowa Nations."

Running Fox, even at a young age, was a very important scout for the Kiowa nation. As such he was often sent on special missions. On this particular mission he was searching for a buffalo herd. The tribe was in need of fresh meat, and additional hides to make new tepees for the expanding tribe.

Soft Rain sat in silence for a time. She did not know if she should feel relief or fear. She decided that she must trust these braves. She was weak from hunger and her leg gave her great pain.

"My illness is only a great hunger, my pain is only in my foot. I slipped on a stone, and injured it to the point that I cannot walk. I had escaped from the Apache, and was trying to avoid being recaptured."

Running Fox came forward and examined the injured foot. He concluded that it was not broken but only sprained. However, it was swollen to twice the normal size.

"There is a Zuni Pueblo not so far from this place. This is the closest village. It is there that we will take you, under the sign of peace. I know of a woman called Misty Night that will care for you until such time as you are able to travel to your own village. After we have carried you to this place, we will then return to our own village many days to the east."

After this was decided, Running Fox placed Soft Rain on the back of his pony and started to the west. A short distance from where they started, they came across a running stream. The stream was filled with the cool water from the mountains that spanned the horizon to the Northwest. He placed Soft Rain on a rock and instructed her to keep her injured foot in the cool water. She knew that this would help get rid of the swelling, and shortly she began to feel better.

Meanwhile two of the other braves had left the group, and soon returned with the fresh meat from a small deer.

After soaking her foot in the stream, and eating the first real food that she had had in a very long time, she began to feel a little better about her situation.

She was told that they would rest there for a few days, and then she would be carried to the canyon pueblo of the Zuni people.

She knew of this woman, Misty Night. She had seen her on several occasions at the celebration of the snake dance. She also knew that the Zuni were not a hostile tribe, and her chances of returning home were greatly improved.

For many days Running Fox and his followers tended the injured woman's foot. She was well fed and provided with a new blanket with which she fashioned a make shift dress.

With the return of her strength came the renewed hope that at last she was going to be returned to her home. She was looking forward to the time that she could again walk, and be on her way to the Zuni Pueblo.

Early one morning Running Fox approached her. He told her that this was the day that they would start for the land of the Zuni. It was with great excitement that she prepared to leave this camp beside the river.

Running Fox had dispatched a runner, under the sign of peace, to the pueblo of the Zuni. It was the objective, of this runner, to advise the people, of the pueblo of their mission into their land.

With the confidence that they would be received in good faith, the small party of Kiowa escorting Soft Rain headed west toward the canyon of the Zuni Pueblo.

The runner, Crazy Owl, was riding under the sign of peace. All the while he was aware that there were many eyes watching him. He felt no danger because it was the way of all Red Men to honor the sign of peace. As he entered the valley, to the east, of the canyon, he began to see that the lookouts were now showing themselves to him. This was the good sign that told him soon they would soon make contact with him.

As he approached the place, where the canyon entered the valley, he came face to face with three armed warriors.

"I am Crazy Owl of the Kiowa Nation, I have a message for Misty Night, of your pueblo. We have rescued a woman captive from an Apache. She is in need of care. It is our wish that Misty Night might see to her until she can be returned to her home."

After telling the others of his mission, Crazy Owl laid down his weapons.

The three Zuni braves discussed this message for a few moments, and invited Crazy Owl to follow them. They led him up the trail into the canyon, and to the trail that led to the place where the ladder could be lowered.

After giving the signal, some unknown person lowered the ladder that would take them to the first level of the pueblo. When they reached the place of the council fire, just outside the big room, they told him to sit and wait.

A brave, named Many Elk, went inside the big room. He soon returned with a fine looking middle age squaw.

"This is Misty Night, and I have told her your story. She has informed me that she must hear more of this woman that you have taken from the Apache. After hearing the story, she will hold council with her husband and give you her answer."

Crazy Owl proceeded to repeat the story of how they had found the Hopi woman. He told Misty Night of the woman's injury, and the progress that she was making. He said that they had chosen this pueblo because the leader of their group, Running Fox, said that he knew your people from the dance of the snake, in the land of the Hopi. Also, that this pueblo was much closer to where they found the woman than was their own village. He said that it was their desire to see that the woman got the proper care, and then be returned to her own pueblo on the great canyon.

After hearing all that this Zuni had to say, Misty Night returned to the big room. There she summoned her husband, Walks Long, from the Kiva. Misty Night then repeated the story of Crazy Owl.

"This must be the same woman that our son, Red Feather is searching for," said Walks Long. "We will take and heal her, we will also send a runner to her village to inform them that she is here. That she will be returned to them when she is able to travel. Also I will send several braves to find Red Feather to tell him that this woman is here at our pueblo."

Misty Night returned to tell Crazy Owl that they were welcome to bring the woman to them only if they approached the canyon under the universal sign of peace.

While returning to the camp on the river, Crazy Owl met Running Fox and the others. He gave them the message. Running Fox decided that they would continue the journey to the canyon.

Running Fox was anxious to conclude this journey. He had tribal business that needed to be attended.

The trip to the canyon was a slow one because they made frequent stops to allow Soft Rain to get off her pony and rest. She was still very weak from the long period of having little food and water.

Finally they arrived at the entrance of the canyon in the valley. There they set up their camp. There was no need to advise Misty Night that they had arrived. They had been aware of many eyes watching them for several days.

Running Fox and four of the braves lay aside their weapons, and under the sign of peace proceeded up the canyon on foot.

When they reached the trail that would take them up to the pueblo they were met by Walks Long.

"You are welcome my Kiowa brothers. It is a good thing that you have done. We will deliver the woman to my wife. Then you are welcome to share a meal with us, after which we will enter the Kiva to talk and smoke the pipe."

After this was done, Running Fox and his braves returned to the valley. The next morning they departed the valley under the watchful eyes of many Zuni braves. These eyes were not seen but Running Fox knew that they were present.

Chapter 12

The land was very unforgiving, and the signs were very difficult to read. There were many times that the trail disappeared completely. At these times Red Feather would have to double back, and began the process of making wide circles until he once again found a sign that would tell him that he was once again on the right trail. The trail of the woman wandered everywhere, indicating that she knew not where she was. Red Feather could tell that the Apache was having the same difficulty following the trail.

All the doubling back and circling took much time. Red Feather felt that he was loosing ground, and that he would not overtake the Apache before Soft Rain was again captured.

At one time he withdrew into a shallow depression as he observed a party of Apache braves passing. They were riding very fast. He decided that they were heading back to their land. He knew, for a fact, that he was now in Kiowa territory.

He was also certain that the Apache he was searching for was not with this party. The one ahead of him was on foot, and there was no pony carrying double.

For a while, the trail he was following disappeared in the hoof prints of the many ponies.

Once again he had to employ the circling tactic in an effort to regain the path that the fleeing woman and the Apache had used.

After nearly a half day he found not one but three trails. One was going in the same direction he was traveling, and had been made by many ponies. Another was coming toward him. This trail also had been made by many riders. The third trail was some distance from the others, and was the one he was searching for. This trail was going away from him. With renewed energy, and determination, he started in the direction of an unknown future. He could read from the trail that the woman was still traveling ahead of the man. He also saw that the trail showed signs that both of the travelers ahead of him were showing signs of being very weary.

He continued on, often he was filled with anxiety and despair. However, he was always determined that he would over take those that he pursued, and rescue the woman, if she had been recaptured.

After following the trail for over a half day, Red Feather began to wonder why it was leading further into Kiowa territory. Could it be possible that he had misread the signs when he had first discovered the original trail? Was it perhaps a Kiowa; and not an Apache that he was following? He reassured himself that he had read the signs correctly. It was then that he came across a fourth trail. This trail told him of two ponies and a man on foot. The track of the man walking was the trail of the Apache. This trail showed the imprint of the stick. This trail was headed in a southwest direction. This trail aroused his interest, but he decided not to abandon the trail he was following. It appeared that the Apache was being driven from the place where he had apparently been captured. Red Feather concluded that the woman was probably not one of the riders.

It was not until he found the place that Soft Rain had been discovered by Running Fox that the entire picture came to his mind. It was here that he found signs of the Apache and several Kiowa, along with the signs of the woman. From this place he followed the trail to the west until he came to the camp on the banks of the river. At this camp he was able to determine that it had been used for several days.

Red Feather began to circle the camp until he found the signs that several ponies had departed, heading to the northwest. There were also signs that one pony had used this trail a few days prior to the rest of the ponies.

The finding of this trail puzzled Fed Feather. It seemed that he was being led in the direction of his own pueblo. It was not long before this puzzle was solved. After a days ride to the northwest, he met the band of Kiowa led by Running Fox. When he inquired about the woman, he was told the following.

"We discovered the woman that is called Soft Rain, being held by an Apache called Two Coyotes. We tended her injured foot and carried her to the pueblo of the Canyon Zuni. There she is being cared for by a woman that is called Misty Night. We have also sent the Apache, that had her captive, from this land."

"The woman called Misty Night is my mother, and the pueblo you speak of is my home. It makes me glad to hear that the woman is safe, and that the Apache has been banished from this land. I will now follow the Apache to make certain that he captures no more of our women", Red Feather told Running Fox. "I desire to see this man that has caused this trouble to us all, and the pain to Soft Rain".

Running Fox invited Red Feather to spend the night in their camp, which they were in the process of establishing.

After having a good meal and a restful night Red Feather departed on the trail of the two ponies and the Apache. This trail was easy to follow because it had been made only a short time earlier, and the winds had not completely devoured it. It was going in a straight line in the direction of Apache land, and had been laid in a hurry.

After a short ride, Red Feather met the two Kiowa braves that had been assigned the task of delivering Two Coyotes from their land. From them he learned that they had parted with the Apache only a half days ride to the southwest.

After gaining all the information from the two that he could, Red Feather picked up his pace in the direction of the spot they described.

When he at last came to the spot where the two ponies had turned around, it was not difficult to pick up the trail of the Apache on foot.

Mean while back at the pueblo, Misty Night was busy with the chore of returning Soft Rain to health. Soft rain was very weak from the hunger that she had endured over the past experiences. She was totally exhausted, both mentally and physically, from her many days of running and hiding from Two Coyotes.

Walks Long had dispatched two runners to the land of the Hopi to inform them that Soft Rain had been found. They were to tell them of her condition, and that she would be escorted back to her home when she was able to travel. They traveled under the sign of peace, since it was not time for the snake dance celebration it was unusual for Zuni's to enter the land of the Hopi.

By the time the runners had delivered their message, and made their way back to their village, Soft Rain was greatly improved. They informed Walks Long and Misty Night that the Hopi would welcome the party, of Zuni, when they returned Soft Rain to them.

Soft Rain had regained some of her strength, and her foot was healing somewhat. She began to take short walks around the pueblo. She asks many questions about the customs of Misty Night's people. She felt very comfortable here and enjoyed the company of Misty Night.

One day when Soft Rain returned from one of her walks, Misty Night informed her that her son, Red Feather, had gone into the desert in search of her. This pleased Soft Rain because she had made friends with Red Feather during the trips he had made to her pueblo. She now began to wonder where Red Feather might be, and if he was safe in the land of other tribes. Why had this man taken on himself to go alone, into a strange land, in search of her? Each day Soft Rain would go out on to the ledge in front of the pueblo, and peer down into the canyon. All the while she knew that she could not see anything in the canyon below.

Red Feather was making great progress in his attempt to overtake the Apache. Each day he could tell that the trail was fresher than the day before. It now appeared that the one he was searching for was only about a half days ride in front of him.

Two Coyotes progress was not a good. He was getting weak from fatigue and hunger. He had been stripped of his weapons. He had no way to obtain fresh meat to give him the strength. Therefore, he could not move very fast. With each step he was now dragging his feet. This left a long track that clearly showed that he was not in good shape. He had reached a small stream, and was attempting to drink. His tongue was so swollen from thirst that drinking was difficult. After he had finished drinking, he dragged himself to the base of a nearby willow tree and propped himself against the trunk and went to sleep.

It was here, at the stream, that Red Feather found his body the next morning. It was not the end that Red Feather had wanted but he told himself that it was a just end to such a man. He had wanted to confront the man to make him suffer for all the trouble and hardship he had brought on the people of three tribes. When red Feather examined the body of the Apache, he discovered that this had been one of the young braves in the raiding party that had stolen their ponies and supplies long ago. He was sure of this because the man had a deep scar across the side of his face.

Although it was not to his liking or custom, Red Feather removed the scalp from Two Coyotes. He did this to insure that this Apache could not enter the next world. He was certain now that no one except himself and the Spirits would ever know what had happened to this man that would bring hardship to a woman. It was one thing to cause pain in battle or when raiding, but quite different to inflict pain on one that was not capable of fighting.

Chapter 13

Red Feather went up stream a little ways and made camp. He was going to spend the necessary time here to refresh himself, and build up his strength before he started the long journey back to his pueblo.

The night seemed long, but Red Feather had a restful sleep. He was content in knowing that Soft Rain was safely in the pueblo of his mother. He was satisfied with himself for having seen the task, that he had chosen, completed.

The hawk had been with him through the entire ordeal, and it was perched on a low limb near the sleeping man. Some how the bird knew that it's search was over that it could rest also. It was looking forward to returning to it regular hunting grounds and the warm and dry perch in the pueblo.

The restful sleep brought pleasant dreams. Red Feather was once again enjoying the lessons taught him by his father. Finally the dream focused on the first trip to the land of the Hopi. He was once again on his way down the trail that led to the bottom of the big canyon. He was in the company of several other young people from the Hopi pueblo. One of which was a young girl named Soft Rain. This girl had taken a special interest in teaching him the ways of her people. She had explained the snake dance, and was going to the fields below to explain the raising of crops Hopi style.

She explained that her travels had been limited to the area surrounding the pueblo and big canyon. She was very interested in hearing of the ways of the Zuni people. Therefore, Red Feather carefully answered her every question. They had spent long hours discussing everything from their origin to the present living conditions. When he left the big canyon they both had a fairly complete knowledge of the other's ways and customs. He had carried this knowledge with him throughout the ensuing years. He had taken every opportunity to pass it to the people of his village. Without knowing it, or doing it intentionally, these two young people had done much to further the relationship between the two tribes.

His dreams raced forward to the meeting with Running Fox of the Kiowa tribe. He wondered why this stranger, from another tribe, had befriended a woman that was not of his people. He was sure that this must be an exceptional man that would go far in the world.

Finally the dream settled on the dead Apache that could not enter the land of the spirits because of the missing scalp lock.

The sun was up and the day was crisp and bright when Misty Night came out on the ledge to join Soft Rain.

"Your progress has been good, therefore, it has been decided by my husband that when the sun rises next there will be a party of our braves organized. This party will take you to the land of the big canyon where you will again be united with your people".

This was welcome news to Soft Rain. This was the day she had been waiting for. She had hoped that, by this time, there would have been some news of Red Feather.

It was with mixed emotions that Soft Rain departed the pueblo in the canyon, and started the journey to her own pueblo. As she rode she was constantly looking back at the trail behind her. This was to be a long and tiring journey because of the rough territory that she must cross. There would be many rest camps along the way. She had not fully regained the strength of her former self.

She was amazed as they passed the huge field of soft rocks. She was familiar with the yellow rocks but had never seen them in such quantity before. Then came the valley of the fire rocks; these she had never seen before. The travel was difficult across the valley of fire, and there was no rest until they had reached the other side. Still with all the rigors of the trip, Soft Rain was gaining much knowledge of the land outside her own world.

Finally after many torturous days on the trail, they were approaching the pueblo on the rim of the big canyon. Hopi scouts had been watching their progress ever since they had crossed onto Hopi land. When the party, of Zuni braves escorting soft Rain, reached a point just a half days ride from the pueblo a rider was sent to the village to inform Soft Rain's family that she was arriving. There was a great celebration planned for her return.

As they reached the summit of a rise, Soft Rain was amazed to see that the entire Hopi tribe was lining both sides of the trail. That night there was much singing, dancing, and story telling around the huge fire in front of the pueblo.

Soft Rain was overcome with relief and emotion. She was asked no questions because it was their custom to wait until such time as she was ready to tell her story. The Zuni braves were honored, and invited to stay in the village as long as they wished.

Red Feather awoke from his dream world, and was preparing to start the long trek back to his home village. He was disappointed that he was not the one that had rescued Soft Rain. Still he had comfort in the knowledge that she was safe, in the home of his mother. As he mounted his pony, the day seemed brighter than it had in several moons. Soon his journey would be over. He would once again enjoy seeing Soft Rain, and have long conversations as in the years past. He knew that she must be returned to her people. He knew that it would be next summer before he could travel to the land of the Hopi and participate in the dance of the maidens. However, he could wait with light heart.

The days were getting shorter. It seemed that he was making slow progress. In reality he was pushing his pony to its limit. Finally he returned to reality; slowed his pace, and stopped often to allow the pony to rest, eat, and drink.

When he entered the south end of the valley he felt greatly relieved, he was now only a short distance from his home.

A scout had first spotted the hawk, and then Red Feather the day before, and had returned to the pueblo with the news for Walks Long and Misty Night.

When Red Feather arrived at the pueblo, he was greeted as one who had accomplished a great deed. It was true that he had not succeeded in finding Soft Rain himself. However, he had made the necessary sacrifice. He had returned only when he had received word that she had been liberated from the Apache.

"Where is Soft Rain, and how is her condition?"

It was only after he had asked this question that it was learned that she had departed for the land of her people. His spirits were lifted somewhat when he learned that she had recovered enough to make the journey. But he was also saddened to learn that she was no longer in the pueblo of the Zuni.

On the second day after her return to her home, Soft Rain returned to her favorite spot on the rim of the canyon to enjoy once more the beauty that lay in the canyon and beyond. As she sat there her mind began to wander. She recalled the day of her capture, and the horror of being held by the Apache. Then her thoughts turned to Red Feather, her friend. She wondered what he had endured in his search for her. She was very concerned for his health and safety. Would she ever see her friend again? These questions would have no answer in the near future.

The following week she accompanied the other women to the bottom of the canyon. There she busied herself with the tending of the crops. For the next several moons her life returned to the normal dull routine of her everyday life. To occupy her time she again returned to the art of writing pictures stories, and through these she began to tell the story of her experiences as a captive, of her escape, and ultimate rescue. Never were her thoughts far from the outcome of Red Feathers journey.

After a prolonged rest Red Feather was up and about the pueblo and the canyon, in an attempt to occupy his time. The braves of the village were preparing to go on the annual buffalo hunt. This hunt would be conducted on the vast grasslands several days ride to the north. As the women were getting ready for the trip, the braves were busy preparing their hunting equipment. Red Feather decided that he would join the hunting party. For this he would need a new stronger bow.

The hawk seemed to know what was happening, and it was flying around in excited circles. He showed more energy now than he had on their long search for Soft Rain. He would dart high into the sky, and then dive down to the spot where Red Feather was working. He did this repeatedly as though telling Red Feather to hurry.

Finally all was ready, and the hunting party was assembled in the valley. They were waiting for the signal from the leader to be off. Red Feather, with the hawk perched on his shoulder, was riding at the rear of the party. This was to be a long and difficult journey, so his thoughts were taken away from Soft Rain and her people. He began to devote his time to scouting and searching for the herd that they were looking for. After four days and three night camps, he was rewarded with the discovery of the massive herd of buffalo just a half days ride to the north of their last camp. He returned to the hunting party and reported his findings. Immediately the women began to set up camp and prepare for the arrival of the meat and hides.

At dawn the next day the men were near the summit of a small rise. When the sunlight came they surveyed the situation, and decided on their plan of attack. There was no place in the area that a corral could be constructed. And there were no huge cliffs that they could stampede the herd over. This would be a hunt requiring much riding and shooting from the backs of their ponies. This would leave the slain animals scattered over a large area. It was decided that they would attack in such a manner as to circle the herd if possible to confine the kill to a smaller area. The herd consisted of two main parts. The bulls were grazing apart from the cows. Most of the mature cows had young calves at their side. The bulls were the objects of the hunt. The hunters would attempt to separate them further from the cows. No cows or calves would be taken. These were vital to the continued growth of the herd. Only part of the bulls would be harvested, and these would be mostly the older ones.

Red Feather had been on several hunts before. He knew that this was the most demanding type of hunt.

As the hunters topped the rise, the herd began to get nervous. Even though they had poor eyesight they could smell the grease and sweat of the hunters. When the hunters were about half way down the side of the rise, the herd started to stampede. Soon the braves were riding among them and selecting their targets. This stampede was controlled somewhat and forced in a wide circle.

Finally the hunters had depleted their supply of arrows, and the hunt was over. There were dead and injured animals scattered across the wide prairie. At this point in time the women joined the men in the killing field. They began to prepare their bounty for transportation back to the pueblo. While the women were in the process of doing this, the men went to a nearby river and secured poles for the construction of the many travois needed to carry all useable portions of the buffalo back to their home.

It had been several long and tiring days but at last they were ready to return to the pueblo in the canyon. It would be there that the real work would be required. They would have to carry everything up the narrow ladders. Then the final drying of the meat, and the processing of the hides would be completed.

While the women were engaged in this, the men set about replenishing their arrows. The only arrows that they now had were the ones set aside in case they were attacked by a hostile tribe on their return trip. It was not unusual for some of the hostile tribes, from outside their land, to steal rather than hunt for their food.

While Red Feather was engaged in the making of arrows, it was quite common for the hawk to fly out for an extended time. One day when the hawk returned there was a second hawk with him.

"I see that you have taken a mate my feathered friend. This is good, for all living things need a mate and companion to further the growth of their species. It is my desire to do the same when next I visit the dance of the snake."

From that time forward the two hawks were together. The new addition seemed to know what was expected of it, and conducted itself as if it too had been raised with the people of the pueblo.

Now when Red Feather went into the wilderness, he had the spirit of two hawks to assist him. This was good he thought to himself, the use of four eyes scouting above him was a welcome addition. The three made a rather unusual, but effective combination. Red Feather had always depended on the wise hawk spirit to assist him in everything he undertook. To him the spirit of the hawk was more powerful than that of the eagle. This was probably because he had learned, during childhood, to understand the hawk's actions.

With the task of making new weapons completed; and the meat and hides from the hunt prepared, and stored, it was now time to return to the task of everyday living.

Walks long was getting older and his body would no longer allow him and Red Feather to do the things together that they had done in the past. Red Feather had come to Misty Night late in life. She too was beginning to show the slowness of the years. Nevertheless, their spirit was still bright and alert.

Walks Long spent much time now in the Kiva telling stories with the other older men. Misty Night was busy now weaving and making baskets from the reeds gathered in the valley.

Red Feather and his two companions went for long walks along the river. Occasionally they would hunt, but more often they would just enjoy the beauty of the coming spring. He was always thinking and planning for the trip to the land of the Dance of the Snake. It never occurred to him that Soft Rain might not enter the circle of unwed maidens.

Misty Night knew of her son desires. She set about selecting the finest deer hides, and making the finest pair of leggings and a vest for him. She wanted Red Feather to be the best dressed brave at the celebration; regardless, of the out come of his quest to secure Soft Rain as his wife. When she had finished the clothing, she proudly presented them to her son. Red Feather accepted the new clothing. He was in agreement with her that these were the finest that she had ever made. He would indeed wear these in the land of the Hopi. These, along with headband she had made him many years ago, made him feel that he was the best dressed brave in the village.

Finally the time had come for the people of his pueblo to prepare for the long journey across the wild land to the west. This journey would end when they joined the many other tribes. This would be in the land of the big canyon. The horses were brought down from the mesa above and placed in the holding area, at the entrance of the canyon. There they were groomed and painted with the traditional markings of the Zuni People. New travois were constructed, and loaded with the poles and hides for tepees that would be their temporary home while they were attending the celebrations. After all the necessities for the trip were loaded, it was now time for them to make what Walks Long considered his last visit to the land of the big canyon.

With the two hawks circling high above the tribe, they started the long climb from the valley to the mesa above. There they would turn to the west and cross the edge of the field of the soft rocks. Red Feather was leading five of his finest ponies. These he would give to the father of Soft Rain in the event that she accepted his invitation to be his wife. He felt confident that she would accept, but then there were many young braves that would attend the wedding celebration. It had been two years since he had spoken to Soft Rain. Much had happened in both their lives.

Red Feather was so embedded in his thoughts of the future that he hardly noticed the circling hawks, or the rough rocks of lava, in the valley of fire.

The days drug by ever so slowly, and he thought that perhaps the Great Spirits had moved the big canyon. He knew that this was a foolish thought brought about by his anxiety and desire to quickly reach the pueblo of the Hopi.

"Foolish ideas, I am acting like a child," he thought to himself. Never the less these thoughts would reoccur from time to time.

Being burdened with the extra ponies he would not scout ahead, but remained in his position in the traveling unit. After what seemed endless days in the land of rock and cactus, one of the scouts returned to report that they were only a short ride from their final destination.

This news brought new life to the thoughts of Red Feather. His pulse quickened and for the first time in his life he was getting nervous. All this was strange to him because he had never felt this before. Until now he had never known that such a condition even existed.

The next few days were spent setting up their temporary home, to the south of the main Hopi Pueblo. There was much work to be done. Most of which was the duties of the women. The Tepees were set in place. This was the somewhat unfamiliar work that was performed only during hunting trips, or a trip such as this every two years. The men were invited into the Kiva for smoking and story telling. No one would enter any Kiva that was not their own without being invited. The Kiva was reserved for special councils, and social events for the men of the village. After what seemed an eternity, to Red Feather, the day arrived for the beginning of the Snake Dance. It did not seem practical that this celebration should last so long, and Red Feather grew very restless. To him the dance went on and on. There seemed no end to the celebration.

Many tribes were represented, and a group of dancers from each was invited to take a part in the dance. The beauty of the costumes and the ceremony was completely lost to Red Feather. His mind could not focus on the proceedings. He was only looking for the end of this celebration, and the beginning of the Dance of the Maidens.

Chapter 14

Late in the night the Snake Dance was completed. The people returned to their temporary homes. The following day the snakes were carried far from the village, and turned back into the wild. The work of the people was completed, now it was time for the snake spirits to carry the message to the outer world.

After two days of resting and preparing, it was time to once again assemble for the second celebration. After nearly two years, and a long and demanding search, it was time for Red Feather to see if his dreams would be fulfilled.

All the tribes assembled in the large outer circle. There was a loud cheer sent up at the sight of the first maiden entering the circle.

The procession was long, and Red Feather could not remember a time when there had been so many women entering the dance. He held his breath as they each one entered the circle, and began their slow dance around the inner circle. His heart fell as Soft Rain emerged from the women's compound and came forward. To his dismay, she did not enter the circle of dancers. She found a place in the outer circle and sat. He grew very sad as he realized that maybe this was not the year that Soft Rain would choose to become a wife. The dance continued as the number of maidens grew smaller when each chose her future husband.

The number of dancers was reduced to only four, and the number of braves had also dwindled, to a point where, there were only a few of proper age left in the outer circle.

Soft Rain rose from her place in the outer circle. She slowly began to dance as she approached the circle of remaining maidens.

Red Feather had never fully realized the profound beauty of this woman. She was dressed in a white doeskin dress that was decorated with all the colors of a rainbow. There were many ornaments of hammered gold on her dress and the headband. The likes of which, Red Feather had ever seen. To him this was truly a woman among women.

Red Feather sat silently, as if in a trance, and watched as this thing of beauty made a complete circle. When she reached the opposite side of the circle she had to pause as the maiden in front of her chose a husband.

Soft Rain then began the dance again. When she reached a point directly in front of Red Feather, she fixed her eyes on his face, and extended her hand in his direction. Red Feather stumbled, and almost fell as he jumped to his feet.

He took the extended hand and they retired from the circle. In his excitement he never knew anything about the completion of the ceremony. The next morning Red Feather joined Soft Rain as she emerged from the woman's compound. All the wedding ceremonies were just a blur to him as they waited their turn to be married.

As was the custom, they were first married in the tradition of her tribe. Then there was a second ceremony in the tradition of the Zuni. The women of each tribe had prepared a special place for the newly wed couples to stay until the various tribes departed the pueblo. It was an understood custom that the bride would become a member of the tribe of her husband. Now Soft Rain was no longer a Hopi, but had become a Zuni. She knew that she would have no difficulty adjusting to their way of life. Had she not already spent time in the pueblo of her future home? The transition would not have been difficult anyway because the Zuni lived, and had many customs that were not unlike those of her own people.

The next few days were spent preparing for the journey back across the prairie to the pueblo, just off the valley. Once there it would become necessary for a new room to be built onto the existing pueblo.

Misty Night and Walks Long were very proud to have Soft Rain as a member of their family and tribe. They had become very fond of her while she lived in their home.

Two snows had come and gone, the flowers and trees were putting on their yearly color. The bear had returned to the land from its long sleep. The creatures of the land had brought, or were about to bring new life to their species. The two hawks had prepared a nest just outside the pueblo. They had brought into the world two off springs of their own. The giver of life had presented Soft Rain with a fine son. He had been given the temporary name of Little Feather.

Soft Rain was preparing to make her first return to her people since she had become the wife of Red Feather. At first she had though that she would leave Little Feather in the care of Misty Night. Later she decided that it would not be fair to deprive her parents of the joy of seeing their only grandchild.

Walks Long and Misty Night had decided to remain behind, neither felt that it was in the best interest of their health to make the demanding journey. The years had taken much of their energy, and had greatly reduced their activities. Therefore, they stood happily at the mouth of the canyon, and wished them a good journey.

The demanding journey was very hard on the youngster. Riding on the back of his mother was not a happy thing for him. The arrival at the temporary village site was a welcome sight to all.

There was great joy and celebrating in the village by all the Hopi Tribe. After all the celebration was over Red Feather, Soft rain, and Little Feather knew that now a complete circle had been made. They were looking forward to next phase of their life.

Another day had been completed and Rain Cloud rose and faced these gathered before him. "That completes the story of the first lifetime. It is important that all of you retain what you have heard. You must pass it on to future generations. The lessons that Red Feather learned must be learned by each of you, and taught to the younger ones of tribe that will come in the future. When we meet again I will tell you of a second lifetime. It will be the story of a Kiowa Apache Warrior and his efforts to retain our way of life".

Part Three

The Last of the Buffalo

Chapter 15

Rain Cloud had returned to the center of the council circle. He was preparing to continue with the second of the stories he was going to tell.

Running Fox lay behind a huge bolder on the crest of a small knoll, looking down and across a large rolling prairie that extended into the fading sunset to the west. He could hardly believe what his eyes were seeing. There before him were hundreds of buffalo grazing peacefully from left to right across his line of sight. They were feeding on the tall prairie grass that had just reached maturity and was showing signs of going to seed. It was approaching the mating season. The animals of all sizes and ages were gathered into large herds. Even though only the older and stronger bulls would mate with the cows, the younger bulls had gathered as though they were to take part. Also these bulls wanted to establish their place in the herd. This was the normal time of the year for the older mature bull to join with the younger bulls and cows. This was the annual, and only time during the year that the great bulls would be gathered with the cows. For the rest of the year they would remain in separate herd on a separate section of the feeding area. On occasions Running Fox would see a fight break out between a dominant bull and a lesser youngster. This was the largest herd to have passed through the land in over ten summers. It was the herd that he believed that the Great Spirits had assembled to save the tribe, from the prolonged hunger that they were enduring. It was as if by magic that the herd had appeared before him as he lay on the eastern side of this small knoll. He decided that he would stay here for a while to observe the herd. He must determine which direction they were traveling. For the most part a group such as this would graze in a straight line following a lead animal. This did not mean that they would be one behind the other, but would fan out to each side and slightly to the rear of the leader. As the herd passed there would not be a blade of grass left standing behind them. This intense grazing made it necessary for the herd to be forever on the move.

Following the buffalo was a way of life for the Kiowa people, therefore they must continually be moving as well. These moving herds provided most of the necessities of life for all of the people of the plains. The meat, of course, was their main staple. The hide was used for clothing and the lightweight portable shelter that protected them from the weather. The bones were fashioned into weapons and tools. Often the skulls and horns were made into headdresses used in the various ceremonies that were an essential part of their life. There was nothing pertaining to the buffalo that was not used. It seemed that the Great Spirits intended that the buffalo be the sole supporter for the Red Man, of the plains. Even the dung was made use of, providing fuel for the cooking and heating fires of the villages. This was a very important item because on much of the prairie there was not enough wood to maintain one cooking fire. It certainly would support enough fires to serve an entire village.

As he lay there watching the herd he became aware that there was something very unusual about their movement, the animals seemed to floating in space. All the time he was watching them, the entire herd remained directly in front of him. It appeared that the prairie was moving or changing.

While the animals remained directly in front of him, the rolling hills and grasses kept changing.

What a thing of beauty these creatures were to him. The massive shoulders with their longer, darker, hair and the relative smaller hips glistened in the afternoon sun. The blue black colored horns curved gently upward, and caught the rays of the sun. A grown bull stood as tall as a man. It represented the most powerful thing that the Great Spirits had placed on the land.

He had been watching for a very long time and still while the herd was moving it seemed to remain in the same place. All this was very unreal to him, and he searched his mind for some explanation.

Suddenly he was awakened. He blinked his eyes, because as he peered out across the prairie the huge herd of buffalo had vanished. It was then that he realized that the strange actions of the herd had been in a dream world. There had been no buffalo; in fact he had not seen a buffalo sign in over ten suns. The place where he now found himself was the place of the dream, but the prairie of the dream was in reality the prairie of the prairie dog and the antelope. The only sign of the buffalo was a few chips that had long since dried and become only a sign that there had been no herd here for quite a long time.

Running Fox was one of several Kiowa Apache braves that had been sent out in search of the buffalo, the means of survival for the entire village. There was no longer enough dried meat to feed the people. New hides were needed for repair to the tepees, and make new robes for the coming winter. For an extended period of time, the tribe had been without their main source of meat and clothing. There had been a decline in the number of buffalo in the Kiowa land for a couple of winters. They had survived this period by eating the meat of dogs and horses, as well as that of deer and antelope. The meat from these sources was now running low and was not very satisfying. The meat of the horse was too sweet for their taste. The other animals in the land contained too much fat. To these people the strong lean meat of the buffalo was the preferred diet.

The Kiowa people were continually moving either, following the buffalo, or searching for another tribe to engage in battle. They had little time for the raising of corn and squash. They depended on the wild oats and wheat. They ground into a type of flour or meal. There were several types of gourds growing in this land that also provided them food as well as containers for carrying water and for holding food.

In ancient times the buffalo had crossed a great ice bridge to the north. From a distant land, that lay to the north. They had, over several generations, come to the land that they now made the home. It was told that the land from which they had come had so many animals, that some of them had left their land in search of food. With the moving of these animals it became necessary for some of the people to follow the moving herd into this new unknown land. The move was not made over a short period of time, but rather it took many lifetimes. During this time the animals of the North had adapted and evolved into what was now known as the buffalo. While on the trail of these animals the people of the tribe had also changed many times. With each new generation came new ideas. From time to time smaller groups would break away and form separate tribes. Some even attempted to return to their homeland only to find that over the years the ice had melted, and there no longer existed a path between the two great lands.

As the buffalo moved it also grew in number, and split to form different herds. Eventually there were both buffalo and Red Men spread from the great salt water of the East to the other great salt water on the West. From the great ice fields of the North to the barren desert of the South, they traveled. Both the people and the animals had over time adapted to the different environment of the area where they had eventually established their territory.

Running Fox had been sitting in front of his tepee carefully shaping arrowheads from a supply of flint that he had gathered in the spring, when he was called to the tepee of the Chief.

He was called Running Fox because when he was a boy he had shown the ability to out run all the others in the tribe. While the other boys could run for over half a sun, he could run from the rise of the sun until it went to sleep. Like other Kiowa boys he had been sent out alone to search for his vision. This vision was supposed to determine his destiny. During this period of fasting and talking to The Great Spirits, he had had no vision or sign as to what he was to do. When he returned to the village, and reported to the Medicine Man of his lack of a vision.

He was given his name based on the ability he had displayed through out his youth.

Inside the tepee were Running Fox's Mother, Leaning Tree, and his small son. The Father of Running Fox had been killed long ago when his pony had stumbled during battle. Leaning Tree had lived with Running Fox since. She had raised the boy. The boy was called Small Fox until such time that the Great Spirits sent a vision to offer him a new name. White

Deer, the wife of Running Fox had died during the birth of their second child. The child also had died at birth.

Small Fox would soon be moved to the compound that was set aside for the training of young braves. It would be while he was in training that he would be sent out alone to fast, and wait for a vision that might rename him. If he received no vision then he would retain the name of Small Fox. It was the custom of the tribe to train youngsters apart from their family. The training of the young girls was similar except that some of them would be sent to live with other tribes such as the Navaho. There the girls would work under the supervision of the women to learn the customs and ways of others. Navaho was the main choice because they were very adapted to the raising of food crops and tobacco.

It was well known that the Kiowa Apache could run as well as or better than the Chirichua Apache and could ride as well as the Comanche.

It was said that a long time ago there had been an invasion, to the south, of brown skinned men from another land. These men had brought with them the horse. After seeing these men riding this thing called a horse, the Comanche decided to declare war on these people to steal their horses. The horse had become a symbol of wealth, and was soon prized, by the people of the plains. After many years of raiding and stealing from each other all the tribes had great numbers of these horses. As new horses were raised the older ones were often used for meat. This meat was not as good as that of the buffalo, but it served to sustain life when the buffalo was not available.

The art of making the arrowheads was a very boring task for a young brave, full of energy and ambition. However, it was a job that had to be done on a continuing basis. Therefore, Running Fox was carefully chipping small flakes from a larger piece of flint. For this he was using the tip of a deer antler. There were times that he used small droplets of water placed at just the right spot on the flint after it had been heated. On this day it was too hot to use the fire method; so he was steadily shaping the various sizes from the available flint.

Chief Big Bear summoned Running Fox to his lodge along with several other braves. He gave them instructions to spread out to the four winds and search for the diminishing buffalo herds. It had been to the

Northwest, that Running Fox was told to search. That had been over a moon ago, and he had not as yet found any fresh signs that there were buffalo in this part of the vast land that surrounded his home village.

It had been along time since he had discovered a woman in the area just south of where he was now located. He had often wondered what had become of her, and the Zuni Warrior that was searching for her. He did not have to wonder about the Apache that had captured Soft Rain. They had learned of his fate while hunting to the south earlier that year.

While he was preparing for the days search, a gentle breeze coming from west brought a foul odor to him. He decided that he would ride to the west, and find the source of this strange smell. Out in front of him the land looked the same as the land he had covered the day before. He could see a gentle rise of the prairie ahead about a quarter of a days ride from him. It was to this rise that he would ride. The direction he rode really made no difference, because in the past no day had provided any clue to the location of the object of his search.

The farther he rode the stronger the foul odor became, and he was quite sure that something was terribly wrong just over the rise of the earth. It was only then that he noticed the great masses of vultures circling over a spot just beyond his field of vision.

When he reached the crest of the hill he could see a large basin beyond, the sight that greeted him was beyond belief. He saw that the basin was covered with the carcasses of dead buffalo. Each had been stripped of the hide and the meat left to rot.

Running Fox had heard, in the singings at tribal councils, of a large band of strange men with white skin. These men had come into the land, and hunted the buffalo only for the hides. He had to assume that this was what had happened here. There could be no other reason for so many animals to be killed and left in this shape. There was enough wasted meat in this basin to feed the entire Kiowa Nation for several summers. The thought of all these wonderful animals being slaughtered, and left to waste away brought a foul taste to his mouth so strong, that he felt sick. It was not the way of the people of the plains to destroy or waste anything that the Great Spirits provided.

He rode in a slow circle around the basin in search of answers to this mystery. He found the place where the herd had casually entered the basin. It was evident that there had been nothing to indicate danger for the animals as they entered the basin. At the point where he was now located it was clear to him that the buffalo had simply entered the basin while feeding. Farther along he found the trail where the surviving animals had left from the basin. The trail told him that they had stampeded, and were running from something. Here he also found the signs of many ponies that had passed a few days after the departing buffalo. After the ponies had passed there had been something else following them. Running Fox could see deep cuts in the earth that were about four fingers wide, and separated by about the length of a mans body. He could read almost any trail that had ever been made but this trail puzzled him. He had never seen anything that left such a trail. He decided that he must follow this strange trail, and learn for himself what could make such a track. The trail led into the wind. After a short time the foul odor of the rotted flesh was left behind. As he rode he wondered why he had not seen evidence of how the animals were killed. Usually, on a killing field there were pieces of broken arrows or lances, yet he had noticed none of these among the dead animals.

By the time he had determined that this was a trail that must be followed, the night had arrived. He camped by one of the few running streams that were available in this area. The night proved to be too short for his tired body. However, when daylight fell on the land he was up filling his water gourd, and making preparations to continue along the trail before him. The small paint pony seemed reluctant to continue up the trail. Running Fox assumed that the horse was reacting to a strange odor that man could not detect. Being well trained, the pony did proceed after a minimum of urging by its rider. After leveling out on the trail, the pony settled in to a gait that it could maintain for hours.

Running Fox could see a great distance in front of them, and there was no rising dust to indicate any movement. Being assured that there was nothing in his near future he again began to think of the scene that he had wandered onto the day before. How had so many animals been killed without some kind of sign being left behind to tell the story of how they had been killed? He knew that this had to be the work of some kind of man. If the Great Spirits had taken these buffalo for some reason they would not have removed the hides. When the Greats Spirits took the life of something they took only the spirit and left the body behind. If it had been some sort of animal, they would have devoured the flesh and left only the bones.

After much thought about what he had seen, Running Fox could not come up with a logical answer. There was nothing he had ever experienced that would justify such an event that must have taken place in that basin. He would call on the Great Spirits to send him a vision, and if they did not he would talk to the much wiser Medicine Man when he returned to his village. There had to be an answer, and he must learn of it. For now he would follow the trail before him to learn of the fate of the remaining buffalo.

He followed the strange lines in the sand all day only stopping to rest for a while in the middle of the night. He was so excited that he did not want to do this, but he knew that the must save the strength of his pony. He was running short of dried meat, parched corn, and his water gourd was less than half full. There were no berries or melons left at this time of the year. He had to seek out seeds, nuts, and the fruit of the cactus to retain his strength.

At daybreak he was getting ready to continue on his mission, when he heard a noise coming from beyond an outcropping of rock. He quietly eased to the rocks and peered over. There in the bottom of a shallow gully he spotted a rattlesnake engaged in a death struggle with a badger. He had never seen such a fight before, and was interested in the outcome. It was a typical struggle of two enemies. One was capable of death with a single well-placed blow. The other with the ability to move faster, and had a greater striking range. As he watched the snake would coil and strike. The badger would dart just out of range of the deadly head. As the snake reached its full out stretched length, the badger would strike at a point just behind the head. This back and forth battle continued for what seemed hours, but in reality it was only a matter of minutes. It was quite obvious that the snake was up against superior odds, however it would not give up the struggle and submit to defeat. The snake was making ever effort to protect its territory and drive the invader from his land. It soon became apparent that both parties, to this struggle, were getting very tired. The strikes of the snake were getting shorter and less often, and the teeth of the badger were getting closer to finding the flesh of the snake. Finally the badger succeeded in getting its teeth into the snake just behind the head. With one great motion it bit completely through the neck, and threw the doomed snake high into the air.

As Running Fox lay there recalling what he had just witnessed, he was sure that there was a message from The Great Spirits hidden in this event. He could not believe that he had just happened upon this fight by chance. It must have been a sign sent to him by The Spirits to foretell of some future event.

Chapter 16

The Americans had won the war that had been fought against the English several years earlier. They were now beginning to flex their muscles, and were seeking to expand their territory into what they called Indian Territory. The name Indian had been brought from Europe with the arriving settlers. It was said that the first man to set foot on this new land had called them Indians in error. He carried the name back to his homeland. However, the name Indian would forever be retained, when referring to the Native People. Prior to this there had been limited exploration of the wilderness to the west of the Mississippi River. Along the west side of the river a large nation of natives called the Mississippians had built a large group of villages. In fact the White Men had limited their activities to the forest that surrounded the River. A few men had once ventured out into the vast prairie never to return.

It was believed that these men had been discovered and killed by the Indians. The Indians along and east of the river, at first, had offered some resistance to the advancing white man, but in time the two races had learned that trading and living together was far better than the constant fighting. One of the main trade items that the natives had was the buffalo hide. For the most part these natives were of the Chickasaw, to the north, and the Choctaw, to the south. Some of these tribes had joined forces with the Whites to defeat the English. The Whites had learned from the natives that this animal, called the buffalo, existed in great numbers on the open country to the west. These buffalo skins brought a good price when sold to the people of the northeast. The merchants of the Northeast gained even greater profits by exporting the leather to Europe. The leather was superior to that of the domestic cattle owned by the Americans. This knowledge, combined with their natural greed, spurred the men of the east to begin their exploration farther and farther beyond the safety of their towns and settlements. There had been one group of adventurers that had made a journey to the edge of the Great Plains, and returned with one cart loaded with buffalo hides. After seeing the hides and hearing of the vast herds, there was a group of about twenty men preparing to attempt a journey far out onto the plains in search of these vast herds, that the returning hunters had told them about. They were equipped with five carts that had large wheels made of solid wood. They were aware that in time the center holes of these wheels would wear, and would have to be replaced so they carried extra wheels. These carts were pulled by oxen and carried their supplies on the first half of the trip. They would transport the buffalo skins back to the river after the hunt was completed.

Finally they were ready to set out on this experiment that they were certain would make them all rich men. After crossing the river they traveled for several days through the forest and finally came to the edge of the great rolling plains of the south central part of the country.

They had been told of a tribe of natives that lived on these plains. It was said that these Red Men were very hostile to any that came into their territory. Unlike the natives of the east, these natives of the prairie rode horses they had acquired from the Comanche.

The Comanche had stolen the horses from the Spaniards that had once tried to invade their territory. Over time the natives of the plains had massed great number of these horses to the extent that there were great herds of wild horses spread out over the entire south and west. Having the experience of dealing with the natives of the forest, these white men could foresee no danger in dealing with those of the plains. However, their experiences could not have prepared them for any encounter with the Kiowa Tribe. The Kiowa would be the first natives they would encounter as they moved across the great plains of the mid west.

During their first two weeks the hunters saw no sign of hostiles, or any other human. They had come across a herd of the buffalo that they had been told about. They began to slaughter every animal they could, until the herd had stampeded out of the basin where they were feeding. Then began the unpleasant task of removing and cleaning the skins. By the time they had removed all the skins the odor from the dead animals was so foul that they loaded the skins on their carts and moved out of the basin following the path that had been used by the herd. Their plans were to make another kill when they caught up with the herd. Their carts were not yet full and with the animals being so plentiful they were determined to continue to amass enough hides to make them all rich when they returned to the river. They followed the trail of the departing herd to a point where the rocks of the foothills prevented them to follow further. They swung to the South and set up camp to finish preparing their skins and to relocate the herd. It was at this camp that a lookout posted high in the rocks spotted the first Red Man that they had encountered.

Each day at sunup there was a guard sent onto the rocks to guard against the approach of anyone. On this day the guard was sitting on top of a huge rock and as the sun rose he could see the figure of a man lying prone and peering down onto the camp. This man was clad only in a loincloth and carried the usual bow and arrow of the Native American. After carefully surveying the area the lookout was satisfied that there was only this one man. He decided that he would handle the situation himself. There would be no need to alert the rest of the camp.

Chapter 17

The trail was always the same; first there had been the tracks of the buffalo followed by the tracks of horses and then the strange lines that ran side by side after the horses. Running Fox could read all the signs except the ones represented by the strange lines cut into the earth. He could tell that the tracks of the horses and the strange lines had been made several days after the buffalo had passed. The further he went the more determined he became to solve this mystery.

Finally after two suns of travel he could detect some movement ahead of him when he placed his ear to the ground. The sounds were faint and he could not determine what made the sounds that traveled through the earth. He proceeded slowly leading his pony until he topped a rise in the trail.

By this time the prairie had joined the foothills. This area was mostly large stones that had been pushed out of the earth by some unknown force. These stones were so large and piled so close together that there were only several narrow trails through the area. When Running Fox reached the edge of these foothills, he could see that the trail divided. The buffalo had gone through the narrow openings between the rocks. These openings were so narrow that they would permit only a few animals at a time to pass. With so many animals passing such narrow points the trails had been worn into deep notches between the rocks. The horses had followed to this point and then turned aside and headed south. The strange lines had followed the horses to the south. The maker of the strange trail would have to remain a mystery at least for the time being. The buffalo must be found and their location reported to the people of his village. With this in mind Running Fox began to work his way through the rocks. He had never before known buffalo to travel through this type of country, unless being driven by some outside force. These buffalo were not running from anything when they had reached this area. It was also true that the horses and the strange lines were not chasing the buffalo but rather following several days later. Another thing that puzzled Running Fox was the fact that the trail was always pointed to the North and West. Normally the buffalo trail would wander across the prairie to wherever the grass grew. This trail seemed to ignore the best feeding grounds at times in favor of continuing toward a particular destination. While puzzling over this, he was working his way ever deeper into the maze of rocks and trails. He no longer recalled his starting point nor could he see a possible end to this strange trail.

Just as the sun slipped away for its night sleep, Running Fox came upon a small level opening in the rocks and it was here that he would remain until he could once again see the path before him. His thoughts of the past few days were so strong in his mind that the sounds of the night were completely lost. He was so exhausted from the day of travel that he fell asleep almost as soon as he closed his eyes. How long he had been asleep he did not know. When he was awakened by the sounds of strange voices drifting through the night. They were the voices of men, but he could not recognize any of the words. As was the way of all his people he woke with out a start. In fact his body had been trained just to remain as though asleep until he was aware of what was surrounding him. When he had determined that the noise was far away, he slowly opened his eyes to only the darkness that had been there before. He slowly stood up and looked around. Again he heard the strange sounds. This time he could tell that it was several voices singing in a strange tongue. Also he could see the glow of a fire some where off to the Southwest. He must examine this while the darkness would cover his movements.

He carefully worked his way between and around the maze of boulders taking special precautions so as to not make any noise. He worked himself in a direction that would put him down wind so that his approach would not alert the horses that he knew must be near the camp. Finally after much difficulty he was in position to see the fire.

In the glow of the fire he could see the movement of several people but could not make out their features. They were talking very loud in a strange tongue that he did not know. Their movements were very strange and from time to time one of them would stumble and fall. Also at times they would lift something to their mouth as if drinking. Being unable to really see enough to tell how many there were or what they were doing, he decided that he would remain in this hiding place until the sun came. It was obvious that they had no one stationed outside the camp standing guard. Running Fox settled down for what he expected to be a long wait.

Sometime in the late hours of the night the camp finally settled down and everyone seemed to be asleep. He knew that he needed the rest also, so he took a series of short naps.

The call of the blue quail began to signal that the day had arrived. Running Fox had found a place where he was completely hidden from sight. The only things that were visible from his hiding place were the three eagle feathers that were made into his headband. The camp below him began to show signs of life. When the people of the camp arose and began to move about he could tell that there were about twenty men. He had never seen such men. They were clad in strange clothing and had long dirty looking hair. Their skin color was very pale compared to that of his people and they had long hair on their faces. They wore a strange headdress that covered their heads. It had a wide part that stuck out from their heads in every direction. He could not see any spears or bows but some of the men carried a long object that was part wood and the rest was made of a shiny material that he could not identify. They were drinking something that came from some kind of black pot that was sitting on the fire. After a while the men began to remove rolls of buffalo hides from some kind of platform and unroll them. After they had placed them all on the ground they began to remove any meat that was still attached to the hides. They were using a strange looking scraping tool to remove the flesh, while they were crawling around in the dust. While they were doing this, Running Fox turned his attention to the platform where the hides had been. It stood above the ground on two things that were shaped like a full moon except they were flat and made of wood. There was one of these wooden objects on each side of the platform. He noticed that there were about five of the strange looking things but only three of them had had hides on them. One of these objects had many hides that were dried and lay flat, one on top of the other.

Running Fox lay for a long while without moving. He did not want any movement or sound to give away his presence. The strangers worked on the hides one at a time stopping every once in a while to drink out of a gourd looking thing made of clay. It appeared that they had no idea that there was anyone in the area. There were several horses hobbled nearby and also some strange looking animals. These other animals looked somewhat like buffalo except they did not have the hump on their backs or the long shaggy hair across their shoulders. Their horns were bigger than that of the buffalo and stuck out to the side.

Suddenly a sharp pain pierced Running Fox's side. The pain was followed by a loud booming sound from behind and above him. As he turned to look in the direction of the sound bits of rock sprayed across his back followed by a second boom. In the rocks above him he could see one of these strange men holding one of the strange sticks that they all carried. Looking back toward the camp he could see that all of the men had grabbed their sticks and were running toward him.

There was nothing he could do except run and seek safety. As he ran he could hear more booming sounds behind him. All of these men were running and yelling to one another that there were Indians about. This was the first time that Running Fox had ever herd the name Indian. As he ran, Running Fox could feel the pain in his side and the blood rushing from his body, but he kept running and dodging through the rocks. There was no way that he could reach his pony so he ran in the direction of his village knowing that it would take several days to reach it. He knew that he could run for a very long time if the loss of blood did not rob him of his strength.

He ran and hid for the entire day and then finally came to a small stream. By this time he was sure that the strange men were no longer following him. From a pool out of the main flow of the water he gathered moss and placed it over the cut in his side. By this time the blood flow had slowed somewhat but the area around it was very hot and tender to the touch. He would remain by this pool for the better part of the night. He would replace the moss at regular intervals and take short naps in between. By morning his entire body was hot and he knew that he did not have the strength to run this day. However he knew that he could not remain here very long without food to give him back his energy. Maybe, he thought, this was where the Great Sprits were going to call him to them.

Around the middle of the afternoon he decided that he had to move on regardless of the wound in his side. As he moved carefully along the edge of the stream he held the moss tightly to his side. Finally he came to a small pool that was large enough for him to lie down in. He lay in the cool water for a long time in an effort to cool his body. He tried to figure out a plan but the only thing that was clear to him was the fact that he must get back to his village. He was certain that the strangers had long since given up the chase but he must still travel with caution. He located a large growth of water crest in the stream and the nuts from a nearby patch of nettles. After he had eaten these he felt his strength returning. There was nothing else he could do but continue his journey. He started off in a steady trot that he knew he could maintain for hours if his strength did not leave him. At this pace he could cover much distance but the trip back to the village would take several days. He ran until the breath was gone from his body and then sought the shelter of the nearby rocks. He could feel his heart pounding inside his chest and it echoed in his ears like the sound of a giant roll of thunder. He examined the wound in his side and after he was satisfied that the bleeding had stopped, he relaxed and slipped off to sleep. When for some reason he was awakened he remained very still and opened his eyes slowly to examine the surrounding rocks. There just a few feet away he discovered a rattlesnake coiled on top of a flat rock. The snake was apparently asleep as he had been. He believed that The Great Spirits had sent this snake to him. The flesh would give his body the strength needed to continue.

With a stick in one hand and his flint knife in the other he prepared to capture the snake. He slowly began to tease the snake with the stick as he got himself in position for the kill. Each time the snake struck at the stick he moved it a little further away. Finally the snake was so engrossed in the stick that it was paying no attention to Running Fox. With one final strike the snake was uncoiled the full length of its body and Running Fox struck with the knife. This was a method that he had used many times, and as usual he was successful this time. He quickly skinned the snake with his flint stone knife and thus he had the fresh meat that he needed. He quickly ate part of the meat and stored the rest in the pouch that he carried around his waist. The pain in his side was getting worst and his vision was getting blurred, he must sleep for a while. After a series of fitful naps he pulled himself up into a sitting position against a huge rock and began to ponder his next move. During one of the times when he was in a deep sleep he had dreamed that he was out on the open prairie. There were many vultures circling over him and while he lay there looking up at them, an Eagle appeared and cleared the sky of these creatures. Running Fox was sure that this was a vision intended to tell him that he would survive and rid his body of the sickness that was robbing him of his will to carry on. Now he knew that he would live but for the first time in his life Running Fox could not run.

The time passed slowly, and with the fever he had no way of knowing how long he had been asleep. It could have been a short time or maybe even days. Only the Spirits knew just how long he had been alone on the prairie. He got to his feet and started once more to complete the journey before him. His feet felt as if they were made of stone. However, he would continue to make his way home even though his pony and lance were far behind at the place where he had last seen the strange men. As he slowly walked along the bank of the steam the stiffness began to leave his legs. With the stiffness leaving his body his fighting spirit was also returning. Finally the slow walk of an old man became the trot of a young dog. After he had set this running into motion he began to feel much better. He was now doing what an Indian Brave should do under these circumstances.

He ran on until once again the strength of his legs began to leave him. By this time he was far from the stream that offered the cooling water. Nevertheless he must rest and recover from the day's run. He was asleep almost as soon as he stretched out in the shade of a outcropping of rock.

How long he slept he did not know but when he awoke it was dark with only the light of the moon to show the way. This was good he thought because the air was much cooler and would refresh him both inside and out. He ate a portion of the snake meat that he had in his pouch and drank only a small amount of water from his water gourd.

He had been so preoccupied with his wound and the desire to run, that up until now he had given no thought to his weapons. He knew that he had left his lance near the spot where his pony was grazing. However, his long bow was still draped across his shoulder from left to right. He did not remember ever removing or placing it there but he knew that he had not slept with the bow in such a position. Also his quiver of arrows was in place just over his right shoulder. His knife he knew he had because he remembered the killing of the snake. He realized that he had done all of these things not because of logic but rather by instinct. With his body somewhat rested and his mind beginning to function once again he got up and ran into the night.

With each passing night the distance he could cover grew less and less. The sleep during the days brought with it disturbing dreams. One such dream kept coming back time after time. In this dream he would see a giant herd of buffalo grazing peacefully across the prairie and in an instant the herd would disappear and be replaced with a huge gathering of vultures over a field of dead and rotting flesh and bones. The horror of this last sight would wake him and when he returned to his sleep the same dream would reenter his world.

The wound in his side was getting more painful.

Fluid was beginning to seep from the moss covering he kept over it. Also there was a foul odor that accompanied this fluid. He was getting quite light headed and would on occasions stumble and fall. Each time he fell it was more difficult for him to regain his footing.

By this time he was in the general area of his home village, but was not within range to signal for help. On this night he stumbled and fell to the ground and was unable to regain his feet. He rolled over on his back and while looking at the full moon he called on all The Great Spirits to send him strength to continue his journey. While in the middle of his prayer to his Gods he slipped into total dreamless darkness.

Chapter 18

Bitter Water was on the long trail back to his village. He was very discouraged because he had spent many days searching for some sign of the buffalo. Not only had he not found the herd. He had not seen any sign that was fresher than two moons old. He was slumped low on the back of his little paint pony, and feeling that the disappointment of his people would be a bitter one, unless one of the other Kiowa Braves had had better success. His best friend Running Fox had been searching to the north. It was his hope that the Spirits had rewarded Running Fox with a sign of the buffalo. For some unknown reason he raised his head and looked to his left. That was the direction that Running Fox had been searching. The prairie was open and flat, and off to the north he spotted something that he could not identify. With nothing better to do he decided to investigate to see what it was that he had spotted. Besides, this would delay his return to the village with the bad news. As he approached the object he could see it was a man lying in the sand. After he identified the object he rushed to see if the man was alive and if it was a friend or an enemy. As he was dismounting from his pony, he recognized the clothing and weapons as those belonging to Running Fox. It was apparent that Running Fox was near death. After using what water he had in an attempt to cool down the body temperature of his friend, he quickly loaded the lifeless body on to his pony and started for the nearest water. He knew that there was a stream about a quarter of a days ride away.

When he got to the water hole, he placed his friend into the cool water. He proceeded to clean the wound in Running Fox's side. He could tell that the wound had gotten infected and was in need of attention. He must get his friend back to the Medicine Man back at their village.

Burning Water rested himself and his pony for the remainder of the day in the shade of the small trees that lined the water hole. As the darkness fell and the air became cooler he loaded the still lifeless body onto the pony and started off at a steady trot. He knew that if he could maintain this pace he would be in the village by the time the sun came up the next morning.

Running Fox could hear muffled voices from somewhere in the distance, but he could not understand what was being said. He could also feel movement about him, but at first he could not get his eyes open to see what was taking place about him. He supposed that this was another visit from the dream world. After much effort he managed to open his eyes. The brightness burned his eyes and his head was spinning. There were several people about him, but he was unable to focus enough to tell who these people were or what they were doing.

Something or someone raised his head and placed a cool and bitter tasting liquid to his lips. His instincts told him to drink from this container. After he had consumed the liquid he lay back and again drifted into the welcome darkness.

After an undetermined time he was again aroused by movement. When he opened his eyes this time, not brightness but the darkness greeted him. He heard a familiar voice coming to him from out of the dimness. Whether it was real, or just another dream he knew that this voice was that of the Medicine Man, Walks With A Stick. It finally became apparent to him that he was indeed in the company of his people. When his strength returned he must find out how he had returned to his people.

For several days Running Fox was in and out of the real world. He would slip into a foggy dream world in which he was again in the killing field or the camp of the strange men. For most of the time he did not know what was real or what was a dream. The only clue he had was the fact that the dreams were unpleasant and very disturbing. When he was in the real world he was given much to drink. Some of these drinks were distasteful, while others were broths that he recognized. He could feel his strength returning and his head had stopped spinning and aching.

Early one morning he was aroused by the voice of Walks With A Stick.

"Wake up my son it is time that you started getting yourself back into shape to perform the duties of a Brave."

This time when he opened his eyes he could see the features of the Medicine Man, and make sense of the words that were said to him. "You have been away from us for a long while. You have wandered in the world of illusions and pain. With the aid of the Great Spirits and the power, of the healing herb, I have been able to start the healing of your wounds and return you to reality. The rotted flesh has been removed from your side, now the wound will heal leaving only a sign where it has been".

"How is it that I am in this place of my people? The last I recall is falling to the earth in the middle of the prairie, only to wake up here with you. Where are my Mother and my son?"

Walks With a Stick then began to tell him the story of his return to the village. It was another of the Braves, Bitter Water, who had discovered him lying in the dirt. Bitter Water had also been sent in search of the buffalo with no success. He was returning to the village with the bad news when he happened upon Running Fox. At first Bitter Water thought Running Fox to be dead. He was preparing to carry his friend back to the village for the death dance. He dismounted his pony and was preparing to place his Indian brother on the pony. As he approached the body he could detect a slight movement of Running Fox's chest. Filled with excitement from the fact that there was still life, within the body, he quickly loaded Running Fox onto the pony. He started leading it in the direction of the village. Bitter Water carried Running Fox directly to the tepee of the Medicine Man. Walks With A Stick had donned his buffalo skull headdress and his necklace of bear claws. After which he preformed a dance. He called on The Great Spirits to assist him in the restoration of health to this very sick Brave. For days he had kept fresh powder sprinkled over the wound. He had kept wet blankets over the body to remove the heat caused by the fever.

Now he was rewarded for his efforts with the signs of life returning to this young man. Still it would be several suns before Running Fox would be strong enough to sing the story of his experiences. He was told that his Mother was in her tepee and doing well. His son had been transferred to the camp for young boys and was in training.

It took about one moon for Running Fox to gain enough strength to walk about the village. After this time, he was to appear before a council of the village to tell of his adventure and how he became wounded. Up until this time there had been no questions put to him by anyone.

The tribe was assembled and the smoking of the pipe had been completed. Chief Big Bear stood in the center of the council circle. He gave thanks to The Spirits for returning this brave, Running Fox to the people.

"At our last council it was decided that I must send Warriors into the field to search for the buffalo. I do not believe that The Spirits are angry with us, and are removing the buffalo from our land. There has to be some other reason that the buffalo are moving. All the Braves sent out have now returned and most were met with no success. The last to return was Running Fox. Today he will sing his story to this council."

Having said this, Big Bear returned to his honored place within the circle. Running Fox sat for a while in deep thought. He then rose and took his place before the council.

"I am Running Fox, one of the Braves sent on this mission. I have come here to tell of what I have seen. I have seen things that we have not known to exist. When I left the village I rode in search for the feeding fields of the great buffalo herds. Through light and darkness I searched without finding any sign of the buffalo. For many suns I searched and hoped that The Spirits would guide my pony to a place where I might find the object of our need. One morning the gentle wind of the west brought to me a strange smell. Being unable to identify this smell I decided to investigate to determine the source of such a foul odor. With the aid of the wind and the circling of vultures, I was able to find a huge basin. When this basin came into full view I could see that this was a perfect place for the buffalo to feed. However, feeding buffalo was not what greeted my eyes. Before me I saw the remains of many buffalo that had been killed and left to rot. These great animals had been skinned, and left to feed the vultures and the animals of the wild. There were more dead animals than a band of braves would have fingers. They lay from rim to rim of the basin. There were no signs to tell me how the buffalo had been killed. After searching through the dead buffalo, I decided to circle the basin to see if I could read the signs of what might have happened there. It was quite evident that what happened had been the work of a force that had no regard for the buffalo. I did find the place where the buffalo had peacefully entered the basin. And after further searching, I found where the buffalo had run from the area. I also found signs that many horses had followed them. The sign of the buffalo and the horses were made at different times. I also found a strange sign that I have never seen before. There were several sets of deep line cut into the earth. These lines came in pairs and ran together, about the length of a man apart. I followed this strange trail for a great distance. Finally the two trails separated with the buffalo going through the rocks of the foothills and the horses and strange lines going to the southern side. It was here that I abandoned the path of the strange lines and followed the buffalo.

After following the buffalo trail for a long period of time I grew very weary and decided that I must sleep. I was awakened from this sleep by strange singing. This singing I had never heard before and decided to investigate. I saw signs of a fire glowing in the darkness. It was there by this fire that I discovered strange men. They wore strange clothing and their skin was pale. They had long hair on both their heads and their faces. They were singing and drinking from an odd shaped gourd thing. They were staggering and falling the same as a horse that had eaten from the loco weed. In the darkness and the dim fire light I could not see all that I wanted so I settled into a hidden spot to wait for the light of the day.

When the light came I could see these men drinking something from a strange looking pot that sat on the fire. After a while they began to remove buffalo skins from a platform that stood on two round things. The two round things that supported the platform were shaped like the moon only they were made of wood and were flatten. When these men moved the platforms these objects rolled along the ground in the same manner as a tumbleweed rolls. It was these that had made the strange lines in the earth. One of the platforms had dried flat hides piled on it.

These strange looking men unrolled other hides and began to remove the remaining flesh.

It was while I was watching this that I felt something hit my side and then heard a loud sound. As I looked back over my shoulder I saw one of these men holding a long stick like thing. Then small pieces of rock sprayed my body and again I heard the booming noise. This was followed by a puff of smoke coming from the stick. These sticks were throwing something at me that I could not see. They were throwing these things farther than an arrow can fly. There was nothing I could do but run to safety. All the men began to chase after me. All of them were carrying the same kind of thunder stick. I managed to stay away from them until the weakness finally overtook me at the point where Bitter Water found me."

Chapter 19

Running Fox finished telling his story and returned to his place in the inner circle. Chief Big Bear returned to the center of the council circle. He raised his hand to silent the mutterings of the people, who were amazed at the story they had just heard.

"We have just heard a brave story from the lips of Running Fox. I have heard of such men from our Choctaw and Chickasaw Brothers, of the big river country. When I sat in council with these brothers they told of such men. It was said that a great number of these men live on the east side of the river. There they lived in huts along the river in the same manner as our Red Brothers. There was one such white man that had crossed the river with packhorses carrying beads, colored cloth, and thunder sticks. These thunder sticks were called guns. This man offered these things to our brothers in trade for the fur skins of the beaver, fox, as well as other small animals skins. It was told me, that after a time this man took a Choctaw woman to be his squaw. In time he taught her and others of the tribe to speak in his strange tongue, while in turn he learned to speak as a Choctaw. Our brothers said that they had seen some white men bring a number of buffalo hides to the river on a things they called carts. They had strange animals called oxen that pulled these carts. At the river the hides were placed on large boats and carried down the river, to the salt water in the south. It was said that there were more of the pale skinned men coming into their land all the time. At this council, I also heard of the return of the brown skinned people, coming from the south. I have been considering this ever since being told of these men at the Choctaw council. These pale and brown skinned men are stealing all the buffalo from our land; we must act before they complete the job. This double threat to our land must be eliminated.

I will discuss this matter with my War Chiefs and we will lay a plan to stop the killing of our buffalo. While we are making the plan I want all Warriors to prepare for war by adding the paint to themselves and their horses. It will be necessary for each Warrior to have an extra supply of arrows that may be needed for a long journey. In three suns we will leave the village and search out those that destroy our land and buffalo. In the past the Choctaw and Chickasaw have been a war like tribe the same as the Kiowa, but now they have reached a trade alliance with these strange invaders from the east. We have no such agreement with any people except our Indian Brothers, and not all of these. Therefore, it is my wish to eliminate all who are not welcome in our land."

There was great excitement among the people of the village, as they prepared for battle. To the Kiowa Indian, war was a way of life and they thrived on the excitement. The best horses were selected and all their weapons were carefully prepared. Each night there was a dance around the main village fire. They called on The Great Spirits to give them both the strength and wisdom, necessary for the raid that they were about to make on the white man.

On the morning of the third sun the people of the village gathered for the departing of the war party. There were fifty men painted and prepared for battle. The war bonnets were place outside the tepee of all that were going as symbol of the great mission that the Warrior was going on. Running Fox was in the lead as they left. It was his duty to lead the war party to the spot where he had last seen the intruders. From that point they would find the trail and follow it where ever it took them.

For the better part of four suns the band rode in silence. As each day passed the excitement grew within the hearts of all. They were each determined to rid the entire country of this white thief that stole what belonged to them.

When at last they arrived at the spot where Running Fox had been wounded, they found the remains of a cooking fire along with bits and pieces of dried flesh and buffalo hide. They also found the strange trail that Running Fox had told of. This trail was going to the northwest. It was apparently made at a slow pace. They set up camp at this point and several scouts were sent down the trail to determine where the enemy was now located.

For the better part of three suns the braves searched for the sign of the enemy camp. Again it was Bitter Water, along with Tall Tree that discovered the thing they were searching for, in a small valley, just to the west of the foothills.

After they had reported the location of the enemy to Big Bear, there was again a war council held. This time there would be no singing or dancing. They did not want to alert the strange men as to their presence. At this council Big Bear presented his plan to the Warriors. They would surround the enemy and attack them with the element of surprise being their main weapon.

The night was very dark with only a small slice of the moon showing across the prairie. The white men were settling down for their night of sleep. These men were so engrossed in the drinking from their clay gourds and getting sleepy that they did not notice the new circle of brush that surrounded them. As they fell deeper into their sleep the bushes moved slowly and quietly ever closer to the unsuspecting camp. The thunder sticks had been stacked together in the shape of the poles of a tepee, and were out of the reach of the sleeping men. Each warrior had selected a sleeping target. Half were armed with their arrows and the other half stood by with their lances. The second half was ready for close hand battle if it became necessary. They all knew that even an arrow would not kill immediately. Now the circle of brush had moved as close as half the distance of the flight of the arrow.

At once the bowmen stood up and fired their arrows. They had moved as one without a verbal signal. Some of the enemy did not rise from their bedrolls. Others rose to their feet only to stumble and fall while trying to reach their thunder sticks. Almost instantly the warriors with their spears finished the job started with shooting of the arrows. There had been no battle the entire destruction of the enemy had been accomplished with the strangers not having time to realize that they were under attack.

Big Bear gave the command. "We will take no scalps from this battle. We are not sure of what these men represent, and cannot be sure of how The Spirits of these people will react. The scalps will be removed and buried in the ground so that their spirits will wander forever. We will take every thing that is in this camp that has a use and leave the rest. We will take the horses and the buffalo looking animals. When the sun again returns we will take the hides that were stolen from our buffalo then return to our village. Each Warrior will cut poles that we will need to drag the hides back to our village. The buffalo hides that we have recovered will be made use of by our women. They will make many robes and moccasins for our people. There will be no singing or dancing until our people have heard of our successful mission". When the war party left the camp there was nothing left but the naked bodies and the burned carts.

Big Bear took the lead and was very proud that they had cleaned this strange man from the earth. He had been on many raids, but this was the most complete victory he had ever seen. They took the thunder sticks even though they had no idea how to use them. Little did they know at the time that they would have many occasions to observe these in use at sometime in the future that was ahead of them.

Running Fox and Bitter Water were dispatched to continue the search for the buffalo herds. The rest of the party started on the long ride to the village with their plunder. They did not feel that they had stolen the hides, but simply regained that which was theirs.

When the Warriors returned to the village there was much joy among the people. There would be two suns of celebrating and a great feast. The feast would have to be of deer and antelope meat as there was no buffalo to be had until Running Fox and Bitter Water returned with news that they had located the herds. The entire village dressed and painted themselves for the ceremony and the celebration. Then the music and dancing started that would last through two nights.

After the celebration the women set about the work of dividing and preparing all the newly acquired buffalo hides. The men were busy making new arrows dividing the thunder sticks and knives that they had recovered from the dead enemies. These new knives were made of something similar to the flattened copper that was made from ore found in the hills. The difference was, that these knives were made of a much harder material and could be sharpened to a finer edge. They carefully examined the thunder sticks and soon discovered how these things worked. These were given to the most worthy of the Braves that had been involved in the raid.

While all this activity had been going on back at the village, Running Fox and Bitter Water had continued their search for a sign as to where the buffalo had gone. They carefully circled every basin and open meadow searching for the sign. For many days they rode without once seeing the fresh sign of the buffalo.

Running Fox was sitting on his pony at the top of a small knoll when he spotted Bitter Water racing across the prairie toward him. When he pulled up near Running Fox, he was very excited.

"I have discovered the trail of the buffalo going to the north west. They appear to be traveling at a normal pace. There is no sign of anything following them. This sign shows that there is still a large number together."

The two of them hurriedly started back down the trail that Bitter Water had arrived on. After riding for the better part of a half-day they were at last on the scene of the buffalo trail that Bitter Water had described. It was indeed the trail of a large herd of buffalo, feeding across the land. The trail was in the center of a large valley that appeared to split as they looked to the north. By the time they arrived at the trail, night was approaching and they made camp for the night. They had not taken time to secure anything to eat during the last several days. Therefore, they had to eat some dried antelope meat and parched corn that they carried in a pouch tied to their waist. They had chosen a campsite that was on the downwind side of a large outcropping of rocks. As it turned out this had been a wise choice because during the night a thunderstorm passed through the area. There was torrential rain with a lot of cloud to ground lightening. This storm lasted most of the night. When daylight came they could see that the floor of the valley had experienced a flash flood. There was still water everywhere. They did not have to go into the valley to know that the trail of the buffalo had been washed out. It was as if The Spirits did not wish for them to find the buffalo.

When they reached the point where the valley split, into two valleys, there was no indication as to which way the herd had gone. Running Fox took the valley that pointed more to the west, while Bitter Water took the remaining valley.

Running Fox now realized that they had been searching too hard and they were getting very tired. More important was the fact that his pony needed rest. Therefore, he decided to travel at a slower pace. He would ride for a while and then walk for a time. The heavy rain had left no signs that could be seen. Even the grass was no longer standing up with the seed heads reaching for the sky. Running Fox knew that the buffalo could not have vanished. Somewhere they would discover a sign. But it was two days before he reached the outer limits of the storm area and again old signs began to return to the earth. He laid a crossing path across the valley crossing from one side to the other and back. He was sure that if anything had passed through this valley he could pick up the trail.

Meanwhile Bitter Water had encountered the same situation. The only difference was that his valley had run its course, and had gradually become level rolling prairie. He decided that he would ride to the west and try to intercept Running Fox.

Resting on the rim of the east side of the valley Running Fox could see Bitter Water approaching a great distance away. He prepared a small fire and sent a smoke signal into the sky so that Bitter Water could join him.

"I have searched the valley to the east until it vanished into the prairie of its beginning, There is no sign that the buffalo has ever been in that valley."

"I too have searched the length of this valley. I am sure that no herd has passed this way. It must be that before the rain came they left the valley. They seemed to be always traveling to the north and west. We must ride the rim of the valley back the way we have come to find where they left the valley."

The valley that had been searched by Running Fox had grown so wide that it was impossible for one brave to cover it completely. As the two young warriors rode back to the southeast they came upon a wide depression in the western rim of the valley. Even after the rain it was possible to detect that something had left the valley at this point. The grass across this depression had been cropped very low. This depression continued for some distance to the west and they followed it for sometime until it opened into another valley. Here they found signs that the herd had spent some time feeding there. They rode for the remainder of the day. Just at dust they rode within sight of the feeding buffalo. With their spirits lifted by the discovery of the buffalo herd they decided to camp for the night, and would start back to their village at first light, the next day. They knew that the news of their discovery would give their people renewed energy. The return ride to their village would be a joyful ride because of their successful search.

Chapter 20

Unknown to these two happy Braves, to the east at the great river there was another group of the strange white men preparing to move into their land. These men were quite different from the ones that had been killed on the prairie. They were using larger carts with covered tops. They also had women and children with them. They were moving as would an Indian village would move. Their intent was to make their home in the land to the west of the river. These men were equipped with many thunder sticks, which they called rifles. They also had with them domestic cattle and chickens. Also they had seeds for planting. They were uncertain about their future the same as the Indian was uncertain about his future. Neither group suspected that their paths would cross out on the great open country that covered the central part of this land.

The return of Running Fox and Bitter Water brought great joy to the village. Big Bear called a council of the tribe, and passed the news of their success to the entire village. He laid plans to move the village to a place closer to the buffalo herd.

With the plans made, the entire village was quickly disassembled preparing for the journey to the northwest. With their belongings loaded behind their ponies and the extra animals gathered, the tribe moved away from their village, in search of a new home. Like the white men, they were carrying seeds so that they could plant corn and squash when they established a new village.

With Running Fox and Bitter Water leading the way, it was a happy tribe that took to the trail. Behind them came Chief Big Bear, next the War Chiefs, followed by the remaining Warriors. None of the men shared the burden of carrying any of the village property. The men must be able to move quickly if any occasion should arise. Behind the Warriors came the women and children and the remaining extra horses and dogs. The entire tribe was strung out for a great distance. There was an air if excitement and celebration among these people as they looked to the future to bring them once again the prize buffalo. They all knew of the White Men that had been slain, but they thought that this had been an isolated event. They had no idea that there would be another encounter. In fact there were many encounters, with the whites in, their future.

For the first few days the tribe traveled to the northwest. Due to the size of the tribe, the distance covered each day was short in comparison to the distance covered earlier by the war party. They set up camp early each day, but got an early start the next. Every fourth day the entire group rested, with the exception of a few advance scouts. The weather presented no problems. On the travel days their only meal was after the evening camp had been established. Each day the excitement would build, as they were ever closer to the buffalo, the giver of life. Their journey took them into and out of the valley that had been searched by Running Fox and Bitter Water. Finally the scouts reported that they were within two days ride of the herd. Big Bear decided that they would travel one more day and establish their village on the bank of a river that ran from the west to the east.

Once the village was established and the tepees were all in place a hunting party was selected to be the first sent out to secure the fresh meat that they had been without for so long. The hunting party consisted of twenty braves and as many women and extra horses. The herd was located and the men set about building a stockade or corral at the end of a trail that went through a cut in the prairie. When the preparations were completed the braves began to separate a small group of buffalo from the main body. They worked them toward the final killing area. Once they had their prey herded into the killing area the braves took very little time completing their part of the work.

With the buffalo now on the ground it was time for the women to prepare the meat and skins for the return trip to the new village. The work of the women was very tiring and slow mainly because of the crude stone knives they had to work with.

With the spoils of their hunt properly prepared the hunting party returned to the village and received a regal welcome. After the meat and other parts of the kill had been divided among all the families, there were plans made for a great celebration. It had been a long time since the people had had cause to celebrate. This was a happy time. All the hunters would gather inside of the council circle, and each in turn would sing and demonstrate his part of the great hunt. Some of the events that were demonstrated were expanded adding flavor to the occasion. To the people this was not telling a lie, rather, it was just part of regular story telling. Everyone realized that there was not much glory in killing a buffalo that had been trapped inside of an enclosed area. The singing and dancing lasted for the better part of two days. After this time, the men set about replacing their supply of arrows and attending their horses. The women were busy working the buffalo hides to make them soft for future use. A few of the more talented women of the tribe would record the stories of the hunt by painting pictures on prepared skins that were placed on the sides of tepees so all could see. For a time life returned to normal within the village. Little did the people know at the time that their life was about to forever change, but this was no time for them to speculate on the future.

To the east the wagon train, of the strange white men, was making steady progress toward the very spot where the village was located. The men had seen the vast riches that could be made from the sale of buffalo hides. They were determined to have their share. The money obtained from the sale of buffalo hides would enable them to establish new homes along this new frontier. These men gave little thought as to the preservation of the buffalo. They did not even consider the fact that it would take years for the herd to replace the animals they were going to slaughter. As was the nature of the white man, greed was their only motivation. They did not consider the buffalo as a source of life but only a source of wealth. To these people everything was theirs for the taking.

There had been small groups of men before that had traveled to the west of the great river, but this was the first of many wagon trails. The wagons contained men from all walks of life. There were farmers, merchants, hunters, and a lot of people that had no real purpose in life. They had hired a guide that had once before traveled to the west as far as the wide prairie, and said that he could find the large herds that was to bring riches to those that could successfully make the journey. The one thing that this guide could not prepare them for was the difficulty they would encounter along the trail. He did not know the exact places where there was water or shelter from the challenging weather. The air was already showing signs of the approaching winter. This would be a winter that would be one to remain in the memory of all who survived the trip.

After a few days on the trail, they found themselves faced with the open country that stretched out as far as the eye could see. They would travel for days not seeing any sign of water, and their supply was getting very low. The heat and dust of the day, along with the cold nights was beginning to take its toll on the women and children. At the end of this journey there would be many that had not survived.

The first major problem that faced them was the illness of the guide. He grew so sick that he was confined to one of the wagons. Therefore the entire train was left to wander aimlessly across the barren wilderness. With no guide and no knowledge of the area they wandered across the land in search of water, or a trail that would make the traveling easier. The end results being, that they traveled almost in a circle. They made little progress to the west. After several days of wandering they spotted what appeared to be a line of trees, which, to them, indicated a stream and the much needed water.

Indeed their assumption was correct, but they were not prepared for what came next. As they drew up on the edge of the trees, a band of strange red men appeared around them. Before they could get their rifles several of the people had been wounded and, fire arrows were lodged in two of the wagons. They began to shoot at these red men. After the Indians heard the loud reports of the rifles, and several of them were killed the Indians recognized the bad medicine of these people. The Indians retreated into the trees and left the area on their ponies.

Both parties to the battle were equally surprised at this event. These white men and the Indians had never seen anyone like their enemy before. The end result was that several of both sides lay dead on the ground. Two of the wagons with their contents were lost to the fire. Under the cover of darkness that night, the Indians returned to the wagon train and retrieved their dead so that their Spirits could receive a proper send off to The Spirit World.

This was the first of many such battles that would take place between the Indian and the invading whites. It was never determined which tribe had started the war between the Indians and the whites. It was the first battle on the west side of the great river.

After burying their dead, the people of the wagon train regrouped and restocked their water supply. They decided that they would continue to the west. They had gone too far to return to the east. They the idea that the riches to be obtained was worth the effort. That combined with their greed spurred them on. However, from that day forward the men always had their rifles at hand. They were determined that they would not be surprised again. No one suspected that surprise was the main weapon used by these strange red men.

The people of this wagon train had been warned that there were hostile savages in the new land. They were also told that the first they would encounter would be the Kiowa. The people of the white world would soon learn that the Kiowa were one of the more hostile tribes in the west.

For several days the train continued west without a second encounter with the Indians. Having seen nothing since the first attack they soon began to relax their alertness and concentrate more on the hardships of the trail. This would later be a fatal error in judgment.

While the people of the train saw no sign of the Indian, the Indian, on the other hand, had kept a constant watch on the activities of these strange people that were invading their land. It was their plan to either kill these people, or at the very least drive them back to the land of the big river.

The wagon train had come across a wide game trail and had decided to follow it as long as it went in the general direction that they wished to go.

The area that surrounded them was flat with only small bushes, about half knee high. It was possible for them to see a great distance in every direction. All of this caused them to relax. Some of the men who stood night watch even dozed in the wagons. Having detected no danger in their immediate future they begin to relax somewhat. They were completely unaware of the small reeds that rose from the sand behind most of the bushes. Had they been accustomed to prairie they would have noticed that these small hollow sticks were not native to this barren land. There was no movement anywhere within eyesight. Even the hot gentle breeze had stopped blowing.

Suddenly there rose from the very ground a multitude of Indians and the air was full of war cries. The air was also full of flying arrows, most of which struck either the people or their animals. Just as quickly as they had struck, the Indians turned and ran from the scene. Once again the raid had been a complete surprise leaving behind many dead and wounded people and animals. At the end of this battle it was discovered that the white people had not had time to fire a single shot from their dreaded thunder sticks. Now the number of people on the train had been reduced to nearly half.

The only reward that the raiding party had was the fact that they had killed many of the invaders. This was not a typical raid. Therefore, there was no bounty to mark the success of the Warriors. No scalps had been taken and no horses had been stolen. This, however, did not dim the excitement of having won another battle. This was the second attack on the white man by two entirely different tribes of the Kiowa Nation. Still from these attacks there had been little of the death chant in the villages.

A lot of the belongings of the people of the wagon train had to be abandoned because there were not enough horses to pull all of the wagons. After such a major defeat the remaining people of the expedition decided that it was fruitless to attempt to go further. They had to return to the east without the riches that they had dreamed of. Most of the people had lost part of their families and at least two families had been completely eliminated.

Under the watchful eyes of the Indian the remaining group reluctantly turned their path to the east, back down the trail that had once promised them riches and happiness. They had had problems with the Indian before along the river, but after a time these problems had been resolved. They must return and report their fate to the army stationed on the east side of the river. This was the first that the army would hear of the great numbers of the Indian population and the fierce way they defended their land from all invaders. By the time that the word reached the army the number of attackers had grown to thousands in the memory of the travelers. These red men presented a great problem to anyone that hoped to move to the west. But even now they did not know just how great this problem would become for both the white man and the red man.

Chapter 21

The daily lives of the people of Big Bear's village had settled back to their normal activities. It had been several moons since a Kiowa Brave had rode in with the message that the White Man had left the land. He said that they were told of the incident as if it had been a fierce battle, being decided by the superior fighting of a Kiowa war party.

The next news that Big Bear received of the White Man came when a small party of Chickasaw hunters arrived in the village. A Sub Chief called Standing Tree was leading this band of hunters. After smoking the pipe with the leaders of the village he told of the return of the wagon train to the land of the big river. He also told of a large group of men wearing blue coats that had left the river and were riding to the area where the train had been attacked. This large group of men all carried thunder sticks and wore long knives on their side. These knives were about the length of a man's arm and could cut through a large melon in a single blow. It was said that these men were sent to rid the west of all Indians that would not sign a treaty with the Whites. It seemed that the Whites had declared war on all that would not bend to their will.

While this story was being told to the people of Big Bear's village, there was in fact a detachment of White Soldiers making their way out of the forest onto the great plains of the west. The soldiers were under the leadership of Lieutenant Amon G. Briggs. He had received orders to ride west and eliminate any opposition that they encountered along the trail.

Thereby, making it safe for future exploration of the entire land. No one in the entire White world had any concept of what a problem this would be. This was the first military operation to be attempted west of the river, called the Mississippi. Up until now this river had been the outer boundary of the white civilization. Lieutenant Briggs was very proud of his assignment. He knew that his name would go down in history as being the man that had secured the entire west, for his nation. With little knowledge of what was ahead, and filled with dreams of glory and much ambition the Lieutenant forged into an adventure that would be his last in this world. Of this entire detachment, there would be only a handful that would ever see the Mississippi again.

Each day, after their march, Lieutenant Briggs would record the events of the day in his journal. Thus far there had been nothing of notable interest to record. On the second night that their camp was made on the open prairie, he sat down to record the day. "There has been nothing out of the ordinary to record for this day. We have left the forest and rivers behind and are now looking across a vast wasteland. There is nothing in front of us that stands over waist tall. This condition extends to the North, West, and South from where we are camped. Between the horizon and us there is nothing. There has been nothing more hostile than antelope, rabbits, or rattlesnakes sighted. And these only move at dusk or in the early morning. I am afraid that the stories told by the returning civilians have been blown out of portions. We will continue to the west for several more days. If we encounter nothing, we will return to the river country. My men are already getting restless. The excitement of an upcoming battle with an inferior enemy has vanished".

All the chiefs, of the Kiowa villages, gathered at the camp of Big Bear with the purpose of forming an alliance among all tribes, to combat this growing danger. At the conclusion of this council it was decided that a small group would travel to the land of the Choctaw. They would invite the white trader, from Ireland, to their land and bring with him guns and long knives for trade. This trader had lived among the Indians many years. He was accustomed to the Indian way. The Indians were not aware that the trading of guns to the Indian was against the law of the Whites. Had they had known, it would have made no difference to them anyway. They had realized that the white man had superior weapons with very strong medicine. Having made this decision, a small group of braves was selected and dispatched to the land of the Big River. They were to ride across the land showing the sign of peace to show all the tribes of the plains that they meant no harm.

When the group of braves reached the camp of the Choctaw, they met with the white trader and his Indian Squaw. They told them of their mission. They were very interested in what they found out. The trader would travel back to the Kiowa nation under the protection of the Kiowa people. He told them that he could supply them with the desired fire sticks and teach them to use them, however, first he must make certain of his safety. Also he wanted to know how the Indians proposed to pay for the guns, and just how many they would need. He also said that this trade would have to be made in secret, because the white government had a law that forbid the sale of guns, or whisky to the Indians. He advised them that it would take about two moons for him to get the guns back to their territory. The Indians, in return, were to trade him many beaver hides, that they had obtained in the hills and river to the west. They would also have to agree to allow him and his workers free access to their country. The agreement was made with the various Kiowa Chiefs and the pipe was smoked to seal the deal.

There was no question in the mind of the Kiowa that with equal weapons they could conquer the invading people from the south and the east. They were preparing for the greatest war that had ever taken place on the west side of the Mississippi. They would call on The Great Spirits to assist them in the upcoming battle.

While waiting for the delivery of the guns, all of the Kiowa villages were preparing for the great battle. This was to be the first major encounter between the Indian and the White Long Knives.

The progress of the Long Knives was observed from the first day at the river. From the very beginning there had not been a minute that there had not been several sets of Indian eyes on every man in the troop. It had been determined by observation which of these strange men, who was the chief. The soldiers had been studied very closely. It was determined that these men were men of habit. Now that the soldiers had reached the open country the responsibility of watching them had fallen to the people of the Kiowa village to the north.

Not once, during the trip, from the river to their present location, had the soldiers seen any movement or sign that told them that they were being watched.

The second in command was a Sergeant Foster, and he always rode to the right and slightly to the rear of the Lieutenant. This knowledge was very important in the plans of the Indian. It was always the plan in any battle to kill the chief and war chiefs first with the first shots.

The advance scouts had returned to the troop and reported that there was a shallow valley about a quarter of a days ride ahead. This valley was covered with massive numbers of buffalo bones. After making their report they had assumed their regular place in the formation. Lieutenant Briggs was sitting very tall in the saddle even though he was not very alert he gave the appearance of being the complete commander. Sergeant Forest was half asleep as well, as was of the rest of the men. Most of the men were lost in their thoughts of returning to their post and enjoying a long rest after so many days in the saddle.

Approaching the valley there was a slight rise to the ground. It had a large field of brush that overlooked the valley, which was covered with the white bones. Lieutenant Briggs spotted a trail through the brush, and without any thought about the safety of his men, he led the way through the waist high brush. He was thinking how he could record this expedition in his journal. He must make himself look good to his superiors.

This particular patch of brush would be the final resting place of many of the unsuspecting soldiers. Also the last battle of a few Kiowa braves. The braves had been hidden in this brush since the darkness had covered the land. They had laid in wait completely motionless for hours, and now the time to act was very near. There would be no signal, but the entire band would act as one when the battle began.

The lieutenant took out the journal from his jacket and was gazing at it while deep in thought. With a slight jerk he slumped forward and fell from the saddle. His journal fell into a small bush. There the recorded history would remain. When he hit the ground he struggled to his feet grasping the shaft of the arrow that was lodged just below his breastbone. As he staggered to his feet a second arrow struck him full in the chest. No one saw where these two arrows came from. At the same instant the sergeant was knocked from his mount. The entire area erupted with a mass of Indians, and the air was filled with the war cries of the hostiles. By the time the sergeant hit the ground the entire troop was firing at anything that moved. For several minutes they fought in a disorganized manner, and not as they had been trained. Just as quickly there came from the valley a large group of Indians on horseback. The soldiers at the rear of the troop immediately discharged their weapons. Recognizing that they were defeated, before the battle had hardly begun, they turned and retreated the way that they had come. The mounted Indians pursued these men for a short way, and managed to kill a few more before they gave up the chase. In all there were only five of the soldiers that lived through the battle. Within minutes the fight was over. The loss to the Kiowa was only seven braves. The Indians set about scalping the slain soldiers and removing their jackets, boots, guns, and long knives. The most valuable of the bounty recovered from the dead Whites was the short hunting knives that they all carried on their belts. These knives were more suitable to the methods that were employed by the Indians. Before the end of the day the Braves had recovered their dead and started back to their village to sing of the victory, and to give honor to their fallen brothers. The entire event would be told in detail. The women of the village would record the story in picture paintings, for future generations.

When news of the battle reached the village of Big Bear, there was much excitement. It was decided that Big Bear and his War Chiefs would travel to the village of their brothers to the north. It was their desire to learn of these strange men with the long knives. Also they must honor their brothers for their outstanding victory. The Kiowa people were sure now that the white man would no longer attempt to enter their land after being defeated three times. They overlooked the fact that the whites could have not known of the first group that had been killed.

Never could the Indians have been more wrong. At the very moment that they were discussing these things, the five soldiers that had escaped with their lives, were reporting to their superiors back at their fort on the river. A dispatch would be sent to the head of the army. More soldiers would be sent to confront the savages that blocked progress to the west. The description of the battle was very vague, but it was quite evident that they were not dealing with an ordinary enemy.

Chapter 22

There had been no sign of the white man now for over two moons. Life in the Kiowa Nation returned to normal. New robes had been made and the tepees repaired. The braves were busy scouting the buffalo herd, and making new arrows and spears. Big Bear, had been given one of the long knives, by his counterpart of the northern village. He had held a council of all his people and told them of the great victory. He told his people that even with the thunder sticks and long knives of the white man, they could not match the fighting ability of the Kiowa Warriors. He cautioned them to be ever watchful just in case the whites were foolish enough to again enter their territory.

The daily reports of the buffalo herd indicated that it was moving, ever so slowly, to the north and west. There was no explanation for this because the grass was equally as good in the other three directions. It was determined that the buffalo knew something that the Indian did not know. It seemed that it was the will of The Great Spirits that ruled the buffalo for the herd to move in a certain direction.

While the Kiowa were experiencing the normal life, things were far from normal at the fort on the river, There was expected a great number of soldiers to arrive in the near future and plans were being made for an all out war against the red men, of the west.

Word had gotten out that there was a movement on to place the army west of the river. Would be settlers from all walks of life were gathering on the east side of the Mississippi. They were just waiting for the courage to make the big move into the west. As the numbers grew so did the excitement. The rumors of the vast wealth that could be obtained from the fur and leather trade, gave even the meek a false feeling of security. That, combined with the knowledge that the powerful army that had defeated the English was going to clear out the west, made the move even more enticing.

One such settler was a man named Jacob Miles. He was a farmer by trade. He had brought with him tools and seeds. He was not searching for the wealth expected from the harvest of fur. He was planning to discover a section of land where the soil was suitable for the growing of crops. He had with him small fruit trees, grape vines, and berry bushes that he was expecting to plant on his new farm. He had with him every thing that he and his family processed. Jacob his wife Martha, and their two young daughters were not looking to become rich. They only wanted a safe secure place to live and establish their farm. They had heard of a range of mountains that ran from the North to the South. These mountains were supposed to be a day, or so north of the river of the red water. It was with joy, and a heart full of hope, that they had left their small farm in the far Northeast.

By the time the army had assembled on the

East side of the river there were hundreds of civilian people waiting to make the push westward. At first there was no official orders to the army as to the protection of these people. The people knew this but the leaders of the groups decided that if they stayed close to the advancing army they would be safe. This would prove a false security that would be fatal too many.

Large rafts were constructed to transport wagons across the river. The only great wealth that was acquired, by this expedition, was that of the owners of the rafts. They took their fee, for carrying the wagons across, in every thing from money to household goods. With these goods they established trading post that would serve future adventurers.

The army was the first to cross the river. By the time that the civilians had crossed and regrouped, the army was two days ride ahead of them. This poised no problem at first. The civilians supposed that they would overtake the army shortly. This was the first mistake that was made in a long series of mistakes this first settler group would make.

The commander, of this expedition, was Captain Leggett. He had a staff of three lieutenants and half a dozen sergeants. These ten men were experienced soldiers that had seen battle before. They had fought the English, French, and small bands of Indians. They presumed that this experience would be sufficient to carry out their orders. They had no way of knowing the vastness of the country to the west, or the numbers of the hostile tribes that they were to encounter. This detachment had with it two officers, whose sole responsibility it was to record the events of each day. They were to carefully map the territory that was covered. This would be the first recorded map of any land west of the river. The purpose was to make a permanent record of both the historical and geographical facts of the first white man's venture into what was to become a future part of the United States. The mapmaker had plenty of time to perform his job because of the slow progress that the army was making.

The civilians, who were on the wagon train that was attempting to follow the army, on the other hand gave very little thought to the possible danger. Their only desire was to get to the land of the buffalo and start down the path to wealth. Most of these people had very little of material things and were chasing a dream, while others had definite goals.

There was a Charles Melborne, who came from a wealthy family back East. He had his wagon loaded with trade goods. These goods were not for trade to the Indian, but he proposed to buy furs from the other settlers. He would resell them back at the river. Another in the group was Amon Armstrong. Amon was a gunsmith and merchant. He had with him three wagons of supplies, his wife, two grown sons, and their families. He proposed to make his fortune by repairing guns and selling ammunition to others. The bulk of his stock consisted of rifle balls and kegs of black powder He also had a large assortment of knives. This huge stock of gunpowder dictated that he and his wagons travel to the rear and somewhat behind the rest of the wagons.

There was no doctor among these people, but there was an army surgeon with Captain Leggett and his detachment. Over half of the men in the group had left their families behind and traveled alone. Another merchant, Bryce Baron, had two wagons loaded with barrels of whiskey. He proposed to make his fortune by selling, or trading with the others traveling with him. This would be a false assumption, because all but a few were traveling with only the bare necessities. These would not be able to purchase anything. For the most part, these people all expected to be able to live off the land until a settlement could be established.

After a crooked and slow journey this odd assortment of people had just reached the outer limits of the forest area. By this time, they were at least four days behind the army. When they reached the open country they all felt a little safer because they could see to the horizon in three directions. From time to time they could see small puffs of smoke rising in the distance but had no idea what these meant. They were sure that they could catch the army now because they could travel in a more or less straight line if only they could pick up the trail of the soldiers. They would make shorter night camps. The only other thing slowing them down was the necessity to grease the wagon wheels and to make minor repairs. They had not counted on the occasional dust storms, or the flash floods, when it rained. They soon learned that this was a violent and unforgiving land.

The Miles family had from the very beginning intended to leave the train and travel to the South and West. After they had been on the open prairie for two days, they pulled away and headed to their promised land near the rumored mountains. They reasoned that the cooler climate of the mountains would be beneficial to their fruit trees. They traveled for days, and finally they could see the hills rising in front of them. It was then that the excitement began to grow and give them renewed energy. When they finally reached the mountains they discovered a river of cool clean running spring water. There was an abundance of hard wood timber in the river bottom to construct a log cabin. The first order of business was to get their plants into the ground. Once they had completed this task they proceeded to build a large one-room cabin. Only then did they feel that they had arrived in the place where they would spend the rest of their lives. During all this time they had encountered no living person. However, unknown to them they had been watched ever since they left the wagon train. While they were confident that this was a safe haven that they had established, there were always the unseen eyes that were determined to observe their ways and then destroy their home.

From the very beginning both the army, and the people of the wagon train, had been under the watchful eye of the Indians. At first it was the tribes of the forest that was slipping thru the woods, and then it was the Kiowa who were watching for the proper time to ambush the train. The complete destruction of the white people was ever on the minds of the Kiowa Nation, with its many tribes. They were waiting until the train was far enough from the forest that it would be impossible for anyone to retreat back, to the cover of the dense woods. The Indians had determined that the three wagons at the rear were carrying something special because of their position, and the care and special attention that the men gave it. The other reason they were interested in these wagons was the simple fact that they were the easiest to attack and hardest to defend. Therefore, the plan was laid to allow the wagon train to pass a designated point and then cut it off from the last three wagons. The site was selected and the raiders were well hidden the day before the proposed attack. The spot was well chosen and the scouts for the wagons failed to detect any thing amiss. It was a long and restless wait for the wagons to approach and pass. However, the spot had been chosen carefully, and because of the extra weight of the targeted wagons they were further behind than normal. The unsuspecting travelers were surrounded and killed almost before the remainder of the train knew it was happening. With hundreds of fierce warriors between them and the captured wagons there was little attempt made to recapture the wagons, or even engage the hostiles. This time the scalps were taken from the entire Armstrong family and their bodies stripped and left on the prairie.

Another encounter with the Whites had resulted in very little loss to the Indians. They were beginning to believe that it would be a simple matter to master these invaders. So far their experiences had told them that the White Men were inferior fighters. Therefore, would be easily defeated. The raiders led the wagons off across the open country to a large valley that surrounded a small river. It was only then that the Kiowa took the time to examine what they had captured. It was also the first time an Indian had ever made use of anything that had wheels. They had no idea of how to free the horses from the wagon so they proceeded to cut them loose thereby eliminating the further use of the wagons. When they discovered what was inside of the wagons they found that they had captured something very valuable. This made them determined to learn the use of the guns. This was the first time that the northern Kiowa had come in possession of the white man's thunder sticks, and the raw powder to make new ammunition. They did not really know the true value of their captured bounty, but were certain that now they had furthered their superiority over this strange enemy.

Meanwhile the tribes to the south had completed their trade with the white trader, and were becoming more confident in the use of their new weapons. The Kiowa were a war like people, and at one time, or the other had been to battle with every tribe in the Midwest.

The loss of the merchant and his family was a major loss to the wagon train, but in their greed these people did not realize it at the time. To eliminate the possibility of another attack from the rear, most of the out riders were pulled back and rode to the rear of the wagons. The number of advance scouts was reduced, and for the most part each rode alone. This also was an error in planning. Almost daily there would be one, or more of the scouts that would not return to the train. Some of them would later be found naked and scalped out on the seemingly barren prairie. Due to size of the wagon train the losses did not appear to make a difference at first. Finally the train camped near a natural lake where they proposed to spend several days resting and repairing equipment. A meeting of all the men was called. The necessity for better organization was discussed at length. They held an election and selected a leader. It was decided that they would reorganize the train in such a way as to put the weaker sections of the train in the middle with the stronger to the front and rear. Prior to this each place in the train depended only on one's ability to get ready and move out. This effort effectively shortened the train by requiring everyone to stay close to the wagon in front of them. This proved to be a good plan with poor execution. With the daily loss of scouts and their horses and weapons, the leading portion of the train grew to be the weakest part of the assembly.

The unseen eyes along the trail recognized this weakness even before the travelers did. It was then that the Indian Warriors changed their tactics and laid plans for a frontal attack. Late one afternoon with out any warning a large band of warriors rode out of the glare of the setting sun. They hit with such suddenness that every one in the wagon train was caught off guard. The time and place had been selected with much care. The Whites were weary from their travel that they were very lax in their perception of what was going on around them. The attack was planned so carefully that even the most alert might not have noticed it coming. The Warriors rode with such swiftness that they hit the train, and were gone before there were more than a dozen shots fired, by the members of the train. Then the most damaging part of the battle took place. While the Whites attended their wounded, and watched the departing band of hostiles, a second wave came from out of the sunset. This wave was larger in number and stayed longer. When this second charge was over there were many dead and wounded and several of the wagons were burning. How the Indian had ridden in so fast, with burning arrows, was then and remained a mystery to those that present. This encounter fared a little better for the wagon train. The end results were that they had been able to shoot about a half dozen of their attackers.

After the second wave, the Indians seemed to vanish. How these warriors had managed to disappear, on this seemingly flat open country, was also a mystery that would remain unsolved. The group set about the task of tending their wounded, and repairing the damage to their equipment. At this point, they discovered that more of their horses had been killed than had their people. They finally realized that this had been a major part of the entire plan.

With the reduction of their number of horses their progress would be greatly impaired. In the future, they would have to place more emphasis on the protection of their livestock. Gradually day after day the Indian was winning the battle. The Indian was very patient. He did not engage the settler without first preparing a battle plan. It was seemingly impossible to predetermine when, where, or how new attacks would occur.

Captain Leggett and his troops were now about six days travel ahead of the slower moving wagon train. They were totally unaware of the problems that had been encountered by the civilians. This would have made no difference even if they had known, because they had their orders. They expected to fulfill these orders, thereby gaining fame and glory for themselves and the mighty United States Army. They expected to reach the same status as the troops of George Washington, and establish complete control of all lands as far as they went. These were visions of arrogance and not reality. Their enemy had been underestimated. There was no hope of reinforcements, or supplies being able to reach them. However most of the men were experienced frontiersmen, and could live off the land, under most circumstances.

The Army had encountered no Indians. They had, on several occasions, come upon sites where villages had been recently abandoned. They could not understand how their enemy could move on the spur of the moment. As was the case of most Indians, these Plains Indians could move an entire village in just a day's time. They simply seemed to vanish into the landscape.

By this time, Captain Leggett had reached the valley of the buffalo bones. He decided that he would establish his headquarters on the ridge above and to the north of the valley. From this vantage point, he could survey the country for a great distance in all directions. To add to this, was the fact that the headquarters could be defended easier than any place that he had encountered, on this journey into the west.

The advance scouts had not gone beyond this point in any direction. As he dismounted at the spot where he would place his tent, Captain Leggett could not be aware that at that very moment there were at least a hundred pairs of eyes watching his every move. Nor could he know that what seemed to be a vast flat rolling landscape, actually contained many hidden valleys and depressions that contained hundreds of the very enemy he was searching for. This lack of knowledge would cost him dearly in the coming weeks.

Chapter 23

Running Fox and the warriors of the village of Big Bear had spent many days training in the art of using the thunder sticks and the gunpowder, they had obtained thru trade with the White Trader, from the river.

Word of the advancing Army of Long Knives, and the great wagon train that followed it reached the village. Big Bear was aware that the Long Knives had established their village about three days to the south and east of the new village, of his people. This was information that Captain Leggett did not have. At the time the headquarters was established the Captain had no idea where this enemy, he was searching for, was located.

Big Bear called a council of war. " A great band of Long Knives has entered our land. They have established a village overlooking the valley of the buffalo bones. With each rising of the sun they send out a small band of scouts to search the land beyond. They are coming closer each time, to our village. It is my wish, that all warriors prepare themselves with the paint of war. After the dance we will engage and destroy these scouts one by one as they are sent into the field. It is my belief that each time we kill the scouts that the number in each band will be increased for the next visit into the land. We will dispose of as many as possible in this manner. When the Long Knives change their methods, we will engage and destroy the remainder of their village."

The long ceremonial war bonnets were placed on a pole outside of the tepee of each Warrior, and replaced with the single feather of battle. Now it was time to stop the invasion of the White Long Knives, into the Kiowa Nation.

The plan of Big Bear was a good one. The word, of this plan, was sent to their brothers to the north and the west. The entire Indian population, of the central plains, was now united as one Nation to rid the land of a common enemy. The Apache of the mountain country to the southwest were aware of these invaders but so far the Whites had not come close enough to their territory to cause more than mere concern.

For about a half moon this plan worked well and many Long knives were surprised and killed. There was not the loss of a single Warrior. Big Bear knew that this success would be short lived. He was busy making plans for the attack on the village of the buffalo bones.

Captain Leggett was also making such plans, while he was attempting to learn the location of the main Indian village. He was totally unaware that the plains contained many villages that had declared war on him.

While the preparation for war continued for the two factions in the west, back at the river a second large wagon train was being formed. This train was not made up entirely of hunters and settlers. It was mainly made up of fortune seekers that would kill anyone and steal anything. These were mostly men of violence and could not get along, even with themselves. The self appointed leader of this expedition was a man named Rafe Pettigrew. In fact Rafe had a second motive for going west. He was running from the law back in New England. Moreover, he had arrived in the United States after fleeing the law in Europe. Rafe was a mountain of a man, standing six foot seven, and weighed in at well over three hundred. He had become the leader of this group by brute force, and subduing lesser men. Rafe had surrounded himself with a group of seven others that were equally as vile as was he. They had no homes and were so unclean that they produced an odor from their bodies that could be detected several feet away. The majority of the people on the train were traveling by horseback, because they processed nothing that required the use of a wagon. Those that traveled by wagon had paid Rafe a hundred dollars each to travel with him and his men. Rafe had no intention of staying with this group of people. Once they had cleared the river country, it was his intention to abandon them and go his own way.

This excursion was doomed from the start as they crossed the river. With money in his pocket Rafe was in a hurry to get far enough from the river so that he could execute the next phase of his plan. Therefore, he only allowed short over night camps. He would not tolerate anyone that had a tendency to lag behind. If anyone fell behind, they were abandoned to fend for themselves. This would prove to be fatal to those unfortunate, would be, settlers. This was of no concern to Rafe, or his small band of cutthroats. The fewer people that remained with him, the easier it would be to abandon them. They were traveling much faster than the first train and the army. They were out of the river country and on to the prairie very quickly. Rafe did not employ the use of advance scouts therefore he had no idea of what was ahead. He had drained the last dollar from these people, and was on the look out for a good spot to slip away for good. They were following the trail laid by the army and the first train. One night the settlers camped early in a grove of willow trees next to a river. There was no questions ask, when told that they could relax and sleep in the next day. They were advised that they would spend the next day getting much needed rest.

When the first man arose, the next morning, he found that Rafe and his men had slipped away during the night. The wagon train was left at the mercy of the wild country. This would later prove to be the biggest mistake Rafe could make. In fact it would be the final mistake he would make.

Meanwhile, Big Bear had completed his final plans for the attack on the army at the valley of the buffalo bones. He had the full support of all the Kiowa villages from the north. This huge war party had encircled the entire valley, and the first attack would come out of the glare of the rising sun. Every warrior was aware of the danger that such an attack would cause, but they felt no fear for their personal safety.

Captain Leggett and his men were completely at a loss for knowledge, of the impending attack. They were not familiar with the Indian style of warfare. Therefore, the men were very lax in their daily activities. Those that had money were busy gambling and drinking most of the time. On this particular morning there was no bugle call to wake the troops. Most of them would not have responded, even if there had been. The sun crept over the horizon. With no morning fog the rising sun presented a blinding glare across the land to the west, of the first wave of the Indian war party. As the lower rim of the sun reached the upper rim of the horizon, Big Bear lifted his spear as a signal to begin the attack.

Instantly a wave of several hundred Indians descended on the camp with a chilling war cry. Even though the soldiers were looking down on the advancing horde, they were instantly driven to panic by the sheer volume of the noise and the multitudes of Indians.

Those that could gain their wits began to fire wildly at the advancing hostiles. After the first volley of arrows and gunfire, the battle was reduced to hand-to-hand fighting. Even their swords proved to be very ineffective. The lances of the Indians were longer, therefore, more effective out of range of the shorter sabers. Each soldier that lived beyond the gunfire and arrow stage was left staring in the face of certain death. The painted faces of each of their enemies represented the last image that they would take into eternity. Those warriors that were equipped with guns were in the first wave, and then came the archers. The arrow proved to be the most effective because they could be reloaded faster than the guns. After the fist wave had gained the confines of the camp, a second and more devastating wave came. This wave consisted of three groups of equal size, coming from the three other directions. The final results of this encounter were never in doubt.

The mapmaker and the historian had gotten up early. They were away from the camp before the sunrise as a result they were the only survivors of the entire detachment of soldiers.

There were many scalps that would hang on lodge poles this night. Also there were many squaws that would have to sing the death chant. The entire contents of the camp were removed, and the bounty carried to the various villages. All that remained was the grim reminder that the mighty army had suffered a complete defeat.

There was much singing and dancing in all the Kiowa villages that night. Many more braves now had guns and long knives.

Running Fox had been rewarded for his discovery of the buffalo and was made a senior War Chief. A few days after the battle of the valley of the bones he took a small band of warriors, and was scouting the back trail of the army. Four days out, he discovered the remainder of the first wagon train. This train was not nearly as large as had been reported by the scouts. Running Fox did not know of the attacks on the train by the warriors of another village. It was his desire to learn more of the advancing Whites. He carefully circled the camp of this wagon train and continued his journey to the East. One night, while his band was camped out on the open prairie, he discovered the glow of a fire in the distance. Closer examination disclosed the camp of eight white men.

Around this small campfire Rafe and his men were drinking and generally enjoying their success at abandoning the settlers. They had no concept as to what was going on in the darkness around them. Silently the warriors of Running Fox crept thru the night. They over run the camp, in a matter of seconds. Rafe left this world without ever knowing his fate. When he was slain by a tomahawk, the pouch with the ill-gotten riches fell to the ground and split open. Some of the coins were buried forever in the sands of time. Others would be found by settlers, generations later. Most however were recovered by the Indians of Running Fox's war party. The coins would be worn proudly around the necks, or adorn the belts of the Kiowa Warriors. By daybreak there was no sign that this camp had ever existed. A few days later the abandoned settlers were discovered, roaming aimlessly across the prairie, headed in the general direction of the forest from which they had come. After determining that these people were retreating from their land the Indians chose to let them continue east.

Out in the vast brush country the two remaining survivors of the army detachment were struggling with the elements and fear. The mapmaker and the historian were attempting to find their way back to the fort on the river. They would travel by darkness and remain hidden for the entire daylight hours. Armed with only their long knife and a pistol they knew that they were defenseless, if discovered. During the night they would struggle through the sagebrush. By day they would lay motionless under a pile of brush or cover themselves with sand. They found little water and nothing to eat in the darkness. It was only by chance that they found themselves on the very trail that the retreating wagon train survivors were using. Lying completely covered with sand they were nearly over run by the retreating settlers. After receiving food and water they were placed on one of the wagons, and transported back to the river.

After completing his mission Running Fox returned to his village beyond the valley of the bones. At council, after his return, he reported his findings to Big Bear. He had no way of knowing that these people were carrying information, and pictures of their land that would later cause the Indian nation much grief.

Once again the Kiowa people would turn their attention to the buffalo migration. It was as if the spirits were directing the herds to move further from the river country.

Chapter 24

It had been several moons since the last battle with the Long Knives. Big Bear was getting very old. He realized that his days were short. He had summoned the tribe together, and declared that with his passing Running Fox was to become Chief. The Medicine Man had just moved on to his final resting place. The Medicine man was replaced with his daughter, Quick Beaver. She had been training since childhood, a period of over forty summers. She quickly gained the confidence of the entire Kiowa Nation. This was the first time that a Squaw had held such an important position.

Word had reached the village that another valley of bones had been discovered to the Northeast. Apparently the Whites had entered the land from another direction. And they destroyed another buffalo herd without being detected. Running Fox was dispatched to investigate to determine how such a thing could have happened.

After riding for many days the band, led by Running Fox, came upon a field of bones. Apparently there had been more killed at this place than had been at the valley of the bones. After examining the killing field, and the surrounding area it was determined that this kill had taken place before that of the valley. It was also determined, after much searching, that the remainder of the herd had also left the area by going in a Northwestern direction.

When Running Fox returned to the village he was informed of the passing of Big Bear. There was to be a council called to confirm that he was indeed the Chief of the village.

After the brief ceremony, Running Fox placed the necklace of bear claws around his neck and addressed the tribe.

"It is with a sad heart that I assume the leadership of the tribe. We have lost a great Chief that I am sure will be of greater service to the Great Spirits that guide the Indian Nations. I have been to the second killing field, of the Northeast. I am quite sure that the Whites have done more damage than we are aware of. Their numbers are greater than we expected. They are as determined to conquer our land as we are to rid the land of them. It is my order that all warriors go into the field and seek out and kill any White that is west of the river. The only exception shall be that of the peaceful white trader and his helpers, who help transport his goods. I am certain that we cannot remove the Whites from the land East of the river. However, we can keep them from entering new land on our side of the great river. We will not enter into a peace with these people because they are greedy, and cannot be trusted to keep their word.

I believe that the spirits that guide the buffalo have warned the herds of the coming Whites, and therefore they are moving to the Big Sky country, to the Northwest. Their movement is slow. In time they will be overtaken if we do not stop the advancing killers of buffalo.

I will hold council with the Indians of the west, including the Apache and the Shoshone. I will seek an alliance with them to assist our people in our struggle to rid the land of this destructive force that has descended on our way of life. We will continue to follow the migration of the buffalo, while keeping a close watch along our back trail. We will keep the buffalo, and the White Man separated until such time that the great spirits have delivered the buffalo to their destination. When they have reached this place we will establish our new nation and return to the normal life that we have enjoyed for all time. I am sure by the time that this happens the Great Spirits will send forth a vision to determine our future."

When the council was over, Running Fox made plans to seek out, and confer with the Indians of the North and the West. He would smoke the pipe with the leaders of each tribe. He explains what was happening among the tribes, of his land.

Running Fox first went to the main village of the Jicarilla Apache. There he sat and smoked with their Chief, Pale Sky. He told the many stories of the Whites, of their efforts to invade the land to the east of the Apache domain. He and Pale Sky reached an accord to band together to prevent further intrusion of this white menace. The Jicarilla Apache was a fierce and hostile tribe, but the news brought by their Kiowa brothers had appealed to their better sense. At least for the time being they were to join forces with other tribes, to ward off a greater enemy.

Pale Sky sent several of his War Chiefs along with Running Fox, to visit the land of the Navaho. This would assure the Navaho that the two nations were united.

Chief Tall Man of the Navaho received the envoy composed of representatives of the two tribes. He invited them to council, and to smoke the pipe. The smoke in itself proved to be enjoyable, because the Navaho grew a fine grade of tobacco. Once again the story was repeated about the White killers of the buffalo. After the assurance of the War Chiefs from the Apache Nation, Chief Tall Man agreed that they must unite at least for this one purpose. "It is said that brothers may fight among themselves but in time of crisis they must unite to fight side by side. This is a threat that may destroy our way of life. if it is not put aside at this time."

The same was true with the Zuni and the Blackfoot tribes. However it was not quite the same with the Lakota. Even though their name really meant allies, they were reluctant to join forces with the other tribes. Running Fox spent several days in the council with White Buffalo, the Chief of one of the tribes. There were three main tribes in the Lakota Nation. After the third day with Running Fox, White Buffalo sent to the other tribes, and requested that the Chiefs of those tribes meet with him, Running Fox, and the other Chiefs. After the arrival of the Lakota Chiefs, there were three more days of talks. While these talks were in progress, word arrived in the village that there was a wagon train headed across the northern part of the land. It was said that this train was coming not from the land of the Choctaw, but from the land of the five lakes region. This was the first such attempt, of the Whites, to cross the northern portion of the land. With this information the Lakota decided to join, with the rest of the Indians of the Great Plains, in their war against the Whites. The Indians, beyond the great mountains to the west, were not as yet aware that the White Man even existed. They were not included in this pact.

With the knowledge that they had the support of many thousands of Warriors behind them, the Kiowa returned to their village and prepared a plan for the passing of information from one tribe to the other.

When he reached his village, Running Fox had been advised, by the White Trader that the army was preparing to send many troops into the west. They were to establish what they called forts in many locations. He was quite sure that once these forts were established the Whites would invade the land in vast numbers.

Meanwhile the Whites were spilling across the Mississippi like water from a split gourd. As they advanced they destroyed everything that they encountered. The destruction was almost as complete as burning rocks descending from the fire mountain.

Quick Beaver sent word that she wished to talk with Running Fox. He went to her tepee, and listened to what this wise old woman had to say.

"I have spent many moons alone in my tepee searching for a message from The Great Spirits. At last a great vision was sent to me. In this vision a great eagle was sent to warn me of the future. The mere fact that an eagle brought the messages tells me that it is of the greatest importance. The eagle, the greatest of all spirits, is and has always been used by The Spirits to send messages, which must not be ignored.

In this vision, the eagle told me of the threat presented by the advancing hoards of Whites. He also told me of the of the existing threat from a similar group of brown men that were crossing the land to the south of the great river, called The Rio Bravo. It told me that the first group would be men all dressed in the same type of clothing. These men were the dreaded Long Knives. They would enter the land a little way at first and establish a camp. Then they would move a little more and establish a camp. This would continue until these camps would reach across the entire land, even beyond the great mountains where it is said that the land divides.

These camps will not be the same, as we know camps to be. They will first build great walls of logs. Then build many small places inside for the Whites to seek safety. These walls will be so tall that it will be difficult for a man to climb. Once a camp has been established, there will come other Whites to take from the earth and rivers.

The number of the Long Knives will be many but will be only a small portion when compared to the numbers of the Whites that will dig in the earth and hunt the forest.

The Great Spirits have directed that we, and our Red Brothers guide, and protect the buffalo from the wasteful slaughter of such greedy people".

Chapter 25

It had been almost three summers since his meeting with Quick Beaver. The Long Knives had established two of their camps at the edge of the forest country. They were now making preparations to move about two days ride to the West. There had been several occasions where a small group of these Long Knives had been sent into the field. Some of these groups had been discovered and destroyed. It was the Indian custom to leave signs to warn off any enemy from their land. On these occasions the killed, or captured soldiers were staked to the ground over anthills and left to be killed, or devoured by the beast of the land. The end results were that the next scouting parties would be larger. Finally the scouting soldiers were so large in number that a single raiding party of Warriors could not contain them.

The villages, to the north, had received the word telling them that a large column of soldiers was exploring the area to the Northeast. A huge war party was formed to intercept the Long Knives. All able bodied braves were called on to join this expedition. After much dancing, the warriors were painted for war, and rode off to do battle. Unknown to the Kiowa a second column of soldiers was marching at a slower pace. They were headed directly west. After the army scouts determined that war party had left the village, the column picked up its pace and headed directly toward the village. They had learned from the Indian, that a force that utilized the element of surprise usually became the victor. The troops traveled all day, on this occasion they traveled the entire night also. As the early light of dawn made it possible to see, the army swept down on the village. It was their intent to kill every one left in the village. With only old men, women, and children in the village it was only a matter of minutes before the entire population of the village was destroyed. After the initial charge every Kiowa in the camp lay on the ground, either dead, or mortally wounded. This massacre would be recorded in the journal as a massive battle with a glorious victory. The truth of the battle would be lost in the memory of the soldiers. They would tell of the battle so many times that eventually every man began to believe that they had in fact fought a decisive battle with the Red Man.

Meanwhile, to the South Running Fox had received information that there was new movement of the White Army. He chose a few of his bravest warriors and was going to the village to the North to hold council with the chief there. They were far enough away that they did not hear the battle and were not aware that anything had happened in the village, of his Red Brothers. When he rode in and saw the death and destruction, he knew immediately that this had not been the work of an Indian raid. There had been no scalps taken and the tracks of the horses were different from the tracks that would have been made by the unshod hooves of Indian ponies. He also noticed that there had not been a single brave capable of fighting found among the dead. Even the ponies and dogs had been left behind.

Running Fox immediately sent runners to advise the other villages, in the nation. He and the rest of his party followed the trail of retreat and discovered, after three days ride, that another of the forts was being built. This brought the known number of forts to three. It was now evident that the Whites were going to push into their land in greater numbers. After the army had sufficient numbers of these forts, Running Fox knew that the greedy hunters and settlers would swarm across the prairie. He had also sent a runner after the warriors of the village to advise them of the destruction of their homes and families.

A council of war was called and all the tribes of the area attended. Running Fox was the first to speak at this council.

"The evil people, of the county to the east of the big river, have apparently decided to mount an all out invasion into our land. It was the fault of our brothers on the east side of the river for not stopping the first Whites that arrived in their land. Now there are so many Whites that nothing short of complete and decisive victory will stop the destruction, of our way of life. This we will do by attacking every settlement and fort west of the big river. In the meantime we must follow, and secure the remaining herds of buffalo that are now moving slowly to the west. We must assist these herds with their journey to safety. My village will move to the western limits of the Kiowa Nation to a point where our Nation joins the eastern limits of the Jicarilla Apache Nation. I urge all Kiowa villages to do the same. There we will set up a line of defense between the advancing Whites and the buffalo herds. From this point we will wage all out war in three directions. We will continue this war until the forts are destroyed, or the Long Knives are returned to the big river, or further."

Chief Pale Sky was the next to rise and talk to the members of the council. "I have heard the words of Running Fox. I also have heard of the forts being built by the Long Knives. It is the intent of all Apaches that we will defend our land, and all that belongs to us. To do this it will be necessary for our brothers to band together to fight as one. Only after the defeat of the Whites can we return to our lands to resume a normal life. To accomplish this end, I feel that it is necessary to appoint a common leader to gather information, and direct our efforts. All other Chiefs will act as sub chiefs until the battle is won."

"I am Tall Man, Chief of all Navaho people, I too feel that it is necessary for all tribes to unite. It is my wish that Running Fox be appointed to guide us through this difficult time. It is his land that was first affected by these outsiders. It is his land that now stands abandoned so that we can present a better defense by being closely united. I pledge the support of my people in future efforts concerning the inhuman acts of these merciless outsider Whites."

So it was that Running Fox became the leader of the massive combine of Indian Nations. His first order of business was to select and dispatch a large group, of the best-equipped Warriors, to scout the various herds of buffalo. They were to act as a security unit for these remaining animals. He then selected a band of Kiowa Warriors to go back into the lands that they had just left to determine the location of all white settlers, or army posts. He was to be kept posted on their findings.

The Kiowa Warriors, that had been in the field when their village was attacked returned to their village and performed the proper ceremonies for their dead. The leader of this band was a younger warrior called Dark Water. Dark Water vowed to avenge the death of his sons and set about immediately to destroy the fort that was now being built, by the attacking Long knives.

Dark Water led his Warriors to the site of the new fort, and devised his war plan. The walls of the fort had not as yet been completed and he determined that he should attack at once and prevent the completion of the giant log wall. The Warriors attacked in waves. First, armed with fire arrows they swarmed the fort. It was soon determined that the logs used in the construction of the wall were too green to burn rapidly. This plan having failed, he came up with a second plan. Next, his Warriors began to charge the fort dragging large piles of dry brush. There would first be an attack by armed Warriors. Then the second wave would drag the brush, and deposit it next to the wall. The armed Warriors would keep the soldiers busy so as to prevent them from removing the brush. This operation took the entire day. Finally, fire arrows were sent into the brush. The heat from the burning brush finally started the logs of the wall to burn. By this time Dark Water had received reinforcements that were sent to their aid by Running Fox. When the walls began to crumble, the efforts of the soldiers to stop the fire were abandoned. Now all that was left to do was to fight and die. Fight and die they did for two days. In hand-to-hand combat the army was no match for the hoard of Warriors that came at them from all sides. At the end of the second day there remained only burning logs and many dead. The numbers of the dead seemed to be about the same for both the army and the Indians. The surviving Indians prepared their dead and carried them to their final resting place. They then gathered all of the weapons of the troops and withdrew to the West to regroup, and plan their next battle. There had been no one to escape the fort. Therefore, word of the attack never reached the headquarters of the army to the East. The wounded Warriors were attended too and honored for their bravery in battle.

When Running Fox received the word of the victory, he was pleased and called the remaining Warriors to him to hold council pertaining to their next encounter with the Long Knives. He realized now that this was going to be a long war. The two sides had equally good reasons to fight to the death. The Indian was fighting to preserve the land, and their simpler way of life. The Whites were fighting to gain as much land, and material wealth as possible. Neither side considered the other to be a civilized people.

All the Apache Tribes, including the Kiowa, moved their villages to established a line of camps that extended from North to South along the imaginary line that was the boundary between the two nations. The Lakota were preparing for war and would move close to the boundary to the North. By the time all this was done, every Indian Tribe from the west bank of the Mississippi to the shores of the great salt water had been made aware of what was happening out on the Great Plains.

The white soldiers had fought a great army when they defeated the English, but that had been organized warfare. The battles that they were now engaged in were nothing similar to that type of battle. There were no bugles or drums to signal a charge. In these battles, a peaceful day would suddenly erupt in total disaster, for one side or the other. The Indians would win a battle and move forward only to have the Whites win a battle, and the tribes would have to fall back.

Back at the villages the Squaws would spend much time engaged in preparing the dead and singing the death chant. It was the custom of all tribes to remove the dead, and wounded from any battlefield. The proper ceremonies would be preformed in order that the spirits of the slain warriors would depart this world with the just honor that these brave men deserved.

The line of defense, the tribes had established, was still in tact, but they were gaining no ground to the East. While their numbers were getting smaller the number of Soldiers was growing. Running Fox had underestimated how many Whites would be sent into the land. In the past when at war with another tribe, and had had complete victory, the other tribe would either retreat to another part of the land, or join the victorious tribe. This would not be the case in this war. It seemed that for ever soldier killed they were replaced with two more.

The Indians were gaining many guns and long knives. Every Warrior that returned from battle brought with him a new supply of blue coats and shiny buttons. The taking of these items had replaced the taking of scalps as a symbol of the kill.

Many ponies had also been lost and some of the battles had to be fought on foot, with a different deception tactic.

While the battles were taking place the non- military settlers were crossing the river in great numbers. It had been discovered that another herd of buffalo had been destroyed in the area between the forts. There was a massive field of rotting buffalo left behind to signify that the intent of the Whites was to kill every buffalo they could find. From this field, the trail of the invaders was followed and after three days of fast riding the Warriors discovered the hunting party in a grove of trees along side a river. The hunters were preparing to move out to the East. A series of hit and run attacks was begun. After several waves had hit, the White Men had abandoned the carts and wagons and began to run. The Indians followed them for a short distance, and then returned to the wagons. They proceeded to recover the buffalo hides that had been stolen from their land. This was a shallow victory, but a victory nevertheless. They took the recovered hides and returned to the area of safety where the tribes had established their main villages. Not only was there safety in the huge numbers that occupied the area but also they were in the foothills of the Apache land. The huge outcropping of rocks gave them cover from attack.

Meanwhile the original herds of buffalo were slowly moving to the Northwest guided and protected by the Apache and Lakota. All tribes knew that the preservation of the buffalo was critical to the survival of all. It had been thus, ever since the Ancient Ones had followed a similar beast across the ice field many generations ago. In fact all tribes were descendents of these Ancient Ones. This made all red men brothers in their way of thinking. Being brothers made it now necessary to rejoin as one against a common enemy.

The Sioux had at first tried to live along side the Whites in the land of the Five Big Lakes. Now they had become so dissatisfied with the arrangement that they had begun to sell their land to the settlers and they were making the move to the west. As they were moving west it became impossible for them to continue a peaceful relationship with the settlers. Finally open warfare broke out between the two sides. This would later prove to be to the advantage of the tribes controlled by Running Fox. Now the soldiers of the forts had hostile Indians on both the east and the west. This divided their attention and for the time, made their whole position weaker.

Chapter 26

Rain Cloud rose from his place within the council circle. "The stories of these battles are so many that it would take an entire summer to relate them to you. Another sun has set and I must retire to my tepee and rest for a while. When the sun returns I will return also and complete this story that I have been telling you." Having heard these words the entire assembly retired to their homes and awaited the rising sun to hear the completion of the saga of Running Fox.

With the return of the sun, Rain Cloud made his way back to the center of the council and continued his story.

The numbers of whites that arrived at the forts increased almost monthly. The soldiers were gaining a firmer hold on the land around the forts. There had been many killed on both sides of the battles. It seemed to Running Fox that each White killed there would be two or three to replace him. Now it became evident that the entire west was the objective of the invading Whites.

The Shoshone from the North West and their blood brothers, The Comanche, from the South had joined the Indian alliance and gave Running Fox new hope for victory. Being more familiar with the land to the west, the Shoshone and the Lakota took on the responsibility of protecting the great buffalo herd. With this burden lifted Running Fox could now devote his entire efforts to the many battles that were being fought daily. Most of these battles were only small raids conducted by either side. This would in fact weaken the Indians ability to protect the entire land. The Warriors of the alliance were spread over such a vast area that it was impossible to pass word of the movement of the Long Knives.

The tribes now had many captured guns and long knives but ample ammunition was a problem. Trading for these has been stopped when the army captured their source.

The Irish Trader had been sent to a stockade at one of the forts, and his Indian wife had returned to her people. Now the people of the tribes had no one with which to trade for rifle balls and powder.

A General, from the fort nearest to the big river, had entered the area. Under the sign of peace, he had held council with Running Fox. There were times that they seemed to have reached an agreement only to have a few from one side or the other breech the treaty. Not all the people in the army were in favor of making peace with the Indians. Some of the men in power at the headquarters in Washington were determined to rid the country of the Red Man. Regardless of the agreements made at the local level, orders would be issued to kill all Indians where ever they were found. These orders made no distinction between age and the sex of the victims. Therefore, most of the first to die were women and children.

There had been no time, for the Braves to hunt and provide food for the villages. All were getting short in the necessities of life. The corn and squash along with the tobacco fields were destroyed. It came the time for Running Fox to withdraw a large number of his Warriors to dispatch them to the fields, to the west, to secure food enough to carry the tribes through the coming winter. This would greatly enhance the ability of the Army, and the civilian settlers to advance further into the land once occupied by the Kiowa. The winter was long and severe and the hardships for the tribes grew daily.

There were times when no one could venture into the fields for days on end. Meanwhile reinforcements for the Army were gathering along their line of temporary forts.

While the bitter winds from the north cut across the prairie, it greatly hampered the daily activities of the tribes. Much of their time was spent preparing their weapons for the coming spring. There was a great need for arrows, spears, and tomahawks. The supply of ammunition for their captured guns was in short supply. The only supply of fresh ammunition came from the raids killing the Whites.

The brown skinned people from south of the Rio Bravo were now beginning to move to the North and West. These people were not as well organized as the Armies of the East. They came in smaller numbers and were easier to control. However, with them added to the problems facing the Indians, it became evident that the Indian forces were being spread too thin to adequately protect their land.

Running Fox called a council of all the Chiefs from all the tribes. All that attended the council gathered to smoke the pipe of war. After all the formalities were over, Running Fox stood in the center of the group.

"We have reached a point where we can not control both the flow of the Whites, of the East, and the Spanish of the South. You have been called to this council to offer plans as to how we must now act to save what is ours. If the buffalo herds are destroyed, then the very way we live will be destroyed. This we must not allow to happen. It appears to me that we must give up a portion of our land and devote our energy to the preservation of the buffalo. We must assist the herds in relocating to a different part of the land. We will move them to the land of the big sky. Where they can live in the safety of the black hills and badlands. We will split the herds into smaller groups. We will place them in separate parts of our land. We will place some of them in the land of the Shoshone, which is to the north of the lakes of the salt. Also we will move some of the buffalo to the south of the Lake of Salt. There they will be placed under the protection of the Utes and the Piaute tribes. Some will be placed in the land of the Navaho and the Lakota. Others will be driven across the great mountains into the land of the mighty tribes to the west. Once we have divided the herds, and have them in places where they can live in peace, we will again turn our attention to the outsiders that are determined to destroy the people and the buffalo. They see our land as a means to obtain many riches. That is true it is a means of riches, but it is our riches that they are trying to take from us. We must prepare a better plan to preserve and protect these riches. I now call on each of you to offer your own plan as to what must be done."

"It is I, Chief Many Fires of the Lakota that now speaks to this council. It has been the duty of my Braves to look after the buffalo herds and in so doing I have determined also that these herds must be split onto smaller groups, and sent in different directions. There is at this time enough buffalo in our lands to support all our people for all time. However, if the Whites are allowed into the land they will kill every buffalo that they find. The hides are a source of wealth for them. They leave behind the remainder of the animal to rot away where they fall. It is the wish of all my people to fight to the death, if necessary, to preserve what The Great Spirits have given us. It would be my plan to send smaller bands of Warriors into the field, and with a series of hit and run attacks to keep the invaders busy while we guide the great herds to a safer place."

This council went on for four days, with each one present giving his version of what he thought. The end results being, that they would continue the fight in the manner as suggested by the Lakota Chief. While this was being done, a great effort would be made to gather the herds to gently drive them to the land of the salt lakes, and the black hills. It never occurred to them that the White man would continue to cross the land until the land disappeared into the great salt water to the west.

The plan being devised, the tribes set about the task of putting it into operation. It would be the more experienced warriors that would carry out the fighting. Naturally these would have to be the better equipped. The younger less experienced braves would locate the herds. They would devise a way to direct the buffalo to the chosen destination, without disturbing them enough to cause a stampede. The plan was simple, but the execution was far from simple. Engaging the soldiers would cause much loss of life. Many more would suffer serious injury. Yet there was no fear displayed among the Warriors.

To move the herds was also a difficult task. At times the prevailing winds would be used to send their scent into the feeding grounds, thus causing the animals to divert from a given path to a path away from the scent. On other occasions the slow movement of the Braves off in the distance would divert the herd from their chosen path. Great care was taken to always head the animals in the direction of known good grazing.

171

Even the Indian people had, up until this time, not realized the great numbers of animals that they were to deal with. Some of the herds were small and could easily be handled others were so large that one could not see them all at one time. This was indeed a monumental task, such as had never been attempted before. Many Fires had gathered his braves for the task of removing the buffalo from the plains of the Midwest. First they must survey the herds and determine how many of these animals must be gathered and moved. They had already determined that the spirits had warned the buffalo. The leaders of all the groups were in the process of moving to the northwest. However, this process of nature was slow in developing. The movement of the buffalo must be speeded up. To Their knowledge there had never before been an effort by man to move a beast of nature. The task would be great and the progress would be slow. Nevertheless, this was a task that had been decided on at the great council of all tribes.

With the assurance that befitted a man of his position, he set about the job before him and his people.

The Lakota braves circled the plains far to the east and while most of the buffalo had already moved to the west, they gathered the remainder and gently urged them toward the setting sun.

As each, of the remaining groups, was discovered, the leader or dominant bull would be directed in the desired direction. They would employ many tricks and use much deception to redirect the travel of the buffalo. As each group was gently moved to the west, they were joined by other groups of Lakota braves with other buffalo. After many suns, there was the largest herd of buffalo ever assembled, headed in the general direction of the badlands of the Black Hills.

The movement was awkward and the progress was slow, however the desired results were being achieved.

Many Fires was pleased by the overall performance of his people, but had to devise a new plan almost daily. It was his intent to have the herd across the mountains before the snow came. This was not to be, because of the multitudes of animals, and the various dominant bulls that had joined the herd.

When they reached the wide-open flat land to the east of the foothills, the herd was allowed several days to graze to build up their strength for the long climb through the mountains.

The buffalo was a creature of the plains. It would be reluctant to go into the mountains. Many Fires dispatched scouts into the hills to determine the better trail to follow.

The winds were blowing from the north. Many Fires had positioned himself, on the south, atop a rise in the earth. This was the place that he could observe the animals without them being able to detect his scent. As the day wore on he could see that some of the bulls were getting restless. This was not normal, because of the extra care taken by his people to not arouse the inquisitive nature of the herd. The buffalo was known to have poor eyesight but they had the keenest sense of smell.

Carefully searching the horizon for the cause, his eyes caught the sight of movement to the northeast. As he watched this movement it became apparent that there was a hunting party from some other tribe stalking the animals.

There were several groups, of two each, easing across the prairie. Each group was covered with a buffalo hide complete with the skull and horns. This was a common practice of small hunting parties searching for only a few kills. He further noticed that these hunters were not very well trained in the art of stalking on the open prairie. The herd was continually moving away from the stalking hunters. Finally the hunting party became discouraged. And they retreated back the way that they had come.

It was at this point, that Many Fires took a small band of warriors, and went around the herd and approached the hunting party under the universal sign of peace.

"Why have you attempted to stalk and kill the buffalo when it is seen that you are not experienced in this?"

"I am Little Mountain of the Blackfoot Tribe, I have come here to take food for my tribe. The elk have moved away from our village. We are in need of food to feed our people," said the leader of the hunting party. "We did not know that these animals were under your protection. It is not the way of our people to steal from brothers."

Many Fires stood for a while in silence and observed the hunters for the clue as to why they would arouse the nature of the buffalo.

"The buffalo is not like any other game that you will ever hunt. They are governed by what smells are sent to them by the winds. When they smell something that is not normal to them they will move away. If the scent is that of real danger then they will stampede to safety. When attempting to stalk as you were, you must first wash from your body the grease of the bear. You must replace the moccasins that are darkened with the ash of the fire, with fresh ones. These blackened moccasins give off the odor of a prairie fire, which is the enemy of all prairie animals. I am aware that this is the mark of the Blackfoot, however there are times when we must depart from our ways to achieve a goal."

Many Fires then proceeded to tell Little Mountain the nature of their actions concerning the buffalo. He advised him that the buffalo must be moved from the east to a place of safety in the badlands of the west.

After much talk it was determined that in the land of the Blackfoot there was a huge valley containing much tall grass.

"I will give you the gift of a herd of buffalo if you will assure me that they will be cared for, and only those needed for food will be killed. The rest must be protected, and allowed to roam free and raise their young."

The word of Little Mountain was given. There was the exchange of blood from their wrist to seal the agreement. They were now blood brothers. This being the case, Many Fires knew that the word of the Black Foot would never be broken.

The following morning the scouts returned with the news that a pass through the mountains had been discovered. It would difficult to coax the herd though the pass, because it would be a strange land for the buffalo.

The weather gods had taken over. Now the snow was falling. Many Fires knew that before they reached the summit that the snow would cover the ground. This was just one of the many hardships that had, or would delay the delivery of the herd to their destination.

Now it was time for Many Fires to make the decision of how the herd would be divided. From this point there were several destinations. Now the herd must be split into one larger herd and smaller herd. The smaller of the herds must cross the mountains, beyond where it was said that the land divides. He called Crooked Stick to him and told him of his plan.

"I will take a smaller portion of the herd and cross the great mountains. On the other side I will cross to the land of the Shoshone. It is with them I will leave some of the buffalo. Then I will continue to the south beyond the lake of the salt, into the land of the Utes. There I will leave a second portion of my herd. The remaining portion I will take still further south to the big canyon. There I will leave them under the protection of the Hopi. When I return here we will take the large herd to the land of the black hills, and send some still further north to the land of the big sky."

After dividing the herd into two parts, and the selection of the braves to make the journey, Many Fires left the prairie. They started the climb into the high mountains. He had chosen to make the ride to the west, and south because he knew that this would be the more difficult portion of their task. He was never one to shirk a difficult job, by giving the assignment to another.

The climb to the summit of the mountains was a strain on both man and beast. The snow was getting heavier with each passing day. The air was very cold and thin. This made the breathing very difficult, thus slowing progress. There was not much grass along the trail on the east side of the mountains. What there was, lay deep in the snow. Many times the buffalo attempted to return to flat land behind them.

When the summit was reached, the snow was frozen on top; even the hooves of the buffalo could not reach the grass below this blanket, of snow and ice.

The massive shoulders, of each animal, were matted with snow. There was ice hanging from each of their horns. The blanket of each Brave was frozen stiff. and provided little protection from the great wind from the north.

At the place where the lands divided, Many Fires would not give in to the fatigue of his braves, or his charges. From this point he knew that they would be descending to better grazing for the buffalo. The rivers and streams would flow to the west for the first time. When they reached the foothills to the west, the winds would be warm from the sands of the desert, and the land would offer the needed grass for the herd.

It was decided that they must start down immediately. The first several days of the descent were equally as difficult. While the travel was down hill, the snow was still a major factor. Several days into their journey down the west side of the mountains, the lead bull got the scent of the warmer air and grass below. Even though they were lank from hunger, the entire herd gathered new strength and quickened their pace. Once they reached the flat land below the snow had disappeared. The grass stood tall in the soft southerly wind. It would be here that they would be allowed to feed for as long as it took them to regain their strength.

After several days resting their ponies and the herd, it was time to move across into the land of the Shoshone. There they would make the necessary treaty to leave a portion of the buffalo on their land.

When they arrived at the village of the chief of the Shoshone, they met Two Knives. The great chief was engaged in teaching his twin sons the art of making arrowheads.

Many Fires sat and smoked the pipe with Two Knives. After a short time he began to tell of his mission.

"We have been on the trail for many suns. The chiefs of the eastern side of the mountains held council, and determined that the buffalo must be moved to a safer place. It is my mission to deliver a portion of these animals to each tribe of the west. I am to secure their assurance that they would guard the buffalo from future harm. There has come to the land of your brothers, of the Great Plains, the white men that are destroying our way of life. The Spirits have told us that we must move the last of the buffalo to a new land."

Two Knives sat for a long while, thinking about what he had just heard, as he watched the twin boys that were waiting just outside the council area.

"The land of the Shoshone reaches from the place where the three rivers meet, across the flat land to the north of the lake of the salt. We have many buffalo of our own. I can see the possible fate that has come upon your people. I will make a place for part of your buffalo. After you have rid your land of the white plague, I will return your animals to the land of their birth. I, Two Knives, have spoken."

Again Two Knives took out the pipe and they smoked to seal the agreement. After they had finished the smoke, he gave the pipe to Many Fires as a gift of brotherhood.

After separating a portion of the herd, it was time for Many Fires to leave for the land of the Utes. By the time that all this was done, the rest of the great herd had full stomachs and had regained their strength. The braves were also rested and prepared for the journey to the south. For many suns they traveled, from the village of the Shoshone on the three rivers, to the canyons where the villages of the Utes were located.

Hidden Beaver, the chief of the Ute Nation, received them under the sign of peace. It was here that Many Fires again told his story of plight of the buffalo, and the Nations of the east side of the mountains.

"We are a people of the rocks and canyons, and also depend on the buffalo as a main source of life. We have many buffalo, deer, and antelope. It would please us to have new blood in our herd of buffalo. When the proper time arrives we will return a share of the herd to land of the Kiowa. I am sure that with the aid of all our red brothers, the white invaders will be forced back across the big river. It will be at that time that all things will return to the way that they were."

It was there that another great bull, and his group was left to enjoy the grasses that were abundant on the upper rims of the canyons and the land of the great stone statues.

As they were preparing to leave the land of the Ute, Many Fires called his braves to council.

"We will follow along the south side of these canyons. There is a great canyon several suns ride from here. This is the mother of all canyons, where the Hopi people make their home. At the bottom of this great canyon they raise much squash, corn, and beans. They are not as dependent on the buffalo as are others of our brothers, however I am sure that they will make good keepers for the remainder of this herd. After we have safely placed the remaining buffalo on the prairie above their canyon, we will return across the mountain and join the rest of our people for the journey to the Bad Lands, and the land of the big sky."

The days were hot and the nights were cold. The land was very unforgiving, but finally they were on the south rim of the great Canyon. It was here that Many Fires met with the chief of the Hopi. The Hopi were raisers of crops and for the most part they were a peaceful people. It was with much interest that they listened to the story of the white man. They had heard of the brown men of the south, but had not had any contact with them. They had not heard of the white invasion to the east, nor were they aware of the massive killing of the buffalo. Being blood brothers of the Kiowa, they never doubted the story told them by Many Fires.

Even though that they had endured much hardship and pain, the entire group that had made the journey with Many Fires, were still with him. They would remain in the villages of the Hopi for a period of seven suns. Then it would be back over the great mountains. There they would join the rest of their people with the buffalo for the trip to the north.

It was with great anticipation and lighter hearts that they now were again at the place where the land divides. The rivers were now again flowing toward the rising sun. It would be a difficult descent, but a joyful one.

The summer had come and gone. Once more the leaves of the trees were turning to many different colors. This was a sign that the snow spirits would soon be upon the land again. Many Fires and his braves had once again joined the people that were keeping the remainder of the buffalo. While they were resting from their journey, plans were made for the trip to the north.

The trip to the north was not nearly as difficult as the one to the west. The land was not as hostile, or as unforgiving. Half of the remaining herd was placed on the open plains that surrounded the black hills. The second half was placed under the watchful eyes of the Cheyenne, in the land of the big sky.

Chapter 27

Back to the East, the Kiowa led Warriors were carrying out their assigned task of attacking the Whites wherever they found them. Whenever possible, they would ambush the Whites so as to inflict as much damage as possible while exposing them selves to as little danger as possible. When ambush was not possible, they would ride in waves. The warriors armed with the White Mans guns would launch the first wave. They would be followed by those equipped with bow and arrow. Some times there would be many of such waves. Finally there would be the final wave of those equipped with tomahawks and lances for hand-to-hand battle. The results were not always the same. There would be times when the Warriors would be repelled and forced to flee the area. Other times the Whites would be killed, or forced to flee to safety. These attacks were repeated many times across the entire frontier.

The Red Man was fighting to retain what he believed was his, while the Whites objective was to conquer and obtain. During all this time there was not any other attempts to establish a peace between the two forces. Peace indeed would only come when one side, or the other realized that theirs was a lost cause. Such a realization was far in the distant future. At this time both sides believed that they would obtain complete and final victory. Neither had any idea of the size of the forces that they were opposing.

The battles would be suspended for a while. This was because Many Fires and his Braves had returned to their homes and families. His tribe had come to the village of Running Fox to report of their success. Meanwhile, to the South the Comanche was waging a similar battle with the brown skinned Spanish, now known as Mexicans. These Mexicans were crossing the Rio Bravo in great numbers.

The Comanche had been at war with the Apache for many years. They had finally forced the Apache Nation to move to the mountains of the southwest. Now their main enemy was the Mexicans. While the concern of the Comanche was not to move the great herds of buffalo, but to retain the great herds of horses that they had captured, and retain the buffalo where it was. The Spaniards, or Mexicans, were not as well equipped as the Whites of the East. This was because they had not established supply routes, therefore were less effective in battle. However they were just as determined to over run the holders of the land, on the North side of the river. Their goal was to retrieve the horses that had been taken from them, and to establish settlements claiming the land for their country.

A small Comanche scouting party had ventured across the river with the red water and discovered the home of the Miles family. Jacob and his family were going about their daily task of developing a farm. This family had no idea that there was impending danger, in the area. They had encountered no one during all the time they were in this country. The Comanche observed for a short time to determine that there were only the four people in and around the cabin. While Jacob and his wife were carrying water from the river to water their plants, the Comanche braves descended on the unsuspecting family. Being unarmed except for their water buckets, Jacob and his wife were killed immediately. The two young girls were captured and would be returned to the main village and given as a gift to the chief, Forked River. Forked river had many captive slaves, however most of them were young Indian girls. There were a few Spanish girls, who had been captured, while the Comanche was raiding across the Rio Bravo. The fields of the small farm were destroyed and the log cabin burned. Everything of value, to an Indian, was removed. The young girls did not know at the time, but it would have been better if they had been slain also. The pain and horror of their lives was just beginning. They would be beaten, and abused by the women of the village. In addition they would be required to work from dawn until after dark taking care of the chores of the village. Their position in life was called slavery in other parts of the world, but to the Indian the term was simply captive.

The activities, of the Comanche, were known to Running Fox, but as yet there had been no alliance between him and that nation. They were conducting separate wars with different enemies.

While the Comanche was fighting the Spanish to the South, the Sioux were engaging the Whiles from the Northeast. Running Fox was leading constant raids on the Long Knives in the central section of the plains. One such raid almost proved to be fatal to him. He and his group of Warriors had come upon a large detachment of soldiers, and launched their attack.

As the Warriors approached they could see a long line of soldiers kneeling. Immediately behind them there was another long line standing. As the Warriors rode in the first line fired their guns. While they were reloading, the second line would fire. This was a different style of battle that the Indians had not seen before. This procedure was repeated over and over.

Riding at the head of the attack, Running Fox had been the first to be wounded. As he rode in upon the troops, a rifle ball had knocked him from his pony. The Warriors immediately surrounded their Chief placing him on a pony with one of the Warriors. He was taken immediately to the rear of the charging band. During the confusion caused by the wounding of their Chief, the Warriors lost the advantage that they had enjoyed. Therefore, they would not loose the battle, but would retreat to reorganize and fight another time.

When Running Fox was returned to the village, it was discovered that the rifle ball had lodged in his left shoulder. He could no longer use his left arm. If the use of this arm did not return then he would no longer be able to be an active part of future battles. After a couple of days, he was up and conducting his duties with only one arm.

The constant fighting was reducing the numbers of Warriors within the tribes, and there seemed to be no end to numbers of soldiers that were coming into the land. There were many small forts being built deeper and deeper into the land. These forts were spaced about a days ride apart.

Each fort had enough men to withstand a normal attack. Running Fox and those that followed him were forced to retreat further into the hills to the West. Greater numbers from other tribes were joining him all the time, but it seemed that Whites were gradually gaining the upper hand.

Quick Beaver went into the mountain to confer with The Great Spirits, and seek a vision that would tell her of a plan to overcome the rapid approach of the ever-advancing Whites. She spent many days chanting, and searching for a solution to this great problem. Finally after receiving no vision she returned to the village and called Running Fox to her.

"I have called On The Spirits to send me a message. There was no vision sent, no eagle to direct me. It would appear that The Spirits have no solution, or they are sure that the people can overcome and solve this problem. I believe that they are confident that you, our leader, will become the master over the Whites."

Running Fox was beginning to regain the use of his left arm and with the return of his arm his confidence was also returning. He would hold a war council again and call upon the Chiefs of the other tribes to assist him in the laying of a new plan. At council, Many Fires made his report. "It was with some difficulty that the Shoshone and Lakota braves have moved the massive numbers of the buffalo. However they gradually had a great success. They were able to direct a large herd toward the southwest, and to the area north of the great lake of the salt water. There they were put under the protection of the Shoshone tribe. This also included the Hopi, who were to the south of the salt lake. The Hopi were farmers and craftsmen, and were not adapted to the ways of the buffalo of the plains, but they were willing to take on the task of supervising the herd brought to them. Since they were the raiser of corn, beans, and squash, and lived in pueblos this would be a major change in their way of life.

Another large group of buffalo were moved into the land of the Black Foot. There was already a few buffalo in this area but the people of the villages agreed that this was a proper place to leave the new animals. They were sure that there was enough open grassland to support the increased numbers."

After the report was completed, Running Fox declared that there would be fourteen days of singing and dancing.

It had taken a very long time to get the herds moved, and to locate them, in what was believed to be a safe place. Even with this giant effort to gather all the buffalo, there were still many animals remaining on the land of the Kiowa.

"I, Running Fox, have made it clear to you before what must be done with the outsiders that invade our land. I now find that the situation is getting even worse. The numbers of Whites into our land is increasing with the rising of each new sun. They are racing across the land, as do the floodwaters in a dry creek bed after a spring storm. The only hope we have is to stop these people before they reach the great mountains. Once they have reached the cover of the rocks and timber of the mountains it will be more difficult to find and destroy them. We must place a wall of Warriors across the land, and with one mighty effort stop these outsiders. If it is the will of The Great Spirits, this will be done. If not, then we will live with their will no matter where they direct us. I have had a vision that some day the Red Man will live in peace with those of the different colored skin. However, now is not the time. The circumstances are certainly not right, at this time. Until that time, if it is to come to past, we will continue to fight and die for the protection of our lands that were given to us by The Spirits that govern all men. For now we must go forth and paint ourselves for continued war. Knowing full well that we must fight until we see the eagle disappear from our sky. As long as the eagle can be seen circling out in front of us, we are assured that this is the path we must take."

All at the council were in agreement with the words of Running Fox. They gave him the sign of agreement. Now that all had agreed on their continued course of action, each tribe went on their way to paint and dance in preparation for even a greater battle than any they had fought before.

Two days after the completion of the council a brave reported, to Running Fox, that a small group of Long Knives were riding across the prairie carrying a large white cloth above them on a stick.

He studied these men and determined that they carried no weapons, and that they had with them the gun trader.

Running Fox gave the command to allow these men to progress to their destination, or until it could be determined what was the purpose for this visit into their land. These men were watched carefully, as was directed by Running Fox. The Irish trader was riding out in front of the group. From time to time he would give the universal Indian sign of peace. Seeing, or hearing no response the group would proceed forward. Running Fox was certain that these men were seeking to hold council with him. This he would not do until they had been observed for several days. He sent scouts to circle the group to examine their back trail. He must be certain that these men were not decoys with the purpose of distracting attention from a raiding party elsewhere.

The Long Knives had reached a shallow depression in the prairie. There they set up an overnight camp. Everything seemed to be peaceful enough, and they were sure that they would be safe. They knew that the Indians were watching even though they had not seen any around for days.

When the sun rose the next morning the soldiers found that a complete circle of Kiowa Warriors were around them. These Warriors had slipped in during the night. The warriors were certainly close enough to have killed them if they desired. This was the first indication the army had that the Indians were men of honor.

The gun trader came forward under the sign of peace. "I have been brought from the stockade of the army to this place. It was because they know that I speak the universal language of the Indian. I have been instructed to advise you that the army wishes to discuss the terms of peace with the Great Running Fox. The Chief of all White men wishes to make a treaty with all the red men of the country. In return for peace he is offering many guns for hunting and also many blankets and beads. But before this can happen there is to be a treaty signed by all the Chiefs of the land. A treaty is an agreement between the two sides that had been recorded on a thing called paper. The Indian in return is to remove the paint of war and cease to raid the forts and settlements, of the Whites. With this treaty it would be possible for both the Red Man and the White Man to go about their daily lives with out fear."

"I, Chiefs Running Fox, have been chosen to lead all the people that you have named Indians. It is our wish to only live in peace, and to resume our way of life. The only thing that is proposed by the Whites, that we could use would be rifle balls and powder. Our women provide the people with beads and blankets. Our braves provide the protection and food. I see no way that the White Man can be allowed to roam our land to destroy the buffalo, just for personal gain. You have spoken and now I have spoken. You will be allowed to return to that place from which you have come. Take with you the message that we are not interested in the treaty that is offered. Also take the knowledge that your safety was and is only preserved by the waving white flag above your heads. If you return to our villages again it must be under the flag of war. This is my final word at this council."

The soldiers were allowed to return along the trail from which they had entered the area. Running Fox dispatched some of his Braves to follow and assure themselves that the White Soldiers returned to the confines of their fort. This had been the second attempt at securing a peace treaty and had failed.

Back at his village Running Fox advised the other Chiefs of his talks with the White Trader. He explained to them that the only reason he had observed the sign of peace was because he knew the trader to be a trusted friend, of the Red Man. One of the Chiefs asked what was this name, Indian, that the Whites called all Red men? Running Fox told them that this was a name that was given them by the first white man to set foot ashore from the Great Salt Water to the East. This name was distasteful to all. They wanted to be known by their tribal names, not by a name given them by an enemy.

For many moons there was a relative peace in the land. All the while the villages were preparing for the eventual battle that all knew was coming.

A dispatch had been sent to the Chief of the Whites in Washington, and the army was waiting for further orders.

Finally a detachment of soldiers arrived, at the western most of the fort, with the orders. The General in charge was ordered to gather all available men and pursue the Indians until they would finally have to agree to a peace treaty. This was an order issued out of ignorance. There was no way that any man so far from the frontier could have understood the devastating effect this would have on the tribal nations, or the soldiers on the front lines. Although the army had the superior weapons, the greater numbers of the Indian alone, would allow them to hold on to their land for a long time.

When Running Fox received word that the army was gathering for battle, he sent runners to all the villages and amassed such a number of able Warriors as the world had never before seen. As he surveyed the assembled group it was impossible to know the exact number of those assembled. They were camped from the horizon to horizon. To the last man, all were painted and prepared for war. The war cries and dances continued through out the day and night for an extended period time. This would be so until word came that the army of Long Knives was marching.

In the mind of Running Fox the outcome was never in doubt. The soldiers marched in close order and their tactics were quite different of that of the Warriors that were waiting along the entire frontier.

The experienced Warriors were prepared to fight as they had been taught. The younger braves were given a different assignment. Running Fox had decided that in order to stop the movement of the army they must be stripped of their horses. He had given instructions that every horse, that could be found, be killed. Even though the younger braves had not experienced actual battle, they had been train since childhood the ways of war. These young men were placed under a War Chief named Half Moon. They were to go into the field, and seek out the horses and steal them, and if this was not practical they were to destroy them. This was no easy task, as they would for the most part have to work under the cover of darkness. The days were spent scouting, and the nights raiding the various locations. It was soon discovered that these animals were of little value to the tribes. They were not adapted to the type of terrain that the Indians traveled. Soon the mission became one of search and kill.

For a period of time this tactic seemed to be working. Once the horses were removed from the detachment of soldiers, the Warriors would attack and most of the time they would come away with a victory. The men that were in the process of building the forts were the easiest to confront and destroy. For the most part they were armed only with a pistol and their axes. Once they had fired their pistols, they were faced with certain death.

With the supply of rifle balls and powder running low, and no reinforcements arriving the army was facing a very serious problem. The same was true of the forces under the leadership of Running Fox. With the constant battles that were being fought, the supply of arrows had grown short. The end results were that a great many of the battles were fought hand-to-hand. This type of fighting caused many more death and injuries to both sides.

After surveying the conditions in the field it was the decision of Running Fox that his people must fall back to the villages for the needed rest. While there they were to replenish their weapons. While this period of rest was in progress many more soldiers were arriving at the forts. These men were not trained soldiers, but men that had volunteered, and were rushed to the mid west. Great wagon trains were arriving with many more men and guns. These people that had visions of riches and land were now faced with the fight for survival.

Running Fox had regained the use of his arm and was constantly on the move from village to village gathering information as to the progress being made. The news that he received was not at all reassuring. It took no vision for him to realize that the Red Man was loosing ground. That the frontier of the Whites was spreading both to the west and to the south. The Spanish people, to the South, now called Mexicans, were gaining more land and position in the land of the Comanche. All of the Apache Nation to the southwest entered into the battle and against their nature they were fighting with the Comanche to over come the advancing Mexicans.

While the Red Man to the east of the big river had adjusted to the conditions of living with the presence of the Whites, the entire Red population to the west was joined in a common cause.

There had been no further attempt to reach peace between the two factions, and would not be for several years.

Chapter 28

Many summers had passed since the first Long Knives had entered the land. Running Fox was getting slower, due to his age. He was suffering the effects of many scars received in battle. During all this time the White Man was covering his beloved land. It seemed to him that there were as many Whites in the land as there were trees in a forest. After the move of the buffalo had been made, it was found that a great number had been overlooked and remained across the land. These animals had raised many young and therefore there were large herds reappearing in the mid western section of the country. Running Fox now was sure that it would be impossible to move more of the buffalo from their grazing land. He was sure that at some point in time he would have to reach some kind of agreement with the Whites. He knew that if he did not then all his people would vanish from the earth. Most of the younger chief of the various tribes were not in favor of negotiating a peace. They wanted to continue the fight regardless of the cost in lives. Now not only was he loosing part of the land to the Whites, he was beginning to loose the confidence of some of his red Brothers. For the first time some of the decisions, were challenged by other tribes. As yet none of them had refused to follow his direction, but he knew that it was only a matter of time until this would come to past.

Small Fox had now reached manhood, and returned to the tepee of his father. He had received no vision that would justify the change of his name. He was now a well-qualified Junior Warrior and had joined in several battles with Running Fox. Small Fox quickly gained the reputation of a fearless and capable man of battle. It was now time for Running Fox to put his son to a real test. There had been a small detachment of soldiers that had returned to the valley of the bones. They were attempting to build a fort there. This in itself was a major task because of the limited supply of timber in the area. Small Fox was placed in charge of a band of Warriors. They were sent to destroy this detachment of Long Knives.

After they arrived in the general area of the valley, Small Fox spent two days studying the movement of the troops. He must devise a plan that would assure the quick and decisive victory. He would split his forces into two halves. One half he sent in a wide circle around to the East. There they were to make a feeble attempt at attacking the camp. With the attention of the soldiers diverted to the East he would then lead the second half from the West. After he had launched his attack then the other Warriors would attack in force. This plan worked mostly because most of the soldiers lacked the proper training. Soon the battle had evolved into hand-to-hand fighting, at which the Warriors were very proficient. Therefore after a battle of short duration the entire camp was over run. All the soldiers were either dead or mortally wounded. It would have been better for them to have all been killed because those that lived faced a slow and painful death. When Small Fox returned to his village carrying the scalps, and other bounty he had obtained he was immediately elevated to the position of War Chief. There was no particular significance to this title. However it did carry with it the knowledge that he had shown outstanding cunning and leadership in battle. He otherwise carried no battle scars to signify his deeds. Therefore, he had a tattoo placed on his left cheek. This he wore as a badge of honor to show that he had been engaged in a major battle, and with the help of The Spirits he had escaped injury. This honor was short lived. A short time later he was leading a band of Warriors to the north to assist another War Chief. As he and his Warriors emerged from a deep canyon they were ambushed by another detachment of Long Knives and Small Fox was the first to fall. He was riding at the front of his group and suddenly a rifle ball tore into the left side of his head. After a short battle his followers became disorganized. They took the body of Little Fox, and retreated back to the village. After his body was placed on a raised platform in a place of honor at the burial site there was a week of mourning declared. During which time Running Fox went into the hills to confer with The Spirits.

After a week, Running Fox returned to the village and reported that he had received no vision. He had to assume that the future actions were to be left entirely to him. While he was fasting alone on the prairie searching for this vision, the memory of the snake and badger would come to his mind. He now knew the meaning of the sign given him by that event. He knew that these two enemies were representatives of the Kiowa and the White Man. The only thing that remained to learn was which side of this conflict was to be represented by the badger. He pondered this for days and the Spirits would not offer an answer. With the death of his son, Running Fox became even more depressed. He vowed to avenge the death by destroying every thing that reminded him of the White Man. As was human nature, the bitterness faded with time. Therefore, after a short time, the thoughts of Running Fox returned to the great problems that faced the tribe.

The Kiowa and their followers were not the only tribes facing great problems. To the south the Comanche was facing an enemy that could not be defeated. There had come upon the land of the Comanche a great sickness. There was no cure that the Medicine Man could find. The Great Spirits of the Comanche had failed to come forth with a vision to assist them to over come this sickness. Over a period of time the number of Comanche had been reduced by half and then reduced by half again. This sickness had caused the once great powerful tribe, to become one that no longer poised a great threat to the Mexicans.

It was at this point in time that the Comanche people were forced again to unite with their enemies to protect their land from the invader from the outside world. They had at one time been at peace with the Apache. Later, seemingly for no reason, the Apache had broken away from the combine.

A War Chief named Little River was sent, under the sign of peace, to council with Running Fox.

"We are a proud people that have fought, and been victorious over the Apache and the Mexican. We have lived our entire lives as a superior force on the plains of the Southwest. However, now there has descended on our nation a plague that the great medicine of our leaders cannot cure. It is under the sign of peace that I am here asking you that my people be allowed to enter into your combine. So that together we will defeat both the White and Mexican People."

Running Fox listened with great interest to what this man had to say.

"It is with a heavy heart that I hear of the sickness that has spread across the Southwest. This is an enemy that we have not yet had to face. I would like to be of assistance to your people, but I cannot allow this sickness be brought into our land. I will however offer protection to the Comanche people by keeping the Whites from your land. You must deal with the Mexican from the south."

The Spanish-speaking people who had entered the land from the south were now called Mexicans and were establishing settlements around a thing they called a Mission. At first they were very hostile and wanted to conquer the men of the plains. They were now trying to forge out a trade union with the Comanche. They were buying female slaves from the Chiefs of the various villages.

During one of these exchanges Forked River sold, the Mexicans, the Miles girls to a General. He found that these white girls would bring much more in trade than the Apache and Navaho girls. It then became his mission to save and capture white women when he raided a White settlement.

This was a decision that had led to the contact of the plague that was destroying his Nation. He did not realize it at the time. Rather he thought that The Great Spirits had become angry for some reason and placed this curse on his people.

There had always been a series of war, and then peace among the Kiowa and The Comanche. Now it was evident that a greater enemy threatened the entire world of the Red Man.

With this knowledge, both nations formed a lasting pact to unite. While the movement of the Whites was mostly contained in the central plains of the country, the Mexicans were spreading across the rough mountainous section from the Rio Grand to the Salt Water of the West.

With the destruction of a single White or Mexican settlement there seemed to be two to take its place. And with the destruction of an Indian village, their numbers decreased. The Warriors were killed and their squaws were either killed or captured. However, for the most part the taking of captives was only the practice of the Mexicans or Comanche. Like in any society there were always a few men that were that processed more greed than others. These men soon learned that the trading of female slaves to Mexico brought them more riches with less work than the killing of buffalo.

Chapter 29

Running fox was getting older and the constant strain of battle was making the winters seem longer and colder. He had seen his once beautiful and powerful homeland become a blood stained field of many wars. He had spent many long days, in the village Kiva, seeking a vision. He wondered had the spirits abandoned his people for some unknown reason. He had called for a vision and none had come. He was in doubt as to his ability to lead his people out of this seemingly lost situation.

Meanwhile, the numbers of settlers were increasing. The forts were being established further and further west. There was no question in the minds of the leaders of the White Army that their will would prevail.

It appeared to Running Fox that the death of a soldier meant nothing to the Army Chiefs. While he, on the other hand, mourned the loss of a single member of his people.

What, or who, could have created such a being as these people. A people, whose only thoughts were of killing to acquire material things, Only the Mexicans showed any signs of having any form of god. These Mexicans were just as eager to gain material things, but one of the first things to be built, in their settlements, was a place to worship their gods.

The great herds of buffalo, that once covered his land, had vanished entirely from the mountains of the west to the rivers of the east. Only those that had been removed to other locations remained. Running Fox feared that these too would soon be discovered and destroyed.

The Cherokee had signed a peace treaty with the Whites many winters before and there was talk in Washington of placing all natives on things called reservations. This would make them wards of the government. This action was violently opposed by the Apache of the Southwest, and the Sioux of the North.

Only the Havasupai Tribes, of the great canyon, were unaffected by these outside forces at this time. Their concern was not the buffalo. These were people that depended on the raising of crops and domestic animals in the floor of this great canyon with a strong river. This too was about to change.

With the aging process and the disappearance of the buffalo, came a new wave of excitement that was sweeping the world of the white man. They had discovered a yellow metal in the mountains. They called it gold. Even the weakest of men were fighting to obtain as much of this metal as they could. The immediate change was made, from the hunt of the buffalo, to the hunt for gold. In place of raiding and killing the natives, the Whites were now engaged in raiding the gold camps, and killing the prospectors.

This gave Running Fox ample time to examine his position and to lay future plans. On several occasions, he had been, approached by representatives of the Army under the sign of the white flag. Each time what they offered was not acceptable. It appeared to him that all that the Whites wanted was to take and give nothing in return. In any case these meetings were only with a small group of Whites. As yet there had been no formal proposal from the main Chief of the United States. Each time one of the meetings proved unsuccessful, there would be a long period of unrest between the two factions.

The Mexicans were placing more of their efforts on collecting land. They had rapidly expanded to the great salt water that they called The Pacific. They had stopped in an area that they called California. There they had established many Missions and were gradually moving along the coast to the north.

While this movement was in progress, there had been another group of white skinned people that were getting established to the north. These

Whites called themselves French and were from another country across the other ocean to the east.

It was to be only a matter of time until the four groups were to converge and meet in a major conflict. This was very alarming to Running Fox. He knew that his people would be trapped in the middle of the other three and would suffer both direct and indirect consequences.

In other events that had taken place in his world, Running Fox had learned of a young Brave to the Southwest called Cochise. Also there was a young brave in the black hills that was a year younger. This brave was named Tatanka Yotaka, but was called Sitting Bull. When these names were first heard, Running Fox placed no special importance on it. Also in the White world there was a young adventurer named William Cody. He was called Buffalo Bill.

Unknown to Running Fox at the time, these three men were to play a great part in the final outcome of what was happening in the world around him.

It would be this Buffalo Bill that would gain a sort of fame for destroying the western Buffalo.

Prior to his gaining this so called fame, he would be part of a mail route across the country. The establishing of this Pony Express dealt a severe blow to the native pride. It served to confirm that the Whites were gaining dominance over the land.

Nevertheless this dominance would suffer many set backs before it was finally accomplished.

This Cochise would rise to become a great Chief and lead his Warriors on many successful battles for years.

Sitting Bull would gather the greatest fighting coalition of Lakota Warriors that had been known to that time. He would lead these Warriors in an attack of long knives at a place that would later be called The Battle of the Little Big Horn. It was there that he defeated a General called Custer.

George Armstrong Custer had gained a reputation from several previous battles. He had fought in the civil war that the Whites had waged against each other in prior years.

The Army had been dispatched to protect the gold seekers in the Dakota Territory. It was here in this territory that another Chief Red Cloud and Crazy Horse, of the Oglala Sioux tribe, had fought off the establishment of the Bozeman trail for quite a while. It was when the three Sioux leaders joined that they had been able to kill the three hundred soldiers commanded by Custer.

Two years before the Little Big Horn, Custer had subdued the Kiowa people. They were moved to a reservation in Oklahoma. They had been given a section of land where there was no water for growing, and there was nothing left to hunt. After enduring these conditions for a period of two or so years, and by choice, Running Fox and some of his followers left the area assigned to them and moved into the black hills of the Dakotas.

The government in Washington was overwhelmed by the problems that face it with the great number of natives. With the changing of the administrations the policies would also change. It seemed that no one had a solution or a permanent fix. Tribes were moved from the desert of the southwest to the Everglades of Florida. Then marched to the plains of Oklahoma. The tribes around the Mississippi River were also moved to reservations in the Indian Territory, of Oklahoma. While all this was being done the government was also offering land grants in Oklahoma to white settlers.

The Zuni were placed on a reservation that was located half in the New Mexico Territory and half in the Arizona Territory. The Hualapai were left in the area of the great canyon in The Northern Arizona Territory. With the Hopi being left just to the east of the canyons. The Navaho were left in the general vicinity of the Utah and Arizona borders. The Sioux were located across a northern tier of states including the Dakotas.

After the capture of some of the escaped Kiowa's most of their chiefs and leaders were removed to Florida with the others were located in the Indian territory of Oklahoma.

Chapter 30

It had been fifty summers since Running Fox had discovered the valley of the bones. As he was sitting in the predawn light that surrounded him high on a mountain in the black hills, he was reflecting back to all that had transpired in his life. He gazed to the North and off in the distance he could visualize the land of the Cheyenne where he knew that their people were suffering the same hardships, as were all Reservation Indians. Far to the west he could see the outline of the forest of the black hills. He was well aware that The Great Spirits had allowed him to remain on the land far longer than most of his people had ever remained.

After he and his people had left the reservation in The Oklahoma territory, they had traveled for many days to get to this place. They had endured many freezing days and nights, suffered much hunger. They had left without food or weapons. They had left what meager supplies that the government provided to those that chose to stay on the reservation.

It was their intent to return to their old way of life. Then live off the land as they had for hundreds of generation. This, they soon found to be almost impossible. However it did prove to be better than the reservations at that time. All the land that was assigned to the reservations was barren and useless for human habitation.

They had first traveled north into the Kansas Territory. Then they went into the land of the Oglala. It was here that they first found friendly Red Brothers who took them in and fed them to restore their strength and determination. After spending one winter and summer in the Nebraska Territory, they were now ready to take the final trip to the black hills. For many days the army tried to follow them and return them to the reservation, but the stronger and more determined managed to elude capture. Those that followed their aging Chief were devoted to his ideas and cherished his leadership. They were quite sure that their great leader would find a way for them to return to the old life.

After several weeks of searching the army finally turned back just a days ride from where the Indians were camped. As yet there were not many whites that had ventured into the badlands. Those that had done so had never returned to what the white man called civilization.

All this Running Fox knew, and he was sure that he at least could live out his remaining years in peace.

His thoughts then turned back to the coming of the Iron Horse to his land. There were multitudes of funny little men with yellow skins and they brought two lines along behind them that went back as far as the eye could see. With the coming of the iron horse had also came the singing wire. Running Fox was certain that these two things would ruin the entire land across the universe.

With the coming of the Iron Horse and the singing wire, there came a man called Buffalo Bill. He had killed the remaining buffalo in the original territory of the Kiowa.

The thought of this slaughter brought a bitter taste to his mouth. But even as the bile rose from his throat there was a trace of a smile on his face. This was because he had had the forethought to remove great numbers of these marvelous animals to a safe place in Utah, and in the badlands of The Dakotas. There he knew that they could be protected and preserved for maybe all time.

He had wondered why there was a need for so many people to travel so far in such a manner. He had watched as the wooden roads crossed the land, and then watched when they were replaced with roads of iron. He recalled the many times he had moved his entire tribe with out the necessity of such things. Haste and discomfort to his people, or others on the land had forever been a factor.

The idea of sending messages from one side of the land to the other side seemed of no value. The people on the other end could, neither see, nor help what was happening on the other side of this land. There were indeed many things that the Whites did that he knew he would never live to understand. This however did not really matter for he did not wish to know more about their strange world than he had already witnessed.

The beautiful rolling prairie where he had often hunted the buffalo was now being invaded with a strange form of animal. These were called longhorn cattle. They were brought great distances from the land of the Rio Grande and placed on what once was occupied by the buffalo and the antelope. These cattle seemed to be sturdy and well adjusted to the type of range they were now living on. They, however, did not have near the beauty or the useful qualities of the buffalo.

He had seen the forest destroyed under the axe of the white man, and the earth torn open with a thing they called a plow. In this earth they planted massive amounts of the various food crops that they used.

The invading strangers were not in the least bit concerned with the conservation of anything. The earth, where they removed their yellow metal, was left to wash away down the mountainside when the rains came. This was causing all the clear running streams to become blocked and stagnant. The fish and water crest were lying dead along the shore.

He recalled the horrible sound of the thunder sticks that was called a rifle. Also, in his memory there were the faces of young boys as they faced death under the chop of a flint tomahawk. These memories also brought back the many nights that he observed the death dance, and heard the chants of his people after a battle that many Warriors had not survived.

He paused for a while just taking in the grandeur of the land that the Great Spirits had provided for all mankind.

When he returned to the thoughts of an old man he was once again back in his childhood where there was nothing, but peaceful happiness. He was running through the land with the determination to out run all the other boys. He was looking back at those trailing him and saying to them. "You can't catch he that runs like a fox."

It was these races that had given him his name after he had failed to have a vision when he was sent out to become a man. Then there was his first long bow and the tiny arrows made for birds and small animals. They were his first real possessions that he could call his own. They had been preserved through the years until he was sent to Oklahoma. More than any thing else he hated the long knives for taking away his childhood treasures.

Through the years he had lost his wife and son, along with his youth and vigor. The one thing he had retained was the Kiowa spirit. He had been, was, and would forever be a Kiowa Native American.

With these memories drifting through his head, Running Fox rose and mounted his pony and started down the mountain to the rolling valley below. Reaching the lower level he rode ever so slowly around the peacefully grazing herd of buffalo. They seemed to not realize that he was even in the area. It was as if they realized that this man alone had saved them from destruction by moving them to this great range that they were now enjoying.

As he rode, he carefully examined each one individually as if it was a personal friend. To him, each had a majestic character that must at all cost be retained throughout eternity to represent the past, and to endure the future. He continued his slow ride around the entire herd and then started back up the mountain.

A Kiowa man was not suppose to show signs of weakness, however he could not hold back the emotion that weld up inside his chest and brought moisture to his eyes.

Running Fox returned to the very spot where he had started the day and once again sat and looked out across the valley that he had just ridden through. The afternoon sun was just beginning to lower it's self to the rim of the opposite mountains.

While he sat, lost in his memories and pride, a majestic eagle rose from the opposite mountaintop and flew directly to him. Running Fox knew that he was about to receive a vision from The Greatest of all Spirits. The eagle flew to within an arms length of him and suddenly turned and circled the entire herd of buffalo below. Completing the circle the eagle returned and perched on a large rock in front of the old Kiowa. After peering into the eyes of this great man, the eagle rose and flew directly away to the horizon. Running Fox watched the great bird until it had completely disappeared in the distance.

When the bird disappeared he told himself that the Spirits were telling him that the buffalo were coming back, and would go on forever on the great prairies of this land.

Running Fox got slowly up and removed the hobbles from his pony and also the rawhide rope from its muzzle. Returning to his chosen spot he picked up the White Man's rifle that he carried. He threw it off into the canyon. He carefully laid his long war bonnet out on the ground. Beside the bonnet he placed his longbow and quiver of arrows. Next he placed his flint knife and tomahawk carefully beside the other things. Running Fox looked once more at the last of the buffalo. He then lay down beside these treasures and closed his eyes for his last run.

Part Four

The Legend of Two Knives

Chapter 31

Again Rain Cloud rose from his sitting place. He looked around the entire circle that surrounded him. "That is the story of the buffalo. The day has been long and I must retire to my tepee and gather my strength with some sleep that my body and spirit need. I will return in two suns to tell you of another lifetime that took place many summers later.

The story that I will tell on that day will explain to all, why I chose to go to the White Man's school and learn the language of the whites. When I attended this school my life was half over. The stories from the past made it necessary for me to learn the white language, and of the ways of the outside world. This story will serve to show you that anything is possible for the Red Man. But first, it must be in the mind and heart of the individual. From this last story, you will gain a deeper knowledge of the history of the Native American as well as the history of those that arrived here from other countries, across the great salt water.

While I am resting for two days, it will give this council time to conduct its business".

Rain Cloud then turned and retired in the direction of his humble tepee.

The third day arrived, and what a glorious day it was. Rain Cloud emerged from his tepee, and to all he looked many years younger. Today he stood straight and walked with sort of a swagger. It was as if the telling the stories of the past had restored his energy. Maybe he was revived in spirit. Maybe he was looking forward to the next council, when he would again be the center of the attention. He sat in his usual place and told the following story.

The afternoon sun was very bright and hot as it hung about midway in the western sky. He sat casually in the old worn Mexican saddle with his head slouched down so that the brim of his hat would shade his eyes. His appearance betrayed who he really was, and the ever alertness of his dark eyes was hidden in the shadow offered by the hat. Eyes that took in every movement that surrounded him in the vast open nothingness of the wasteland where this day had found him. Eyes, that at this moment were watching a red tail hawk dart low across the sand and scrub brush, searching for something to complete its afternoon meal. These same eyes also were noting the flight of a Mexican Eagle circling high in the sky, far above the horizon to the south.

His tall frame and broad shoulders cast a long shadow across the endless sands of west Texas. He was allowing his black mustang pony to wander at a casual pace, to take advantage of the sparsely spaced clumps of grass along the way. He allowed the pony to do this, because the area that they were traveling had very little plant growth of any type. They had been on the trail for a long time.

They were in the vast sand hills, just southeast of where the Pecos River entered the territory from the land of the great bat caves, in the place known as the New Mexico Territory. They were now in the western section of the country known as Texas. It seemed that the hot drifting sand would go on forever. However, the young man knew that this was not the case because he was familiar with this section of the world. He had been born and raised just southeast of where he was now riding. He dismounted and walked for a while, leading the pony to give his faithful mount a rest. Also he needed to get his bearings. There existed no trails across the sand. The pony and the few items it carried, was all he owned. As he walked slowly along, his high heel store bought boots cut deep in the soft earth. The loose sand made difficult traveling for both man and beast. The tracks would be filled with sand as soon as their feet were lifted.

Just ahead, through the heat waves, he could see giant pools of water shimmering in the afternoon sun. But as he approached these pools, the water retreated, always staying in front of them, sometimes disappearing completely. He knew that this was just the sun and heat waves playing tricks on his eyes. He wondered how many men had died out here chasing the non-existing water. With the knowledge of what time of the year it was, and observing the location of the sun, he was told that he must go more to the east to reach his destination.

Shortly after sunset he reached a place where the ever-shifting sand gave way to a firmer ground. This ground was very rocky and rough and it was covered with cactus and greasewood, thus making the walking just as difficult as the sand. After finding a shallow depression in the earth he decided that he would stop for the night.

He unsaddled his horse, and with clumps of dry grass he carefully wiped the sweat and dust from the sturdy mustang.

Laying in the soft sand at the bottom of the depression, looking into the clear starlit sky he began to drift off to sleep. The distant call of the night birds, along with the sound of an entire pack of coyotes chasing their prey, was the music that assured him that there was no danger, for him, in the area. He had spent many nights like this during the long weeks of this journey that had brought him full circle to this country. He knew that the warm sand would soon cool and he would be able to sleep in comfort.

On such nights as this, he had recalled the twenty summers that had been the sum total of his life.

Early memories were faded and incomplete. He could not remember his Father, but he did recall a tall Indian in full paint and headdress, but could not remember the features of his face. He could, however, remember his Mother and could recall her face and features.

His Mother was a fine looking half white squaw. She had spent many teaching hours with him. She had taught him that his Grandmother was a white woman captured at an early age by his Grandfather. His Grandmother had never returned to her people and thus his Mother had been raised as an Indian Squaw. In secret his Mother had taught him the white man's words that had been handed down in a like manner to her. Although he had never known his Father, he had been told that his Father was a Great War Chief and had been killed while on a raid into Mexico.

He painfully recalled the night that his Mother had been killed. They had been awakened around midnight by a band of Mexicans that had slipped into the camp and killed many of the tribe. When he woke up there were Mexican riders everywhere. They were riding through the village tearing down the tepees and shooting everyone they saw. Most of the tribe had been able to escape, the onslaught, in the dark, but there were many killed including women and children as well as the older men of the village. Most of the braves were away from the village conducting a raid of their own. In fact the Mexicans were killing everyone they could find that had not escaped from the village. His Mother had thrown herself on top of him to protect him from harm therefore he saw little of the battle.

He was a boy of six summers at the time. He was called Boy with the Brown Hair. Just before she died, his Mother had reached inside her skirts. She handed him something wrapped in buckskin. Her last words to him were. "Search out the other knife". He did not know the meaning of this. His mother died before she could explain. He later unwrapped the buckskin and found that it contained a necklace of bear claws, a smooth stone, and a beautiful Mexican style knife. This knife was made of fine steel. The handle was carved in the image of a mountain lion. The handle was also decorated with Mexican silver and some beautifully colored stones. He vowed to himself from that day forward that the knife would never be out of his sight. Some of the older braves owned knives similar to this that they had stolen from Mexicans, which they had killed in raids or battles. However, none of their knives could compare to the beauty of the one his mother had given him. To his knowledge no other young boy had such a knife as the one he owned. For the most part there were not many steel knives in the village.

Following the death of his mother, he had been raised as an orphan in the Indian camp. He was raised along with Tonka the son of a Caddo Squaw. Cracked Corn, Tonka's mother had also been taken from her tribe when she was very young. The Comanche Tribes were always raiding the Caddo villages. He and the Caddo boy, Tonka, were raised as brothers. The braves, of the tribe, had taught the two boys to hunt and fish as well as to make arrows and the other things a young boy must learn. They had spent many hours in training, preparing their bodies. A lot of time was spent running through the country. They would run for several hours at a time with out stopping. By the time they were grown they must be able to run nonstop all day if such an occasion should arise, and doing this became necessary. The braves were very strict and the training was very hard, but it was the necessary way to prepare a boy for whatever might be ahead in his life.

The village, of his tribe of Comanche's, was moved frequently but usually it was located in the general area near the spot where the Pecos River emptied into the Rio Bravo. While being taught the necessary skills by the braves of the tribe, it seemed to him that at times they set him apart. At other times they treated him as any other Indian boy. He knew that he was part white, but he did not know the meaning of this, only that his hair was a deep brown rather than black, like most of the other boys his age.

He also remembered the long journeys to the salt hills for their supply of salt. Salt was necessary for all living things. It could be found in large quantities in some parts of the country. It was the custom, when they were very young, for the children to accompany the squaws when these trips became necessary. After he grew older he remained at the village while the salt was gathered. It was while some members of the tribe were away gathering salt that he was sent into the wilderness alone to seek out his vision and to become a man.

He was provided with nothing to eat or any weapon. He was to survive for sevens suns without help or advice from anyone. His mother had told him, when he was very young, that the Indian visions were very important to their belief. However, she said that the white man called them dreams or memories and not visions. On his fifth day alone, he dreamed of walking among the rocks and seeing a cougar following him. The lion did everything he did. When he would stop the lion would stop, if he sat the lion would sit, when he slept the lion would sleep close by. The Boy With the Brown Hair was not afraid of the lion, because fear was unknown to the Indian. On the sixth day another vision came to him. The vision was of a group of people, all were different, and all wore different cloths. In this vision there were four squaws and five men surrounded by many Indians, from different tribes. He could not see the faces of these people but could tell that some had different colored skin.

When he returned to the village he was questioned at length by the Medicine Man, Crooked Stick. The Medicine Man told him that this was a sign that the animal was a friendly lion. That the Spirits were saying that he was to be called Friendly Lion or Puma Teyas (Tejas). The Medicine Man also told him that he was truly gifted because most boys never had a vision such as his second vision. As soon as his story was told at council that night his name was immediately changed to Puma.

His Caddo brother had told him that Teyas was a Caddo word for friend. This brother also taught him to speak the Caddo tongue. The medicine man told him that he did not know the meaning of the second vision, but he was sure that in time the Great Spirits would again come with a vision that would explain it.

On the trips to the salt hills the women went to gather the salt and performed the work while the men protected them. The children were needed to help carry the large pouches of salt back to the village.

He also had been a part of several buffalo hunts to the north. It was during his thirteenth summer while the tribe was preparing to move north that he learned that he was going to be included in this, his first hunt. The entire village was going to the hunting grounds. The women would be needed to prepare the meat for food and the hides for clothing and trading. The men would do the hunting and provide the necessary protection. The journey would be a long one with no chance of returning before the winter came. Therefore, it was necessary to carry everything with them as they traveled.

The tepees were taken apart and the poles were secured behind the horses, these provided a crude but ample means of dragging every thing along the long trail. While the women were doing this, the men were busy making arrowheads and arrow shafts to insure that they would have enough for both protection and the hunt.

The art of making arrows was very demanding and consumed much time. First the flint had to be gathered from a secret place known only to a few War Chiefs. Because of this secret, one of the War Chiefs would always stay in the village when a raid was being made so that the secret would always be safe.

Back in the village the pieces of flint were given the crude shape of an arrowhead by chipping them with a larger stone axe. When the final shape was formed it was then refined and sharpened by chipping away very small chips with the tip of deer antler. Finally the flint was heated and given a final edge with small droplets of water. The shafts were carefully selected, and shaved to a smooth finish with a sharp stone knife. Some of the shafts had to be soaked in water and tied to a form and allowed to dry to the straightness required. After the feathers were gathered all of the parts were stored separately. The arrowheads and feathers were placed in separate deer skin pouches. The shafts were bundled together and tied with long strips of rawhide.

It was the responsibility of each warrior to keep himself armed with the necessary equipment for a hunt, or a raid. The arrows were of different sizes. The size was dependent on the purpose that they were to be used for. Some of the warriors had guns that had been taken from the white men and Mexicans during the various raids. The guns were seldom used because of the limited supply of ammunition. Therefore, the braves were not very good at using the white man's weapons. What little they knew they had learned by watching the white man use them during battle.

Finally the day came for their departure. The entire village headed northwest. The senior War Chief rode out front followed by the Medicine Man. Next came the other War Chiefs and then the Braves and extra horses. The women and small ones were the last in line. Everyone had a special place in the procession and was required to stay in it.

The horses were hand picked from the many taken in various raids into Mexico. Only the best horses were selected. The others were allowed to roam free or used for food.

The Comanche warriors were known to be among the best horsemen in the land. They were members of a band of the Shoshone Indians that had split off from the main tribe to the north. They had left the mountains west of the Colorado Territory, in favor of the arid plains of the southwest. In this vast open land, the horse was a sign of a man's wealth. Most of the men of the tribe chose painted horses and would add more color with paint made from different berries and plants they would gather for this purpose. He had chosen a solid black mount every time, because in his mind it would be safer at night. It would blend into the shadows.

He was awakened by the morning call of the blue quail. In took a few seconds for him to shake off the sleep and return from the past that had occupied his dreams. He stood up and gazed to the north across the vast sand hills that he had passed through the day before. Unlike the white sand that could be found to the west of the big bat caves, this sand was a light color of tan. As is the case of all sand, the hills took on a different appearance with each passing moment of time. He dusted the sand from his clothing and gathered himself for the day ahead. The first order of business was to find something to eat. Looking for a likely spot he found a trail leading into an opening at the bottom of a large clump of brush. He removed a small strip of rawhide, he always carried, from his pouch and made a small snare. After carefully setting the snare he moved a short distance away. He then began to circle the brush. Shortly he was rewarded for his effort, when a long eared rabbit jumped and loped to the brush. The snare had been properly placed. The rabbit was trapped. Using the two fire sticks that he carried he finally got a fire started by the friction caused by rubbing them together. He also carried two small pieces of flint to start a fire in case the sticks would not do the trick. He dressed and roasted the rabbit on a spit over the small fire.

While he was preparing the rabbit he was reminded of the many lessons in trapping and hunting small game with a small bow and arrows made for this purpose. The braves of the village had spent many hours teaching him and his Caddo brother the art of tracking and hunting. Having fulfilled one of the two necessities for survival he must now search for water. He still had a small amount in his water pouch, but was reluctant to drink because he did not want to use his supply until a new supply could be found. The previous two days had not afforded him the opportunity to gather fresh water. He had last filled his water pouches in some shallow rapids of the Brazos River. But even after selecting a place where the water had run over a long stretch of sand and stones, the water of the Brazos, was not of the best quality. Prior to the Brazos he had replenished his water as he crossed the Red River. The water from the Red was certainly not ideal water for drinking. He knew that the Pecos was about a days ride to the west but the water from the Pecos was too salty to drink. He knew that the area in front and around him had good water if you were lucky enough to be near it in the early hours of the day. From where he was this day and the rest of the way to the Rio Bravo, there were creeks and small rivers that had the unique quality of the water rising and running in the morning hours, then retreating back into the sand by noon. This process was repeated daily for most of the summer months.

He finished his meal and called his horse and prepared for a leisure ride to the southeast. As he rode he would continually sniff the wind for some indication that there might be water near.

Riding along in the rising heat of the day he was reminded of the events of the morning. And then of the lessons in hunting and trapping that had been given as a small boy. Once again he drifted into the world of his past. A world in which a small Indian boy was about to go on his first buffalo hunt. This hunt would determine if he was indeed ready to enter into the world of manhood.

Chapter 32

After many days of travel the tribe had set up their village on the east side of a range of hills near a small running stream. The scouts had located a large herd of buffalo a few days earlier. The reasons that they had chosen the east side of these hills were twofold. To the east of the stream the flat grass lands gave way to a stand of trees that extended for about a day's ride to both the north and the south. Also the prevailing winds were usually from the south, or the southwest. By choosing such a spot it was almost impossible for the buffalo to get wind of them, or their camp. While the women and younger kids were setting up the Tepees, some of the braves were selected for the first hunt. Puma and his Caddo brother were selected for the first day. It had been learned many years before that the first day was more likely to afford the best chance for a first time hunter to score his first kill. They were both given heavier bows and arrows, by the older braves. In turn they gave their lighter equipment to a younger boy that he could learn to hunt birds and small game.

The time had arrived for him to find out if he was worthy of the faith that had been placed in him. He secured his blanket on the horse with strips of rawhide. Now he was ready for the great adventure. He had his arrows in a quiver over and just behind his right shoulder. His newly acquired bow was in his left hand. He sat straight with his shoulder back so as to look as big as possible.

They rode to the north for some distance, beyond where the buffalo were grazing peacefully out on the vast grassland. Once they were beyond the herd, they swung to the west then to the south. The buffalo was known to have poor eyesight, but could smell danger for a great distance. Therefore, by riding to the south into the wind they would be able to get relatively close to the herd before spooking them. The hunters fanned out in a long half circle line. Each end was ahead and closer to the herd than the middle. As they approached closer the herd, the dominant bull began to get restless. A dominant bull was always the larger and wiser bull. It was always the leader of the herd. As the bull snorted and scraped the ground, with his feet, the signal was given for the charge. One of the more experienced braves had been assigned the task of killing the dominant bull. By killing this bull the herd would become confused and more easily controlled.

Puma was assigned to the last position on the right end of the half circle of hunters. As the herd started to run every hunter picked out and chased a particular animal. Nothing could be heard above the sounds of the running herd. The dust was so thick that one could hardly see as they charged across the flatland. A large bull broke to the right and crossed in front of Puma. He was sure that the gods had selected this bull to be his first kill. He clamped his knees tightly about his horse and reached for an arrow. The bull was charging straight to the west. Puma's horse seemed to know what to do. It was apparently enjoying the chase. In all the excitement, he found it difficult to get the arrow fitted onto his bowstring. As they raced along, Puma gradually gained on the bull until at last he was almost even and along the right side of it. They were racing side by side, with the bull on his left, when the bull turned to the left. After again getting along side the bull, the bull ran very close to a clump of mesquite. Puma had to go around the other side. He again was able to get into position. He slowly drew the bow to the full length of the arrow shaft. Just as he released the arrow the bull made a sharp turn to it's left. His arrow flew harmlessly in front and beyond the fleeing bull. He was almost thrown from his mount as the horse turned sharply in an effort to stay with the buffalo. Finally he was alongside the bull again and prepared to make a second shot. He was embarrassed hoping that no one had seen him miss such a large target at such a close range. He saw that in the distance in front of them there was a huge prairie dog town. This presented a great danger. If his pony stepped into a prairie dog hole it would most likely break a leg. He hurriedly strung a second arrow and let it fly. With the second arrow he scored a hit in the bulls neck just in front of the shoulder. The bull seemed not to be affected. Puma prepared another arrow and repeated the shot. This shot caused the bull to stumble and turn to the left. After running for a great distance his prey began to stumble and slow down. Finally the bull sank slowly to his knees at the edge of the prairie dog town. Puma got off his pony to examine his kill and noticed that the path that they had taken was colored red with much blood.

The bull was very large and had the scars left from many battles. As he stood looking at the final trembling of the dying bull, he removed his knife. Looking at the knife it was as if he had seen it for the first time. He recalled his Mothers final words wondering what she meant by the "other knife." This was a thought that would cross his mind many times in the coming years. He had learned that the flat stone that his mother gave him was used to keep the knife sharp.

After he had field dressed his kill, and had eaten a portion of the bull's heart, as was the custom among his people, he could no longer hear the sounds of the running herd. He looked around and could see many ponies standing along side a brave preparing a downed buffalo, He could see the arrival of the squaws to skin and prepare the meat for transporting it back to camp. From where he stood, he could see that every hunter had had success. If this had not been so the hunt would still be going on. In fact the hunt had been so successful that another days hunt would not be necessary. He retrieved the two arrows from the bull. Then he searched the area until he found the arrow that had fallen harmlessly to the ground. The preservation of the arrow was vital.

In camp that night there was much dancing and singing. Each brave told his story. The entire village celebrated the first kill of the two young hunters.

It was at this celebration that the senior War Chief announced that the two young hunters were now to be promoted to the status of Junior Brave.

Sometimes the hunt would go quite differently. There were times when an entire herd was stampeded off a bluff. This would cause the entire kill to be in the same location. This method was only employed when working with a small herd because an Indian would not kill more than was needed, or could be used. However, most of the hunts were in an area where there were no bluffs or cliffs.

He was brought back to the present by a movement off to his right. The memory of the hunt faded and he realized that that hunt had been many years ago. In the distance he could see the white flags of a small band of antelope. He knew that this was a sign of danger. No danger to him, but they were warning the other antelope in the area of danger to them. Also between, and beyond the antelope he could see several dust devils rising through the heat waves. A dust devil was nothing more than a small cone shaped column of dust dancing across the ground by a twisting wind. These cause no harm and usually disappeared in a short period of time. The only other movement in this land was the rolling of the tumbleweeds that were moving with the wind, this was the way nature had provided for the weeds to spread their dry seeds to assure that there would be new life the next year. Puma was amazed at the various ways nature had of helping the various livings things reproduce.

He had been riding for most of the day. By sundown he had reached a dry creek bed. After looking over the creek bed he decided that this was a good place to camp for the night

After he had finished hobbling and rubbing down his pony. He had a cold meal of dried meat and parched corn. He settled down for the night. As he settled down on a small ledge near the top of the creek bed, he listened to the sounds of the night. There was no moon and the stillness told him that there would be no danger this night. Like most nights when he had assured himself that he and his pony were safe, he slipped into a deep sleep. This was the sleep that always brought dreams or visions. He had determined that his dreams were of things past and that his visions were things of the future.

On this particular night the dreams took him back to a point in time when he was preparing to leave the village and explore the outside world. The Comanche had reached an agreement, or treaty with the White Man several years earlier. This treaty meant that they would no longer go on raids against one another and would live in peace. This treaty, did allow raids by both Indians and Mexicans on each other because neither the Indian, nor the White Man was at peace with the Mexicans that lived across the Rio Bravo. There were some Mexicans that lived north of the river that were accepted by both the Indian and the White Man.

The White Men had fought a great war among themselves. This war was to free the Black Men. They had also defeated the Mexicans. They run the hostile ones back across the river. There still continued to be raids by the Mexican outlaws, and the Apache Indian from the west. These raids were usually not made by war parties but were simply to steal horses. The Mexicans would steal horses in Texas. Take them back across the river to large ranches in Mexico. The Comanche would slip across the river and steal horses and bring them back. Some times these raids did turn violent if the raiding party was discovered. The Indian had little use for cattle. Therefore, would not take the slower moving animals. The white man had more use for the cattle. They would gather them across the river and bring them to Texas.

Puma was tired of stealing and raiding. He wanted to learn more about the world around him. On this particular day he said his good byes to the village. He selected his best pony, and equipped with a supply dried meat and pouch of water, he rode out of the village to the east. He carried no weapon except his knife. He was dressed in buckskin breeches, shirt, and leggings. As he looked back at the village and then to the place where his Mother slept, he again wondered what was the meaning of her last words to him. "Search out the other knife."

He had heard of a place where the Spanish people had built a great mission many summers ago. He knew by the teachings of his Mother that the white man called each summer a year and each sun a day. The place he sought was a place where the Mexicans had overrun the Texans and killed them all before finally being defeated by the white man in a later battle, at another place.

Puma, or Friendly Lion, was only seventeen summers old but had been a brave for over four summers. He was in no hurry as he rode, because his purpose was to see and learn what lay outside his world. It was early spring and the grasses and trees were beginning to show their new growth. The bird and animal life was preparing to raise their young.

As the days passed and he got further and further from his village, he began to see more white men. Some were in small settlements. Other families lived alone and apart from others. He was not armed and could speak the white tongue therefore he had no problems while passing these places. In fact these people gave him the chance to practice the language that had been asleep for nearly eleven summers. He rode slowly and stopped often to enjoy the wonders of this large new land. After many days of studying the land and the people, he arrived at the city of the Alamo.

While this journey by Puma was in progress, a young black man was enjoying the cool shade of the deep woods near a large cotton plantation south of Montgomery Alabama. He was hungry and dirty from days of travel. He was recalling the past few days. It was near here that the Confederate Capitol had been when the War was going on. The Southern States were trying desperately to hold on to the belief that they could own the black people that had been brought to this country from Africa.

The surrender of the Southern States, and the aftermath of the war had brought devastation to the economy of the South. However, it had been even worst for most of the black people. They had been set free without homes, education, or any means of feeding themselves. There was little work to be had for a long period after the war. Many of the once rich landowners had been reduced to poverty, and could not afford to rebuild their homes. What work there was for the Black Man only paid two or three dollars a week.

The Blacks had nothing of their own. In fact most of them only had one name. It was the practice of black families to take the last name of their previous owner. This had been the case for Amos Treemont. His family had been house servants on the huge Treemont plantation. Most of his family had been allowed to remain on the plantation on a small piece of land. They had become sharecroppers, and could barely support the nine kids in the family.

When Amos reached the age of sixteen or seventeen he had decided that it was best for him and the other kids for him to leave and fend for himself. He was not sure of his age because no one really knew what year it was when he was born.

Late one night in late winter he had left the only home he had ever known. He left while the rest of the family was asleep. He knew not where to go or what he would do. He took nothing with him except the few rags of clothing that he owned. He wandered for weeks sleeping in old abandoned barns, and houses that had been destroyed by the war. He kept to the woods for the most part, because he did not fully understand what being free meant. He did not trust the White Man. He had little to eat. There was nothing growing this time of the year except a few turnips. He occasionally found a chicken that had survived and was roaming free among the ruins.

He was huddled in the corner of an abandoned pig shed, a few nights later, when he heard a sound coming through the bushes to the rear of the shed. Then he saw the movement of a man darting from shadow to shadow. He knew that he had selected a place where there lived no one. He called out to the man.

"Hello out there, my name is Amos Treemont and I am alone in the pig shed to your right. Come on in, it's warm and dry in here and I have some cold chicken that I will share if you are hungry."

The figure reappeared in the dim light and started to the shed. Amos could see that this man was also black. The approaching man held his arms outstretched to show that he meant no harm.

"My name is Lazarus Brookside and I too am alone. I have been searching for a place to sleep and something to eat. I have come far from the plantation where my family once lived and worked. It has been several days since I have had anything to eat."

Amos could see that the man was about the same age as himself. He offered the man the remainder of a chicken that he had cooked earlier in the day. After Lazarus had eaten the chicken, they began to talk, in order to better acquaint themselves with each other. Finally they slept for a short while. When daylight came Amos asked. "What are your plans? Where are you going and what do you expect to do when you get there?"

"I really don't know where to go, or what to do. There are so many Black People here that are in the same shape that we are. There seems to be no way that all of us can survive under these conditions. I have heard of a place called Texas to the west. It is said that there are not as many people there and that there might be work for those that are willing to travel that far."

It was decided that the two if them would make the long trip to Texas. They knew not where this place, Texas, was so they decided to walk away from the sun in the morning and into the sun in the afternoon. These two young men had no education. That was the only way they knew where the west could be. They would just keep going until someone told them that they were in Texas. They would encounter many people along the way, some were friendly, some were not, but for the most part the people they met were just indifferent.

After they had crossed the Alabama River and the border into Mississippi they found that most of the people were black. However, these people were in no better shape than they were. When the wind was strong from the south they could pick up the strong scent of salt. They were completely unaware that the great salt water of the Gulf was just a day or so away.

Days later they found themselves in the swamplands of Louisiana. These swamps made travel more difficult than before. It was not until they crossed the Sabine River that they learned that they were in the place called Texas.

A few days later, they came across a lone white man on horseback. He told them that he was going to San Antonio, He had heard that one could find work if they were willing to make a long ride with the cattle herds going north. Amos and Lazarus decided that this was the place for them to go.

Days later, after they had passed through the pine woodlands and crossed many rivers, they were in the town that had become their destination. Things looked pretty good the first day there. A man had approached them and said that he had a job for one man. The two young men drew straws to see who would accept the job. Lazarus won, and a short time later they separated.

Chapter 33

Tyson Morris returned home after a long day at his shop. He was better known in the area as Ty and was the local blacksmith as well as a gunsmith. He lived in a small village on the western side of the Connecticut River, at the point where it emptied into the Sound that separated New York and Connecticut. His wife Ena was a schoolteacher. They had a son, about thirteen years old, named Charles.

Business had been slow for the past year, and Ty was getting very restless.

"Ena I think that it is time that we considered a move to a place where we can be of more service to ourselves and others. The country is spreading to the west. I feel that along the frontier we can earn a better living. There should be a greater need for my services in a place where the men live by the gun. Also there will be a greater need for school teachers where people from different parts of the world settle."

The two of them discussed the idea for the next week and finally decided that this was what they should do. Ty traded his smaller wagon for a large Prairie Schooner, and purchased extra horses. The larger wagon was necessary because of the equipment that he must carry to pursue his trade. The prairie schooner required six horses rather than the two, or four for normal wagons.

Charles was very excited by the prospect of seeing Indians, and exploring the west. He could hardly contain himself while helping with the preparations. They carefully loaded their belongings and equipment, discarding things that were not necessary.

They headed west across the Susquehanna River and into Pennsylvania. They had planned the trip very carefully. They planned to end up in Independence Missouri. There they hoped to join a wagon train headed west. The trip was uneventful as they crossed Ohio and down into Kentucky.

However they had misjudged the distance and the time it would take to make such a journey with the heavy wagon. When it rained the wagon would become mired in mud and often took hours to free it. Once it was stuck so bad that they had to work several days to free it.

Their first real disappointment came when they arrived at Independence. They found that a wagon train had departed a few days earlier. There was no other train forming at the time. Knowing that the train had many wagons and would have to travel very slowly, they decided that they would try to overtake it. They paid a man to take them across the Mississippi, on a huge log raft.

On the west side of the river it was easy to pick up the trail to follow. With their spirits lifted they were off alone into the wilderness, and to the unknown adventure.

Somewhere along the way they lost their sense of direction. They wandered for days across the desolate country known as the Indian Territory, and into the panhandle of Texas. It was here during a sand storm that Ty became very ill. There was something in the area that made breathing very difficult. He lost the ability function. They remained in this lonely spot for a very long time. Ty got sicker by the day and finally there was nothing Ena could do to help him.

Ena and Charles buried Ty along side the trail. It seemed that their journey had come to an end.

They did not know where they were. They knew it was not likely that a wagon train would pass their way because somehow they had lost the main trail. To make matters worse they were running out of food and water and a rainstorm had put out their fire. Neither Ena nor Charles could get another started.

About the same time that the Morris family was making the crossing on the Mississippi there was another couple preparing to leave their home in Tennessee. The man was Paul Jefferson and his wife Marylin. Paul was a preacher and his wife a music teacher. With the masses heading west in search of land and gold, the attendance at the church had dropped. It was no longer practical for Paul to continue as minister there. They had loaded their wagon, and joined a small group of wagons headed towards Independence. Marylin was a frail woman and could not stand the rigors of the daily travel. One morning Paul woke to find that she had died during the night. Funeral services were held and she was buried just beyond the west bank of the Mississippi. After a few days the small wagon train where Paul was camped started west again. They were determined to reach a place called Pikes Peak. Everything went fairly smooth, until one afternoon one of the wagons broke a wheel when it dropped into a hole. The group decided that since they could not repair the wheel that they would shift the contents to other wagons. After which they would proceed to their destination.

Mean while, far to the southwest, Puma just sat on his pony looking with wonder at the buildings and activity around him. He had never seen a white man's town, or been inside a wooden building. He was curious enough to leave his pony and go inside. It became apparent to him that these people were used to seeing strangers, because they paid no attention to him. He walked along between the racks of tools, clothing, and weapons. There were many items that he could not identify. But he was determined to learn of these things before leaving this town.

He wandered along the streets, stopping often to look at the strange things that the white man had that his people did not. There was clothing made of a woven material similar to a blanket. However most of it was not as thick as an Indian blanket, and the weaving was of a finer quality. The men's shirts and the women's dresses were very colorful. The men wore boots that had pointed toes and high heels, these did not have to be laced or tied. The men wore large hats, but were not nearly as big as the Mexican sombrero. The women wore something they called bonnets that were tied under their chins. All the horses that were tied to poles along the street wore saddles over their blankets. There was a thing attached to each side that was called a stirrup. These stirrups made it easy to mount the horse and provided a footrest allowing better balance while riding. He assumed that the White Man was not as good as the Indian when it came to riding. The women used a different type of saddle. It allowed both legs to be on the same side of the horse.

Puma worked his way to the end of the street until he came to a building that was set apart from the rest of the buildings. It had a large pen in the back and several smaller pens to the side. Inside these pens were many horses, none of which wore a saddle. He wandered over to the wooden rail fence and squatted facing the town. He remained there for several hours just looking at the activity all around him.

After a few hours a Mexican boy, about his age and size, joined Puma. The boy said that his name was Pedro Chavez, and that he had been born and raised in the San Antonio area. He said that made him a Texan. After learning that this boy also spoke the white man's tongue, they began to talk about what was happening around them. The words came slowly at first to Puma. After a while he became more comfortable using them. Pedro told Puma that his family had come from a very poor section of central Mexico.

"They traveled far in search of work and a better way of life. My people in Mexico have very little to eat and live very much in the same manner of the Maya Civilization, of long ago. It is said that a large part of the people in my country originated from the mixture of the Maya and the African people that were brought to our country during the slave trading days. The others of Central Mexico are of Spanish Blood and had arrived in our country from a far away place called Spain. I am of Spanish Blood and therefore I speak the language of those people as well as that of the White Man."

While they were talking, a black man joined them. This was the first black man that Puma had ever seen. He was very curious to learn more about this man. The black man said that his name was Amos Treemont and he had just arrived from Alabama. Puma did not know this place, Alabama, but knew that it must be far away. The three of them talked in the white man's tongue, which Puma learned was called English. English was the only language that the black man could speak. Puma wanted to know more about this Alabama. He began to question the man about it. Amos was willing to talk about his home, and his people because being one of the few black people in the area he had had little chance to talk to any one.

"Alabama is a farming section of the country where there is much cotton and food crops grown. The land there is owned by white men and is worked by black people. The Black Man was brought to this country about two hundred years ago. They were captured in their home country of Africa and brought to this country in large ships. Those that survived the trip were then sold to the plantation owners of the south. There they were forced to do the work, they were in fact slaves and were confined to the property of their owners. They had to live under the worst of conditions. There was never enough to eat and they lived in large groups in small houses, of poor construction. Even this was not as bad as what is happening to the Indians, of this country. By this I mean that only those captured were subjected to this type of treatment, not the whole black race. Here the entire Indian race is robbed of everything including their land and pride.

Ours was not the first type of slavery in this country. Many white people had suffered a form of slavery when they came across the oceans. These people from many countries were brought here at the expense of the rich already here. They were forced to work for a long period of time to repay the cost of their transportation. Even the poor Mexicans across the Rio Bravo are forced to work for the rich landowners just to survive. Finally, a short time ago the black man was set free, this, was after a long war between the Northern and the Southern parts of the country. This left the black man in worse shape than he had been in before. He now had no education, and no way to provide the food that he had been furnished before. I was more fortunate than others because my family had been house servants. They had leaned much from their masters. This left me in a better shape to enter the outside world, however I am not accepted as an equal by the Whites."

When darkness came the three young men withdrew to a small stand of trees outside the town and camped for the night. Puma learned that his two new friends had nothing to eat, so he shared his dried meat with them. Puma lay for a long time thinking of the many things these two new friends could teach him.

When daylight came the three returned to the same place they had been the afternoon before. Things looked pretty much as the day before. They began to wonder what to do next, and how to go about looking for work. While they were discussing the prospects of the coming day, a huge white man approached them.

This man walked as one of authority. One that was always sure of what to do. He reminded Puma of a Great War Chief from his village. He said that his name was Ben Harvey, and asked the black man if he spoke English, Amos replied that they all spoke the language. This seemed to please the big man. He asked if they had ever worked cattle. The reply was no from two of them, but the Mexican said that he had worked for a time on a cattle ranch. They were asked if they were looking for work? They all replied that they were, and could learn the ways of the cattle.

The big man told them that he had a large herd of cattle that he had gathered in Mexico and south Texas. He said that he was going to drive them to a place in Kansas. They did not know of this place, Kansas, but knew that it must be far away. He said that he did not have enough men to make the drive. He would give them each a white man's dollar for each day of the drive. Amos explained to Puma that the white man used the dollar to get things they needed. Puma knew that this was to be a new learning experience for the three young men. They eagerly accepted the job.

After a few days of preparation, the herd was ready to start north. They were to spend many days on the Chisholm Trail. This was a trail that had been established from San Antonio to Abilene by Jesse Chisholm, a Cherokee Indian. Puma was given an old Mexican saddle and bridle and instructed on how to use them. It took a while for Puma and his pony to get the hang of using the saddle. Their first assignment was to ride with the extra horses and keep them together while following the cattle. To pass the time during the long days the three young men decided that they would teach each other their native tongues. Puma knew the language of several of the Indian tribes. He also knew the universal sign language of the Red Man. He set about teaching these, while he was learning Spanish.

The first few days were spent getting the cattle into one large herd. When this task was done, the lead animals were pointed north, and the long drive was underway. The progress was very slow because they allowed the cattle and horses graze as they went. At the end of the first day they were only a short ride from the starting point. However, as the days passed the distance traveled each day grew longer. By this time the cattle and horses had settled into the routine, and were easier to control.

Puma, Pedro, and Amos had to ride night herd for two hours every third night. The nightriders usually sang to keep the herd settled. Puma knew nothing of this singing so he just rode and listened to the others.

The cowboys called anything to eat grub or chuck, this was prepared at a wagon called the chuck wagon. After they had their grub at night the three young men would work on the learning of new words.

He was awakened out of the dream by the soft rattling of stones on the opposite side of the creek bed. It took a few moments for him to return to the present, from the dream of the cattle drive. He lay very still until he was able locate the source of the noise. As he lay there peering across the creek he was able to detect movement. At last he was able to identify the outline of a large desert mule deer. Seeing the deer told him two things. One, he was not in danger. Two, the water was rising out of the sand. He lay there reviewing the dreams of the night until it was finally light enough for him to see. He got down from the small ledge, and went to the edge of the small stream of water in the bottom of the creek bed. He could see by the tracks that his pony had already discovered the water. The pony was quietly grazing nearby. He selected a spot and began to scoop out the sand and stones from a spot where he would fill his water pouches. When he had a hole large enough he sat back and waited for the water to clear. After he refilled his pouches he proceeded to wash his face and hair. After a cold meal he felt rested and refreshed. He was about to catch up his pony, when he spotted a lone wagon along the creek to the south. He sat on a large rock and watched until he could determine that there were only two people with the wagon. They apparently were gathering water and putting it in large wooden barrels. Although there was a relative peace in the area, he decided he would circle around and beyond these people. He was set on getting to his home village to see the friends that he had left behind three years before.

Shortly after he completed his circle he came to a point where the Pecos changed directions. Instead of going southeast the river was now going south and flowed past an abandoned fort. Ft. Lancaster, he recalled had been abandoned several years ago, but there remained a few white settlers in the general vicinity. After realizing where he was, the mystery of the lone wagon was solved. About an hour later he rode upon a Black Man that was crawling along the edge of the creek.

"Man I am glad to see you friend, my name is Lazarus Brookside and I have been here nearly three days. My horse stepped in a hole and threw me and broke my leg and I can't get up on my horse. There are no people in this country that know, or care where I might be. So there will be no one out looking for me. I came to this country from Alabama with my friend, Amos Treemont. We separated in a place called San Antonio. I have been traveling alone ever since."

Puma got down and examined the leg. It was a clean break. It needed to be set and braced. Puma went to the stream and cut several willow branches. From these he formed a splint. He set the leg and secured the splint in place with pieces of rawhide from his saddle pouch. After this was done, he gave Lazarus some of the dried meat and parched corn and water from his pouches.

"I know your friend, Amos, in fact he and I have spent many days together on a cattle drive, from the place where you last saw him, to a place called Kansas."

They rested the rest of the day and Puma unsaddled Lazarus's horse and gave him a good rub down with a handful of soft grass. The following morning he loaded Lazarus on his horse, and returned to Ft Lancaster with him.

After leaving Lazarus with the people at the fort he continued his journey. As he rode along the east side of the Pecos his thoughts returned to the dreams of two nights ago. In these thoughts he was again on a cattle drive just north of San Antonio. The horses had settled down and it took only a couple of men to drive the horses behind the herd. He, Pedro, and Amos had been moved up to help with the cattle. From time to time they would pick up stray cows that had apparently been left behind by previous drives. The herd was so large and spread out that one could not see from one side to the other.

The young men were awakened along about midnight for their turn of riding night herd. Some time during the evening hours a thunderstorm had blown in. The night was very dark and you could only see when a bolt of lightening would light up the sky. The cattle were very nervous. They began to mill around which was uncommon in the middle of the night. Then came a loud clap of rolling thunder and many flashes of lightening. Lightening struck a mesquite tree near the lead animals. The stampede was on. Along with the thunder and lightening came driving rain and wind. The entire camp was up and in the saddle, but there was no controlling the running cattle. Puma was bent low in the saddle trying to work himself to the outside edge of the herd, but all he could see was a mass of running cattle and thousands of lightening flashes. They ran on into the night stumbling over rocks, brush, and fallen cows. Finally the riders had to stop, because their horses were completely spent. After failing to stop the stampede, there was nothing to do but seek shelter from the wind and rain and wait until daylight, or the end of the storm.

By the time daylight came the horses were somewhat rested, and the storm had passed. Most of the herd had followed the leaders. They were gathered in groups. The entire prairie was a complete mud hole making it very difficult for the horses. The next few days were spent searching for the rest of the herd. Some of the strays had gone several miles and some were dead or injured. By the time the herd was once again assembled the ground was dry. It was decided that a few days were needed for rest and to repair tack.

Several days later they started the herd toward a spot just west of the old Fort Worth. It was here that they were to meet some more cowboys with more cattle. While they were at the meeting spot the cattle were allowed to graze in the tall grass that was abundant in the area. It was here that Harvey became fully aware that Puma was indeed an Indian. That he knew much about the Indian ways of scouting and tracking. He told Puma that in a few days they would cross a river into Indian Territory. He then assigned Puma as forward scout and allowed Pedro to help him.

The scouts usually worked about a half days ride ahead of the herd, and had reached the Red River. They worked the river both directions looking for a safe place for the cattle to cross. Both sides of the river had large deposits of sand that had been washed down stream. Some places had quick sand that would not allow crossing. When they found a likely spot they rode back to the herd, and headed it toward the crossing point. They held the herd on the south side of the Red for two days. During this two-day period the scouts worked far into the territory. On two occasions they encountered small parties of Indians that gave the sign of peace. They were assured that the herd could pass without any problems. They returned to the Red, and the following morning they proceeded to start the herd across. The crossing took two full days and nights. The cowboys were all very tired, wet, and in need of rest.

The second day after crossing the Red, a small band of Indians rode into the camp. They appeared to be in a very bad way, and they were showing the sign of peace. They were allowed to ride into the camp where they explained that they had nothing to eat. Their women and children were in need of fresh meat. Harvey had several head of the weaker cows cut from the herd. These gave to the Indians. He did not know it at the time, but he had gained friends that would be very helpful during his trips across the Territory.

Finally after Puma had selected the best camping spots ahead they started north again. As usual the camping spots were located near good water, and offered good grass to keep the herd content. One night they camped in one such place located right in the middle of the Indian Territory. They were about half way between the Red and the Cimarron Rivers, and every thing seemed peaceful enough. From seemingly out of nowhere, a small band of Indians rode into the herd at the far northwest side. They ran off about two-dozen cows. Harvey at first wanted to go after them, but later decided that if he took enough men to regain the lost cattle it would leave the rest of the herd with out proper protection. He sent Puma, along two other cowboys out to determine which trail the Indians had taken. Two days later they met the cattle being returned by the same band that Harvey had given the cattle to at the Red. To show his appreciation Harvey gave the leader of the band half of the cattle that they had returned.

The plains in the area they were traveling were very dry and the grass offered little nourishment for the livestock. In addition there were daily sand storms. The winds were out of the west, and when the sand blew in you could see it coming from the horizon. At times the sand was so thick that you could not see over ten feet. It felt as if it would strip the hide off both man and beast.

Finally they arrived at the crossing spot that had been selected on the Cimarron. It was here that they were thankful for the dry conditions. The river was very low, and the crossing was made relatively easy. The only thing that slowed the progress was allowing the cattle, and horses to drink all they wanted. By this time Puma had earned the respect of most of the crew, and for the most part he was working alone. Harvey trusted his judgment. Puma was a very fast learner, and had mastered the art of using the rope. He had also mastered the Spanish language. To satisfy his hunger to learn more, he asked Harvey if the man called Pepe could assist him for a while.

Pepe was a slightly built Frenchman with a long mustache. He was from Louisiana and Puma wanted to learn the French language and more about this place, Louisiana. Pepe was very good with a knife, and had often admired the knife with the carved lion handle. Each time he mentioned the knife Puma would think back to his mother's words. "Search out the other knife".

By the time they had crossed out of the Indian Territory, and reached the Arkansas River, Puma had just about mastered the French language and was looking for something else to occupy his mind during the long dusty days. The area they were in was not much different than the Indian Territory. Dry, desolate, and wind blown.

The days had been long, and the men were getting very weary. A few had dropped out along the way thus forfeiting their pay. Finally one day, just before sunset, Puma was riding out front of the herd about a half a days ride when he spotted a town that he knew must be Abilene. He could see two long shiny lines leading to the east. He returned to the herd and told Harvey what he had seen. Harvey assured him this was in fact where they were going.

They bedded the herd down about a half days ride south of town. Harvey took Puma with him into town to search for a buyer for the cattle. Puma knew nothing about selling anything, but he could speak several languages and that might prove useful.

Abilene was quite different from San Antonio. There were mostly just cowboys and a few men that wore pants and coats to match. These, he leaned were the buyers and the strange clothing was called a suit. Harvey talked to several of these men while Puma took in the sights of the town. When they arrived back at the camp, some of the men who had money were allowed to go into town. Harvey told the crew that the train would be there in a couple of days. Most of the men were broke and just stayed in camp and rested. Harvey said that they would hold the herd here until the train arrived. The noise of the train might spook the cattle and horses. Two days later they heard a strange noise, coming from the direction of the town. This must be the train that Harvey had spoken of. Puma wondered what was this thing called a train.

Early the next morning the herd was gathered, and driven toward town. When they arrived, there was a large black metal thing sitting in front of many large wooden boxes. The boxes were all tied together, behind the black metal machine.

The big iron horse sat breathing slowly. With each breath it would send a puff of smoke into the air. This reminded Puma of a smoke signal being sent into the sky, by one of the lookouts for the tribe. This thing also sent a small stream of smoke out to the side of things that Amos said were wheels. The cattle were driven into large pens, and then into the wooden boxes. After the last of the cattle were driven into the pens, most of the crew returned to camp. There they began to bath and change their cloths. Then some of them did a strange thing called shaving. Puma wondered why the white man had hair on his face that had to be cut with a thing called a razor, but made no comment.

Shortly Harvey returned, and sat down on the back of the chuck wagon the entire crew gathered around. This was called payday, and he was preparing to pay the crew. Before he paid them, he told them that he would be making another drive in a couple of years. If anyone was interested in working another drive, they should meet him in San Antonio the following spring to help gather the herd. He said that they would be going to Dodge City the next time, because the railroad would be in Dodge by then. When he paid them he gave each their choice of any horse they wanted because he was going to sell the rest. When it came his turn to get paid, Puma was asked if he would return the next year. When Puma replied that he would not, Harvey asked what he planned to do. Puma said, " I will search out the other knife". When Harvey counted out the money, Puma had nearly two hundred dollars, which he did not know how to use. Most of the men were off to town immediately to drink and gamble. Of these two things he had no knowledge, and he ask Amos if he would go with him to show him how to get the things that he wanted, with the white man's dollars. After Amos had explained the use of the white man's dollar, they went into town. He had now learned many of the white man ways. He now wanted to look the part. This was a decision that he would later come to regret, and would return to his Indian ways and appearance.

Amos went with him into town, and while there Puma bought himself a couple of outfits of the white man's cloths, a pair of boots, and a hat. He also bought himself a hatchet made of the same material that his knife was made of. Next he went to the gunsmith and got a pistol, a rifle, and ammunition. At the suggestion of Amos he got a pistol and rifle that would shoot the same bullets.

While they were at the gunsmiths, they encountered some problems. After they had entered the shop, the owner told them to leave, that he did not sell his services to Indians and Blacks. However, not wanting to cause any kind of trouble the two of them was about to leave when Harvey walked in. When Harvey found out what was going on, he quickly grabbed the gunsmith by the vest and slammed him against workbench. He quietly told the man that he would sell to these two men, and any others that might come into his shop in the future. After this they encountered no difficulty, because the storekeepers knew that Harvey and his cowboys brought a lot of money to the town.

Back at camp, Puma removed and stored his buckskins in his bedroll, except for his jacket. He dressed himself as a white man. He looked and felt different with the stiff denim pants turned up at the bottom exposing the shiny boots that at first were difficult to walk in. With his pistol tied down western style and his extra money tucked inside his shirt he said goodbye to Amos and Pedro, and headed out toward the Rio Bravo, which he had now had learned to call the Rio Grande.

By the time his thoughts returned to the present he was quite a distance south of Ft. Lancaster. In another day he would be home at the mouth of the Pecos. Since leaving Abilene, he had practiced sparingly with his new weapons. He did not want to use any more of his bullets than necessary. Because he had no idea where he could get more. Being anxious to learn of the use of his new weapons he had taken great care with these practice sessions.

When he finally reached the Rio Grande he had been gone nearly three summers. When he reached the spot where the village had been, he discovered that the area was abandoned. It appeared that his people had been gone for a long while. He sat there in the saddle looking around, and wondered where they might have gone. It was not time for the buffalo hunt, and he could see no other reason why the people would leave. The place was clean, and showed no sign that the village had been raided. Now the search for the other knife became the search for his people.

He decided that he would spend the night there, and tomorrow he would try to find some sign to tell him where his people had gone. He lay in the darkness listening to the sounds of the night. There was the call of the whippoorwill nearby, and the answer of another still farther down the river. Off in the distance he could pick up the sound of the coyote, and the occasional bray of a burro, drifted across the river from Mexico. He was very disappointed and tired when he drifted off to sleep. There would be no visions or dreams this night.

Chapter 34

During the first summer after Puma had left the village, there was to be a great important council in the village on the banks of the Rio Bravo and Pecos. Tonka was preparing to attend, because the entire village had been summoned. As he was preparing him self, he allowed his thoughts to wander to his friend and brother. It had been a whole summer since Puma had rode away to the east. A smile crossed his lips as he recalled the many happy times the two of them had shared. The long runs through the hills, and along the river. He recalled the long hours spent making the small arrows for hunting birds and small game. He wondered if he would again see his brother, and what great adventure Puma might have had. He had wanted to go with Puma, but had felt it his duty to remain with the people of the village. His father had long since died, and he knew that his mother needed a man about the tepee.

His thoughts returned to the present as he entered the council circle. The Medicine Man was already giving thanks, and praise to the Great Spirits. He sat down and quietly listened to the words of this wise man.

"Today it is with a saddened heart, that I must speak to you. To me has come a great vision of which you must be made aware. In this vision I have seen a barren land where there is no hope for a living thing to exist. The coyote. and the mountain lion are lank from hunger. The leaves have been stripped from even the greasewood by the remaining deer that also suffer from hunger. The buffalo vanished before my eyes and the antelope has retreated to the north. The Rio Bravo is very low and the bad water from the Pecos makes it unfit for our people. In this vision, I see a land to the north and west where another tribe of our people is now living. They are calling for us to join them. To do so would require us to make a long, and very hard journey. If such a journey is made, it will mean that we would have to leave the only place that most of us here have lived for our entire lives? To undertake such a move would cause much heartache, and the days and nights will be long and hard. There are some here that would not be able to complete such a journey. The Great Spirits tell me, that for those that complete this journey, there will be a better life. There would again be enough food for all, and there would no longer be raids from the Mexican bandits. Since we have no Chief in this village I will take those that wish to follow me to the land of my vision."

There was a great silence over the village as the people were recalling the words of Crooked Stick. It was as if they were looking back into darkness and then forward into the sunlight. Finally Tonka rose to his feet, and announced that he and his mother would follow the Medicine Man to this new land. Almost as one the entire tribe voiced the same decision.

Their fate was decided, and the preparations were begun immediately. Within a day's time, the village was dismantled, and everything that the people possessed was secured on the poles attached behind the extra horses. During this process there was little talk, some were happy at the turn of events, while others were not so sure of their future.

With the coming of the new day, all the people gathered in silence and listened as the Medicine Man gave praise to The Great Spirits. He asked for their assistance in guiding the people safely across the unknown land, to the place of the vision. This was to be a long walk for the women and children, and the burden of carrying the remaining items of their lives was great. Some of the Braves were assigned as forward scouts. It was their duty was to find a proper trail, and to provide food for the entire group. The Medicine Man took his place at the front of the group. They headed north along the east side of the Pecos to the crossing place a short distance from the abandoned site of the village. Once the people had all crossed the river, they turned back to the south to the bank of the Rio Bravo. They would follow the river through the rugged mountains until they came to the flat lands to the west.

The river led them through deep canyons, and over high peaks until they passed the village of three tongues. Another three long days and they were passing the place where it was said that a White Man had killed many Indians while they were feasting in his giant eating area. Then it was to a place known as The Presidio. On the barren flat land east of The Presidio they again turned away from the Rio Bravo and headed into the unknown, to the north. The tribe was getting weary, when they passed a small settlement where some of the white settlers were still digging for gold. The very limited supply of gold had all but disappeared under the frantic digging of many. A woman ran the run down trading post, and it was from her that Tonka learned, that for the most part, all the people had abandoned the search for the gold, and had departed for the promise of riches in the mountains of Colorado. There had been two major gold rushes before, one in California and one in Colorado. Now there was the beginning of a second rush in the mountains in the southwest mountains of Colorado.

The travel was very slow, and the tribe getting very low on food. On the high plains of Texas they came to the Pecos again. Just north of the river the people stopped and set up camp, on the shores of a small lake. The winds were blowing from the southwest and there was not a sign of a cloud in the high sky. Before they could complete the camp a sand storm started to blow in. Within an hour, the area was in darkness as the sand hid the afternoon sun. The area was flat and barren except for a small stand of trees near the lake. The people took the horses into the trees, and huddled together as a defense against the driving sand. For a day and a night the winds beat down on them and ripped at their clothing and skin. It seemed to them that the Great Spirits were angry with them for traveling through this land. Suddenly the sun returned, and the giant wall of sand could be seen moving away to the east. The people emerged from the trees, and found that much of their camp had been destroyed. The rest covered with a layer of sand. It was decided that they must rest, and regroup for a while even though they were anxious to move out of the area of the angry winds and sand.

Several days later they found themselves along the border of New Mexico and Texas. They were just east of where they knew the giant bat caves to be. The surrounding land was hostile and afforded nothing to make their journey easier. The Braves had managed to kill enough antelope to feed the tribe for a few days. This did not present much of a problem because the animals had been subdued by the storm also.

Tonka was in the process of cleaning, and sharpening his knife. His thoughts returned to his brother Puma, and the knife that he carried. He could not help but wonder where Puma was, and what had happened to him, if anything. He had no way of knowing that at that very moment Puma was on his way to a far away place called Kansas.

After preparing the meat, and letting it dry for a few days in the sun, they were once again ready to start their endless march into the unknown future.

The ground over which the tribe was now traveling was beginning to show signs of change. There began to appear small patches of lava rock. This made for difficult walking for both the people and the horses. Their moccasins were already worn and even some of the people were barefoot.

The lava bed grew thicker, and they could see a single large hill rising before them to the north. When they approached the base of this hill they could see that it was the remains of a volcano that had long since become inactive. This was a sign that they must turn to the west. They were to cross into Colorado through Raton Pass, the smaller of the passes that they would encounter before their journey would end. The air was getting thin, and this made the travel even more difficult, and the distance covered each day became less and less.

Their next major set back came when they reached the pass of the wolf creek. By the time they reached the summit, the winds were very cold and strong. While camped on top to rest for a day or two, it began to snow. None of the people had ever been this high in the mountains before, and none had experienced this much snow. Even though they were among the trees seeking shelter, the snow grew so deep that it was almost impossible for them to move about. The horses could not find anything to eat. It was determined that they must seek a lower camp sight before the strength of the animals was gone. They started down the west side in a driving snowstorm. Some of the people were getting sick from the exposure to the cold, but still they struggled forward. After what seemed an eternity they reached the meadows of the valleys below. There they set up the camp that must serve as their home for the remainder of the winter. There were many elk and deer in the lower valleys, and they were able to restock their food supply, which by this time consisted of only corn and dried onions.

Not only was their food supply now in good shape but the skins had been prepared and new clothing and moccasins had been made for all that needed them. While the leather was not of the same quality as that of the buffalo, it would make moccasins and clothing that would enable them to continue their journey. The weather was harsh, and the nights long, but the people fully knew the need for the work that they were doing.

With warmer days, and brighter skies the tribe felt the urge to move on. They again broke camp. And after several moons they were on the high green mesas overlooking the dwelling of the Pueblo. It was here, that they met the first real friendly people of the journey. They were welcomed into the village, and there was a council held by the leaders of both tribes. After the council there was much singing and dancing.

Gentle Dove, the daughter of the Chief, was especially happy to see these new people. It was her first diversion from the boring daily life she had led, since the departure of the White Holy Man. She asked many question of the women visitors and in return they inquired of the strange way that the Pueblo lived.

It was here in this village that they learned for the first time of the exact location of the Shoshone Tribe they were seeking.

Tonka was relieved to hear of the place they were seeking, but was saddened when his mother grew ill. She died while they were in the land of the cliff people. He decided that this was not the proper place for his mother to rest. He prepared her body for travel. He would take her to a proper place for a Caddo Woman to rest, and meet The Great Spirits.

After he had selected the proper resting place for his mother, a period of mourning was observed, and then the Tribe moved to the north along the border of the Utah Territory.

Tonka was scouting out in front of the people when he finally discovered a village on the Strawberry River. He rode in, and told the people of this village of the arrival of his people from the south. When he brought his people into the village they were greeted with a celebration that lasted for seven suns.

When Puma woke up, he was surprised to find that he had slept past sunrise. This he had not done since he was a small boy in the tepee of the Caddo Woman. He was now faced with the problem of where to start his day. But first he must eat to maintain his strength. He went to the river and squatted in the thick reeds along the shore. Finally he succeeded in spearing a couple of fish with a sharpened stick that he had made with his knife. Again the knife brought back the mysterious words of his Mother. "Search out the other knife." Puma shook this thought, or memory from his mind and went back to the small fire that he had prepared. After cooking and eating the fish, he felt refreshed, and was ready to continue his journey to wherever it might lead. While saddling his horse he thought of the possible direction his people might have gone. He knew that they had not gone to the south across the river. There were the Mexican enemies there. They had probably not gone east, because of the white settlements, or north because there was not enough water to the north to support the entire village. To the east there was the growing number of white settlers that continued to push to the west. He mounted his horse and carefully searched the area once more for some sign. Finding nothing, he started back up the Pecos in search of a shallow place to cross. Once he had crossed the Pecos he headed back to the Rio Grande. He had decided that he would ride along the big river until some sign or vision told him otherwise. This ride took him west for a couple of days to a point where the river was coming from the south. He had never known that this river ever flowed north. He had always suspected that the river rose in the great mountains somewhere in the land of the Utes, and Shoshone then flowed from the west to the southeast, and emptied into the great salt water to the east. The route he was taking took him into the Chisos Mountains. It was here that the river passed through three great canyons. This was a part of the area where he had never been; therefore, he rode slowly and observed everything around him. While passing through these great canyons, the river began to turn again, and finally it was flowing southeast again. He was getting low on fresh water. He had not filled his water pouch since he had crossed the Calamity, to the northwest of the great canyons.

He rode into a settlement called Terlingua, or the town of three tongues. It was in this settlement of mud houses that he was able to purchase dried meat, dried corn, and wild onions from a trading post there. It was the first time that he had tested the power of the white mans dollar since he left Kansas. While in this settlement he had learned that a band of Indians had passed this way two years before. He could not be sure but he supposed that he might be on the right trail that would somehow lead him to his people.

About a days ride to the west he came upon the Frio, and it was here that he would fill his water pouched in the early hours of the next morning.

With fresh water and something to eat he was again riding along the river to the west. The mountains had given way to a flat land. A day or so later he was at an old abandoned fort. The army had moved out of Ft. Leaton. A White family now lived in the old place.

Legend had it that at one time a white man had lived in the old fort, and had invited a band of Renegade Indians to his home for a feast. He was trying to assure the Indians that he posed no danger to them. After the feast the Indians rode away, taking all his horses and cattle. The following year they were invited back to the fort. As they sat in a room enjoying the feast, a huge door was opened, and a cannon fired into the room full of Indians. This had killed most of the band and injured the rest. Puma knew not if this was true, but he found the people that now lived at the fort were friendly, and they too told of a band of Indians passing that way. They could not provide enough information for Puma to identify the band as his people.

After leaving the fort he continued along the river to the west to a place known as The Presidio. While he was hanging around this place trying to get information, he learned of the yellow metal called gold that was favored by the white man. Some of this gold had been found about a day's ride north in a place called Shafter. But the area had mostly been abandoned when news that a great amount of gold had been discovered in the big mountains of the Colorado Territory. On the third day at the Presidio, Puma found an old man that told him of a large band of Indians that had passed about a days ride to the east. This, he said, had been two years ago. He said that they seemed to be headed north perhaps in the direction of the big caves. After thinking about the words of the old man Puma decided that this must have been his people. He decided that the next day he would gather supplies, and head out to the north.

About noon the next day, he was riding through Safter. This was an area where white men had been digging for gold. There were few people left in the area but he managed to get a little information from a woman that ran what was left of the trading post. She told him that the band she had seen was being lead by a Medicine Man, not a chief. Puma felt much better now because the way she described the Medicine Man, he knew that this was his people. He knew now that he was on the trail of the people that might offer some knowledge of "the knife". Something inside of him told him that he must continue north where he would again come to the Pecos River. If he were correct in this he would find the Pecos about a days ride west of where he had passed only a few moons ago. When he got to the Pecos, the land around him was flat and desolate and he could see the beginning of the sand hills to the east of him. There was a small settlement on the Pecos. The settlers were mostly white, with a few Mexicans and a couple of Frenchmen. They had just been raided by a bunch renegade Apache Warriors, and therefore, were very cautious when the stranger rode in.

Puma did not look like an Indian, rather his sun and wind burned face and hands gave the appearance of a typical drifter. Puma spent the better part of two days asking questions without giving away the fact that he was Indian. Since he could speak all three of the languages of the settlement, the people felt at ease with him and talked freely. He sought information about any travelers that might have passed this way over the preceding two years. He found out that there had been many men from the gold mines to the south passing this way in route to the gold fields in the Colorado Territory. He also heard of a gunman that had gained quite a reputation in The New Mexico Territory. It was said that this young man called, Billy the Kid, had killed over twenty men and was feared by many. Having no interest in this kind of information he discarded the stories of this outlaw. After being satisfied that he was still following the trail of his people, he again headed north on a wagon trail that crossed the Pecos. This trail would take him across the southeastern corner of the New Mexico Territory about two days east of the big bat caves. He had never been in this area before, but he knew that the great white sand hills were several days to the west of the big caves. He also knew that the Apache Chief Geronimo, and his renegades roamed the area to the north and west of the white sands. Geronimo had once been a top war chief under Cochise, the chief of the Chirichua Apache tribe. Knowing that the Apache roamed far and wide, and raided Indian as well white settlements he had no desire to encounter these people. He headed up the Texas plains to a point that he knew would put him in the Indian Territory. He knew that somewhere he would cross a trail called the Santa Fe. This was a trail well traveled by the white settlers, from a place called Missouri, to a Spanish settlement that was called Santa Fe.

As he rode Puma tried to imagine what the place where his people were going was like, and where it was located. He had guessed by this time that they were returning to the land of the Shoshone, but he had no idea where this land might be.

It was getting late in the year, and the leaves were taking on their fall colors. He was now on the high plains of the Texas panhandle, the air was thin. The winds were coming from the north, and were very cold in the early morning frost. He had crossed the Canadian River the night before. He had spent the darkness on the north side of the river. He had crossed this river before, but that had been to the east. Therefore, he was not familiar with the land that now surrounded him.

He stretched, and shook off the sleep of the night, then saddled his pony and began his seemingly never to end ride. As he rode he chewed on a bit of dried meat, and pondered what the day might bring. It had been several nights since his last dream or vision.

As he topped a rise, that was a little higher than the surrounding grass, he spotted what seemed to be a lone wagon. The wagon was in front and to the east of where he intended to go. As he rode, he carefully examined the wagon, and all that surrounded it. He saw seven horses but no other sign of life. There was no fire in the camp. He decided that he must investigate this camp, and see if there was anything he could do. As he rode in, he could tell that the camp had been here for several days. He saw the end of a rifle barrel sticking out from under the canvas cover. He raised his hand in a sign of peace, and repeated the word friend in every language that he knew. He could see by the signs that the camp had had very little activity during the last few days. Off some distance from the wagon, he could see a white man style grave with a crude wooden cross at one end. After repeating the word friend several times, he noticed the gun barrel move slightly. He dismounted and removed his pistol and rifle placing them on the ground. After he stepped away from them, he saw the canvas open slightly, and a woman's face appeared behind it. She asked him, in English, what he wanted. He assured her that he was a friend and wanted to know if he could help her, or them. After the brief exchange the woman climbed out of the wagon. She was accompanied by a young boy of about thirteen summers. The woman appeared to be about thirty, but he really could not tell because she was very pale and wrapped in several blankets. The woman told Puma. "We are very cold and hungry. We were on our way west and my husband got very ill. When we reached this spot he was unable to go on. We remained here for many days before he died."

She also said that a rainstorm had put out the fire about a week before, and her and the boy did not know how to start another one. They had had nothing to eat for two days and now their water was gone also. After hearing her story and telling her his own story briefly, Puma set about building a fire. After the fire was going, she brought a cooking pot and he placed some of the water from his pouch into it. He then put some dried meat, dried corn and wild onions into the pot and let them boil for a while.

While the broth was cooking he examined the horses and wagon to see if they were in any shape to travel. By the time he had completed his inspection of the equipment, the woman and boy were eating from the pot. When they had finished they huddled close to the fire and finished telling their story.

They had started from New England to Independence Missouri to join a wagon train to the west. When they arrived at Independence they found that the wagon train had left a couple of days earlier. They thought perhaps they could catch the wagon train so they crossed the river and started out. They had traveled for several days, and had not caught up with the train. Finally coming to the Arkansas River, the trail seemed to split. They knew that the Santa Fe Trail went to the southwest so they chose the trail that went more in that direction. Unknown to them they had chosen the Cimarron cut off that would later rejoin the main trail. Lacking the knowledge of the ways of the frontier and having no way of knowing where they were, they had wandered in the vast open plains for days, and finally had lost the trail completely. They had mistaken a trial coming from the south for a trail going south, and had drifted across the western section of the Indian Territory into Texas, and finally to the spot where Puma had found them. After the woman had eaten, and gotten warm she began to talk freely about their situation. She told Puma that her name was Ena Morris, and that the boy was named Charles.

Puma assured her that he would help her, and the boy find someone, or a wagon train for her to join. He then gathered up his guns and told her that he was going hunting for fresh meat.

After a while he spotted a herd of antelope, which were plentiful in this part of Texas. He circled to get down wind of them. After hobbling his horse near a small patch of grass, he crept closer to the antelope. As he got closer, he began to crawl on his stomach. Finally he decided that he could not get closer, and he settled in a small depression to wait. He remained motionless for what seemed hours while the antelope grazed about. He had as yet not tried to kill game with his new guns. He was not sure if he had mastered the weapons. Therefore, he wanted his prey as close as possible before attempting the shot. Finally a young doe approached to a distance that he was afraid if he did not shoot, the day might be wasted. He carefully slipped his rifle into position. He waited until the doe was standing broad side to him. He aimed at the center of the body because this would allow more room for error. At last he carefully pulled the trigger, and nothing happened. He then remembered that he had forgot to put a bullet in the barrel. He slowly, and as quietly as possible, levered a bullet into the gun. The second try brought better results. The doe jerked and started to run. Just as he thought that he had missed, she stumbled and fell. After preparing the doe for travel he slung it over his shoulder, and started back towards his pony. He had learned that stalking game was not nearly as easy, when wearing the white man's boots, as it was wearing a pair of moccasins. He thought that he must remember to make himself a pair to carry in his saddlebags, to use in such situations. He placed the antelope across his horse and started in the direction of the wagon.

When he got in sight of the wagon he could see no sign of Ena or the boy. He had been hunting to the west and therefore was approaching the wagon from the northwest. When he arrived at camp, he discovered them sitting on the south side of the wagon out of the wind, in the fading sunlight. His first chore was to skin and prepare the meat. While he was doing this, Charles joined him and watched his ever move. He explained to the boy that the skin was as important to them as the meat. That it must be removed very carefully and prepared properly to make a blanket or wrap. He told the boy that the antelope skin was warmer than any other type of large animal skin. The reason he said was that the antelope hair was hollow and filled with air and this would help keep out the cold.

After he finished with the antelope he went to see after the horses and prepare them for the night. When he returned to the wagon he saw Ena holding something that looked like Harvey's tally book, except that it was bigger. He asked her why she needed such a big tally book. She explained that it was not a tally book, but a book for reading. Puma knew nothing about reading so he asked her to explain.

Ena told him that she had been a teacher back east where she had once lived, and that books were tools she used to teach people how to take words from the books turning them into spoken words. She also said that the words in books told a reader how to do things. Puma was very interested in this thing called a book, but ask no more questions that day. The only book that Puma had ever seen was the one that Harvey used to record the number of his cattle in.

Ena prepared some of the fresh meat from the antelope, while Puma and Charles gathered firewood for the night. There was no moon on this night but, the sky was clear and that meant that it would be very cold before morning.

Puma was up and had the fire going when the other two got up at sunrise. Ena said that this was the first restful night she had had in quite a while. Although she knew how to shoot, she said that she would lay awake at night in fear. Puma found out that Charles also knew how to use the guns. He told Puma that they had two rifles, a pistol, and a shotgun. He said that his father called this a scattergun. He also said that his father was a gunsmith, a black smith, and a wheelwright. Puma knew from his days on the cattle drive what a blacksmith was, but he knew nothing of the gunsmith or wheelwright.

He felt more at ease asking Charles questions than he did asking Ena. Charles carefully explained each. He told Puma that they had all his father's tools in the wagon. He said that much of the work was to heavy for a boy, but that his father had taught him how to use these tools.

Puma realized that these people knew many things that he would like to learn. However, that would have to wait. Today they must decide where they were going, and prepare to leave this camp. Ena had said that they were in route to the gold fields in the mountains of southwestern Colorado Territory.

Puma then decided that they would go north across a small portion of the Indian Territory and then to the Arkansas River unless they came across a wagon train on the way.

They spent the rest of the day checking the wagon and harness for the horses and preparing them for the journey. By sun up the next morning they had eaten and hooked up six of the horses to the wagon. They had saddled the remaining horse as well as Puma's pony. When they started out the cold frosty air cut like a knife and was blowing directly in their faces. After about an hour a light snow began to fall. The snow did not hinder their progress because they knew that they were better off moving than sitting in the camp huddled next to the small cooking fire. The first day they only covered about half the distance that would have been a days ride under normal conditions. At first the horses were reluctant to travel into the blowing snow but soon settled in and accepted their fate.

Puma had filled all their water pouches and kegs the day before but it was still necessary to make camp close to water for the horses. However, this time of the year it was not difficult to find water for the horses. They located such a spot about an hour before darkness fell. The grass was dormant but there was sufficient grazing for the horses. When they awoke the next morning they discovered that there was a real blizzard in progress. The wind was so strong that it shook the wagon so bad that Ena ask if it was possible that it would tip over. Puma said that it was unlikely but he thought that they must remain where they were until the storm was over. The snow had extinguished their fire, and was so deep that it was difficult finding wood or buffalo chips to burn. They started a new fire with the little extra wood that they had in the wagon. From time to time the snow would slack off a little. At these times Charles and Puma would trudge thru the snow and gather what fuel they could find. They knew that they would most likely be here for several days. Although the prairie grass was normally tall it was difficult finding places where the horses could dig out enough to eat. It had been months since the horses had had any grain to eat and they were beginning show the effects of this. Puma's pony was the better of the lot because he had never been fed corn like these horses, from back east.

After the third day the snow stopped and the sun came out. This made them feel better but it would still be several days before they could travel. By this time they had burned everything in sight of the camp and were getting low in fresh water. Ena spent a lot of her time melting snow in her cooking pots and pouring it in the water barrels. By the time they were able to travel again it had been seven days, and the time had been well spent. Charles and Ena had explained the use of the books and the tools that they carried. Puma always eager to learn something new absorbed everything that they said.

Finally Ena got the courage to ask where he got the name Puma. Both she and Charles were surprised at his answer. They had assumed that he was white and could hardly believe him when he told them that he was only a quarter white and had been raised as an Indian. By this time they had learned to trust him completely. The knowledge really made no difference to them. Ena ask him if he would like to learn to read and write? She said that she was teaching Charles, and that she needed the practice teaching because this was what she planned to do when they were settled someplace. This was what Puma was hoping for, but had not asked. She told him that when the weather broke she would start teaching him. Ena had many books and Puma wanted to know what was to be learned from each. He was especially interested in the one that told of the White Man's God.

By the time they crossed into the Indian Territory, the snow was almost all gone from the ground. The frozen earth had turned to mud. The soft muddy ground made it even more difficult for the horses to move the heavy wagon. As a results of this they made less progress the following few days. The extra time was used with each one learning what the other could teach. Puma was teaching them the ways of the frontier and they in turn were teaching him the use of the white man's tools and customs.

By the time they had crossed out of the Indian Territory into the Kansas Territory, the weather had changed a little. The days were cold, but the nights were nearly unbearable for the woman and boy. It was here that they found the Cimarron River, and The Santa Fe Trail. At the crossing of the Cimarron they found four wagons of settlers. These people told them that they had left the main wagon train at the point where the major trail divided. The other half of the trail was north and took a less direct route to Santa Fe.

After gathering all the information they could, Puma and Ena decided it was best for them to continue north. It was Ena's intention to settle in The Colorado Territory, not the Kansas Territory. This met with the approval of Puma because he was sure that his people and "the other knife" were somewhere west of where Ena was headed. Besides he was not satisfied that he had gained enough from her books.

They had been on the trail for several days since leaving the Cimarron, and had encountered no other travelers. Late one afternoon they could hear a strange noise ahead of them. Finally they could see, and hear the sound of a train and a large group of people.

When they arrived at the location where all the activity was, Puma saw that most of the men had yellow skin. Ena explained that these were Chinese men that had been hired to build the railroad from the east to the west. When Puma asked where these men with different shin came from, he was told that they came from a place called Asia. He did not know this place, Asia. This gave him something else to ponder and later learn about. Even though Puma knew many languages he could not understand these men. However, there were many white men in the group. The white men seemed to be in charge, and from them he and Ena hoped to obtain information about a wagon train and Puma's people. As it turned out they were not able to find out anything about either.

They did learn of a trail that went to the northwest. The Oregon Trail was the trail used mostly by settlers that were searching for free land. These settlers were mostly farmers, and cattlemen and were not searching for the gold fields.

Puma and Ena knew that they did not want to go that far to the northwest, so they decided to wait in this area for a while in hope that a wagon train going more to the west would pass. But as the days passed there was no sign of a wagon train. However, during this time the weather began to get milder. Puma and Charles continued to learn to read and write. Puma was also teaching Charles, and Ena the ways of the Indian. Charles had shown Puma the use of his Father's tools. They had repaired the wagon, and the harness for the horses. They had purchased, or traded for extra supplies for themselves as well as some grain for the horses. The railroad crew had supplies brought into camp each time that the train returned with material to build the railroad track.

By the time they finally decided that they were going to have to go on alone, the horses were strong and healthy. It was decided that they would go due west. They entered the Colorado Territory north of the Raton Pass. A few days out, they came across a trail heading west. Puma could tell that there had been several wagons on this trail a day or two before. They decided to follow this trail as long as it kept going the way they wanted to go.

Two days later they came upon a large group of wagons camped by a small stream. Several of the men were gathered around one of the wagons. When they reached the wagons, they found that a wheel on the wagon was busted. The men were in the process of moving everything out of it, into another of the wagons. Charles told the men that he had the tools to fix the wheel if they wanted to borrow them. The men were very surprised to find such tools in this desolate country. But they immediately set about to unload the tools. Under the direction of Charles and Puma they had the wheel repaired in about three hours.

Early the next morning, everything was loaded back on the wagons and they were ready to continue their journey. Puma, Ena, and Charles were invited to join the group. They said that they were going to a settlement near the base of Pikes Peak. Ena thought that this was ideal and eagerly accepted the invitation. Puma had no objection, because that was still in the direction he had decided to go. They traveled until darkness overtook them. They made a dry camp for the night, and were on their way at first light the next day. The horses began to labor a little and everyone could tell by the air, that they were climbing a little more each day. After they had been in The Colorado Territory for several days, they turned to the northwest. Ahead of them the trail had not been used in several weeks, but had been used often in the past. To their surprise they again came to the Arkansas River. It was here they camped for a couple of days, while Puma and a man named Paul scouted the area for about a days ride on the other side of the crossing.

While they were scouting, Paul told Puma that he was a man of God. Not knowing the meaning of this, Puma asked what he meant. Paul said that his other name was Jefferson and it was his mission in life to teach religion to others. He said that he and his wife had started out to find a settlement where they could establish a church. He explained that a church was a place where the will, and the ways of the White Man's God were taught. He said that unlike the Indian the White Man had only one God. He went on to tell Puma that these things were written in a book called the Bible. Now Puma remembered that Ena had such a book. Paul said that a few weeks out of Missouri his wife had died of consumption. This left him more determined than ever to continue his journey into the frontier.

When Puma and Paul returned to the camp the entire party was very anxious to be on the move. They had seen a small band of Indians the day before. Puma assured them that there was no danger because the Indians in this Territory had agreed on a treaty with the White Man.

They continued to follow the Arkansas, after first crossing over. Late one afternoon they came to a massive canyon that seemed to go down to the center of the earth. There was a small settlement on the north side of this canyon. The people in this settlement called the settlement Canyon City. After a day there, Puma met an Indian man that said that a band of Comanche's had passed this way about a summer and a half before. He said that they were being led by a Medicine Man. With this knowledge, Puma was assured that he was still following his people.

For days Puma had been able to see the great mountains off to the west. As they had traveled, it seemed that they were getting no closer. Most of the larger mountains were covered with snow. One of the men in the settlement said that several of these mountains were covered with snow all year. He told Puma that most of the people in the area depended on the deer, and elk for fresh meat. When summer approached the snows began to melt and the deer and elk retreated higher and higher into the mountains. Only to return to the lower levels as the snows began to return. The mountains were covered mostly with great trees, and were very different from the mountains in Puma's homeland. After several days resting, and trading in this settlement, most of those in the group were ready to continue their journey. Two or three families decided to remain in Canyon City. Again it was Puma, and Paul who scouted the trail ahead to learn how best for the wagons go. Due to the mountains, it was difficult to find a trail that would allow the passage of some of the larger wagons. Some of the wagons were so large that they had to be pulled by six horses, or oxen. There was one wagon that belonged to a large family that had eight oxen pulling it. Most of the wagons contained only a family of two or three, but this particular family had seventeen members. Most of them rode horses with only the small children riding in the wagon. The trail had been used many times in the preceding months, but still offered many challenges for the settlers.

Each time they came to a creek, or stream there were men working in the water with their gold pans, looking for gold. There were several one and two family camps along the trail, but no larger settlements.

Finally after several days of this rugged trip the party reached Fountain Colony. There it was decided that they would stay. Puma knew that sooner, or later some of these people would get the urge to move on. But for the time being he was the only one that was planning to move farther west.

Chapter 35

Puma spent two days preparing to leave the wagon train at Fountain Colony. He had gathered what supplies he thought that he would need. He also had acquired a second horse from Paul. Finally the time had come for him to leave. It was with a heavy heart, he said his good bye to Ena and Charles. They had been his companions for about half a year. They had taught him many things that he would have never have learned otherwise.

While riding away from the colony, and into the heavy forest, he realized that it had been four years since he had ridden away from his people on the Rio Bravo. Ena's last words to him were. "I hope you find the other knife."

It was early spring and the air was cold, and damp in the forest as he swung to the southwest. He was in the land of the Jicarilla Apache. From time to time he would encounter small bands of hunters. From these hunters, he was able to learn that his people had passed this way. He learned that they were headed in the direction of the ancestral home of the Pueblo People, in the southwest corner of the Colorado Territory.

As he got closer to the mountains he determined that it was still too early in the year to attempt to travel over the top of them. He had also learned that at the top of these mountains the country seemed to divide. The Apache said that this was the place that the earth divided. They had assured him that the land beyond was far different from the land in which he was now traveling.

As he rode, he began to ponder the past year or so. The people that he had traveled with over these months had never treated him any different than they had each other. No one had ever asked about his name or where he was from. He supposed that many of the men that he had come in contact with had a different name than the one they were called. He knew that it was the custom for men to change their name to hide their past.

As he rode in a southwestern direction he was amazed at the size of the mountains, and the difference in the weather from day to day. He was in no hurry. He did not want to over look a pass, or a trail that his people might have used getting through the mountains. He was continually hunting and fishing to provide himself with his daily needs. He was very reluctant to use the supplies that he carried. He had no way of knowing what the future has in store, in a strange land. As was the Indian way, he took only what he needed from the forest and wasted nothing.

Late one afternoon he came upon the camp of a Navajo hunting party on the bank of a river. To his amazement they told him that this was the Rio Grande. It was just as he expected the river started in the mountains a couple of days ride west of their camp. It was hard to realize that after all the traveling he had done that he was again on the river of his childhood. From these hunters he learned that a band of Comanche Indians had passed through this area a little over a year before. They told him that they were going to the south where there was an outlet of water that was very hot. Also he learned that there was a pass through the mountains that was not as high as might be found elsewhere. The Navajo called it the Pass of the Wolf.

After spending a day and night with these hunters, and gaining all the information he could, he rode toward the pass. The mountains were very tall, the trail very difficult, but on the second day he reached the summit and started down. The wind here was very strong, and cold. He was looking forward to the time when he would be at the springs of the hot water. He now was at the point where it was said that the land divided. He spent the next day descending the west side of the mountains. The footing was very hazardous because of the many loose stones. As he arrived at the hot springs the ground had leveled out somewhat.

He found a small band of Navajo camped near the water. This band was complete with women and children and gave the appearance that this was their permanent home. Puma spent many hours talking to the Chief of this band. He had notice, when he arrived that there were small patches of ground that appeared to be fields like those the white man used to raise his food. When he ask the Chief about this he was told that they were indeed used to raise corn, squash and beans. He said that they had learned some of the ways of farming from the white man, but that the tribes to the west had been raising food crops for many life times. The Pueblo people raised their food among the large flat mesas that were on the top, and also in the valleys between the mountains to the west.

The Chief told him that there was a white settlement about a days ride to the west. He said that they were preparing for the arrival of the big iron horse. This settlement was called Durango. Durango was a Spanish word that meant a stopping or watering place. He also told Puma that his people had passed through Durango. They had gone on to the land of the cliff dwellers.

Puma thanked the Chief for the information, and took his leave to continue his journey. He had decided that he would go to this place, Durango.

When he arrived in the settlement, he found that most of the white men were searching for gold. The mountains were so rough that raising large herds of cattle was not a common practice. However, there were large flocks of sheep and goats. As the days got warmer the flocks were driven into the mountains and would continue to climb higher and higher until the cold weather set in. They would then begin their trip back to the lower valleys where they would spend the winter.

The Indians of the area were not happy with the sheep and goats. The sheep would eat the grasses down to ground level thus destroying the chance for new growth. The goats would eat the foliage of all plants from the ground to as high as they could reach. This extensive grazing caused the wild life of the area to migrate to other sections of the mountains. However, some of the Indians would tend these flocks and earn some of the white man's dollars.

Puma stayed in Durango several days, but could not obtain any information about his people. Most of the people in the settlement were to busy trying to find gold. They were so occupied with the gold fever that they would not even talk to one another. Finally Puma decided that to stay here longer would be a waste of time.

After a days ride to the west, the mountains gave way to deep canyons and large flat mesas. On these mesas he could see strange houses made of brush and beside each was a small round Kiva. There were sheep and goats being tended by Indian boys. As he approached, he was halted by a group of braves armed with the white man's guns. They ask him where he was going and what he was doing in this country. When he explained his mission, they invited him to sit with them and smoke.

For the most part these people were dressed in the clothes of the white man. The brave in charge told him that their purpose on the mesa was to guard the village and to keep out unwanted intruders. He said that they were at peace with the whites, and engaged in much trading with them. But they were still raided from time to time by small bands of renegade Indians. Some of the natives had not put aside their differences. He went on to say that these bands would drink the white Man's firewater that was called whiskey. This he said would make the Indian crazy and mean. When they were crazy they would raid both the Indian, and the white villages. The place where Puma now sat was really a small compound of several families, whose purpose was simply be lookouts and warn the village if they were approached by renegades or strangers.

Puma asked where the village was located, and how large the tribe was. He was told that the main village was in the canyons, and there were many families living there. He was also told that when the sun next rose they would take him to the Chief of the village. He was then invited into one of the huts to spend the night. He lay awake far into the night listening to the sounds of the sheep and goats. His mind was busy wondering about these people and their village.

At daybreak two of the braves got their ponies and told Puma to follow them. As they approached the canyon Puma could see several lookouts scattered along the rim. Reaching the rim of the canyon, and looking down Puma saw many houses made of mud and stone under the rims, or ledges of the canyon walls. Some of these places were small but some were quite large. One such house was a huge building that had many rooms. It was to this house that Puma was escorted. It was here in the large Kiva that he would sit in council with Chief Grey Hawk and the Medicine Man.

At this council the Chief explained to Puma the origin of this place. He said that a very long time ago the Ancients Ones had built this place. It had been a place for many families to live safely from the outside world. It was protected from the weather by the canyon walls and the only access to the village was by guarded paths or ladders that were made for that purpose. It was explained that many families occupied each of the houses, and they each shared in the work of the village. Since peace had come to the area, they had obtained and learned to use some of the white man's tools as well as his weapons. He was told that the women of the village made woven baskets and blankets that were traded to the whites for the items that they wanted and needed. The men worked the fields, raised the crops and the sheep. Some of the tribe would work the sheep herds of the whites for the white man's dollar.

Puma asked. "What were these fields and where were they located? He was told that the crops were raised on the floor of the canyons, and that they had learned how to get the water for them during dry days. Other fields were high on the mesa where the crops that needed less water were raised. After nearly a day of council, Puma was taken to a single room of the complex. He was told that this would be his place as long as he was in the village.

Although the people were no longer at war, the various leaders were still called War Chiefs. The following morning one of these War Chiefs took Puma on a tour of the canyon floor. It was determined that he wanted to learn of their ways; therefore, he caused no alarm as he wandered around the village asking questions.

When they arrived on the floor of the canyon he saw many patches of different kinds of corn, squash, and beans. He had eaten beans many time while traveling with the white man, but this was the first time that he had ever seen them growing. He saw other plants that he did not know. He made a mental note to ask of these. Puma was amazed at the size of the corn and squash plants. They were growing much bigger than any he had ever seen before. He was told that this was because of the rich soil, and the available water that was brought in by a system called irrigation. He approached a group of men and women working these crops and found that the group consisted of both Ute and Pueblo people. The strange thing about this group was that the men were working the fields along side the women. This was a practice that Puma had not seen before. One of the braves explained to Puma that the growing of crops, sheep, goats, and cattle had become necessary because the buffalo herds were killed or driven from the area by the white hunters, when the railroad had come to this country.

When they returned to the compound they went to the Kiva, where all religious and other ceremonies were held. There the Medicine man was leading such a ceremony when they arrived. Every one sat quietly on the ground through the entire ceremony, which lasted nearly an hour. After the ceremony, Puma was left to roam freely about the village. He observed that there were buildings on both sides of the canyon, which extended as far as he could see.

The next day he again returned to the floor of the canyon. There he asked many questions about the tools that were being used. After learning the names, and uses of the various tools he decided to learn more of the living habits of these people. His next stop was at the living quarters of the Chief's family. The Chief had no sons and only one daughter.

The daughter of the chief was a princess, named Gentle Dove. She was about the same age as was Puma. She had never married. The Chief explained that she had not taken a husband, because the daughter of the chief must wed a chief or son of a chief. Puma did not question this because this was the custom of many Indian tribes.

Gentle Dove could speak the English of the white man. She had learned the language from a White Holy Man that had spent several summers in their village. He had also taught her of the white man's god even though she was not sure if it was truth or a legend. It was her duty to translate for the tribe as well as teach the younger members of the tribe the language. The new language was necessary to enable them to conduct business with the Whites.

Puma spent many hours talking to Gentle Dove in both English, and also her native tongue. From her he learned many things about how the cliff houses came to be, and how her people had come to live there.

After many suns in the village Puma decided that it was time for him to move on. He went to the Chief, and asked of his people. He was rewarded with more information than could have been expected. He was told that indeed his people had passed this way. They had spent several moons in the area. When they departed they said that they were going to The Utah Territory, the land of many tribes. This Utah territory was the land of many lakes with bad water. The water in the lakes of this territory was filled with salt and was not fit for use by man or beast. It was said that his people were going to join the Shoshone, or Snake tribe as they were sometimes called. These people lived to the east of the greatest of the salt lakes.

Puma was told that there was a strange group of whites in and around the area of the Great Salt Lake. A man, named Brigham Young, had brought these people to this area and adopted the policy of a man having many wives. It was said that he had had as many as twenty-seven wives at one time. The custom of having several wives was far different from that of the Indian and other Whites. The only time that a brave had more than one woman in his home was when a warrior had died or been killed, and left behind a wife. This woman would be taken into another's home during the period of mourning, and remain there until she took another husband.

About thirty summers ago the Chief of the Whites, President Buchanan, had made Young the Territorial Governor of the new territory of Utah. Young had died several summers later but his people still flourished in the area. It was said that his people did not believe in God in the same way that other Whites believed.

Armed with the new knowledge he had gained from the Pueblo People, Puma prepared to leave their land, and continue his search for his people. He must find,

"The knife" his mother spoke of. The trail he must follow would lead northwest across a barren and desolate land.

Shortly after he left the land of the Pueblo he, also left behind the mountains, He entered a flat section of the territory that would take him several days to cross. He was amazed at the correctness of the Chief's description of the country. From time to time he would come across small settlements of Whites, but they only waved or ignored him completely. Based on the words of the Chief, Puma had no desire to learn anything from these people. Therefore, he continued his journey to the north until he reached the Green River at the point where it entered the great canyon lands. After resting for several hours he crossed the river and followed it north. When he had gone a short distance he reached a place where the river almost doubled back on its self. It was at this point he encountered a small group of soldiers that were camped there. He was unable to gain any information about his people, but did learn that there was an army headquarters located about two or three days ride north. They said that it was located where the Green, White, and Strawberry Rivers met. They also told him that there was an Indian Agent located at headquarters that might have the information he was seeking. He was told that an Indian Agent was a man that conducted business between the Whites and the Indians.

Three days later he rode into the headquarters of the soldiers. He found that there were many Indians working peacefully with the white soldiers. The Indians in the headquarters of the soldiers were from different tribes, and it was their duty to scout and hunt for the army. Puma did not know the ways of the army. Therefore, he questioned only the Indian scouts. After several days of observing, and asking many questions he was advised by the leader of the scouts to seek out the man that was the administrator of all dealings between the white government and the Indian leaders. He said that he did not know this man's name. He was simply called The Indian Agent. It was said that this agent did a good job. However, the great council of Whites in a place called Washington did not supply him with enough money, or material to do the job properly.

The headquarters of the army here was not the same as the forts that Puma was familiar with. This place was more like a settlement, or a town. The soldiers here had their families with them and lived in separate houses. Because of the size of the fort there was little chance that any band of renegades would attack.

Puma sought out this man whose name was Philip Petty. When he entered a room called the office, he found Philip Petty sitting at a desk that was covered with books and papers. He was told that these were the records of all supplies coming in or going out. Philip greeted him with the White man's handshake. He offered Puma a cigar, and invited him to smoke. Puma refused the offer. Puma considered smoking a ritual, and as yet they had nothing to smoke about. He had realized during his days on the cattle drive that the white man smoked for pleasure.

At this point, Philip thought that Puma was a white traveler, and it was not until Puma gave his name that he realized that Puma was Indian. That he was here in search of something other than shelter and safety.

Philip asked Puma the nature of his visit and what he could do to help. Puma proceeded to tell Philip the story of the last few years. He said that it had been nearly five summers since he had had contact with any of his people. That he desired to reunite with those he had left behind so long ago. He did not mention " the knife", or his search for knowledge of it. After listening to his story, which took several hours, Philip told him that there was such a band of Comanche in an area to the west. He said that this band was part of a larger group of Indians that he was working with. The larger group consisted of Ute, Snakes, Pueblo, Comanche, Sioux and a few Yuma Indians as well as a large tribe of Shoshone. He said they lived in an area that had been designated for them by The Congress in Washington. Puma knew nothing of this Congress or Washington.

Philip explained that Congress was to the Whites, the same thing as a Chief's Council was to the Indian. That Washington was the settlement, or place where they lived and worked. Puma understood that a Congressman must be to the White Man what a War Chief was to the Indian people.

While Puma was talking to Philip an older man dressed in a uniform came into the room. Philip told Puma that this man was Zackery Brown the army surgeon. Puma asked what were the duties of a surgeon. Doctor Brown explained that a surgeon was a healer of the sick, or wounded, the white version of a medicine man. He told Puma that at the present time he was assigned to the area to tend the Indians as well as the army. He explained that since the coming of the white man many Indians had become sick with some of the white man's diseases. Two of the more deadly diseases were smallpox and consumption. With these came the necessity of the white medicine, thus it was his duty to administer to the affected. He explained that both of these diseases were usually fatal especially if not treated in the early stages.

Philip said that there were settlements like this one scattered through the frontier. The frontier to him was an area that extended far north into The Dakotas and as far west as the white man had traveled in his search for gold, and land. He said that he had been at this post or settlement ever since the Sioux had attacked the army at the Little Big Horn about, five or six years before the Iron Horse had arrived in the Colorado Territory. After this battle the tribes that had been gathered by Sitting Bull and Crazy Horse had separated and gone separate ways. He suspected that some of the braves that had fought in this battle were in fact in the very group that Puma was seeking. Not his people but others that they had joined.

After finding out all he could about the situation of the Indian in the area, Puma ask for direction to this place where it was suspected that his people might be. When he was satisfied that he knew where to go, he departed and headed west along the south bank of the Strawberry River. The further he got from the settlement the more desolate and deserted the land became. All along the river he saw the remains of wagons. There were many bones of dead livestock and also many places that seemed to be graves. These graves had to be those of the whites because an Indian would never place their dead in such a manner. After about a half days ride he began to see small patches of corn, and other various crops. The cattle and sheep that he encountered were in very bad shape. The grasses were very poor. and so scattered that it was difficult for anything to find enough to eat. Finally he began to see brush huts, and tepees scattered about. There would be groups of each but never would the different structures be together. It was as if each band was trying to retain its own identity. The first group that he was able to recognize was a large band of Pueblo Indians living in mud huts with a large Kiva in the center of the compound. He stopped at this place and inquired about the Chief or Medicine Man. A young Squaw took him to the hut of the leader of the band. The man was called Stands Tall but was not really a Chief but only a Sub Chief. Puma and Stands Tall sat and smoked before they entered into talks. Stands Tall listened to Puma's story in silence. After hearing the story and the request for knowledge of his people, he told Puma that there was such a band just to the west.

It was with a happy heart that Puma then mounted his pony and headed to the west. At last he was going to be united again with his people.

His happy heart was saddened as he came in sight of the village. The tepees were ragged and in bad repair. There were no longer the colorful pictures painted on the tepees. Those that remained were faded and no longer showed the pride that the owners once had of their homes. The village was in complete disarray and there was much junk and trash scattered about. Even the dogs looked lean and hungry. The cattle that surrounded the village looked as though they were starving. As he rode through the village he saw many that he recognized but the look of despair in their eyes told Puma that there was something wrong. The people seemed to have lost their will to live.

He asked one young brave if he knew of his Caddo Brother, Tonka. The brave gave no reply but just nodded his head in the direction of a tepee to the south. Puma dismounted in front of the tepee and called out to Tonka. Tonka emerged from the tepee, and stood silent for a moment. It was then that he recognized his brother. Puma noticed that Tonka no longer looked the strong healthy brave that he had remembered. Tonka greeted him and invited him into his tepee. He told Puma that they could not smoke because he no longer could afford to trade for tobacco. They sat around the small fire in the center of the tepee for several minutes before either spoke.

Finally Tonka said, " Welcome, my brother your journey has been long." He told Puma that the many raids by the Mexicans had finally forced the people to leave the land of the Rio Bravo. It was after the death of the Chief during one of these raids that the Medicine Man had decided that they must return to the land of their origin. After many moons they had come to this place, only to find that conditions for the Indian here was far worse than where they had been on the great river. It seemed that, now they were dependent on the white government for the necessities of life. There were no longer the great buffalo herds to hunt and the people had to resort to the ways of the white man by raising crops and cattle just to survive. He said that out of all the different people in this area, there existed not a single Chief to lead them or to deal with the white agent sent from Washington. A council of Medicine Men now governed the people of this camp. He said that it was not the fault of the agent but that the White Chief, Grover Cleveland, and his Congress. They did not send enough supplies for all the people. He said that there was no longer any spirit left, in the tribes, to resist the ever expanding white population. He said that the only time any trouble arose was if some white gave an Indian whiskey and caused the Indian to loose control of his actions. When this happened the Indian was arrested and placed in the army stockade.

When Puma inquired about Tonka's mother, he was told that she had died while they were making the journey through the land of the cliff people. She had been carried for several suns until they could find a proper place for her to sleep.

Puma asked of the Medicine Man, Bent Knee, and was told that he was more or less the head of the band from Texas, and he also took part in the council that was for the time being acting in place of a Chief. After a short rest Puma and Tonka again sat and talked. Tonka talked at length about the loss of spirit by the entire group of bands that were now living at this place. He talked of the Indian Agent and his attempt to gain better treatment for the Indian. Tonka then asked if he would seek out the Medicine Man. When Puma said that he must talk to Bent Knee and ask for necessary directions in his search for " the Knife".

Bent Knee was a man of about fifty summers and had been the medicine man ever since his father had died. He was well respected and trusted by all the Indian Nations. When Puma and Tonka approached him in his Kiva he was wearing the traditional buffalo skull and the necklace of bear claws. He invited them to sit and smoke the pipe. After about an hour of silence he asked. "What can I do for you my son?" Puma told him of the words of his mother and said that he was seeking the meaning of her message. Bent Knee said that he knew of her words and that he was unable to explain them to Puma. He further said that he did know of a man that could give Puma the complete story. He said that the knowledge of the Knife was to be kept secret until such time that some brave came forward seeking out the information. He said that when the sun showed its face next that he would take Puma to the man that held the secret.

The next morning just as the sun was clearing the earth to the east, Bent Knee summoned Puma to his tepee. "Now my friend it is time for you to learn of the secret." They walked together to a tepee that was located on a small hill apart from the rest of the village. The tepee was decorated with the markings of a Shoshone Medicine Man. Beside this tepee was a very large Kiva. This Kiva was where the governing council was held. Just as they approached the tepee the Medicine Man appeared from behind the flap of the tepee. He too had on the buffalo skull and bear claws. Around his neck the necklace held more bear claws than Puma had ever seen before. The Medicine Man was very stooped and stood on legs that looked as if they might fail to carry him further. As was the custom, Puma waited for The Medicine Man to speak first. Puma guessed that this man must be over ninety summers old. He could see much wisdom behind the old man's eyes.

"I am Burning Fire and I have been expecting you for many moons. I have been told of your coming, and also of the reason, by a vision. It is I, who holds the secret of the other knife, but you will have to wait two more suns to hear my words. It was the wish of The Great Spirits that I should live to this age, or until the secret of the Knives is made known to the proper person. After the two day wait there will be a council of all the people of this village. Then the secret will be given to all. Go now and wait while I retire into the Kiva, and seek more visions."

After leaving the tepee of Burning Fire, Puma took the liberty of exploring the village. From time to time he would pass someone from his childhood, and was accepted by all others.

It was said that from child hood Burning Fire had gotten his visions from looking into the fire. He had been so named because when he was very young he would sit and gaze into the flames for hours at a time. No one really knew if this was true or not because there was none other older than he.

On the morning of the third day, a council was called. Everyone in the entire compound was expected to attend. The Medicine Men from all the tribes represented, sat in a circle around a ceremonial fire. These were accompanied by the greatest of their sub chiefs. They all took part in the smoking of the pipe. During the smoking, which took the better part of an hour, the remainder of the people sat quietly in a circle that was with in hearing distance, but several feet behind the leaders.

After the smoking, and the pipe it was put aside, Burning Fire stood in the center and looked out over the assembled group for several minutes without saying anything. He was dressed in the deerskin robe decorated for such an important council. He wore the skull of the buffalo that had been bleached white to simulate the great power of the White Buffalo. About his neck he wore many strings of bear claws. In his hand he had the staff that was the sign of his great position. No other sound was heard. The people knew that this was going to be a long and serious council.

"I am Burning Fire, the Chief Medicine Man of the Shoshone People. I stand today before the member of many tribes that have gathered here under circumstances not because of their own choosing. We have gathered here at this place because of the many treaties that have been made with the White Man. The invasion of the Whites has destroyed our way of life. Over the past many summers we have been trying to adjust to a less simple way of life. This was, and continues to be, very difficult for a proud people such as we are. I have lived over ninety summers, which is much longer than most of our people have ever lived. I will tell you of some of the things I have learned, and seen during these many summers. Before this council is over I will tell you of a great secret that was kept by my father then handed down to me at his death. My father was also a man of many more summers than any of his people. He told me many stories of our people. He passed much of his wisdom to me.

Thousands of summers ago the Ancient Ones passed across a great ice field into this place, from another place far away. As is with all men they were searching for better hunting and living. Many summers after they passed over this path, the ice melted and took what was then a great land and made it two great lands. Now that this path was gone the Ancient Ones began to search further and further south and east. As they traveled through the land they formed smaller groups. There arose many tribes that sought out different places to occupy as their territory. The

Shoshone, soon to be called Snake tribe, and the Ute settled in the area where we are now camped. We are allowed to remain here because the Whites have decided that this land is not fit for the digging of gold, or the raising crops and cattle.

The many tribes that were formed occupied lands from one great ocean to the other great ocean. They also spread from the ice fields in the far north to the deserts of the far south. Then the white man came. Our land became the land of the White settlers. The Tribes fought to hold on to their lands, however the will of the White Man and his superior weapons gradually forced our people to enter into a treaty of peace. After a period of time, many of our people began to help the White Man as he pushed into the frontier. A very famous Shoshone woman, Sacajawea, assisted a group of Whites led by two men called Lewis and Clark. They were attempting to locate a route from the east to the west.

During my many summers I have seen the White Man spread across our land, as does a prairie wild fire. They first sent messages to one another on what they call paper. These papers they carried from one place to another by riders on horseback. They called this The Pony Express. Shortly they began to carry people across the land in boxes on wheels called stagecoaches. With the help of many men with yellow skins they built the railroad and now the numbers of Whites coming into our land are more than ever. I have seen long lines of wagons coming from the great river to the East. Some of these wagon trains, as they were called would go as far as the eye could see.

With the coming of the great Iron Horse called a train, there came a great white hunter and he slaughtered the Buffalo herds for both meat and the hides. It is said that he killed four thousand or more. This gained him the name of Buffalo Bill.

With the Railroad came the singing wire. It was said that men could send messages over this wire for great distances.

After the peace between the Indian and the Whites, the White Men began to fight each other. They did not raid for horses or food. They would shoot each other to settle any disagreement that came between them. They would fight for the yellow metal or even the place to dig for it. They all wore guns, and they would shoot down others in the streets of their towns for what seemed no reason at all. Large groups of men would rob places called banks. I have heard that there was a famous gang of men led by Jessie James that robbed banks and trains. This was shortly after the war between the whites over the black man.

Greed had brought the Whites to the west in search of gold. Their greed caused them to do stupid things. It is said that a group of such people, under the leadership of George Donner was in such a hurry to get to the gold fields that after suffering many hardships crossing The Great Salt Lake, they attempted to cross the Sierra Nevada and were trapped by the weather. It is told that the living of this party had to eat their dead in order to survive.

The Whites brought their own form of law to the area. The ones that enforced these laws were called Marshals who were really just paid gunmen. One I remember the best was called Wild Bill, I don't know if all the stories that are told of Wild Bill are true or not but it is said that he, Buffalo Bill and Sitting Bull later went across the great ocean to another land and showed the people in the land of the Whites how things were in our country. They did this by a thin called playacting.

Chapter 36

Burning Fire stood silent in the center of the council, as if to recall something that had slipped from his memory.

"Sometimes, when I get to telling or singing a story, I wander from the real purpose of the council. This is true of most men of my age because we have more of life behind us than before us. The past is far greater than our present. However, as I stand before you today I will give you reason to look and hope for a better tomorrow.

Many summers ago when the Shoshone was a large and proud tribe, there was a great Chief. He was called Two Knives. It was said, that once on a raiding party into the land of the Spaniards, he killed a Spanish General that carried two Knives that were alike. Having never seen such a knife before he took these knives for his own. He had then changed his name from Red Hawk to Two Knives.

Two Knives was looking forward to the time when his squaw would present him a son. Such a son would some day become the chief of the Shoshone. When it came time for the son to arrive there were two sons not one. This made Two Knives very proud, and gave him a vision for the future. The boys both grew to be fine braves, and one could not tell them apart. One of the sons was called Soaring Eagle, the other Soaring Hawk.

Many summers later as Two Knives lay near death he summoned his sons to his side and told them of the vision he had when they were born. He said, as things now stood there could only be one chief of the tribe.

The vision had told him that the tribe must be divided. Soaring Eagle would remain with half of the tribe in the lands north of the Great Salt Lake. Soaring Hawk would take half of the tribe and travel to the southeast. It was there that Soaring Hawk would establish a tribe called Comanche. The sons did as their father requested, thus a new tribe was established in the area that would one day be called Texas. The old ways and customs would remain the same except for changes that would become necessary by the nature of the new territory. After telling the sons this he passed one of the knives to each son.

For a very long time the tribes maintained their customs and hunted the buffalo as was their way. The only fighting that they did was with raiding parties from other tribes. There was no sickness among the people until the White Man arrived among them. Soaring Eagle had no son's therefore, before his death he called my father to his side and passed his knife along with a story to him. The knife was to be kept by the Medicine Man of the tribe until The Great Spirits told him it was time to pass it on to a future Chief. At his death, my father passed the secret of the knife was passed to me for safety.

Five summers ago a vision came to me and told me that a great Chief was on his journey back to the Shoshone people. This vision told me that when the two knives came together again that the holder of them would again be the Great Chief of all Shoshone tribes.

Three suns ago a brave arrived in our village and he did in fact carry the second knife. This brave has been on a long journey searching for the story of his knife. He has no knowledge of the history, or of the importance of owning the knife.

Puma my son it is my duty to tell you that your father was Soaring Hawk. The knife you carry was to be passed to you when you reached manhood. Due to the circumstances surrounding the death of your father and mother this story was never told you. I have been told that you are indeed the boy with the brown hair that was born the only son of Soaring Hawk. If you will step forward I will determine if you are truly the proper Brave. If you are the son of that Chief, you will have a sign marked on the back of your right shoulder. If you have this mark I will present you with " the other knife" that you have been searching for these many summers."

Puma rose from the outer circle of the council and joined Burning Fire in the center of the Kiva. He was asked to remove his shirt. The Medicine Man then examined his shoulder just where his arm joined his back. There he found a small blue line and a small yellow circle that had been tattooed into the skin. It was then that the old Medicine Man took from his robe an object wrapped in deerskin. He unwrapped a knife that was identical to the one Puma's Mother had given to Puma.

"I see that you have the proper mark and now I present this knife to Puma The Boy With The Brown Hair. Once this knife has joined the other knife on his side he will become Puma Two Knives, the Chief of all Shoshone people."

Burning Fire handed the second knife to Puma and removed a necklace of bear claws from his neck and placed them around the neck of Puma. Puma took the Knife and stood silent for a moment. Burning Fire retired to a blanket spread on the floor of the Kiva. Puma turned slowly and looked everyone present in the eyes. After a long period of silence he raised his arms and face to the sky and had a quite word with the Great Spirit.

"It is true I am the Boy With The Brown Hair, a brave of the Comanche Tribe of the south. I have been seeking to return to my people for a very long time. During this time I have learned many things. I have worked with the White Man. I have learned the language and customs of the many people that I have come in contact with. Some of these customs are good and some are not. I have witnessed many of the things that Burning Fire spoke of. I am what the White Man calls educated in the ways of the world. Not in their schools but rather by living with them and taking the opportunity to learn everything that I was in contact with. I know now that The Great Spirits guided me through these experiences for a purpose. I do not as yet know the full story of my destiny. I will spend many hours in council with Burning Fire, and others to learn the entire story. During this time of council I will remain a Comanche Brave. If I find that I am indeed to be the Chief of the Shoshone, I will accept the responsibility to serve my people with pride. There are many tribes represented in this council, and it is my understanding that there is no Chief among you. It is my wish that each tribe would hold council among them selves to decide if they too would join with the Shoshone in the same manner that all tribes joined with Sitting Bull and Crazy Horse at the Little Big Horn. When I have determined to my satisfaction, if I am to be the Chief I will call another council and advise the entire village of my decision. If I am to be the Chief I will ask, at that council, for the choices of the other people of the village."

For seven days Puma sat in council with Burning Fire and the older braves of his tribe. They spoke of many things, but mostly of the history of the people. Puma needed to know of the past as well as the present. After this period, he had satisfied him self that it was indeed true that he was of the blood of the Great Chief Two Knives. Burning Fire again called a council of the entire village.

"This council has been called for the purpose of honoring the new Chief of the Shoshone. After the ceremony there will be three days of singing and dancing to celebrate this great event".

Burning Fire then preformed the ceremony that confirmed the making of a new Chief. Puma stood in the center of the Kiva. After the ceremony he removed the Jacket and boots of the White Man and replaced them with the deerskin jacket and moccasins that befitted an Indian.

"I am, now Chief Puma Two Knives of the Shoshone People. My first duty as such will be to ask the others here to join with me in my journey to a better life for our People."

With this Puma turned to each tribe represented and ask the leader of each group if they would join him. When they all agreed that they would join with him. The leaders of each tribe represented were invited to smoke the pipe with him. After they had put the pipe aside Puma again stood before the group.

"Since all have confirmed that they stand with me, I now honor each one that smoked the pipe with me by making them Chief of their tribe. This will give each of you a Chief to represent you in council with me, the Chief of all. It will be that each of you keep and use the customs and language of you ancestors. I will in the future have each one present here today taught a common language that can be used among each other as well as with the Whites. The future of this village will be decided in council of Chiefs. Now it is time for everyone to return to their homes and prepare for a better future."

Puma spent many long hours pondering over what he must do first. He would draw upon the experiences he had with the White Man as well as those of his training as a Comanche Brave. He must also call on the wisdom of the elderly Medicine Man, before he would be called to his reward. After much thought, he had decided upon a course of action. The first thing he would do was he would talk with each member of the village to determine the needs and wishes of each. Once he had this knowledge, he would determine the next step he must take.

First he went to the Utes. There he spent several days learning of their customs and found that they had suffered many hardships trying to cope with the changing times. They were unhappy with the strange customs of the Whites that surrounded the Great Salt Lake. They said that it was not in keeping with the customs of the Whites with whom they had made the treaty.

He found this to be true with all the people. Also one of the greatest concerns was the fact that they did not have enough to eat. These were the main complaints. He found that they had no difficulty dealing with the Indian Agent, but that the Agent had difficulty dealing with the Congress in Washington. He supplied them with all the items at his disposal, but this was far less than the needs of the people. These talks with the people, and his observation of the conditions in the village alarmed Puma. He decided that the next step would be to correct this situation.

It was decided that in two days he would travel to the office of Philip Petty. There he would council with him about the problems that faced his people. He would take Tonka with him. He had made Tonka a Sub Chief.

As he and Tonka traveled to the office of Philip, they observed the weary attempts of the people working in the fields of corn and squash.

They were attempting to work with the ancient tools that were made for only a few small patches of corn. He also noticed that there were no longer fields of wild rice, oats, or wild onions. He assumed that these had been the victims of over harvest when the people attempted to feed their families. No longer did there exist large fields of growing grass. For as far as he could see there was not enough grass to feed the cattle and horses.

There was no water crest in the streams and the water supply was filled with dirt and trash. He supposed that he could remedy the grass situation by rotating the livestock over a larger area, a system he had learned from the white cattlemen. He knew that he could clean the water. These two chores would require time and manpower. To get the people to do this he would have to give them hope, and a reason to do the necessary work. He had to convince the people that with their willingness to apply themselves, they could overcome many of their hardships.

As he and Tonka rode toward the white settlement they were in deep thought, and spoke of many things. A great plan began to form in Puma's mind.

When they arrived at the settlement they ask to speak with the Indian Agent. When they entered the office, Philip was seated at his desk behind a huge pile of letters. He explained that the mail had just arrived from Washington, and he was trying to figure out what needed to be done first. He said that the money he was sent was not nearly enough to buy the things he needed to properly perform his job. He invited them to sit, and offered them a long black cigar made of the tobacco from the east. He then asked, "What can I do my friend, to be of service to you?" Puma accepted the cigar and told Philip that they would smoke with him because this was to be a council about the affairs of the Indian People.

"I no longer come to you as a traveler in search of my people. Today I come before you as Puma Two Knives, Chief of all Indians in my village, and the surrounding lands. This position was given me by my birthright in the Shoshone Tribe, and the vote of other Tribes. In the coming days all affairs concerning my people will be conducted with me."

The three of them sat and smoked for a few minutes in silence. Finally Puma decided it was time to discuss the reason for his return visit to the office of the Indian Agent.

"It is quite clear to me that all people of this land are experiencing great hardships. But none are suffering as much as my people. We have common problems just as do the Whites, however during my ride from my village to your office I have noticed many things that are different. For example your people plow their fields with metal plows pulled by horses. They remove the unwanted grasses and weeds with sharp metal tools with wooden handles. My people are still trying to do the same chores with sharpened wood tools. Our cattle and horses are expected to survive on the sparse, and stunted grasses of this barren land. We cannot water our crops because we have none of the wooden water barrels that the Whites use. Without these we are put at a disadvantage. We are not able to feed ourselves properly. It is my understanding that the Treaty for Peace provided that the Government in Washington was supposed to provide supplies for the Indian in return for use of some of the land, and peace. This was accepted by both sides with the smoking of the pipe and the signing of the paper. However, the Indian did not read or write, and he had to depend on the word of the White Man for what the paper contained. Being that the Indian Man was a man of truth, he made his mark on the paper. It has now come to pass that I am the Chief. I can both read and write. Therefore, I now wish to see this paper and examine the contents of the treaty to learn what provisions were made for the Indian."

Philip sat silent, and in thought for a long time. "The paper you speak of is stored in an office in Washington, it is guarded by the Chief of Indian Affairs. I have never seen the paper, nor do I really know what it contains. I am merely a servant of my government, therefore, must do as I am told to distribute the supplies that are sent me".

Puma had expected such an answer, and he had prepared for such an event as this. He replied. "This being the case then I shall travel to this place Washington, and examine the paper."

This took Philip by surprise. He was at a loss for words for a long time. Finally he told Puma that he would use the telegraph, and he would attempt to set up a meeting. He left the office briefly to dispatch an assistant to send the message. They sat in silence for about an hour. The assistant returned with a yellow piece of paper.

Philip read the message on the paper, and said. I have been advised that there is to be a meeting in Congress. This meeting concerns the affairs of the Indian. This meeting is to be held in three weeks time. It is the desire of my boss that you, Tonka and myself travel to Washington to participate in these hearings. We will ride on the railroad that crosses from the west to the east. If this meets with your approval, then return to your village. There you must prepare for the long journey."

When Puma and Tonka returned to the village to prepare for their journey, they were greeted with the sad news that Burning Fire had gone into the hills to die. This caused a problem because Puma was going to leave him in charge of the village while he was away. Now he must select someone to lead the people while he was on his long journey. Burning Fire with all his wisdom was gone, and he needed Tonka to go with him, as a witness to insure that the knowledge gained on the trip would get back to the people in the event that something should happen to him. He decided on the Chief of the Sioux, Running Bear. The Sioux Tribe was the smaller of the tribes among the people but their leader was one of the more experienced. Running Bear had been with Sitting Bull at the Little Big Horn.

Chapter 37

Having made the necessary preparations Puma and Tonka returned to the settlement to meet Philip. Puma was dressed in a buckskin suit that had been made for him by the women of the village. It was made of the best deerskin, and the workmanship was the best he had ever seen. He wore the two knives, one on either side. He walked tall and proud. There was no doubt that he was a man of authority.

They met Philip and his assistant along with a group of six soldiers. The soldiers were under the leadership of a Major Kent. They were to escort them to Washington. There was no need for the escort except that this was a military formality. They went to the train in a horse drawn carriage of fine workmanship.

They were escorted to a special car on the train. Puma was amazed at the decorations within the car. There were large paintings on the walls, and there were soft seats at small table. Also the car was equipped with four small beds along the wall. Philip said that this would be their home for several days. He also said that at the end of the journey they would stay in a place called a hotel. Puma ask what was this hotel? He learned that a hotel is a large building where travelers stay when they are in a strange town.

After about an hour of waiting Puma heard a loud whistle and then the train began to move. He had seen this before but Tonka had not, and Tonka was a bit uneasy until he got the feel of the rocking and bumping motion of the car. This was to be a long journey. Puma intended to learn all he could along the way. It would also be necessary to teach Tonka some of the ways of the White Man. Tonka had never sat at a table. Or ate with the tools of the Whites. They neither one had ever seen the game that the White Man played, called cards. They were amused at this game, but had no interest in learning such a game. They would spend the long hours sitting by the windows to and observe the changing territory as they moved along the never-ending ribbons of steel below them. They were to cross many rivers, and pass through many mountains before they reached the flat farmlands of Colorado and Kansas.

As the train left the mountains behind, the land became more or less the same as any other prairie. The travel was slow, and Puma and Tonka were already getting restless. What made them more restless was they knew that the journey had barely begun. Puma longed to be once again a young brave alone with his pony and with no cares except the condition of the weather. However, he knew that this would never again be the life he would lead.

Tonka on the other hand was absorbing every thing around him. He was seeing things that most Indians would never see. He was seeing large herds of fatted cattle, sheep, and goats. He was seeing grasslands where the grass was so thick that one could not see the earth from which it grew. This flat land went to the east as far as the eye could see and the mountains were continually getting smaller in the west. He wondered what else he might see before returning to their village.

They were offered whiskey on many occasions. This they refused because they believed that whiskey covered the mind as the clouds cover the sun. They believed that if the mind was thus clouded then the wisdom needed could not direct them in their daily activities. It seemed that everyone on the train was having a good time. Maybe this was because they knew what was at the end of the ride. Puma, and Tonka did not know what might be ahead. Therefore, they were in constant conversation, or thought about the future.

When the train approached the border between the states of Colorado, and Kansas everything looked about the same. However, Kansas had been a state longer, and the many cattle herds from the south had caused many more people to settle near the towns that had the railroad. The fields were larger, and were better prepared. A lot of the houses were white washed with children and flowers in the yards.

Tonka asked about a building that had a high pointed shaped thing on top. Puma explained that this was the same thing to the White Man that a Kiva was to the Indian. That it was called a church it was where the Whites honored their God.

When the train reached Dodge City Kansas, they were told that they would be here for a while. The train was going to take a load of cattle. Having never been in Dodge, but being familiar with a cattle town, Puma chose to stay close to the cattle pens. He and Tonka were leaning on the rail fence watching the cows being loaded when Puma heard a familiar voice. He turned and located the source of the sound. To his amazement he was looking into the faces of Amos and Pedro. not twenty feet away. After their greetings they explained that they had gone back to Texas and made a second drive with Harvey.

Puma immediately ask where he could find Harvey. He was directed to the buyer's office. Puma had just come upon a plan. He would need Harvey, and his two friends to make it work. Just as he got to the office, Harvey stepped out carrying a pouch of money, along with his tally book. Harvey was amazed to see the third of his former cowhands. Puma had carried Amos and Pedro with him to see Harvey.

"Harvey my friend I have a great task before me and I need people that I can trust to help me carry out a plan I have for my people. I have found that I am the Chief of a great tribe of mixed Indians in Utah. I am on my way to Washington to settle matters between the Government and my people. It is my desire that Amos and Pedro go with you back to Texas and return with you next summer. When you return here next, I will meet you here with a group of my people and purchase five hundred head of your best cattle. Then with the help of Amos and Pedro I will take the cattle to my land. There I will raise my own herd. I will pay Amos and Pedro for the work they perform while with you."

After completing the arrangements with Harvey, and his two friends, it was time to again return to the train.

As the train moved further east the lands began to change again. There were more fields and other signs of the invasion of the Whites. There were more settlements with many more very small children. To Puma this was a sign that these people had been settled here for a longer period of time. He assumed that for the most part they intended to remain in this area. These were not the people that Puma was concerned with. He was interested in the many wagons that he observed traveling west. He knew that these wagons contained men searching for unclaimed lands, or were in search of gold. The settlers in this area seemed to be at ease with the world. They seemed to have no desire to make trouble for them selves or anyone else.

As they entered Missouri, the land as well as the people, seemed to be the same as in Kansas. Seeing nothing that seemed different, Puma sat looking out the window while returning to his thoughts of his people, and his plans for them. He was trying to determine what he would say to the Congress that would best relay to them the current conditions in the west. He felt that he would have a difficult task trying to convince the White Man to give anything to an unknown people in a distant land. They did not realize that it was beyond the Indian to lie or to misrepresent the facts. They would think that he was begging for things that they really did not need. He must talk with assurance, and determination. He would call on Philip to vouch for what he was telling them. He knew that Philip was an honest man, but he also realized that Philip worked for the white government. Phillip must obey the orders given him. Puma must carefully portray to the congress, the exact needs of the west, and depend on the common sense of men to know, or understand the needs of other men. He must paint a word picture that would best show the Congress the dire condition of the people of the frontier.

When the train reached a place called St. Louis Puma saw a mighty river that ran from the north to the south. He asked Philip what was this river and was told. "This is the Mississippi river, the mightiest of the rivers in the land. It rises in a place called Minnesota. From there it flows to the great salt water in the south. It is joined by another river here in St. Louis, the longest river in the land. That river is called the Missouri. The Missouri

River rises in the mountains of southwestern Montana. Further to the south the Mississippi is joined by the Ohio River. This river comes from the east in Pennsylvania. Still further south it is joined by the Arkansas River. The Arkansas flows from the west. It is the same river that flows through the great canyon at Canyon City."

Puma was well acquainted with the Arkansas River. He appreciated the lesson of the land given him by Philip. He would store it in his memory for further study.

Tonka had not learned the language of the whites. Puma had to interpret all that was said. Tonka asked many questions because he was seeing things that he did not know to exist. Both he, and Puma saw for the first time the large riverboats.

Philip told them that this was the way the whites carried their supplies, and their people from town to town along the river. There was smoke coming from a pipe on the top. This reminded them of the train engine. These boats were not paddled like an Indian canoe but had large wheels on the back that pushed the water out behind. The French had been the first whites to come to this part of the country. But people from many countries in Europe soon joined the French. Puma and Tonka knew that Europe was a place far across the great salt water where many different Whites lived.

The train crossed the river on a huge bridge, and soon left St. Louis behind. Once they had crossed the river things began to change. The land, in the east, as Philip called it was different. But the main difference was the way people went about their daily lives. There were no longer the big covered wagons but smaller wagons and many carriages that carried the people. They used these carriages more than they rode horseback. Their clothing was somewhat different. Their tools were better than in the west. Puma was explaining everything to Tonka the best he could, but he was also placing all these images in his memory for future use.

Tonka was very impressed with what Puma had learned while traveling in search of his vision, or destiny. Now that he had been appointed Sub Chief and was to assist Puma, he was determined to learn as much as possible from Puma, and the experiences that they were having together. At first the ride in the confined space of the train was somewhat boring. But now he realized that he was involved in a changing world. Therefore, he took in everything that was said, and everything he saw. They were now in a place called Illinois. The further they went, the more the country turned from a vast wilderness into a very large settlement.

Phillip had told them that Illinois had been a state for over seventy years. He also told Tonka that what to him was a summer was a year to the Whites. He said that the state was called the Prairie State even though it did not look like the prairie that they both were familiar with. Tonka noticed that the people in this area had cows that were different from the cows being driven into their country. He learned that these cows were raised to supply milk along with a thing called butter for the farmers. They also raised birds that were called chickens. The supply of eggs that the Whites needed did not have to be gathered from the nest of wild birds. They also had turkeys that were different from the wild ones from the land of the Rio Bravo. Many of the homes had holes dug in the ground that were called wells. Tonka learned that a well was a source of water. and the water was removed from the well by a wooden bucket attached to a rope. He also noticed that some of the wells were covered with a wooden structure with a large wheel on top. The wind would turn the wheel pulling the water from the ground. The whites called these windmills. Philip said that many of the houses had water inside. Water was also pumped from the ground by using small hand pumps. Puma and Tonka noticed that at night there was light coming from the inside of them that was obviously not created by a large fire. Philip explained the use of the gaslight and kerosene lamp to make light. He said that in some parts further east there was a light created by a new power source called electricity.

Tonka was beginning to learn the tongue of the Whites and hoped some day that he could also learn to read and write these English words, the same as did Puma. After turning this trip into a learning adventure the days did not seem to be so long. In fact he would lay awake at night wondering what the next day would bring.

The next day did bring them into a country called Indiana. There they were told that this state was a couple of years older than Illinois. It was here that the Whites had factories. A factory was a building where the cloths and tools were made. As they passed through the settlements, they noticed that the country surrounding the factories was not as clean as the area to the west.

While traveling through the state of Ohio and then into West Virginia they saw much the same things only more of them. It was when they arrived in Washington D.C. that they began to see a major change in the people. They were told that this city had been the capitol of the United States since 1800. When asked about this 1800, they were told that this meant that it was 1800 years since the death of Jesus, the son of the White Man's God. That the Whites measured the years before the birth of Christ with a number followed with the letters B. C. and the years after his death with the letters A.D.

There were many people on the streets of Washington, and there were carriages everywhere. Some of these were made of the finest material and carried people, while others were plain and used to transport material and supplies.

The clothing that the people wore was also somewhat different. A lot of the men wore pants and coats made of the same material with white ruffled shirts under the coat. Many of the coats had long split tails that came down around the knees. The hats of the men were usually black in color. Some of these were very tall and some of them were shorter and more rounded. A lot of the men carried a short stick with a fancy knob on top. These they learned were called canes. The women wore long dresses that were usually very colorful. These dresses came almost to the ground. Their shoes were high top and appeared to be buttoned around their legs. The women wore very colorful hats. And they carried a thing called a parasol that when opened it would provide shade over them, but for the most part these were just for show.

There were many large buildings along the streets. As they passed a large building located on a big piece of land, Philip told them that this was the Capitol and where the Congress met to conduct the countries business. This would be where they would go to make their presentation at the scheduled time. The carriage that they were riding in stopped in front of a large building. They were told that this was their hotel. It was here that they would stay while they were in Washington. When they were shown their room they were given a small metal object called a key. When they asked what the key was used for they were told that it opened the door to their room. Philip said that in the city it was necessary to keep buildings and rooms locked. He said that the locks were placed there to keep out people that were not supposed to be there. He knew that Puma and Tonka would not understand the act of theft. The only thing that the Indian ever took that did not belong to him was taken on large raids.

The first order of business for Puma was to seek out the main office of Indian Affairs. He requested to see the original treaty. At first his request was ignored until he advised them that he was going before their Congress in two days.

For the next two days they walked around this large town, where they drew the attention of the people on the streets. They paid no attention to the stares of the people because they were too busy observing and learning.

Shortly after sun rise on the third day a carriage took them to the Capitol, and they were escorted inside.

They were escorted into a large room that was filled with men all dressed in dark suits. They were placed in a row of seats near a large platform that was at the front of the room. There were several men on the platform. After several minutes one of the men rose and walked to a small desk like thing in the center of the platform. He picked up a wooden hammer, and struck the top of the desk. After the room grew silent he began to speak.

"Gentlemen, we today are assembled to take up the subject of the affairs of the American Indian. We have here today the honor of hosting a great Chief who represents a large nation of his people. It is my understanding that he will address us on behalf of all Indians in our great country. But first let me call on Mr. Philip Petty, our agent from the territory of Utah."

Phillip rose and climbed up to the platform and quietly looked around the room.

"Distinguished Gentlemen, I have been honored, over the past several years, to be the placed in the job of representing my government in the affairs of the Indian, in the west. I have found that for the most part, all of these people are honorable and trustworthy. One who is more qualified to make this presentation than any other man I know has come this great distance to address this group. It is he that I have brought to this session of Congress. And it is he that I will allow to state their case."

Philip then called on Puma to come forward. Puma took Philips place on the platform and gave the Indian sign of greeting.

"I am Chief Puma Two Knives Chief of a large Indian Nation in the north eastern portion of the territory you call Utah. I am not a savage as many have called me. In fact there are no savages among my people. This you will soon see to be true. I have traveled much, learned much of the ways of the White Man. I have learned the native language of most of you. I can read and write the words of the English. In spite of this I was raised as an Indian and will remain true to my people as long as I live.

You did not call yourselves savages when you fought for this country against the Powers of England, France, and Mexico. You did not call the men of the South savages when they fought to keep the Blackman their slaves. Rather you simply called them Rebels. Therefore, I tell you that my people are not savages for standing up for what they think is theirs. My people have owned this land ever since the Ancient Ones crossed the great ice fields to the north. In fact this very place where we are today did not exist just a hundred of your years ago.

Many years ago my people entered into a treaty with the Whites, a treaty of peace. In return for the land, we were promise land of our own and the necessary provisions needed to replace the buffalo that the White hunters have almost destroyed. The leaders who signed the treaty were honorable men and did so in good faith. The Indians that signed the paper could neither read nor write. Therefore, they made their mark on faith alone. I have come here and have read this paper. The provisions of this treaty were not sufficient, or were misused from time to time. It is now necessary for me to enter into an agreement, or new treaty that will be fair to both the Indian, and also to the White settlers in our land.

The greed of some of your people has caused them to spread out across this mighty land like a wild prairie fire. In passing they have over killed the buffalo, many times leaving the meat to rot away. They killed only for the profit that could be gained by taking the hides. The same is true with all wildlife in the land. Soon even the beaver will disappear from the streams. They have taken the gold from the streams and mountains with out any regard as to the conditions they left behind. The spread of these people is so great that your laws, and your Army cannot control them.

A White Holy Man once told me that your God teaches that all people were created equally. If this is truly the belief, I ask then why is it that the women of your nation do not have the same rights to select their elected leaders, as do the men. Even the countries across the ocean have had women leaders called Queens. Many Indian tribes have had women Chiefs.

Your people came to this country in much the same manner, as did our Ancient Ones. Both were looking to expand their worlds and looking for a better place. The Black Man on the other hand was brought to this country by force. He was placed in slavery for the profit of some Whites. They may have come to this world on their own in time, but were captured like animals and shipped to this part of the world.

I realize that by the nature of the way you choose your leaders that the different men in this place have different goals. These differences have brought about conflicting decisions to be made. For example the Indian Territory called Oklahoma was created for the purpose of moving the Indian from one part of this land to another. In fact the very name was taken from the words of the Choctaw word meaning Land of The Red People. After this territory was created, a great number of our people were moved from their homes on the east side of the great Mississippi River to this new territory. The move created what is now known as The Trail of Tears. These people were from some of our more famous tribes. They included the Choctaw, Chickasaw, Creek, Seminole, and Cherokee. After this move you then opened the land and gave it freely to the White Settlers. This effort caused the greed of the Whites to take from their own by claiming some of the land before the legal date. This gave the people the nickname, Sooners. After you had shipped the Indian people from the east side of the great river, you then took the Apache from his home in the west and moved him to the east to a place called Florida.

I have told you of some of the things I have seen. I am now prepared to tell you how your government has fallen short of the provisions that the treaty contained.

First and foremost, you gave us the land to the east of the Great Salt Lake and then allowed the settlers to continue to occupy part of this land. You offered food and supplies to take the place of the vanishing herds of buffalo. This you did in part, however, you did not realize how many of my people occupied this area. This mistake, in not knowing the numbers, led to the hunger now being suffered by my nation. The shipments of cattle were far too small; therefore, they had to be used for food thereby leaving none with which to raise our own herds. The seeds and tools for raising our food were so limited that we cannot produce corn and squash as do the Whites. I fully realize that the error was due in part to the fact that your government did not have enough information. I also realize that your agent in our land cannot properly relay our condition back here over the singing wire, or writing one of his letters.

Our people now occupy a portion of The Utah territory that is located around the meeting of the Green, White, and Strawberry Rivers. I have had your Army mapmaker prepare a detailed map of this area and will submit it, along with a written copy of the following proposal, to the leaders of this gathering.

Our Nation is much like yours. We are a nation of many tribes with one main Chief. Each tribe has it's own Chief and they all join together to decide all matters that concerns the Nation as a whole. I believe that there are those that rule, as well as there are those that are ruled. I also believe, as do you that those that are ruled must select the ones that rule, and abide by their decisions. We enforce the laws and rules of the nation much in the same way that the Whites enforce theirs.

There is much talk in the Territory about Statehood. Therefore, I propose to you that before you allow Statehood you, set aside the lands described on the map for an Indian Nation to be governed by Indians. Also that you give the Agent of that area the proper dollars to provide the supplies, tools, and materials needed by my people, as were promised. I have taken the opportunity to buy a herd of cattle being brought out of Texas as we speak. I also propose that the dollars be enough to make the necessary payment to the owner of this herd. If this is done as I have requested I will assure you that my people will honor all agreements made by me. Then it will be the duty of your Army to make sure that the advancing settlers honor the agreement." Puma then raised his right hand and looked at each man in the room one by one then stepped down from the platform.

There was a moment of silence in the room and then every man rose to his feet and raised his right hand in a salute to the Indian Chief. Then there were shouts, then the clapping of their hands for a long time. Puma knew that this was the White Man's sign of approval. The first man then returned to the desk and hit it with hammer once again.

"We give our thanks to The Great Chief from Utah. And assure him that we will consider his proposal and advise him of our action in due time."

Puma, Tonka, and Philip took leave of the chamber and returned to their hotel. It was the belief of all three that Puma had presented a just and accurate description without casting a shadow on anyone.

Three days passed without any word as to the decision of the congress. Puma was very uneasy, as the time had come for them to prepare to leave Washington. Finally on the morning of the fourth day a detachment of soldiers came to their room. They said that the President wished for them to join him.

President Grover Cleveland sat behind a huge desk in a very large office.

"Welcome Gentlemen it is with great pleasure that I receive such a Great Chief. I am what is known, in politics, as a lame duck President. In a few weeks, I am to be replaced by the newly elected President Benjamin Harrison. However, before I am retired I must continue to attend to the Nation's business. I have before me a bill that was brought before the Congress, and was passed. I am sure that you will find it to your satisfaction. If you do indeed find that it meets the needs of the people of the Indian Nation then I will sign it in to law."

He handed the documents that were several pages long to both Puma and Philip. After they had studied these pages for a long while they advised the President that this bill did in fact cover the needs as Puma had presented them. The President then signed the papers and gave a copy to each and then excused them.

Chapter 38

The next day they were on the train headed west. Puma was again studying the papers he had. As he read the words aloud to Tonka one could see the satisfaction on his brothers face. They were to have the cattle and tools that were equal to those used by the Whites. They also would have the title to the land as was mapped. It was to be called a reservation but to Puma and Tonka it was called a Nation.

The trip west to St. Louis and then to Dodge City was equally as long as the trip east, but to the two proud Indians it did not seem as long.

It was at Dodge City that they were to separate. Philip was returning to Utah and Puma and Tonka were to go on to the Fountain Colony. Puma had plans that he must talk to Ena and Paul about. When they arrived in Dodge, Philip went to the bank and cashed a Government draft and gave the money to Puma to purchase two horses and supplies enough for Puma and Tonka to make the rest of their journey to the Fountain colony, then to their Nation. Puma was very careful with the money. He spent only what they had to spend for the necessary supplies.

When they had everything that they would need, they headed west on the trail that would take them to Fountain Colony.

It was getting late into the winter and the strong north wind carried with it occasional snow flurries. Off in the distance one could see that the great mountains were covered with a deep blanket of snow. The bear had gone to sleep for the winter, and the rest of the wild life had come down to the lower levels. Puma's head was filled with so many thoughts that he hardly noticed the cold. On the second day one of the horses came up lame and they had to seek out a settlement to get another. Most of the settlement was nothing more than a ghost town and when they asked about this they were told that most people had moved to a place called Cripple Creek after hearing of a new gold strike there. After securing another horse. They rested for a part of a day then again set out. The long hours passed unnoticed for the two Indians. They were accustomed to being out in the elements, and were thinking ahead to all that must be done, in the coming months and years. Between long periods of thought, Puma continued to teach Tonka the English language. Tonka was a good student. He knew that Puma depended on him to act for him, if the occasion should arise.

It was far into the night when they arrived at the Colony. They made camp just outside of the settlement. Before they slept that night, Puma gave Tonka a brief outline of his immediate plans. When they woke the next morning their blankets were covered with a light dusting of snow. After they had a breakfast of dried meat and parched corn, they went into the settlement to put the plan to work. They searched for a schoolhouse, or a church. When they found them, they found both abandoned. It appeared that neither had been used for several weeks. Puma began to look elsewhere for Ena and Charles, or Paul. Finally, he found an old crippled drunk near the one remaining general store. It was with much effort that they got the information that they were seeking. It seemed that when most of the settlers left for the Cripple Creek area, there was no need for a teacher or preacher. Ena, Charles, and Paul had followed the rest to the gold fields. They were told that the trail to the southwest would take them to this place called Cripple Creek. It was decided that they would seek out this place, and try to locate the friends from Puma's past. The journey was not long. When they arrived, the gold hungry settlement was full of wagons and makeshift huts. They finally located the blacksmith to inquire about the schoolteacher. They were told that there was such a woman in town, and she was using a large tent for her school. The tent was located next to a building that was being used as a church. Puma then knew that he had found his three friends.

When they rode into the churchyard, Paul was standing in the doorway drinking a cup of coffee. His face lit up in a smile as he recognized his old friend from the past.

"Welcome my friend, are you still searching for the knife?"

Puma raised his right hand in greeting and replied that he had found the knife, and was now searching for many other things. He told Paul that the reason he was in this place he was searching for him and Ena.

"You have found us both, and it our desire to make you welcome to our home. You see, since we last saw you, Ena and I have gotten married and Charles has gone back East to study to be a Doctor."

Puma introduced Tonka, and then they went inside the building. He found that they were using the back of the building for a place to live. Inside Ena greeted them; she was very excited to see her old friend and began to ask questions so fast that Puma had no time to answer any of them. Finally she grew silent, and embarrassed by her actions. Puma said. "Sit my friends and I will tell you my story, and of my plans for the future.

I followed my people for many days. At last I found them in a large village located in the Utah Territory, near the Uinta Mountains. It was there that I found the other knife. I also found that I was the son and grandson of Great Chiefs. By their wishes the knives were held for me after their deaths, and that I was destined to be the Chief of my people. The village I had found was a part of a large nation of many tribes. There was not a chief among any of these people. We held council. There it was decided that all would join to make one large nation, and that I would be chief over all. I have been to Washington, and held council with the White Congress and the White President. There it was decided that the White Government would assist me in my efforts to help my people, and help them make the adjustments to a different way of life. This now brings me to the reason I am now visiting with you. I propose to start a school and a church in my Nation, and I am here to ask the two of you to return with me to Utah to teach my people the ways and customs of the White Man. I know that this is a great challenge; the money will be little but the rewards will be many."

Paul then told Puma that one in the business of teaching expected no riches, but gained their rewards from the work. He said that they would think on this proposal, and then give him their answer on the following morning.

The following day Paul and Ena came to the spot where Puma and Tonka were camped. It was Ena that spoke. "We have considered the offer you have put to us. We are now ready to give you our answer. But first I will tell you that I still have the wagon with the tools, of a black smith, and a gunsmith. Also, there is a man and woman here that have the knowledge to use them. They came to this place after the work on the long railroad was completed. They learned to use these tools, repairing the machinery for the railroad. It is my wish if we go with you to Utah; these people are to go with us also. The other people in this place are so hungry for the gold that they have no time, or desire to learn what Paul and I have to teach. If this meets with your approval, we all four will go with you to your Nation. But first you must know that this couple is of yellow skin. They are from a place called China, and have come to this land in search of a better future. Up until now they have been treated much the same as the Black and Indian people."

Puma was very pleased to hear of their decision. He gladly accepted the addition to his plan, as laid out by Ena.

For the next three days they were busy preparing for the long journey to Utah. Puma was introduced to Yung and Ling Chang. He welcomed them to his group. This couple was very happy to be invited to go to this new land, with his group. There they would be treated as equals, and they would act accordingly. The wagons were in good repair. All that was necessary was for them to be loaded with the things belonging to all as well as all the tools. Ena and Paul had many books and the tools needed for teaching. The necessary supplies were obtained. Finally they were ready to leave Cripple Creek.

By sun up on the fourth day, they were on the trail used by many wagon trains and the stagecoaches. The trail was in fair condition, and their progress was good. It was somewhat faster than the other journeys they had shared. This trail would take them Southwest to the Arkansas River at a point to the west of Canyon City. For the first few days the area was relatively level. This allowed them to make the good progress. Puma was very anxious to get back to his Nation with the good news. This would be the first real celebration the people had had in quite a while.

He knew also that he had another long journey to make shortly. He would have to select from the tribes the best horsemen to return with him to Dodge City to meet Harvey and buy the cattle.

The trail they were following would take them across the Arkansas, to the east of Poncha Pass. Then they would cross the Divide at North Pass, which was the lower of the passes. It was only a little over ten thousand feet.

The crossing over the Divide was no simple matter because they encountered strong winds, snow, and countless fallen rocks. Some of these rocks were so large that it took hours to move them. Once they were over the pass they took a turn to the Northwest. This would take them through the Black Canyon, to the Colorado River.

After they reached the Colorado, they followed it for four days over land that was at a higher altitude, but somewhat level. This path would take them to a new settlement called Grand Junction.

Grand Junction was a settlement of farmers for the most part because it offered both land and water suitable for the raising of crops. It was in this settlement that they camped and rested for a few days. They were able to trade for new supplies by using the blacksmith tools, and the skills of Yung Chang. There were no such tools in Grand Junction. The residents tried in vain to get them to settle there. Yung repaired everything from wagons to plows, and this allowed them to obtain enough supplies to carry them the rest of their journey. When the time came for them to leave Grand Junction, they were rested and well prepared for the journey to the north. In another six, or eight days they would be at the White River and another day would bring them to the border between the state of Colorado and the Utah Territory. Crossing this border would then put them in the new Indian Nation. In three or so more days, they would be home. By this time all were getting weary of travel, and living out in the open. However, they left Grand Junction with renewed spirits.

The trip to the White River was uneventful. They encountered no difficulty crossing the Douglas Pass. Even though they were very anxious to get to their destination, they stayed on the banks of the White River a couple of days to refresh the horses. Puma and Tonka were very tired after the long trip to Washington, and the many days in the saddle since. Their bodies were tired, but their spirits were high because of all they had accomplished. By this time Tonka was speaking the English language very well. As time permitted, he was beginning to read and write. He would return to his village a very proud Indian.

Four days later they were back in the village. There they were met with much rejoicing. Puma advised the people that with the rising of the next sun he would hold council, and tell all what they had been able to accomplish. This word spread fast. By sun up the next day, the entire nation had assembled for the great council.

The council was assembled with the masses on the outside of the circle, and the Chiefs in the inner circle. The pipe was passed; nothing was said until all had smoked. Puma then rose, and looked to the people with much pride.

"When I last spoke to you in council, Tonka and I were about to go on a mission to help our people. This we have done, and we have had great success. A treaty has been made with the White Man's Government, and it is the law that the land on which we are now located has been set aside for our people. Our Nation is to begin at the Colorado border. From this point it will extend about two days ride to the south, then three and a half days to the west. It will cover the joining of the White, Green, and Strawberry Rivers. It will include most of the Green to the south, and most of the Strawberry to the west. It will go into the great forest to the north. It had been determined that all white settlers will be removed from this land, and only the Indian Agent and a small portion of the soldiers will be permitted on our land. These soldiers duty will at first be to remove the Whites. Then they will keep new Whites from entering our land. You will hear this land called a reservation, but you will call it a Nation. The new treaty provides that I will purchase a herd of cattle. I will bring them here, so that in the future we can raise our own meat. Until that time the white Government will provide the meat for our nation. It will give the necessary tools to work our land and cattle. We are to have tools, and food supplies that are equal to those of the Whites. Also I have brought with me some people that will be very important to the development of our

Nation. I have brought Ena a white schoolteacher, and her husband Paul, a white man of God. They will teach you the ways of the white man, not to be used as your ways. This will enable you to conduct business with the Whites on an equal basis. In the future I hope to have Ena's son join us as a White Medicine Man. He will attend to the white sickness that might occur in our nation.

Shortly I will be leaving on a journey to Dodge City to acquire the cattle, I have told you of. While I am gone I will leave Tonka in charge and he will be able to answer any questions that you have as well as deal with the Indian Agent.

While I am gone, I want a party of scouts to ride with Tonka. They will explore the exact boundary of our nation. He has a map that was provided us by the army. This map shows the limits of our land. You will not assist the army in their efforts to remove the Whites from our land, but will report their location to the Indian Agent. When I return, I will appoint braves to patrol the land. That is all I have to say at this council for I have much to do in the coming days."

That night there was much singing and dancing in the village. The people were celebrating the news that Puma had brought. Puma had little time for celebrating, because he must prepare for a return trip to Dodge City. He must meet Harvey and conclude the purchase of the cattle. He had each of the Chiefs select two braves from their tribes to go with him to drive the cattle to Utah. He asked that the best horsemen be selected. He told these Braves that this would be a long and hard ride, because time was growing short.

After three days of resting and gathering supplies, they were at last ready to make the trip to Dodge. Puma was very pleased with the Braves selected, and noted that each had an extra horse. They would take the same trail that he had been on only a short time before.

Tonka sat about the task of getting Ena, Paul, Yung, and Ling settled and preparing a place for them to live and work. The people of the Nation accepted them as they would another Indian. They did this because this was the wish of their Chief. In fact there was a ceremony whereby they were made members of the Shoshone Tribe.

Puma stopped at the office of Philip to get the necessary Government draft with which to pay for the cattle. Philip told Puma that the Army had already begun to remove settlers from the land. He said that the settlers were offering some resistance. But that the final outcome would be that the orders of the President would be obeyed. He also told him that he had received a dispatch advising him that many of the supplies that were promised were, already on the way to Utah.

Chapter 39

Paul and Ena continued to live in their wagon while, Paul and Tonka selected a site for their home. It was decided that they would build one large log building with a portion being used for the school and church and a portion for their living quarters. Shortly, the first of the supply wagons began to arrive. There were several wagons with four draft horses for each. After all the supplies were unloaded, these wagons would be used to haul the logs from the forest of the north to the village. Philip had included some things that Puma had overlooked. There was a detachment of soldiers with the wagons. They were to assist in teaching the Indians how to use the axe and saw. They were to show them the proper way to construct a log building. The soldiers were under the leadership Sergeant Murphy. They were very efficient in the art of designing, and building the type of structures needed.

Sergeant Murphy was an Irish Veteran of the Indian wars. He understood the feelings of the Indians. He had left his home in Ireland to escape the religious war that had been there for centuries. He himself had come to this country to have a better way of life; therefore he knew and understood the wishes of the Indian. It was also his wish that the many different people on the frontier could learn to live and work together to build a stronger country.

Tonka carefully selected the work party, paying attention to selecting the same number from each tribe represented. The Braves fell to the task even though they really did not know what a school, or church was. In fact they really did not understand what was happening in their nation. It was not their nature to ask questions when asked to do something they did not understand. After the necessary preparations were made they were off to the forest, for their instructions and labor.

Meanwhile, Puma had left the Army Post. He was traveling East along the White River then South to Grand Junction. By this time the days seemed very long, and he was weary from the many weeks of travel that he had endured prior to this trip. Since they were equipped with an extra horse each, the party made exceptionally good time. Puma was pleased with their progress because he knew that the herd from Texas would soon be in Dodge City. He also knew that the return trip would be long because the Braves were not familiar with driving cattle. He would have to depend on Pedro and Amos to provide much of the necessary instructions. By the time they reached Grand Junction the Braves were getting restless because many of them had never been out of the Utah Territory. They could not understand how far they must travel in a strange land. Off to the East they could see the great mountains that they were to cross. The sight of these mountains told them that they were going to have a very cold journey.

After they came down from the high peaks into the lower levels of the area along the Colorado and Kansas border, the weather got somewhat milder. They were on the Arkansas River riding toward Dodge City. The Braves were wondering about this thing called a cattle drive. It had been explained in detail, but they were not accustomed to riding slow. They knew that the trip back to their Nation would be even longer than the trip they were now on. Although they were familiar with working together when hunting, or in some cases raiding in the past they were not certain of their future assignment. The weather had warmed, and the sun was bright. This was welcomed after the cold diving winds in the mountains.

At last they were on the open prairie just south of Dodge City. There they had set up camp and were resting themselves, and their horses. Puma went into town and found out that the herd had not arrived. but it was expected any day. He returned to camp and prepared to get the rest that his body told him that he needed.

For five days they waited in the camp, and late one afternoon they heard the cattle, they could see the dust to the south. Since his people did not have the skill needed to separate the cattle, Puma rode alone to meet the approaching herd. It seemed to him that this herd was larger than the one he had helped bring to Abilene. As he approached the herd from the center he could not see the outside either to the East, or to the West. He worked his way through the herd and greeted some of the cowboys that he knew from the past. Near the back of the herd he spotted Harvey and the chuck wagon.

"Hello my Indian friend have you come to ride drag with me?" was Harvey's greeting.

After they had exchanged greetings, Puma and Harvey withdrew to the side out of the dust and completed their business. Harvey had already cut out the cattle that were to be transferred to Puma. They were being kept as a smaller herd to the west. When Puma asked about Amos and Pedro, he was told that they were with the smaller herd. They rode out to look at the smaller batch of cows. When they approached, Puma noticed that there were two extra wagons to the rear of the herd.

Just then Pedro rode up and greeted them, and after a short time Amos arrived. "We have news for you my Indian friend. Since we last rode together Pedro and I have each taken a wife, and we have brought them along to travel with us to your new land. It is there that we plan to make our home with your people. My wife is called Rebecca, Pedro's wife is called Rosa"

As if it was a great light, the vision of his childhood returned to Puma. The four squaws and five men now had faces in the vision. He knew for certain that the vision had been of Ena, Charles, Paul, Yung, Ling, Amos, his wife, Pedro, and his wife. Puma now knew that the Great Spirits did send the Indian visions to predict the future events in their lives.

Although they were very weary, the two couples were anxious to be on the trail to Utah. Puma left, and returned shortly with his Indian companions. After explaining to the Braves what each must do, they were on the trail back the way they had come. The Braves learned, and adjusted to the new task very quickly. The element of time was lost to them because each day was the same. Only the earth around them changed. For the time being, travel was very slow. Pedro said that they must allow the cattle to graze their way because soon they would be in the mountains where the grass would not be as plentiful. The two women were quite capable of handling the wagons and providing food for the group. The Braves were not familiar with the type of food that they prepared, but found it to be very tasty. They ate it eagerly. The days turned into weeks and then into months. The trail before them was now growing very short, but of course this could not be known to any but the Indians.

Finally as they camped one night Puma went to the wagons of Amos and Pedro and told them that in one more day they would be at the office of the Indian Agent Philip. And then the next stop would be the main village of the Nation.

After over a year of travel Puma was at last home again, having completed the two journeys successfully. He was so weary that at first he did not notice the change in his village. It was only after being welcomed by Tonka that he was made aware of the changes.

He saw the completed walls of a large log building. Also there was a smaller log hut with a separate Kiva.

It was Tonka that spoke first. "Welcome home Great Chief, your people have been preparing for your return. Much had been accomplished while you were gone. The tools have arrived. With them we have prepared the fields for planting, and have begun the building of your school and church. Tonight there will be singing and dancing to celebrate your safe return. First there is much I must tell you about our new land. There is much land where we can grow good corn and squash. This land can be watered in the same manner as used by the Whites of the Great Salt Lake. There is good hunting in the forest of the north where there are still many onions and berries growing. The turkey and the deer are in good supply in these woodlands. If hunted properly, they will supply our Nation for many years. Also to the west, in the open country, there is still a small herd of Buffalo. It is said that these buffalo are off springs of a herd brought to this land many summers ago by a Kiowa Apache, called Running Fox, and presented to your Grandfather. There are also many Antelope on our land. High in the mountains there are many mountain goats and big horned sheep. There are other things to be told but I will wait for the celebration this night."

Puma was very pleased by the report made by Tonka. He was looking forward to hearing more, but first he must rest for a few hours.

When Puma had had a short rest, he went out into the village to examine the progress that had been made while he was away. He was curious about the completed cabin that stood empty on the outer edge of the village. He was very pleased to find that the larger building only needed the roof to be completed, and then it would be ready for use. Paul told him this would be completed soon and then would be put to use by both he and Ena for the teaching of his people. He also noticed that the village had been cleaned somewhat. The tepees were still faded and ragged but had the appearance of being better kept. This told him that the Indian pride was returning.

By this time darkness was approaching, and a great fire was burning in the center of the village. The people were gathering for the celebration, and to hear what Puma and Tonka would talk about.

Sergeant Murphy and his soldiers were invited to sit in on this celebration because by this time they seemed to be a part of the Nation. There was to be no official Indian business to be brought before a formal council.

Walking Bird the Medicine Man, of the Hopi tribe, was the official in charge of this celebration. He walked to the center of the gathering, and officially opened the celebration. He first gave praise to the Great Spirits, one at a time, for all the good fortune that they had bestowed on the many tribes of the nation. After all the rituals were completed, he called for Tonka to come forward.

Paul was amazed at how much this meeting followed the same format that is usually used in such meetings of his people. While their Gods were different, their beliefs and procedures were very similar to those of all people of the world.

Tonka stepped forward into the light of the great fire. He was dressed in the full attire of a Chief and looked very much the part of a great leader.

"It is I, Tonka, that most of you know very well. Our Great Chief, Two Knives, is not so well known to all of you, Therefore, I feel that I must give you some of his history. He was raised as my brother in the barren country near the Rio Bravo. He is the blood son of a Great Chief and his Mother was part white. He was made an orphan at the age of six summers when his Mother was killed by a band of raiding Mexicans. He has traveled far, and learned many things over the past eight summers. The Great Spirits have guided him to this place in order that he could use this knowledge to lead his people to a better life. He knows the ways of many of the people of the outside world, but practices those ways only when dealing with those people. I tell you that in fact he is really an Indian's Indian. His belief is that of an Indian and he will never believe otherwise. All of these things have given our Chief wisdom far beyond his years.

Today the people of his nation will honor him by giving him the new log hut that was prepared while he was away on his last journey. Also a private Kiva in which he can retire and call on the Great Spirits for the visions to lead the Nation. Also the Braves of the Sioux Tribe have captured and trained a great white stallion that is now presented to him as a symbol of his position in our Nation.

I first knew him as The Boy With Brown Hair, but now we all know that he is Chief Puma Two Knives. I now call our Great Chief forward to present him with the kindling to start his first fire in his new hut."

Puma rose and went to the center of the gathering. All the people crowded closer in order to see and hear their Chief better. He did not look the part of a great leader because he was stilled dressed in the clothing that was covered with the dust of the trail.

"I stand before you today to accept the gifts that you have given me. I am not yet a great Chief. Great is a title that a man must earn, however, I am the son and grandson of Great Chiefs. It is true that I have learned the language and customs of the Whites, Mexicans, French, Chinese, and many more. I knew not at the time I was learning these things that it was for a purpose. The Great Spirits presented me with the opportunity and gave me the inner urge to learn. I have brought these things here to teach my people the necessary things to communicate with the outside world. This is not to change your ways, or your customs but simply to allow you to understand what is happening in this changing world. It is my belief that an Indian must always remain an Indian. I have brought some of the people from other worlds here and made them members of my tribe. They are of different origin and color and represent only a small portion of the great number of different people that live around the world. The reason, for their being here, is to teach and at the same time learn. These that I have assembled here represent the vision that was sent to me when I was alone on the prairie, in the far away place called Texas. I am looking forward to the opportunity of working with these people, as well as all of you here, to make ours the greatest Indian Nation the Spirits have ever created. But for now it is time for much singing and dancing."

Puma and Tonka retired to the outer circle and sat watching the dancing. It was during this ceremony that several of the Braves each took a wife from the group of young maidens that were assembled for the purpose of selecting a husband. This, thought Puma, was a great thing and had not been practiced for several moons. Before the couples were joined, each of the Braves presented gifts to the maiden's father. To the Indian it was a custom to give these gifts. They did not consider it the purchase of a wife, but rather they were honoring the parents for being allowed into their family. It was near dawn when the dancing stopped, and the people retired to their homes. Now Puma could go to his hut to sleep inside for the first time in a long time. When he entered the hut he found that it had been completely furnished with everything that he might need. It had a straw bed covered with several buffalo robes, a fireplace complete with wood and items for eating and drinking. On the wall hung a beautiful buffalo skull headdress. Next to the skull was a decorated long spear. These items were decorated with the different markings of all the tribes of the nation. This told him more than words could. It told him that all of the people here had united as one tribe.

He went to the river to wash the dust, of the trail, from his body. Returning to the hut clad only in a loincloth he lay on his new bed to get the sleep that he had denied himself of over the past months.

When he awoke it was past midday, the village was very active. The roof of the big building was almost completed. The people were working with a renewed pride, and it was as if they were trying to meet a deadline. For the first time in many summers they had hope for the future. The children and dogs were running and playing like he had never seen them do before. The sights of the people assured him that the long journeys had been worthwhile.

He found Tonka and Sergeant Murphy in front of the shed that housed the tools and building materials. Tonka told Puma that Amos had done a great job in teaching the Nation to raise the food crops that were needed. Also gave praise to Pedro for his teaching the young Braves how to manage the cattle.

Puma felt that he now had nearly all the pieces for this great puzzle, and all that remained was to put them all together. The only thing left was that if indeed Charles returned as a doctor to assist the Medicine Men in administering to the needs of all. But for the time being this chore would remain the duty of the Army Surgeon.

Sergeant Murphy told him that the Army had supplied the Nation with guns to be used for hunting. Also, that he was in the process of teaching the Braves the proper care and use of these.

Meanwhile the Army was having some difficulty removing some of the Whites from the reservation. There had been several standoffs in which a few people had been injured, and some settlers had to be removed by force. But the entire Nation was being cleared of all but those that belonged on the land. The cattle had been moved to a place where there was ample grass and water. There was a group of Braves assigned to guard them. Also another group was assigned to watch and protect the small herd of remaining Buffalos. From these two herds only bulls were to be taken and then only at a time designated for this.

Amos, Rebecca, Pedro, and Rosa were getting settled into the village and they seemed to be received well by the Indian population. This was because their chief had made them members of his tribe. Of course there was some resentment by a few, but that seemed to be the natural reactions of all societies.

"With the rising of the next sun I will take Tonka, Amos, and Pedro out into the land to make myself familiar with the land and the task before us." Puma told Sergeant Murphy.

As the days passed Puma spent many hour riding and examining the various areas of his nation. He visited the different tribes to determine their particular needs. He assured them that they were to continue their culture and habits. He assured them that the new things that he had brought into their world was for them to use only if it became necessary. To his surprise he found that all Indians were just as eager to learn, as was he, this pleased him.

Several weeks later he was called back to the village. When he arrived he found a group of men from the people of the Great Salt Lake. It was their desire to have a meeting with the Chief of this new nation. They wished to establish a good relationship with their new neighbors. After their greetings one of the men stepped forward to speak for the group.

"We appreciate the fact that you received us as friends. It is our desire to enter upon a bartering agreement with your people. We realize that you have different customs, and are not necessarily fond of our customs. We do not wish to impose these customs on your people. We do not intend to adopt any of the ways of the Indian. We simply want to establish a trade relationship with your people in order that we can supply some of the things we have in return for things that you might have, that we need. We feel that this would be of benefit to all since we are far from the industrial cities of the East."

Puma told them that that he would take the matter before the council. After which, he would send them word as to their decision. He knew that he had the power to make such a decision, but that was not the way he wanted this Nation to be governed.

It was decided that a trade agreement would be for the good of both the Mormons and the Indians. Therefore Puma sent a runner to the Salt Lake People with the message. This messenger was to be accompanied by three soldiers because the messenger would be going outside of the boundary of his land. Also it would serve to show that this was an official visit. The guidelines for the coming and going of the people from both parties, of this agreement, were established. An official trade route was established by which the trading parties must travel. Thus a trading relationship was established between the Whites and the Indians.

The work continued in the villages. Those that wished to have log houses were building them and those that preferred the Tepee retained them. As far as Puma could determine, there was no conflict among the tribes. However, they were still bothered from time to time by the attempts of the white settlers trying to claim part of the land. Usually these settlers were removed without conflict.

Chapter 40

It was in the early spring and all the creatures of nature were beginning to show the usual activity of the season. The animals and birds were preparing raise their young. The earth was being prepared for planting. The winds were softer and warmer. Puma was taking his usual weekly ride among the people. It had been five summers since he had returned from Dodge City with the cattle. By applying the Indian customs of taking only what was needed, and wasting nothing the herd had tripled in size. The greed of the white man had depleted the buffalo herd in the surrounding lands. In their frantic search for land and gold the vast majority of whites had wasted many of the things that they would need later. The people had grown accustomed to eating beef and making their leather goods from cowhide. The buffalo herd had also expanded because it no longer had to supply all the necessities of life. They had acquired sheep and goats and were kept in the high country away from the cattle. Pedro had done a good job of managing the cattle, sheep, and goats. Amos also had been successful at determining the planting and harvest seasons for this part of the country.

There was much game in the forest, such as the deer, and especially the turkey. There were antelope on the open plains, bear and cougar in the hills and higher rocks.

There were many new children in the nation and family life had greatly improved. All of these things pleased Puma, but inside him there was great unrest. There was something missing and he could not pin it down. He spent many hours alone in the forest, or his Kiva searching for the vision that would supply the missing part or idea. The Army had long since retreated from the Nation. The only person in the nation that was not a part of a tribe was the Indian Agent, Philip with his wife and two children. All of the children that were of age were learning to speak and write the English language. There were also special sessions for the adults. All that desired to learn were urged to attend these sessions. Therefore, all but the very old could speak in at least two tongues.

The trade agreement between the Mormons and the Indians had proven to be a success. Trading was expanded to other settlers outside the Nation. Therefore, the nation now had a good supply of the White Man's gold and money. Still there seemed to be the missing part.

When he returned to his hut he was met by Ena, "I wish to talk to you, Chief Puma about the school. We have outgrown the original building and there are two many students for one teacher. I am in need of a second teacher to assist me with the duties of the school. For this I will really need a person that can speak English as well as the language of the Indian. I myself have learned much over the past five years, but feel that I need help from one of your people. I started this project with only the knowledge that I learned from you while we traveled from Texas to Colorado.

This request is not all that I wanted to talk to about. I have received word that Charles will finish school in another year and it is his wish that he can bring his knowledge here and establish his medical practice among your people."

Puma was very glad to hear of Charles's wish to join them in the Nation. He must think on what else Ena had said. He did not know of such a person as she had described. This was another part of the puzzle that he had not thought about. However, he would give it much though, and call on the Spirits to assist him. He knew that Ena was right and knew that sooner or later this need would surface. With the ever increasing number of children in the Nation, and other Indians from outside the nation moving in a few at a time it would be impossible to operate in the manner that they had in the past. Even Amos had two small children now and Pedro had one.

That night as he lay on his bed he allowed his memory wander back over the past thirteen years. Finally his memory settled on the time he had spent with the people of the ancient cliff dwellings. It was there that the idea of a real Indian Nation had started to form. Then the other piece of the puzzle seemed to fall into place.

He would return to the cliffs, and if Gentle Dove had not taken a husband he would ask her to be his wife for was he now not worthy of a Princess. Suddenly the dark cloud that hung over his mood vanished. Thanks to Ena's request, he found that which was missing from his life.

He called Tonka to him early the next morning and told him of his plans to make the journey to the southwestern section of Colorado. Tonka was very pleased because he too had taken a wife and knew that it was a family that makes a complete man. He said that he would look after the affairs of the Nation while Puma was gone. Both men set about making preparations for Puma's journey.

Being one to never waste time, Puma was ready to leave the next day just as the sun rose. He had acquired the necessary supplies and selected four additional horses besides the four he would use on the journey. Then he was on the trail that he had traveled before. Since it was the beginning of spring he knew that the weather would not be a problem. Now that he had set his course of action, he rode with determination and a light heart. He intended to cross the border into Colorado. Then he would turn to the South. This offered the best route for a man with a bunch of extra horses. He was anxious, but he would not rush on this trip. Tonka was quite capable of taking care of the affairs of the Nation. He really did not know what he was going to do when he got there. In his thoughts he was searching for a vision, or a plan.

When he arrived at the Colorado River, just east of Grand Junction, he located a good place to camp. It offered good grass for the horses and also some shelter among the trees along the river. He hobbled the horses and set them out in the meadow to feed. He kept the one he was riding with him. It was a belief of his that a man should never be on foot. This turned out to be a wise belief. He went to the river to bathe the dust from himself. When he returned to the meadow, he found that his other horses were gone. The camp was not disturbed. It was apparent that who ever took the horses had only found them and not the camp. He quickly hid all his belongings in the tall reeds along the river, and began to try to pick up the trail of his horses. This did not take long because seven horses plus the ones the thieves rode left an easy trail. The trail he was following was that of seven horses with horseshoes and three without. Therefore, he knew that the thieves were renegade Indians. Yung had made shoes for the horses of the Nation. They would not have suspected that these horses could belong to another Indian. Puma thought that it would not have made any difference to them anyway. Besides the people with his horses were more interested in speed than they were anything else. The trail led to the high country where the trees would hide them from being seen.

Puma followed the trail for two days. On the evening of the second day he could smell the scent of smoke. He pulled up and waited until dark. After it got very dark he could see the faint glow of a fire further up the side of the mountain. He tied his horse to a tree beside the trail, and then made his way up the trail, keeping under cover of the trees.

When he came in sight of the fire, he could see three Apache braves stumbling around the camp. He knew immediately that they must have raided a white man's camp and found some firewater, they appeared very drunk. This was confirmed when he saw one of them drinking from a clay jug. He drew his 38-40-colt pistol from his side and approached the three braves.

"I am Chief Two Knives of the Shoshone Nation. Those horses that you have taken on your last raid belong to me. I hold in my hand the fire stick of the White Man and I am prepared to use it if my horses are not returned to me."

The braves did not know of the extent of their danger, and were not willing to take the chance so they dropped their weapons and backed away. The apparent leader told Puma that the horses were hobbled in a small clearing nearby. He directed all three to lead him to these horses. When they arrived at the clearing they removed the hobbles from his horses. He told them to remove them from their own; He would take them a short distance down the trail and turn them loose.

Two days later he was back on the trail at the Colorado River, and was ready to continue his journey to the cliff dwellings. He knew at the rate he would have to travel it would take five to six more days on the trail.

Chapter 41

Gentle Dove arose in the early morning hours and walked out on the ledge in front of the large Kiva that was attached to their dwelling. First she peered down into the dark canyon below. Then she looked across the way to the canyon wall and the dwellings that were below the rim on the west side. She stood motionless for a long time. She just watched as the shadows slowly descended down, with the rising of the sun. She started each day in this manner; and had, ever since a dream or vision had come to her.

She was a woman of slight build but strong heart. On this particular day she was celebrating her birthday. She was beginning her twenty ninth year. There was not much for the daughter of the chief to do in the dwelling high in the east side of canyon. Even at this age she had not taken a husband. It was decreed that she must marry a man worthy of being brought into the Chief's family. Since there was not such a brave in the area she remained the oldest unwed woman in the entire village.

One night several moons ago, a dream had come to her. In this dream she saw a large white cloud in the sky. From this cloud a rider emerged leading several horses. The dream would not produce a face to the rider. However, he rode up to her. He placed her on one of the horses, then, he rode back into the cloud.

When she awoke the next morning, after the dream she went and met with the Medicine Man. He told her that the cloud represented a far away unknown place. He told her that the rider was also unknown because there was no face on him. He told her that she was going to go with this rider to the unknown place, at some point in her life. Beyond this he could offer no further information. He said that at the proper time the Great Spirits would come to her with the completion of this dream.

After discussing the dream with the Medicine Man, she had immediately started to work on a special dress. It was to be made of bleached doeskin. She spent long hours preparing the skin to the proper shade of white. When the skin was ready she set out to make the dress. This was to be no ordinary dress. It was to be decorated with the finest handy work, with all the colors of a rainbow used in the artwork. There was to be many beads of all of the colors placed on this dress. The task of gathering the colors and beads would be great.

Many hours were spent in the preparation to make the dress. Finally she had everything that she needed. She started the project that would take her nearly a complete summer to finish.

Each morning she would repeat the process of going outside and looking above the canyon in search of the cloud. When no such cloud appeared she would retire to her room of the dwelling to work for the remainder of the day, on the special dress. She believed in her heart that the dream would come true. All the while she thought of this rider but could not possibly determine who he could be. She could not think of any rider that she knew that her father would allow too take his daughter away from him.

At last the dress was completed to her satisfaction and there was nothing left for her to do except wait for the great white cloud.

On the next morning she decided to go below to the bottom of the canyon, this she had not done for a long time. She slowly made her way down the narrow trail and out among the people working in the fields there. They were in the process of gathering the last of the corn that had matured enough for storage. As she walked among the working people she would look up at the rim of the canyon on each side, but there was no sign of a cloud in the sky. There she saw only the brilliant bright Colorado sky.

After hundreds of times, peering up she grew weary. With a saddened heart she decided to return to her dwelling above. As she reached the base of the trail, she turned and took one final look at the rim on the west side of the canyon. It was then that she spotted a single large white cloud just appearing over the edge. She sat on a huge bolder and watched as the cloud slowly drifted from west to east. It came in to full view and she could see that it was the only cloud in the sky. She was so busy watching the cloud that she would hardly move. When the cloud reached the rim on the east side of the canyon she had to move out into the center of the canyon so that she might watch the progress as the cloud made it's way to the east.

The cloud was half hidden by the rim by the time she finally decided that this was not the day of her vision. She took one last look and started back to the trail. To her amazement she could see movement outlined in the center of the great cloud. She held her breath as she realized that this was a lone rider with several horses. Could it be that the Great Spirits were at last reveling to her the meaning of the vision that had come to her in her sleep. Her whole being filled with excitement and she wanted to run up the trail and see if the movement on the rim was real or just her imagination. She stumbled on a small stone and when she looked back to the rim the movement had vanished. She sat beside the trail and stared at the cloud as it disappeared beyond the rim and out of her sight.

High upon the mesa Puma pulled up to the edge of the canyon and peered down at the activity below. Satisfied that all was well below he retreated a ways. There on the mesa, he hobbled his horses. He sought out the trail and started down towards the largest of the dwellings. It was his intention to seek out Chief Grey Hawk, He would ask the Chief about Gentle Dove. At this time he had no knowledge of her situation, or if in fact she was still unwed.

Far below Gentle Dove wanted to rush up the trail to meet the person she saw coming down the trail. She still could not tell what this person looked like. To rush up to this person was not the way an Indian woman must conduct herself. Her face was flushed with excitement and her heart felt as if it would burst from her chest. She returned to the large stone and sat. She was trying to get control of her emotions. She still could not see the face of the new arrival as he approached her father's dwelling. In her heart she was sure that this was her future husband.

313

Puma arrived outside the large dwelling. He asks a brave where he could find Chief Grey Hawk. He was directed to the large Kiva that was part of the structure. He stood in the doorway of the Kiva for a long while. He knew that he must not enter until he was invited. After a long while Grey Hawk rose from the floor where he had been sitting. He waved for Puma to enter.

"I welcome your return visit to my village, you have been gone for quite a long time. Come let us smoke and then we will talk. I must hear of your long journey. I must hear the reason that you have returned to the land of my people."

Puma entered the room and sat on the left of the Chief. Grey Hawk took a burning ember from the small fire and started the pipe. After he had it going he drew from it, then handed it to Puma. After they had smoked for a short time, he laid the pipe aside and turned to face his guest.

"Now Puma what is it that brings you to council with me?"

"Great Chief, I have returned here after all this time to make a request of you, and to tell you things that you could not have heard. Since I was last here I have located my people that I was in search of. Also I have learned that I am the Chief of those people by birthright. I have been to a place called Washington and renewed the peace between the people of my nation and the white government. I have four good horses up on the mesa as well as other things that I have brought to you as a gift from my people.

But, that is not the reason that I have returned to your village. I have come seeking information about your daughter, Gentle Dove. If she has not taken a husband I would like your permission to speak to her. This to be done in the presence of her mother, of course."

Grey Hawk sat silent pondering over this last bit of information. He again reached for the pipe and drew from it. This was a sign that he was in council with himself over Puma's request. Finally he spoke.

"Gentle Dove has reached the age of twenty nine summers, and has not taken a husband. I will consult with my daughter. If she wishes this to happen I will give my permission for the two of you to talk. Until that time you may retire to the same room that you used on your last visit. If it goes as you wish then I will accept your gifts."

Puma walked over to the rock wall that separated the courtyard of the dwellings from the edge of the cliff. Far below he could see Grey Hawk and Gentle Dove engaged in conversation. He could not help but wish that he knew what would be the outcome of this talk. Beyond where the two were talking he could see the people working in the fields. It appeared that they were directing water from the stream to the fields. He was amazed at the construction of the system that carried the water. Finally he saw that Grey Hawk and Gentle Dove were returning to the dwellings above. He retired to the room assigned to him to wait word from Grey Hawk.

Grey Hawk summoned Puma to the chamber that he used for his home. "It seems that my daughter has been expecting you. She says that the Great Spirits told her of your coming through a vision while she was sleeping. As for the marriage, we did not discuss this. That is a thing that the two of you must consider between yourselves. Unlike some tribes, here among my people the maiden, not the father will chose the husband. Gentle Dove and her mother, White Wing, have retired to prepare for your visit."

Puma knew that all the formalities must be in accordance with the customs of the Pueblo. This was not to be a causal meeting, and conversation, as were the many that they had had during his first visit to this village.

Gentle Dove and White Wing were soon ready to receive their guest, and summoned Puma to them. Gentle Dove sat on a bench along the side of the room. Her mother had retired to the far corner of the room and sat silently looking as if she were the only person in the room. It was Gentle Dove who first spoke.

"Welcome to our home it has been long. I understand that you have found out that you are a Chief. You are not the traveler as before. Your journey has been long, and my wait has also been long. My father says that you have come all this way to talk to me. I do not understand why you felt that you must ask permission. Have we not talked at length many times before?"

"Yes it is true that we have talked many times and of many things but this is a matter that must be properly done. I have thought of out meetings many times in the past. These thoughts have brought me to this place a second time. I have come to ask that you become my wife, and return with me to my nation and assist me in the work there. I have passed the age when normally a man has a family. I feel that a wife is necessary to fill the void in a man's life. I have much work before me and I need someone of a gentler nature to assist and direct me."

Gentle Dove said that she would be happy and honored to become the wife of such a man as he.

They then engaged in small talk as she ask many questions pertaining to the Nation, and the country where she was to make her home. It was at this point that White Wing joined the conversation. She advised them that the ceremony must be conducted in their village, according to the customs of the Gentle Dove's people. Puma told her that there would be two ceremonies. One here, and another when they arrived back in The Nation. The ceremony was short but the celebrating went on for seven days. Puma had presented the horses to Grey Hawk and jewelry made from gold nuggets to White Wing. They accepted them as gifts because it was not their custom to sell the bride, as was the practice of other tribes. Puma assured them that he would protect and care for their daughter. He invited them, and any of their people to his Nation for a visit or to live, if they should so desire.

The journey had been casual and Gentle Dove had enjoyed the new things that she saw around her as they traveled. She was as a kid, for after all she was outside her little world for the first time. She had many questions about the things she observed. She had no concept of the size of the country. Puma spent many hours telling her of the previous journeys that he had gone on. He knew that being the daughter of the Chief, she had been overly protected and that there was a rush of excitement within her.

He explained the development of the Nation and tried to prepare her for the things that she would find awaiting her when she arrived at her new home. She was very interested when he told her of Ena and the school. They practiced talking in English so that she might refresh her memory to be better prepared to talk with Ena and Paul. He told her of the needs of the church and school. She was excited about the prospect of being a part of the teaching process. While her father had meant well by protecting her from the daily chores of an ordinary Indian Woman, he had in fact denied her the joys of living and learning of real daily life.

After many days of slow travel dragging her belongings along behind one of the horses, they arrived at a camping spot along the Strawberry River. It was here that Puma told her to prepare for the next day. It was to be the day that she would first see her new home and meet her new people.

Word had somehow reached the nation that Puma and Gentle Dove were about to arrive at the main village. The people were preparing for a greeting celebration. All great events were celebrated in an Indian village. The arrival of the Chief and his bride was among the greatest. The people were lining the trail long before the arrivals were in sight. Although Puma had told her that there would be a great celebration, Gentle Dove was still not prepared for the great masses of people that met them. Puma had told her of the people of different color that lived in the nation. She looked at the thong with excitement. She was anxious to see these people for she had never seen anyone except Indians and whites.

For three suns the nation would sing and dance in honor of the arrival their Chief's bride. There had been the arrival, also, of a small band of Utes while Puma was away. The first night Puma was to tell the story of his trip and sing of the adventure. He had to officially receive the new arrivals.

"I have made a successful journey to the land of The Green Meadows and village of the cliff people. It was there that I took Gentle Dove as my wife according to the customs of her people. Tomorrow I will again take her as a wife according to the custom of our nation. It is my wish that she be accepted and treated the same as any other wife of a Chief. But first I wish to make welcome the others that arrived while I was away. It is known that anyone who wishes to become a part of this great nation may do so by the mingling of the blood with a member of the nation. Therefore, we have in this nation members that have different skins from ours. They are to be allowed to follow their customs so long as it does not cause conflict with the laws of the nation. Once their blood has mingled with ours in an official ceremony they are as one people, regardless of the color of their skin. All children then born of these people are members of the nation at birth. The laws of this nation are for all within its borders. We have no reason to set one apart from another. I will now mingle my blood with the leader of the new group of Ute Indians, thus making them all blood brothers."

The following morning the marriage ceremony was conducted between Puma and Gentle Dove in accordance with the Shoshone customs. After another day of celebrating, the people returned to their homes and resumed their daily activities.

Chapter 42

With the irrigation system patterned after that of the Mormon People, the crops and orchards of the nation were providing more than enough vegetables and fruits for the Nation's people. And by the regulation of the hunting, a thing not yet practiced by the White Man, the wild life flourished. After the removal of the white men that were searching for gold, the streams and rivers had cleaned themselves. The water flowing from the melting snows of the mountains, were pure and sweet. The watercress and fishes had returned in great number.

Puma and Gentle Dove were taking a casual ride through the mountains and enjoying the sights of the prospering Nation. Phillip had joined them and had brought news that he wanted to discuss with Puma.

"There has been the discovery of a metal called copper in the area southwest of the Great Salt Lake. It said to be one of the largest yet discovered in the entire world. From the ore of this deposit of copper comes also the ore of gold and silver. It is not yet known what riches all this will bring to the Utah Territory. It suspected that the rewards could be great. It is believed that this deposit of copper extends into the southern section of your nation. The government is willing to send a crew of men into the Nation to examine, and determine if there is copper on your land. There will be many riches for your people if a discovery is made on your land. However, no one will impose this on the nation unless it is with your blessing."

Puma paused for a moment and considered what he had just heard. "I will take this information before the council and together we will study the possible effect on our way of life."

After much deliberation it was decided that they would allow the men from the outside to enter the Nation to search for the copper ore. They would be accompanied by a select group of Braves to make sure that they performed only the work that they were assigned.

The men searched the nation from the desert lands to the top of the granite mountains, it was determined that there was indeed a large deposit of this copper within the borders of the Nation. When they made their report, Puma and Tonka went to inspect the area. The place where the ore was located was largely a wasteland. It was not used in the production of food crops or cattle.

Since they had a good trade relationship with the people of the Salt Lake area, Puma decided to send a group of Braves and Tonka to the southwest to learn of the process of removing the ore.

Tonka reported that the process of mining the ore was relatively simple but that skill to separate it was not nearly as simple. Puma decided to seek the advice of Phillip on how he should pursue the matter.

Phillip advised Puma that perhaps the best solution was to enter into an agreement with a company from the outside that engaged in this type of work. He said by so doing the Nation would only have to oversee the work and the transporting of the ore off the Nation's land. In return the company would give the nation a large portion of the profit in the form of gold and the White Man's dollars. Philip told him that this had been done in center of the New Mexico Territory with great success.

Such a company was engaged and the work begun. In fact there were several companies that attempted to make the deal with the Nation. Knowing of the greed of the Whites, Puma selected his most trusted Braves and put them in charge of the project. The Nation was now so large and diversified that it was impossible for him and Tonka to look after all the details. It was now necessary to shift a lot of the responsibility to the other Sub Chiefs.

The ore was removed from the Nation by wagons along a specific trail that was the shortest route out of the Nation. The impact on the environment was kept to a minimum. The rewards were many. There had been no problem with the whites that worked the copper pits.

Puma was sitting alone the back of his pony, surveying the nation from the highest peak in the Unita Mountains. These mountains were wholly within the nation. These were an east west extension of the Rockies, which by nature extended from north to south. He often came to this place to talk with The Great Spirits.

He was at peace with himself. He was the leader of the most advanced and powerful Indian Nation in the world. His people had learned to cope with changes made necessary by the new way of life. His wisdom was known and respected by all the different people of the outside world. There had been visits from the leaders of Congress in Washington. They had come to see and report back to the President what all had been accomplished by this unique Indian Nation. His ideas, and changes had been recognized and adopted by many other Indian Nations. It was said that in a short time Utah would become a state. If this came to past then it would be the forty-fifth state of the White Nation known as the United States.

Charles had completed his studies. He come to the Nation and started his medical practice. Lazarus had also moved to the Nation bringing with him a wife Bertha and small daughter named Maylin.

Puma had been surrounding himself with many people of different origin. With them, the results were a well-rounded society. This made up a group of people that would be an example to the entire world.

As he sat on the uppermost reaches of this land he looked around at the granite peaks and deep canyons. Below, to the East, he could see the homes and fields of his people. These were people with black, brown, yellow, white, and red skin. Each had their different customs and Gods, or Idols. They had been urged to maintain these from the beginning. They were encouraged not to adopt the way of others but only to exchange knowledge and ideas. He could see the results and accomplishments of the different people working together to make the Nation what it had turned out to be. To Puma this was the fulfillment of a vision that had come to him long ago, when he was a young boy. These people had proved beyond doubt that if all different people through out the world would work and live together there would be nothing that they could not accomplish.

To the South he could see the dust rising from the work being done in the copper pits. This was a sign of the progress and success that the Nation was enjoying.

While the things he saw in these directions represented the new, out to the West the old was about to be relived. There he saw the Indians preparing to make their annual buffalo hunt. Each fall there was a harvest of the older buffalo to insure that the herd stayed healthy, and the numbers could be managed. This hunt was a throwback to the old customs and was enjoyed by all of the people. These hunts were conducted the same way that they had been for hundreds of years. The hunters rode bareback and hunted with the bow and arrow. After the hunt was over there would be a period of celebration. It was important that all people retain their own separate customs and beliefs. These must be continued until the end of time.

To the north there were great forest that represented the way that part of the Nation should remain untouched and set aside for future generation to enjoy.

To insure that there would be the necessary leadership for the Nation, Gentle Dove had presented Puma with a fine son.

Seven days after the birth of the son Puma sat in his cabin with his son across his lap. With a small thorn from a near by tree, and the special dye provided by the Medicine Man, he carefully tattooed a small crooked blue line and a small yellow circle on his son's right shoulder at precisely the same place as was his mark. He knew that Charles had better tools for this but it must be done the original Indian way.

"My son as the blue water of the river and the yellow light of the sun goes on forever so does the legend of Two Knives" live on forever".

With out another word Rain Cloud rose and entered his tepee. The next day when the council assembled, the teepee of Rain Cloud was gone. It was as if the Great Chief Rain Cloud had never existed.

Naturally the people and events related here did not exist. Nor are these stories intended to represent the actual life style of The Native Americans. This is just a simple and clean saga that will take the reader through the experiences of the Native American life as spawned by the imagination. It starts with the training of a young boy. Continues with the struggle for survival and concludes with the building of a great nation. While the people and events never existed, the historical and geographical data is relatively accurate. However, they are not intended to be of any historical value, rather they are used only to establish time and place. Anything, implied was purely by accident and unintended.